A FISTFUL OF ELVEN GOLD

BAEN BOOKS
by ALEX STEWART

Shooting the Rift

A Fistful of Elven Gold

A FISTFUL OF ELVEN GOLD

ALEX STEWART

A FISTFUL OF ELVEN GOLD

A Baen Books Original

Baen Publishing Enterprises
P.O. Box 1403
Riverdale, NY 10471
www.baen.com

ISBN: 978-1481483155

Cover art by Dominic Harman

First Baen printing, April 2018

Distributed by Simon & Schuster
1230 Avenue of the Americas
New York, NY 10020

Printed in the United States of America

10 9 8 7 6 5 4 3 2 1

A FISTFUL OF ELVEN GOLD

CHAPTER ONE
"People gotta cook wi' that."

Drago didn't mind too much about people trying to kill him; what he really resented was how bad most of them were at it. Take the big human leaping over the bench, for instance, his heavy pewter tankard already swinging out and down in an attempt to stove Drago's skull in: he was so slow and clumsy, the strike might as well have sent a note round last week to make an appointment. And the one trying to sneak up behind him, dagger held edge-on to slit his throat, was even worse, making enough noise to rouse a hibernating wyvern—something that never ended well. But that was humans for you—great lumbering masses of muscle, particularly between the ears.

Actually, to be fair, some of them were reasonably bright, especially the few he favored with his friendship, but intelligence was hardly a job requirement to run errands for Ambrose Fallowfield, the softly spoken sociopath who owned this tavern. If your definition of legitimate ownership included buying up all the old landlord's debts, demanding immediate repayment, and sending armed thugs to evict him and his family the same afternoon . . .

Drago was here to talk to him about that. And a number of similar incidents, which had persuaded the Tradesman's Association of the Wharfside District that the mildly extortionate fee Drago was charging to make their problem go away was far less than they'd lose in the long run by letting someone like Fallowfield simply remain unchecked. And, as Drago had pointed out, if he failed they'd hardly be any worse off, as he'd be dead and unable to collect his payment anyway.

1

Not that there seemed much chance of that, if these two clowns were the best Fallowfield had standing between him and almost two foot nine of irritated gnome.

Not that they saw it that way, of course. To humans, the stupid majority anyway, small meant weak, and his assailants positively reeked of overconfidence. What they generally overlooked was that small also meant fast, and agile.

Drago dropped, headbutting the oncoming man in the groin, and rolling aside to make plenty of room for him to fold up just where he was guaranteed to get under the feet of the knife-wielder. They went down together in a tangle of limbs and profanity, while Drago kept on going beneath a nearby table, rolling to his feet on the opposite side and upending it on top of the struggling thugs for good measure. The stevedores sitting there scrambled out of the way the instant the heavy piece of furniture began to tilt, their imperiled drinks snatched aloft with barely a drop spilled, which said a great deal about the night life in this part of the city. None of them seemed inclined to remonstrate with him, which in Drago's book put them in the brighter portion of humanity.

"Fallowfield!" If he'd had any doubts about the identity of his quarry they were instantly dispelled: A foppish young man, in a coat so expensive looking anyone else around here would have been stabbed for it hours ago, stood with an elaborate air of casualness in response to the shout, and slipped through a door at the back of the room.

Leaving only three more thugs to evade between Drago and his prey. Of course the taproom was crowded with customers too, some of whom would probably join in on the gangsters' side if they saw some advantage in it, but the gnome's reputation preceded him, and most of them were simply getting out of the way as quickly as they could. Which would have suited him fine, except none of them were moving in the same direction, cutting him off from the door Fallowfield had disappeared through with an ever-changing tangle of obstructing legs. Trying to crawl through them would only get him kicked in the head, possibly even by accident, and make life unnecessarily easy for the trio of bravos attempting to hem him in— well, good luck with that, the panicking customers were hindering them even more badly than they were Drago.

If he couldn't go down, then, he'd have to go up: an old wagon wheel hung from the ceiling in the center of the room, dripping tallow from the candles spaced around its rim onto the customers below, most of whom seemed used to the inconvenience judging by the spots of grease on their shoulders. Drago vaulted onto the table beneath it, evaded a sword thrust from a young man whose face seemed composed entirely of acne, and yanked the lad's extended arm downwards, trapping the blade beneath the sole of his boot as it rattled against the table. To his faint disappointment the steel was of better quality than he'd expected, failing to deform enough to give him much of a boost upwards, but at least his would-be kebabber was too slow or stupid to let go of the hilt, trapping his fingers against the tabletop; an intensely uncomfortable sensation, judging by the noise he was making. And there was more than one way to eat a mole, as the saying went.

A quick jump took him to the swordsman's shoulder, landing with a crack of breaking collarbone as the youth straightened reflexively, boosting the gnome upwards. The sword fell from his bruised and swelling hand, clattering against the floor.

"You should get a compress on that," Drago told him, grabbing the makeshift chandelier, and pushing off against the back of the young man's head with a kick which neatly dropped his suddenly unconscious form on top of the first two attackers—who, by now, had valiantly fought off the overturned table, and were using one another to haul themselves upright. The rope securing the wagon wheel to the beam it depended from creaked ominously at the unexpected additional load, but held as Drago swooped across the room, scattering candles in his wake; most, fortunately, blown out by the speed of their passage through the air, the few exceptions adding a distinct odor of singed hair to the already rather close atmosphere. One or two customers yelped, or shouted imprecations after him, but Drago ignored both, letting go of the swinging wheel at what he hoped was exactly the right moment.

The two remaining thugs had shown a bit more sense than their colleagues, taking up a defensive stance in front of the door Fallowfield had disappeared through rather than wading into the chaos of the overcrowded taproom. Both had drawn swords, though neither seemed to have much of an idea what to do with them—probably the people they were used to dealing with found the threat of the weapons enough. The stocky woman on the left had taken up something resembling a proper guard position, the blade held out in front of her ready to split the oncoming gnome, though he'd have bet most of his purse that her chances of doing so would have depended more on luck than skill. Then again, he'd lost enough money at dice over the years not to dismiss fortune as a factor in anything. So he aimed his boot heels squarely at the man on the right, an overdressed dandy, whose slender build and violet eyes hinted at a bit of elvish blood somewhere in his ancestry.

A hint confirmed by the speed of his reflexes. He brought his weapon round in a slashing arc as Drago hurtled at his head; quick, but not quite quick enough. As it was, the sword clattered to the worn wooden floor before it could connect, followed almost instantly by its owner, as Drago's sturdy footwear impacted with his face. Nasal cartilage snapped, and a gush of blood made a terrible mess of the tangle of lace clinging to the front of his shirt.

"You need to get that in cold water," Drago said, rolling to his feet, although the chances of the stain not being permanent were negligible. The dandy seemed unappreciative of the advice anyway, although his answer wasn't really recognizable as words: the slurred gargling might have meant "thanks a lot, I'll do that," but Drago rather doubted it. He drew his own blade, parrying a clumsy cut from the woman by the door, and stared up at her, waiting for her to regain her balance. He smiled, in a manner he knew to be far from reassuring. "Just . . . Don't. Really."

She hesitated, glancing down at her erstwhile companion, across to the other three still thrashing on the floor like stranded fish, then back to the diminutive bounty hunter who'd felled them all with such speed and apparent ease. Her tongue flickered across dry lips. "You're really him, aren't you?" she asked, in a voice which hardly trembled at all. "Drago Appleroot."

"Pleased to make your acquaintance." Drago bowed, keeping his eyes raised against the possibility of a sudden strike, but whoever she was, the woman had enough respect for his reputation not to try anything so blatant. Which was the most sensible thing any of Fallowfield's minions had done so far that evening. He nodded at the door behind her. "If you'll excuse me?"

"Oh. Right." She shuffled aside, thoroughly intimidated, the sword hanging from her hand apparently forgotten.

Drago reached up for the latch and yanked it open, finding himself in a steam-filled kitchen, where a couple of cooks barely glanced up from a bubbling pot hanging over an open fire, and a stained wooden table cluttered with kitchen knives and lumps of what had probably once been vegetables or animal parts. The one hacking things to bits was a goblin, a head taller than Drago, and the one stirring the resulting mess another human.

"Back door. Where?" Drago wasn't in the mood for prolonged conversation. Neither, it seemed, was the goblin. She simply jerked her head to indicate the direction he wanted, before returning her attention to a mallet and what looked suspiciously like the head of a chicken.

A flicker of movement behind him warned Drago an instant before the sword thrust arrived where he no longer was; by that time he was already pivoting out of the way, and seizing a saucepan from a nearby shelf. Overextended, the swordswoman stumbled, and Drago stuck out a leg, tripping her neatly. She went down hard on her right knee, which left her head at the ideal height for a swift blow from the solid utensil.

"Oi!" The goblin looked up from the mess in front of her, and wagged an admonishing talon in his direction. "That's unhygienic, that is. People gotta cook wi' that." She wiped a dripping nose with the back of her hand, and started stuffing something from a bowl in front of her into the body cavity of a disemboweled hen.

"My sincere apologies, madam. And for the intrusion," Drago said smoothly, helping himself to the unconscious swordswoman's purse as he straightened up. The mouth around the goblin's tusks widened a little in response, in what he supposed was meant to be a smile. "If you'll excuse me?"

The doorway across the kitchen was still ajar, allowing a refreshing blast of cooler air into the room, freighted with the reassuring odor of the city: a faint salty tang from the sea, smothered almost into oblivion by the far stronger smells of ordure and rotting fish for which Fairhaven was famed far into the surrounding countryside, and by which many veteran mariners swore they could find the port even in the thickest of fogs. A lifelong urbanite, Drago barely noticed it.

The alleyway beyond was squalid even by Fairhaven standards, carpeted in a slippery mush of kitchen refuse and, more than likely, the contents of the local chamber pots. Drago, however, was as sure-footed as all his kind, hardly slowed at all by the treacherous surface, and took off running in what he hoped was the right direction. To his right, the main street was illuminated by the candles and oil lamps of the many businesses scattered along it, and the occasional link boy, carrying a torch for someone rich enough to afford it and unsqueamish enough not to mind seeing what they were stepping in. Fallowfield might have gone that way, hoping to get lost in the crowd, but Drago didn't think so. Too many people in the neighborhood had grudges against him, and he was too spineless to risk being seen without some bodyguards to hide behind.

Which left the other way, into the dark and shadows, where vermin generally scuttled to hide. He'd been on enough rat hunts as a kid to know that. The other thing about rats, of course, was that they were most dangerous when they were cornered . . .

A muffled curse up ahead reassured him that he'd made the right choice, and a smile which would have made the one he'd given the swordswoman in the tavern seem warm and friendly tugged at the corner of his mouth. Fallowfield was trying to cut through the tangle of narrow passages between the street and the wharves, which weren't so much thoroughfares as places where the tightly packed buildings weren't. If he made it as far as the waterside, he'd be able to hide among the bustle of cargoes still being shifted even at this time of night by the light of torches or, in the warehouses of the Merchants' Guild, who skimmed enough from their clients to be able to afford such things, the brighter glow of enchanted rocks dangling from the ceiling. Or find some more of his hired muscle, who were probably hanging around down there looking for something to pilfer.

Unfortunately for the gangster, Drago not only knew every square inch of the district, he was fast and small enough to take short cuts no human could ever have fitted down. That, and the sharp low-light vision bequeathed by generations of burrowing ancestors, gave him an unbeatable edge in this environment. He darted left, right, and a made a quick sprint down a gap so narrow even a gnome's shoulders brushed against the walls hemming him in.

"Damn it!" The expostulation was near, followed almost instantly by the sound of rending cloth, and Drago's grin widened; it seemed that expensive coat wasn't coming off too well against the confined spaces its owner had chosen to take refuge in. But the noise had been enough to let him pinpoint his quarry's location; exactly where he would have chosen to confront him.

A couple more twists and turns, and Drago stepped quietly out into a narrow courtyard, although calling it that would have been architectural flattery of the most egregious kind: little more than a small space between buildings, across which someone had hopefully hung a clothesline. That probably meant there was a resident or two in what, at first sight, he'd taken for nothing more than a conglomeration of sheds tucked behind a couple of larger, brick-built warehouses. If there was anyone else around, though, none of them had been careless enough to leave any garments hanging up after dark; prudent, but rather disappointing, as that would have given him some clue as to the numbers, race, and gender of any potential bystanders.

Taking a step into the shadows of the courtyard, he waited, his sword held easily ready for use. To his right, the wider gap between the warehouses, almost a yard across, leaked light into the confined space from the illuminated dockside beyond, and, to his left, another dark slit between walls, perhaps half that in size. He narrowed his eyes. Any moment now . . .

And there he was, Fallowfield, wriggling out of the confined space like a grub from a manure pile.

"What kept you?" Drago asked, taking another step forward, the light from the bustling wharfside glittering on his blade in a manner guaranteed to attract his quarry's attention. Fallowfield hesitated, giving the gnome enough time to plant himself firmly in the middle of the wider passageway, blocking his hoped-for line of retreat. The gangster hovered for a moment, glancing back at the narrow cleft he'd just emerged from. For the first time that evening, Drago's smile held a hint of genuine amusement. "Good idea. Let's play hide and seek."

On the verge of bolting, Fallowfield froze, clearly picturing a desperate scramble through the dark, narrow labyrinth, where his diminutive pursuer would have all the advantages. That could only end in one way, and he was bright enough to see it. Instead, he took a few steps toward Drago, assuming a nonchalant air he was manifestly far from feeling.

"We're both too old for games," he said, as easily as if the two of them were old friends sharing a bottle of something. The abrupt switch from sweaty panic to bonhomie was faintly disconcerting, or would have been if Drago hadn't studied his quarry beforehand. As it was, this was exactly what he'd been expecting. Ambrose Fallowfield had all the innate empathy of a serpent, but was adept at simulating it when he thought it would serve his interests. He spread his arms, as though welcoming Drago into an opulent parlor rather than a reeking midden. "I'm sure we can sort something out."

"That's why I'm here," Drago said. "To make you an offer."

"An offer?" Fallowfield repeated, as though trying to make sense of an unfamiliar language. "I don't take offers. I make them."

"Then you know how this works," Drago said. He didn't think the man would try to jump him; vermin like Fallowfield generally relied on other people to get their hands dirty. But he'd faced sufficient cornered rats as a child to know just how vicious they could be. Not that it'd done any of them enough good to avoid the cooking pot, but the attempts had drawn blood on more than one occasion.

"Oh, I do." Fallowfield came to a halt just short of the clothesline, as though the chest-high strand of rope was a tangible barrier protecting him from the gnome, who could have walked under it easily without taking his hat off; even if he'd been wearing one of the currently fashionable kind with a ridiculously long feather tucked into the brim. "You talk, I ignore you."

"Who said anything about talking?" Drago said evenly. He pulled a folded letter from the pouch at his belt, and held it out. Then hesitated, as if struck by a sudden thought. "Unless you'd like me to read it to you?"

"I can read." Nettled, as Drago had intended, Fallowfield ducked under the rope and snatched the paper from his hand. He tore it open, with a disdainful glance at the Tradesman's Association seal, and took a perfunctory look at the contents. His face darkened, all pretense at affability discarded. "What the hell's this?"

"I thought you said you could read," Drago said. He picked up the crumpled ball of paper, and smoothed it out, carefully avoiding some of the more aromatic stains. "It's a ticket. One way. To the Icelands." He pretended to study it. "Oh, leaving tonight. Lucky we're right by the wharf, isn't it? Wouldn't want you to miss the ship."

"I'm not going anywhere," Fallowfield said vehemently, taking another step forward. Drago could hardly blame him for that. The Icelands were as desolate as their name implied, fit only for trolls and the handful of humans hardy or desperate enough to settle there, manning the trading posts and fighting off the occasional raid: the only forms of contact with the outside world the locals seemed interested in.

"The thing is," Drago said, "this offer. It's not what you might call negotiable."

"Everything's negotiable," Fallowfield said, changing tack again. He glanced warily at the blade in the gnome's hand, making sure he was still outside the range of a swift thrust. He produced a bulging purse from inside the enveloping coat, and chinked it suggestively. "If you'd never seen me tonight, I could make it well worth your while."

"Tempting," Drago lied, shaking his head with a regretful sigh, "but bad business in the long run. For me, I mean. Too many people saw me come after you."

"You could say you lost me in the dark," Fallowfield said, and Drago laughed with genuine amusement.

"I'm a gnome. I can see just as well now as at noon." Which wasn't quite true, but humans, he knew, were quick to attribute traits they feared or envied to other species, and he'd never seen the downside of being overestimated. It made the people he was paid to go after less likely to make a fight of it. "Besides, you'll be needing that where you're going. Cold weather gear doesn't come cheap."

Fallowfield wasn't used to people saying no to him, that much was plain. He was holding onto his temper with a visible effort, and the mask of affability was beginning to slip. Any moment now he'd lash out, hoping to take Drago by surprise, and be utterly astonished at his failure to do so.

And here it came, a wild swing with the heavy purse, which made the tankard wielder in the tavern look like a model of precision. Drago stepped aside without thinking, raising the flat of his sword to protect his head, and slipped in the admixture of mud and filth coating the narrow courtyard. Cursing, he regained his balance almost instantly, but the damage had been done. The point of his weapon had risen, and Fallowfield, overreaching, lost his footing too. Man and gnome collided, and Drago found himself slammed into the noxious dirt, the full weight of the gangster on top of him.

At least the ground hadn't been cobbled, he thought, the impacted mud beneath the top layer of slime providing a relatively soft landing, with nothing he could crack his skull against. Could have been a lot worse, although the breath had been driven from his body by the mass of a fully grown human suddenly slamming into his ribcage. And he'd landed on his back, so at least he hadn't had a mouthful of whatever vaguely squishy ground cover he'd landed in.

Fallowfield hadn't been so lucky though, landing face down, and was far from happy about it, judging by the muffled choking noises he was making. Drago got both his hands on the gangster's chest, and pushed, exerting all his strength—which was considerable for someone his size. Fallowfield rolled clear, and Drago scrambled to his feet, casting around frantically for his dropped sword. Whichever one of them found it first would have a considerable advantage. True, it would be more like a long knife in the hands of a human, but could still do a lot of damage, and he wasn't about to wrestle for it if he could avoid that.

Oh. There it was, the hilt sticking out of Fallowfield's chest, still catching the light in a few places, despite the layer of muck encrusting it. And not just filth from the ground, either, Drago realized. There was a thick, metallic tang in the air now, and the stain on Fallowfield's coat seemed to be spreading.

"Damn it." This wasn't supposed to happen. Fallowfield should be comfortably tucked away in the hold of a trading vessel by now, not leaking all over some back-alley midden. Not that his employers would be all that distressed by the way things were turning out; gone was gone so far as they were concerned, but to Drago it seemed like shoddy workmanship. Any halfwit with a grudge could settle a disagreement with a blade, but he prided himself on executing his commissions with a little more finesse. It was what his reputation was founded on, after all, and his services wouldn't be in anything like so much demand if his clients thought they could get the same result by giving a couple of dockyard dregs a knife and a handful of pennies.

No point in crying over spilt blood, though. He bent over the recumbent gangster.

"Fallowfield. Can you walk?" They needed to get to a healer. He knew a couple who wouldn't ask too many questions. The problem would be getting the man there in the first place.

Fallowfield responded with a muffled gargling sound, in which a couple of words seemed to be embedded. The second sounded like "you," and Drago reckoned the first was unlikely to be "bless." This didn't look good; a priest would probably be more use than a healer at this stage, although Drago didn't know any of those with flexible ethics.

Then the matter became moot. Fallowfield spasmed, his heels drumming on the ground, raising little splashes of semi-liquid filth, and became still. A last choked breath rattled his throat.

Drago sighed. "Should have taken the boat ticket," he said, bracing a foot against the dead man's ribcage, and tugging on the sword hilt. It came slowly, with a moist sucking sound as he twisted it to open the wound and break the seal of flesh trapping the blade. Finding a relatively unsoiled corner of Fallowfield's coat, he wiped the steel carefully before returning it to the scabbard—it would need oiling as soon as he got it home. He had a cleaning kit in his pouch, of course, but right now he was disinclined to linger here any longer than he needed to.

As he turned away his boot hit something hard, which gave a little and clinked, and he bent down to investigate, already certain of what he was about to find. Fallowfield's purse, dropped in the struggle. He shrugged, and picked it up, pleasantly surprised at the weight of it: chances were he'd need a whole new set of clothes after tonight's little escapade, and even if he didn't, his laundress would demand a healthy bonus.

The rest of the deceased gangster's trappings he left for the neighborhood scavengers, who undoubtedly needed them more than he did, along with the ticket to the Icelands—a new life, rich with opportunity, for any of the local denizens brave enough to take it. He had no doubt someone would be sufficiently desperate.

Then he went to find too much to drink, and a dice game to squander the swordswoman's money on.

That was Fairhaven for you; life went on around you whatever you did, and wherever you died. The trick was to put it off for as long as possible.

CHAPTER TWO
"Who happened to him?"

Drago woke with a pounding headache, and a sense of deep dissatisfaction. After a moment or two it began to dawn on him that not all the pounding was internal, and that the door of his lodgings was shivering on its hinges.

"All right, all right, I'm coming." To his vague surprise, he seemed to have retained the power of speech, although the effort of articulating his jaw required a bit more concentration than usual. Whoever was outside must have heard him, however, because the incessant thumping on the wood moderated in response, to a slower, lighter tempo of impatient drumming.

"Stop that, you big oaf, you'll have the paint off," the familiar voice of his landlady squawked, followed almost at once by the rattling of a key in the lock. Which narrowed down the number of potential callers considerably; by now Mrs. Cravatt would have run most people causing a disturbance like that off the premises at the point of a broom handle, not to mention her tongue, which had been known to reduce hardened street toughs to quivering wrecks at twenty feet. Relative politeness, and cooperation, just had to mean . . .

"Jak. Come on in." Drago hauled himself more or less upright in the tangle of bedding, instantly regretting the sudden movement, and let go of the hilt of the dagger he habitually kept beneath the pillow.

Captain Raegan of the City Watch squeezed his impressive bulk through the narrow doorway, stooping slightly to fit beneath the eaves. The attic of Mrs. Cravatt's lodging house was cramped even for a normal human, let alone one of Raegan's stature and girth, but Drago had always found it roomy enough.

"Not a social call, Drago." Raegan's voice was blunt and businesslike. "Get your britches on, you're nicked."

"What for?" Drago asked, trying to reconstruct the latter half of the previous evening. He couldn't recall any brawls, or outstanding bar tabs, and Raegan would just have sent one of his constables round to talk about those anyway.

"Murder and robbery ring any bells?" Raegan asked. He glanced pointedly at Drago's discarded clothing, still encrusted with the filth he'd rolled in the previous night, and liberally stained with Fallowfield's blood. Both had hardened while he slept, which at least had moderated the smell, but done precious little for their wearability.

"How many times do I have to tell you to put those in to soak as soon as you stab somebody?" his landlady interjected peevishly, her face appearing round the watchman's bulk, bearing its usual expression of irritation. Edna Cravatt was a woman of indeterminate age and species, although human and goblin appeared to predominate, whose vocation of running a lodging house would have been entirely congenial to her if it hadn't been for the unfortunate necessity of the presence of tenants. Mr. Cravatt was long gone, "to a better place" according to his erstwhile helpmeet; opinion among the lodgers was evenly divided as to whether that meant the hereafter or the Icelands, though they were unanimous in the conviction that either would be a definite improvement. "Gloria won't be able to get that lot out without an enchantment now, and you know what money-grubbing bastards wizards are."

"I've got enough if she needs to buy one," Drago assured her, hoping that was true. Fallowfield's purse had been full, right enough, but the dice had been even more unforgiving than usual last night. Easy come, easy go, as the saying went. On the other hand, he knew a mage or two who could probably be persuaded to do him a favor in exchange for his continuing discretion about some previous commissions, and the laundress would never know the difference.

"Hm." His landlady absorbed the assurance with a skeptical sniff, and remained rooted to the spot.

Raegan turned to look down at her. "Haven't you got cabbages to boil, or something?"

She shook her head, sullenly determined to make the most of the entertainment. "Not for ages yet."

"I need to get dressed," Drago said, allowing the blankets enveloping him to slip a little. "And a lady's presence . . ."

Mrs. Cravatt shrugged. "Don't mind me," she said. "I doubt you've got anything I haven't seen before." Raegan's face became preternaturally expressionless. "And I'm not leaving one of my tenants with the likes of him without a witness."

"Very commendable," Raegan said, trying not to look as though the exchange was by far the most amusing thing to befall him that week. "Because you just can't trust the City Watch, can you?"

"Damn right you can't," Edna Cravatt agreed, brimming with righteous indignation. "You're all either on the take, or just can't be arsed to do your jobs properly." She jerked a thumb in Drago's direction. "Just as well, really, 'cos it means he can earn enough doing it for you to cover the rent."

Raegan nodded. "So, you think if you weren't here to keep an eye on us, I could just make up whatever charges I like and drag him off to the watch house?"

"Exactly." Mrs. Cravatt nodded triumphantly.

A thoughtful tone entered the watchman's voice. "Unless I made up a few more, and took you in as well."

The landlady considered this for a moment. Then turned decisively toward the door. "This is all very well, but I can't waste the whole day chatting with the likes of you. I've got cabbages to boil. Tenants don't feed themselves, you know."

"They do round here, if they've got any sense," Drago confided, *sotto voce*, once her receding footsteps had reached the bottom of the stairs. He rolled out of bed, waited for the floor to stop rocking, and started rummaging in the battered chest of drawers for a clean shirt and hose. Raegan watched impassively. "Who am I supposed to have murdered this time?"

"Ambrose Fallowfield." Raegan waited for a reaction, which Drago was too hungover to have given, and which he would have suppressed anyway even if he hadn't been.

"Never heard of him."

"Really?" Raegan responded, in tones of polite skepticism. "Walking sack of sputum, about so high, last seen being chased through the kitchen of the Jolly Rogerer by you, after laying out five of his goons to get to him."

"Must have been some other gnome," Drago said. "We all look alike to you lot. Just the top of a hat."

"Don't try to be clever, Drago." Raegan seated himself on the recently vacated bed, with a sigh of relief at finally being able to stop hunching his shoulders, even though his chin was now almost level with his knees. "You told one of them who you were." Oh, right, the swordswoman. He'd even bowed, like it had been a proper introduction. One of these days he'd learn not to show off so much. "And we've spoken to Clement Wethers." The chairman of the Tradesman's Association, whose name was most definitely not mocked within his hearing. Not if you valued your fingers. "He told us you'd taken a contract on Fallowfield from him and his mates."

"To persuade him to leave town. On a ship, not a bier."

"Which doesn't change the fact that he turned up dead this morning." The watchman looked pointedly at the heap of soiled clothing on the floor. "And if I take these in to our sorcerers, they'll probably find the blood's Fallowfield's, and the . . . rest of it matches the patch of ground where they found him."

"All right, Jak." Drago sighed, giving up the unequal struggle. There didn't seem any options left, apart from the truth. "I did kill him. But it was in self-defense."

"Course it was," Raegan said skeptically. "When isn't it with you?" He hunched forward a little, trying to look like an attentive listener. "What exactly happened?"

"I gave him a one-way ticket for the Icelands; a little present from the Tradesman's Association, to show their appreciation of all he'd done for the local economy." Drago shrugged. "He didn't want it, for some reason. Tried to jump me." He paused, reflectively. "I don't think he was all that bright."

"You'd just taken out five of his bravos without killing anyone. What went wrong with Fallowfield?"

"He slipped in the muck. Landed on top of me." Which wasn't entirely the truth, but considerably less embarrassing than admitting he'd lost his own footing. "When I pushed him off, I found my sword stuck in his chest."

"Hm." Raegan looked thoughtful. "That would be consistent with the entry wound, anyway. Let's pretend I believe you. So what happened to his stuff?"

"What stuff?" Drago asked, surreptitiously nudging the dead gangster's purse a little farther under the bed with his foot as he spoke.

"All of it," Raegan said. "Purse, boots, clothing—the lot. And someone ate part of his arm, though that might just have been dogs."

"Definitely not me," Drago said. "None of his clothes would fit." Though it seemed his initial instinct, to leave them as a charitable contribution to the Wharfside dregs, had been the right one. "And I don't eat human. Not raw, anyway." He smiled, making it clear the last comment had been made in jest. People had enough wrong ideas about gnomes as it was. You eat just one rat in front of the more squeamish species, and you never hear the last of it.

"Fine. We'll call it self-defense. Again." Raegan stood, and banged his head on the ceiling. "Bugger." He rubbed the affected spot reflectively. "Sod of a lot less paperwork that way, anyhow."

"Glad I could help," Drago said, keeping his face straight with less effort than he would normally have required, the throbbing in his temples and turmoil in his stomach taking a predictable toll of his *joie de vivre*.

"I still need you down at the watch house," Raegan said. "To make a statement in writing. You can write, right?"

"And read," Drago confirmed. "Renaissance gnome, me. Turn my hand to anything."

"That's what worries me," Raegan said.

Sorting things out at the watch house took no longer than Drago had expected, which meant the morning had all but gone by the time he stepped out into the open air again. Raegan had been considerate enough to allow him to grab some breakfast before leaving Mrs. Cravatt's, but since that had left him braving the landlady's porridge on a hungover stomach, it had been a distinctly two-edged courtesy. On the plus side, the hasty meal had been solid enough to ballast him, bludgeoning his innards into something approaching quiescence, but it continued to weigh heavily, and the headache was slow to recede.

Which, in turn, had made the business of taking his statement feel longer and more wearisome than usual. Raegan's deputy, Sergeant Waggoner, was a good deal less affable than his boss, with no time for bounty hunters, whom he regarded as essentially no different from their prey: walking problems for the watch to keep under control by any means that came to hand. He quizzed Drago exhaustively, trying to pick holes in his account of events, and writing down the answers in a cramped and barely legible hand.

"Right," he said at last, blowing on the sheet of paper in front of him to hasten the drying of the ink, before handing it across the table to Drago, "just sign the bloody thing so I can get on with some proper work."

Drago, whose nose was level with the tabletop, Waggoner not having bothered to replace the human-sized chair with one he could comfortably sit in, drew up his knees and knelt on the seat, leaning across the planks to take the proffered document. He skimmed through the summary of events the watchman had sketched out from his account, and stretched his arm toward the discarded pen. Waggoner might not have left it almost out of reach on purpose, but Drago wouldn't have bet a particularly large sum on it.

"You left out 'by accident,'" he said mildly, holding up the paper.

Waggoner squinted at it. "What?"

"Here." Drago pointed at a particular sentence, toward the end, where a cursory skim might have missed it. "Where it says 'he fell, and I stabbed him.' I said 'he fell, and I stabbed him by accident.'"

"So?" Waggoner shrugged. "What's the difference?"

"Not much," Drago said, amending the statement as he spoke. "Just that one sounds like reporting an accident, and the other one like a confession. We wouldn't want anyone reading it to get the wrong impression, would we?" Not if he didn't want to end up in a penal gang somewhere the minute Raegan's back was turned.

"Course we wouldn't," Waggoner agreed, in tones so weighted with irony they sank through the floor. He initialed the correction, and signed as well, as far from Drago's signature as he could possibly get while remaining on the same piece of paper. Then he stood, the scrape of his chair legs across the flagstones rasping through the gnome's fragile synapses like a file on a rusty scythe. He looked narrowly at Drago, registering the reflexive flinch. "Want somewhere to sleep it off, do you? I'm sure we can find you a bunk." He glanced across the main room of the watch house, toward the door leading to the cells. "Drunk tank won't be too crowded around this time of day."

"Thanks, but no," Drago said, pretending to take the offer at face value. There was bound to be someone in there who'd taken a pasting from the constables bringing them in, itching to spread the hurt around, and Waggoner knew that. Giving the sergeant an excuse to detain him for brawling would not end well, even once Raegan had sorted out the mess. "Nothing a bit of fresh air won't cure."

"Your choice," Waggoner said, shrugging, already turning away to talk to a couple of young constables, a man with an unfeasible amount of curly dark hair and a tall, stocky goblin whose helmet crest reached almost as high as his partner's shoulder. They'd entered the watch house in a hurry, responding to the greetings of their colleagues in a perfunctory fashion, and began conferring with the sergeant in an urgent undertone as soon as they had his attention.

"I'll see myself out, then," Drago said, hopping down to the floor, but Waggoner ignored the parting shot, too intent on whatever news his subordinates had brought to take any further interest in verbal fisticuffs. The words "third one in as many days" drifted out of the huddled trio behind him as Drago made his way to the street door.

As he regained the open air, a female watchman, whose shoulder patch and pungent-smelling satchel of herbs identified her instantly as a member of the Supernatural, Wizardry and Thaumaturgical squad, ran outside, almost braining him with the cast-iron cauldron slung across her back as she passed. Something was definitely going on, but Drago ignored the commotion farther down the crowded street, preoccupied as he was with the far more urgent question of whether to risk eating something now, or go in search of another drink in the hope that it would moderate what was left of his hangover. Despite his assurances to Waggoner, fresh air wasn't going to get the job done unassisted, even if such a thing was likely to be found in Fairhaven.

That said, where he was now was as good a place as any to start looking for some. The Wharfside watch house was only a couple of streets away from the estuary, where the river the elves called the Silverroad, and everyone else the Geltwash because of the amount of commerce it brought to the city, ambled its easy way between the dozen or so islands clogging up the river mouth. Islands on which docks for the ocean-going ships and the riverboats that took their cargoes inland huddled uneasily together, like guests at a party with nothing much to say to one another, separated by warehouses,

chandleries, and enough taverns, gambling dens and bawdy houses
to relieve sailors of their pay without the inconvenience of walking
more than a few yards from their ships. The upstream islands, where
the water was too shallow for ocean-going vessels to navigate, were
where the bulk of the population lived; the poorer quarters closest to
the docks, the wealthier ones farther from the sea, where less sewage
floated past on its way to oblivion, and life was consequently less
fragrant. Bridges linked the islands into a pair of archipelagos,
mirroring one another across the water, and to their respective banks,
where the really opulent estates and guild halls were. Bridging the river
itself would have impeded the flow of commerce too much to be
considered, so hundreds of ferry boats swarmed across in both
directions at all hours of the day and night, impeding the riverboats,
and occasionally being run down when a heavily laden vessel wasn't
able to come about promptly enough. Where the bankside city limits
petered out into the surrounding salt marshes, the fishermen took
over, venturing out to sea with their nets, or slogging through the mud
at low tide in search of bivalves, their huts and the detritus of their
profession adding their own, almost chewable, grace notes to the
symphony of aroma which marked life in Fairhaven.

Nevertheless, with the wind off the sea, still sharp with the
southern chill at this time of year, it was possible to catch a tang of
salt and the wider world, as invigorating as a plunge in a bucket of ice
water. Drago closed his eyes and inhaled, feeling a welcome dagger of
icy numbness drive deeply into his throbbing head.

"What are you still doing here?" Raegan's voice, harassed and
preoccupied, snapped him back to the present. "Never mind. Just get
out of the way."

Drago complied, the burly watchman staying at his side, while a
quartet of his subordinates double-timed it toward the watch house,
a heavily burdened bundle of sailcloth swaying between the two
parallel pairs. A lifelong denizen of Fairhaven, Drago recognized it
instantly; a body, fresh from the water. The SWaT mage was pacing it,
muttering incantations while she brushed the corpse's staring eyes
with a small bundle of hyssop twigs.

As they passed Drago and Raegan she glanced up at the captain,
and shook her head. "Can't lift any last images, Guv. Too long in the
water."

"Thanks for trying." Raegan sighed. "Looks like we do this the hard way, then." He glanced down at Drago, who was following the progress of the corpse inside the watch house with his eyes. "Why are you still here?"

"That was Leofric," Drago said. "Who happened to him?"

"If I knew that, I wouldn't be standing here, would I?" Raegan's voice took on a momentary trace of asperity, before reverting to a more businesslike tone. "Do you know who he was after, who he was working for?"

"No," Drago answered truthfully to both questions. Bounty hunters weren't that big on sharing when it came to lucrative leads, his recently deceased colleague even less so than most. "Haven't seen him in quite a while." Which suited him fine. Leofric was, or had been, he corrected himself, an arrogant bully with an unhealthy side order of sadism, and an idea of his own fighting ability inflated by a preference for going after smaller and weaker targets. Hardly surprising if he'd finally bitten off more than he could chew.

"Hm." Raegan looked at the gnome speculatively. "Anyone approached you recently with a high price commission?"

"Other than Wethers, you mean?" Drago shook his head. "Not lately."

"I meant higher than Wethers is paying you," Raegan said. "A lot higher."

This time, Drago's head shake was noticeably more emphatic, to his momentary regret. "I don't take those kinds of jobs. You know that." Which was why the watch captain had accepted his version of Fallowfield's death so readily. The sort of money Raegan was implying almost certainly meant the quarry was wanted dead or alive, but don't bother too much about the alive part.

"I do." Raegan nodded. Drago's scruples in that regard were widely known, so no one local would be likely to sound him out about that sort of job anyway. He had no qualms about killing in self-defense if there was no other way, but he preferred to deliver his quarry alive and still able to walk without too much difficulty. When you were two foot nine, almost, the alternatives involved too much heavy lifting for Drago's taste. "But if you hear anything . . ."

"I'll let you know," Drago agreed. He might even actually do so, if there wasn't any pressing financial need to keep his mouth shut. It never hurt to have the watch owe someone like him a favor, and it would be guaranteed to annoy Waggoner, which was always a bonus so far as Drago was concerned. Which reminded him of the last remark he'd heard the sergeant utter. "So, who were the other two?"

"What?" Raegan was looking down at him again, with an expression Drago knew all too well. "What have you heard?"

"Just that Leofric wasn't the first bounty hunter to go for a midnight swim," Drago said, masking the guess behind a tone of quiet assurance.

"He wasn't." Raegan lowered his voice, although the chances of being overheard on the crowded street were minimal. "We pulled Caris Silverthorn out of the dock the night before last. But she didn't drown, I can assure you. Carved up like a kebab."

"Caris?" Drago couldn't keep a note of surprise from his voice. He'd quite liked the elven woman, though he wouldn't have turned his back on her, or had more than a drink or two in her company; Caris was a dyed-in-the-wool sociopath, who would resort to violence the moment it seemed expedient, or fun. She'd been a hell of a swordswoman, though, he knew that for certain; anyone capable of besting her with a blade would be dangerous indeed.

Raegan nodded again. "Took at least three of the buggers to cross her off," he said. "Or three different weapons, anyway." He shrugged. "Someone might have had a knife in both hands, I suppose." The doubt in his voice was obvious. For a fighter like Caris, even three opponents would have been little more than a mild inconvenience if they hadn't been exceptionally skilled. Unfortunately for her, these ones clearly had been.

"And the third one?" Drago asked.

"Torvin. Found out on the mud flats." Raegan hesitated. "What was left of him, anyway. Whoever did it really doesn't like goblins, I can tell you." Or maybe they just hadn't liked Torvin, Drago thought. He'd collected enemies the way a dog collected fleas, which was hardly surprising given his reputation for casual brutality.

"I'm sure you'll get to the bottom of it," Drago said, turning away in the direction of a favorite tavern. The drink had won his internal debate while Raegan was talking. He'd only taken a couple of paces before the watchman called after him, however.

"Drago." The gnome turned, his face a mask of polite enquiry. To his surprise, Raegan seemed almost embarrassed. "Watch your back. If someone really is targeting people in your line of work . . ."

"I'll be careful," Drago assured him, trying to ignore the querulous internal voice asking "be careful of *what*?"

CHAPTER THREE
"You're having a laugh."

The Dancing Footpad was one of Drago's favorite hostelries, not least because the landlord was a gnome, and he could use many of its tables, chairs, and benches without the climbing and stretching necessary in far too many of the other taverns in Fairhaven. Added to which the food wasn't bad, and there was usually something pitched at the gnomish palate, which most certainly wasn't going to be the case in places where the bulk of the clientele were humans, goblins, or elves.

After an ale or two, spirits being a bad idea this early on in the day, Drago was beginning to feel his old self again, and starting to think about food as something other than a source of potential discomfort; especially since a visit to the jakes, which had moved Mrs. Cravatt's porridge a little farther on around his digestive tract, leaving room for something else to fill the gap. The question was what. He'd just about narrowed it down to sautéed mole or a rat in a bun, or perhaps something from the non-gnomish menu, like the Footpad's widely and justly renowned fish pie, when the light from the window was abruptly eclipsed.

"Drago. Top gnome. Thought I'd find you here." Clement Wethers pulled over a nearby table and sat on it, as though it were a bulky stool, cheerfully oblivious to the stares of the other gnomish patrons. None objected, though; most worked in the district, paid their dues to the Tradesman's Association, and were happy enough to have someone like Wethers around to stand between them and the Fallowfields of the world. Not to mention the City Watch, in one or two cases. All right, he had a tendency to settle arguments with his fists, but that wasn't unusual in Fairhaven, particularly round the Wharfside, and fists were better than knives any day.

"Mr. Wethers," Drago said neutrally. He'd been planning to drop in on the Tradesman's Association hall a little later on, to collect the balance of his fee, and was mildly disconcerted to have been sought out in this way before he got the chance. "Care to join me for lunch?" No point overreacting until he knew what this was about.

"Oh. Was you ordering?" Wethers blinked, assimilating the idea that Drago might have priorities of his own with his usual difficulty. One of the qualities which had helped him to his present eminence in the Wharfside district was the automatic assumption that everyone shared his opinion, and acting accordingly; which most people found reassuringly straightforward most of the time. On the rare occasions they didn't, a fair amount of tact and diplomacy were called for, as Wethers tended to view open opposition as a personal challenge.

"Just thinking about it," Drago said. "Hadn't made up my mind yet."

"Go for the pie," Wethers urged. "I would. Fact, I think I will." He turned, and bellowed across the room. "Oi! Shortarse! Two of them fish pies. And whatever my mate here's drinking. Two of them, and all."

"Coming right up, Mr. Wethers," the landlord assured him, bustling over, and giving the Tradesman's Association pin in the front of his shirt a quick polish with the bar cloth as he came. "Anything else I can do you for? Bigger chair?" He glanced at the larger furniture on the other side of the tavern, most of it occupied by human and goblin stevedores who were pretending not to notice what was going on in the gnomish section, clearly hoping they wouldn't be the one to be evicted in favor of the chairman if he decided to take up the offer.

"No thanks, Hob. I'm comfortable here," Wethers declared, to the ill-concealed disappointment of most of the surrounding gnomes, many of whom had visibly bristled at the casual use of the word "shortarse." He pulled a handful of coins from his pocket, enough to have fed half the customers, and nodded affably to everyone in the immediate vicinity. "And see if anyone else here's thirsty. They're all hard workers, they are, and I say they've earned it."

"Can't argue with you there, Mr. Wethers," Hob agreed, and went off to deal with the clamor of orders suddenly erupting around him. Not for the first time, Drago found himself wondering just how much of Wethers's impulsiveness was a genuine character trait, or a careful fabrication. Either way, he'd got everyone in the tavern drinking his health almost in the same breath as getting their backs up, which was a pretty neat trick if you could do it.

"Drago." Wethers returned his attention to the bounty hunter, pausing just long enough to pick up one of the tankards Hob had plunked on the table, and raise it in salute. "Just wanted to say thanks for getting the job done so neat. Bit more than we expected, to be honest, but you never do things by halves, do you?" He drank appreciatively, nailing Drago with his eyes as he lowered the mug. "But we're not paying extra."

"I wasn't going to ask," Drago said, relaxing a little now that he knew what Wethers wanted to talk to him about. "You got what we agreed on. Fallowfield off your backs." He tilted his own mug. Hob had got the good stuff out for Wethers, and he intended to savor as much of it as he could. "I'll be round for my fee later on. The one we shook hands on." He'd already done better than he'd expected anyhow, acquiring the additional purses along the way, and anything more would be greedy. Not to mention giving people the impression that he was willing to kill for money—a rumor which would attract the attention of potential clients it wasn't always good to disappoint.

"Glad to hear it." Wethers nodded approvingly, and dropped his voice to a confidential murmur which could be clearly heard in the farthest corner of the taproom. "Did you really chew his arm off?"

"It was all there when I left him," Drago said, uncomfortably aware of the listening ears.

"Thought so," Wethers said, with a faint air of disappointment. "Not really your style. 'Drago's neater than that,' I said. 'If we'd wanted someone to go at him like a troll at a sheep we'd have got that nutter Torvin instead.'" He paused, taking a slurp of ale. "You heard about Torvin?"

"I heard he's dead," Drago replied, more interested in the plate of fish pie Hob had just slid onto the table in front of him than the fate of a professional rival he'd have crossed the street to avoid if he'd still been alive.

"Only himself to blame if you ask me." Wethers leaned in to pick up his own plate, balanced it on his knee, and continued to talk round a mouthful of pie. "Going on about some big money contract he'd just landed. Pillock."

"You said it, Mr. Wethers," Hob agreed, popping up to refresh their tankards. "Flashing all that cash around. Bound to attract attention."

"You saw him do that?" Drago asked, keeping his voice casual, a job made easier by the plug of half-masticated pie in his mouth. He still wasn't all that interested, but Raegan's parting admonition was still fresh in his mind, and he'd probably sleep a little easier if at least one of the sudden flurry of deaths among his fellow bounty hunters turned out to be nothing more than an over-enthusiastic robbery. And if one, why not all three? Stranger things had happened. In a place like Fairhaven, stranger things tended to happen on a daily basis, particularly around the districts frequented by mages. At any event, it wouldn't hurt to be able to pass on a bit of information to Raegan, if there was some here to be had; the captain could have been a lot less understanding about the Fallowfield episode when all was said and done, and banking a bit of goodwill for later was never a bad idea where the watch was concerned.

Hob nodded. "He was in here a few days back, spending like money was going out of fashion. You know how Torvin was with a bit in his purse." Drago forced an encouraging noise past the obstructing pie, nodded, and the landlord went on. "Every time he collected a bounty, he drank it as fast as he could."

"And he'd just collected one?" Drago asked, after a convulsive swallow.

"That's what I thought at first." Hob shook his head. "But he said it was just a down payment. When he brought in the head he was going to be rich."

"The head?" Drago echoed. That sounded more like outright assassination than the kind of job he preferred to take.

"That's what he said," Hob confirmed.

"He did," Wethers agreed, stepping in to dispel any doubts Drago might have had about him knowing everything that went on in the Wharfside. Drago was pretty sure he didn't really, but the big man's reputation and position in the community relied strongly on fostering the impression that he did: an impression Drago was quite happy to help reinforce. The Tradesman's Association needed someone like him on a fairly regular basis, and Wethers was known to prefer dealing with people he felt well-disposed to. "Not just in here, either."

"Where else?" Drago asked, directing his question to the chairman, keeping his tone casual, and injecting just the right amount of implied flattery. "I suppose if anyone around here knows, it'd be you."

"Not wrong there, my old mate," Wethers agreed. His brow furrowed, in a pantomime of recollection. "He was shooting his mouth off in The Blind Watchman, The Strumpet, and The Mucky Duck." The last two of which were actually called The Lady Grace, after a long-forgotten noblewoman who'd led a dull and blameless life entirely devoted to charitable works before being posthumously endowed with prodigious cleavage by an overly imaginative sign painter, and The White Swan, whose once-apposite sign had been weathered over the years to match its current nickname. All hostelries Drago was familiar with, and in which it was indeed unwise to flaunt it if you'd got it. "Flashing the cash in there, too." He paused for a moment before adding another derisory "pillock," presumably in case Drago had missed the first one. Then his voice softened, taking on a more thoughtful air. "Them other two, though, they were more careful."

"Other two?" Drago asked, concealing a sudden surge of interest behind the same blandly casual tone.

Wethers nodded, pleased to believe himself better informed than a professional investigator. "Leofric and that loony elven bint. Clarice something? You know, easy on the eye, but bloody dangerous. Be like shagging a lamia, that one."

"Caris Silverthorn?" Drago prompted, and Wethers nodded. "They were both spending too?"

"They were." Wethers drained his tankard, and glanced round for a refill. Hob scuttled over, recharged the tankard, and hovered hopefully around Drago's until the bounty hunter waved him away. The more he heard, the more he wanted a clear head. "But not in bars. Not so much, anyway. Mainly on supplies."

"What sort of supplies?" Drago asked, without bothering to ask how he knew. Wethers was acquainted with every storekeeper in the district, and not a few beyond.

"Dried food, bedrolls, that kind of thing. Planning a trip where there aren't many inns, by the look of it. Or none they wanted to be seen in, anyway."

"Together?" Drago asked, already sure of the answer. Leofric and Silverthorn had detested one another, to the point where weapons had been drawn on more than one occasion, and only the swift intervention of the watch (and, on one occasion, a passing mage, with highly entertaining results for everyone in the immediate vicinity except the would-be duelists) had forestalled a clash unlikely to have ended without at least one of them bleeding out on the rancid cobbles of the street.

"You're having a laugh, aren't you?" Wethers chased the last piece of piecrust from his plate, and followed it with the dregs of his ale. "Good as always, Hob. Give that to the lads in the kitchen." He flicked another coin in the landlord's general direction, which Hob snatched out of the air with typically sharp gnomish reflexes, and returned his attention to Drago. "They'd have killed each other before they got outside the walls."

"Good point," Drago said, as though he hadn't already thought of that himself. But if they hadn't been working together, Leofric and Silverthorn might still have been after the same target. There wasn't exactly a shortage of bounties to be collected within the city limits, and neither had shown much inclination to go wandering off into the wilderness before. And if they'd both been hunting the same scofflaw, then perhaps the third dead bounty hunter had too. "What about Torvin?"

"What about him?" Wethers stood, already turning his face toward the door.

"Was he buying the same sort of stuff?"

"Not that I heard." Wethers shrugged, no doubt coming to the same conclusion. "But he was never very big on planning ahead, was he?"

"No, he wasn't," Drago agreed, lapsing into a thoughtful silence for several minutes, before it dawned on him that Wethers had left him with the bill for both their meals.

CHAPTER FOUR
"There is that, I suppose."

"Thought I'd find you here," Raegan said, casting a shadow across Drago as he emerged from the Tradesman's Association hall, his purse now comfortably heavier. He'd added the cost of his meal with Wethers to his list of expenses, which the Association's treasurer had paid without complaint, and, struck by happy inspiration, gone on to charge them for a complete set of new clothes to replace the ones soused in blood and filth by Fallowfield's messy demise. He'd still get the old ones cleaned, of course, and probably drink the difference, but you never knew—a pair of completely watertight boots would be a welcome novelty for a start.

So musing, he'd failed to notice the bulky watchman's approach, which, for someone of Raegan's stature, was a pretty neat trick—and dangerous for someone in Drago's profession, where a moment's inattention could be his last. Particularly if someone really was targeting the bounty hunters of Fairhaven.

"You thought right," Drago replied, hoping to sound as though the watch captain's approach hadn't startled him, and suspecting that he didn't. But Raegan was in no mood for casual banter.

"We've found another one," he said, without preamble.

"And your first thought was to check on me," Drago said. "I'm touched." Then another thought struck him. "Unless I'm a suspect. How many people do you think I can kill in less than a day?"

Raegan shook his head. "Don't joke about it. I've been cleaning up after you for so long I might start to take you seriously."

Drago glanced down the street, to where the effigy of a felon dangling from the gallows marked the welcoming location of The Dancing Footpad, and dismissed the fleeting thought of Hob's ale. Business like this was best discussed in the open, on the move, away from prying ears. "Who was it this time?"

"Jerron the Heron." Another cold-blooded killer, whose tall, thin build had contributed both to his nickname, and the sudden demise of several people incautious enough to have used it in his hearing.

"Let me guess," Drago said, turning away from the Footpad and the Tradesman's hall toward the nearest market place, where the babble of competing voices would mask their own from any potential eavesdroppers. As the mismatched pair came into view, a quiver of alarm swept through the petty criminals happily plying their trades among the shoppers and stallholders thronging the space between the booths, provoking a small exodus through the rest of the avenues and alleyways leading into the square. Drago found it uncannily reminiscent of walking into a cellar full of rats with a lit torch, and watching them scatter, which in turn provoked a smile of nostalgia for the innocent pursuits of his childhood. "You've ruled out suicide, I take it."

"Pretty much," Raegan agreed. "Unless he stabbed himself in the back, cut his own throat from behind with a different knife, and gave them both to a friend to take away."

"Neat trick if you can do it," Drago conceded. "Was he planning a trip out of town, by any chance?"

"How do you know that?" Raegan glanced sharply down at his diminutive companion. "He had a ticket on him for a riverboat, heading up the Geltwash yesterday on the evening tide. Skipper didn't wait, obviously, so we can't ask him why."

Drago shrugged. "Lucky guess. Caris and Leofric were both buying supplies for a long trip, and the chances they were working together are about as good as mine of being the next archmage. So I'm thinking someone with a lot of money to spend wants someone up the river dead, badly enough to be hedging their bets. And the someone upriver is equally determined not to be dead, and getting their retaliation in first."

"And you know about Caris and Leofric's plans how, exactly?" Raegan asked, pausing to stare meaningfully at a braver or more foolhardy cutpurse who'd stayed behind when his fellows fled, silently daring him to ply his trade anywhere in the immediate vicinity: a challenge the felon wisely declined, finding the apples on a nearby stall suddenly of overwhelming interest.

"I asked around," Drago said ingenuously, "like I said I would." No point in admitting the information had more or less fallen into his lap. Not if he expected a future favor in return. "And Torvin had taken a big down payment too, on what sounded like an assassination, although of course he'd been drinking it instead of getting on with the job."

"Sounds like Torvin," Raegan agreed. "Any idea who either of these someones might be?"

"Not a clue," Drago admitted, with a shrug. "But it might give you something to go on."

"Then again, it might not," Raegan said, scowling. That sort of money meant influence, and both of them knew it. Push too hard, and the guilds or the nobility might start pushing back. If it had anything to do with either, of course.

Drago considered that. Both groups were powerful, and certainly not above resorting to those sorts of methods if the stakes were high enough and they thought they could get away with it. On the other hand, Fairhaven gossip was as ubiquitous as the smell; any dispute serious enough to have provoked a guild or noble family into hiring assassins would have been the talk of every tavern in the city. "My guess would be someone from out of town, here on business. Taking the chance to put out a contract before they go home."

"Unless that's the business they came here on in the first place." Raegan shrugged, his attention momentarily diverted by the aroma from a hot sausage stall, and paused to dig a couple of coins out of his purse. "You hungry?"

"I'm a gnome," Drago said, playing up to the partially deserved reputation of his species. To tell the truth, he wasn't feeling particularly peckish at the moment, but would be later, and he might as well put later off for as long as possible. Free food was free food, after all. "What do you think?"

"I think I owe you for the information," Raegan said, "and I haven't had my dinner yet." He exchanged the coins for a couple of snacks, and swapped pleasantries with the stall holder for a moment or two, mentally filing every piece of local gossip for future digestion. Then he resumed walking, at his former leisurely pace, which allowed Drago to keep up by striding out briskly without having to break into a trot.

"If it's someone from outside the city, they won't be that easy to find," Drago said, resuming their interrupted conversation.

"You're telling me." Raegan led the way out of the market square and down to the riverside. "Outsiders are always a pain in the arse." The tide was high, lapping against the pilings of the wharves lining the embankment, and the air was as fresh as it ever got in Fairhaven. At low tide a thin strip of stinking mud would be adding its own distinctive aroma to the general background smell, and Drago gave thanks for small mercies.

Finding a vacant berth between two moored vessels, Raegan seated himself on one of the mooring bollards to eat his impromptu lunch, which brought his face down more or less to the level of Drago's. The gnome remained standing, chewing the gristly meat inside its slightly stale bun, and nodded in agreement.

"So you're going to need a way in," he said. If whoever had been hiring the bounty hunters really was from out of town, and had the sense to be discreet about their activities, the City Watch's network of informers, or the smaller informal ones maintained by people like him, would be unlikely to hear about it.

Raegan nodded, chewing thoughtfully. "If you've got any ideas, I'd be happy to hear them," he said, without visible enthusiasm or expectation.

Drago nodded again, and swallowed the last of his sausage. "I just might," he said. "But it's going to cost you."

"You sure about that?" Wethers asked, sounding as surprised as he ever did. Drago nodded, looking around the chairman's private office, which felt a little cramped even at the best of times: almost half the floor area was occupied by an ornately carved wooden desk, perpetually unsullied by paperwork, across which Wethers liked to lean impressively toward petitioners, or someone who'd inconvenienced a member of the Association in some way and been "invited in for a little chat about it." Though no one would deny he could read and write well enough if he had to, both processes were conducted in a methodical, painstaking manner accompanied by the drawn-out vocalization of the words in a muttered undertone. Fortunately Wethers had been easily persuaded that a man in his position should delegate any paperwork beyond the occasional scrawled signature to the underlings paid to deal with that sort of thing, which left him free to concentrate on the looming at which he undoubtedly excelled. Currently the room felt positively crowded, as, in addition to Drago, Wethers and the desk, it was also occupied by Captain Raegan, who, under most circumstances, could happily have filled most of it alone.

"Yes." Drago peered over the desk, the polished surface of which was almost level with his nose.

"But it's not true." Wethers's eyebrows converged in a puzzled frown, which Drago knew of old. He wavered in his seat as though contemplating looming for a bit, before returning to the vertical, no doubt concluding that there wasn't much point with someone as short as Drago in front of him. "And who's going to believe it anyway? They all know you around here."

"That's not the point," Raegan put in. "The people we want to hear it aren't local."

The chairman's eyebrows began to resemble a pair of mating caterpillars. "Them Temple District pillocks? Even they're not that thick."

"Not even from Fairhaven, we think," Raegan explained patiently, and Wethers's face cleared with dawning comprehension.

"Oh, you mean *forriners*. Yeah, they'll fall for anything."

"We hope," Drago said. This was going more easily than he'd anticipated. Wethers wasn't normally disposed to do favors unless there was something in it for him, or at least the Tradesman's Association.

"So what's in it for us?" Wethers asked, right on cue.

"For one thing," Drago said, in his most reasonable tone, "it'll make anyone with the idea of picking up where Fallowfield left off think twice about it."

"That it would." Wethers nodded approvingly. "Like it. And?"

"There'd be the commission," Raegan added. Wethers began to look puzzled again.

"What commission?"

"Drago's not going to stick his neck out for nothing, is he? But how's it going to look if I have to tell the city council the watch is hiring a bounty hunter to chase down a lead my lads can't?"

"See your point, yeah," Wethers said, nodding judiciously.

"So Jak slips you the money instead," Drago explained, "the Tradesman's Association pays me for another iffy-sounding job, which we make sure the right people hear about, and you get ten percent."

"Fifteen," Wethers replied automatically, and Drago and Raegan exchanged glances of mutual relief—they'd been expecting him to hold out for twenty.

"Fifteen, then," Raegan said.

"And all we'd have to do is put it about we'd paid Drago to top that little troll shagger instead of running him out of town?"

"That's the idea," Drago said. "But don't make it obvious. Just drop a few hints and let people work it out for themselves."

"I'm sure that won't be a problem for a professional negotiator of your calibre," Raegan said, as aware as Drago was of the chairman's susceptibility to flattery.

"Nah." Wethers grinned. "Piece of proverbial. I'll just get a bit ratted at the Guild Masters' Conclave tomorrow night, and pretend to let something slip in front of the right people. Prebbin from Cordwainers'll do. Tell him anything in confidence and it'll be halfway up the Geltwash by nightfall."

Drago and Raegan exchanged glances.

"That sounds about right," Raegan said. "Your cooperation is greatly appreciated."

"Anything to oblige the watch," Wethers said, as if both of them didn't know he spent half his working life obstructing or misdirecting routine enquiries into the failure of items from the docks to find their way to their intended destination. Drago strongly suspected that the desk itself had been en route to the study of a mage or philosopher at the university before being unexpectedly diverted to its present abode.

"Your civic-mindedness does you credit," Raegan said, with carefully studied neutrality. "I'll send Waggoner round with the money after dark." The best possible choice, Drago silently agreed: the sergeant wouldn't be at all happy about the situation, which was another plus so far as he was concerned, but he could be relied on to follow orders and keep his mouth shut about them afterwards—not something which could be said about many of his colleagues. Not to mention that bringing him in on the deception would avoid any awkward complications, like taking it upon himself to re-open the case of Fallowfield's death in the light of the "new evidence" Drago and Raegan were concocting.

Wethers grinned. "Any idea yet what it's supposed to be for?"

"Still working on that," Raegan told him. "We'll let you know."

"I don't like it," Waggoner said, just as Drago had predicted, with a venomous glance at the gnome. "You can't trust either of them."

"When Drago says he'll do a job, he'll do it," Raegan countered. "Or die trying."

"There is that, I suppose," Waggoner said, looking a little more cheerful at the prospect. The three of them were lurking in an alleyway not far from the watch house, narrow enough to be deeply shadowed even at mid-afternoon, and the onshore breeze was developing an edge. "And if somebody has to be bait . . ." He looked down at Drago with narrowed eyes.

"I never said it was a good plan," Drago said, "just the only one we've got."

"At last we agree on something," Waggoner said, taking the purse Raegan handed him, and tucking it away inside his jerkin. "Any idea yet what this is supposed to be for?"

Raegan nodded. "Tosker Barrower. Ring any bells?"

"Thieving little scrote," Waggoner said. "Haven't felt his collar for a while, though. What about him?"

"Stabbed last night in the back room of The Laughing Gnome," Raegan said, "in an argument over a card game. Captain Nellis's lads cleaned up the mess." Drago nodded. Nellis ran the watch house in the Tanneries, a district considered a bit dodgy even by Fairhaven standards, and wasn't above bending the rules a bit where she saw the need. More to the point, she had a soft spot for Raegan, and was happy enough to bend them in his direction if asked nicely, preferably over a meal somewhere upmarket enough to offer a reasonable chance of escaping food poisoning.

"Which helps us how?" Waggoner asked.

"Nell's got everyone from the game tucked away in the cells, pending further enquiries, which she assures me could take several days. So no one else knows about Tosker's unfortunate demise."

"With you so far," Waggoner said. "You want me to ask Clement to get Drago here to do something about him, right?"

"Right," Raegan said. "Put it about that Tosker's been nicking too much from his members, and that's going to stop. Make sure everyone knows he's hired Drago to sort it."

"And in a couple of days we'll dump the scrote's body on the mudflats," Drago finished. "Someone'll find it, and with any luck the people we're looking for will jump to the conclusion I topped him. And with Clement's version of how Fallowfield died in circulation, they might just decide to approach me with a job offer. Especially as they seem to be running out of potential candidates."

"Right," Waggoner said, with more than a trace of skepticism. "Sticking your hand up for a job that's got everyone else showing an interest in it killed. What could possibly go wrong?"

He strolled away, without waiting for a reply.

CHAPTER FIVE
"What's the point of going hunting if the bear won't eat the goat?"

The next week or so passed in a mingled blur of boredom and paranoia. Wethers sent word that he'd started the rumor mill grinding as promised, and the night after that Tosker's body, now somewhat the worse for wear despite the preserving charm one of Nellis's SWaT mages had cast on it at the scene of his murder, was dumped somewhere it was certain to be found.

Drago had spent the time since then oscillating between a few favorite hostelries and his own lodgings, keeping an even more wary eye than usual on the streets connecting them. The longer no one tried to kill him, the more unsettled he became.

"I don't think it's going to work," he said, his back to the door of The Dancing Footpad, trying to ignore the psychosomatic itch between his shoulder blades. No one would be foolish enough to attack him in here, he knew, especially with Raegan looking past him toward the entrance from the other side of the table (human sized, with a high stool to bring Drago up to the same level as his dining companion), but he still couldn't relax enough to enjoy his rat kebab. Raegan was munching his way steadily through a plate of herring sausage, apparently unmoved by his friend's choice of sustenance; no doubt he'd seen far more unsettling sights in the course of his career, possibly even on the shift he'd just concluded.

"Just got to give it time," Raegan advised, taking another bite. His gaze shifted a little as the door banged to, and Drago stiffened reflexively, but Raegan merely nodded a greeting. "George." Drago relaxed.

"Guvnor." Waggoner patted Drago on the back, right in the center of the target the bounty hunter's imagination kept picturing between his shoulder blades. "Not dead yet, then," he added by way of greeting.

"Imagine my disappointment," Drago responded sarcastically, taking a large bite of the rat on his platter. The mouthful was bigger than he wanted, but the necessity of chewing it gave him an excuse not to engage the watchman in conversation—that seldom ended well for either of them.

"Imagine mine," Waggoner riposted, his inflection only half joking. "What's the point of going hunting if the bear won't eat the goat?"

"Still time for them to take a bite," Raegan said. "It's only been a few days since we started." More than enough time, they all knew, for a really juicy rumor to sweep the city from end to end, sprout several conflicting versions, and maybe spark a riot or two if there were sides to be taken. The story they'd planted was, to be fair, nowhere near as exciting as last year's alchemist who'd finally learned how to make gold before getting an abrupt and fatal lesson in the value of scarcity, the sighting of a Leviathan a few miles offshore the year before that, which had taken several warships and a reluctant team of seasick mages to drive off before it ate enough trading vessels to dent the city's economy, or the perennially popular and invariably untrue reports from far upstream that the Lost Queen had been found alive and well, but even so, Drago had been hoping for some kind of response by now.

"Let's hope so," Waggoner said, in tones which made it clear he had few if any expectations, and turned his attention to the menu chalked up behind the bar. "What's good tonight?"

"Rat's pretty fresh," Drago said, swallowing his mouthful, and watching the watchman for a reaction.

Waggoner just shrugged. "See enough vermin at work," he said. He waved, to catch Hob's eye. "Pie and a pint."

"Coming right up." The landlord trotted over, depositing the order on the table almost at once. "Any friend of Drago's don't need to wait."

"Thanks." Waggoner looked faintly uncomfortable, but said nothing to contradict Hob's misapprehension.

The rest of the meal passed in awkward silence, punctuated by a few desultory remarks which never quite flickered into sociability, and once his rat was gone, leaving only a few bones to mark its passing, Drago hopped down from his stool.

"Going so soon?" Raegan asked, and Drago nodded.

"Could do with an early night," he lied. In fact what he could really do with was too much to drink and some dice to roll, but right now the distraction would be too big a risk. The last thing he needed was a knife between the ribs because his attention was fixed on losing money. He'd been prepared for the physical risks of setting himself up as bait, but hadn't counted on it putting quite such a crimp in his social life.

"Where's the real Drago, and what did you do with him?" Raegan asked, not fooled for a moment. He grinned. "All right then, bugger off. I'll pick up the tab." As if he hadn't been going to anyway. Under the circumstances the least he could do was buy Drago a meal; it gave them a plausible reason to be together if anyone was watching.

"And if you can't be good, be careful," Waggoner added.

Drago was careful to follow the sergeant's advice as he made his way back toward his lodgings, keeping an eye out for anyone showing signs of interest in his progress, but the crowds in the main thoroughfares were just too dense—a constantly changing kaleidoscope of bodies, most of them more than twice his own stature, effectively blocking his line of sight any farther than the next elbow. At least his size was working to his advantage; any humans on his trail would be unable to slip through the minuscule gaps between people and shopping baskets that still allowed him to make reasonable progress. Dusk was falling, and with it came a tidal outwash of the respectable heading for home, theatre or temple, their places being taken by the kind of people who preferred their business to be cloaked by the gathering dark—people not entirely unlike Drago, if he was honest.

As he neared home the crowds began to thin out, and his sense of unease began to grow. Mrs. Cravatt's lodging house was halfway down one of the narrowest streets in the district, not quite cramped enough to be considered an alleyway by Fairhaven standards (streets being defined by local custom and ordinance as being wide enough for two people to pass one another without bumping shoulders and starting a fight), but still claustrophobic enough. Nightfall here was always accelerated by the tendency of upper stories to lean out over the cobbles toward their neighbors, sometimes to the point where raindrops had to turn sideways to slip between them, and the illumination afforded by the chinks between shuttered windows would have struggled to merit the description of barely adequate.

For anyone other than a gnome, at any rate; Drago's night vision was well up to the challenge. Only the deepest patches of shadow could have concealed something, and he knew the street well enough to be able to guess what that might be—piles of rubbish and ordure, in most cases.

Nearing the familiar battered door of the lodging house, he began to relax a little, anticipating the security of his own attic. The few people he could see were all local residents, intent on their own business, their faces familiar enough not to register as potential threats. Not that some of them couldn't be dangerous, if they put their minds to it, but he was well enough known in the neighborhood to be sure of attracting little attention from the locals beyond wary respect.

So it was with some surprise that he found himself stepping to one side and drawing his sword without conscious thought, his rational mind only catching up with the warning hiss of air displaced by a descending blade as the weapon clashed against his own. He'd lifted his sword above his head, angled downward to deflect the blow like rain running off a roof, and kept on moving beneath its shelter, grabbing his assailant's arm with his free hand and yanking sharply downward. The attacker was taller than he was, though not for much longer, riding the momentum of the downward swing to the filthy cobbles, landing with an audible smack. Drago swung his sword around his head, brought his second hand to the hilt, and cut downward, meeting the would-be assassin's rising neck as he tried instinctively to get back to his feet. Vertebrae sheared, blood fountained, and Drago swore. His laundry bill this month was going to be extortionate.

No time to worry about that now, though. He glanced round for any other signs of immediate threat. The locals were either running for cover or settling in to enjoy the entertainment, so he could discount the possibility of any of them intervening, which was something of a comfort. None of them had any grudges they might want to settle, at least so far as he was aware, but they wouldn't be rushing to his defense either. Fair enough. It wouldn't exactly enhance his reputation to seem to need the help of a few off-duty stevedores or dolly-mops anyway.

Mind you, if an assailant could get that close without him realizing, perhaps it was about time his reputation did take a dent. He glanced down at the cadaver on the cobbles. Unmistakably a goblin, he would have been about four feet tall with his head attached, making him on the low end of average height for one of his species. The big surprise was that he'd been able to get so close without Drago spotting him. Goblins could certainly move quietly if they wanted to, but he should have been easy to see—especially for a gnome. The hairs on the back of Drago's neck began to prickle. Something was badly wrong . . .

A clump of shadow detached itself from a nearby doorway and charged toward him. Drago turned to meet it instinctively, cutting at the mottled air, and feeling his sword jar against something yielding. With a scream the darkness evaporated, revealing a second goblin clutching at a belly wound with blood-slick hands, his own sword clanging to the cobbles. He fell to his knees, already bleeding out, and Drago turned again, seeing another patch of darkness solidify in front of him, a good four or five paces away. This goblin was female, dressed like the others in tunic and trews in muted colors, but instead of a blade she held a crossbow aimed squarely at his chest.

Even as he started to run, Drago knew he couldn't hope to reach her before she pulled the trigger. His only hope was to throw off her aim, pray she missed, and close to stabbing distance before she had a chance to reload. Once the bolt was shot, a crossbow was nothing more than an elaborate club.

The assassin grinned, anticipating an easy shot, and Drago abruptly changed direction. He kicked out, feeling the jar of impact shiver through every bone in his foot, and swore again. If he got out of this alive, he was definitely buying the new boots he'd been considering. With reinforced toe caps. The decapitated head of the first assassin sailed through the air, impacting on the goblin's chest, and she staggered back, her finger tightening on the trigger. The bow twanged, the bolt vanished into the night, embedding itself in the overhanging second story of a celebrated local bawdy house, and the assassin howled with frustration and revulsion. Flinging the crossbow at Drago, who evaded it easily, she began to draw a sword of her own.

"Drop it!" a voice shouted, echoing off the surrounding walls.

"Shag off!" the goblin yelled back, charging at Drago, cutting down at him as though trying to split a log. But logs don't move. Drago was long gone by the time her blade hit the cobbles, deflecting the cut as easily as the first assassin's. He pivoted, kicking out at the back of the goblin woman's knee, and bringing his own sword round in a neat, flat arc, which bit into the side of her neck. Arterial blood sprayed, and Drago flinched, stepping back as the corpse hit the ground, spasming.

"You took your time," he said, as Raegan and Waggoner strolled into the street, their swords drawn.

"I was finishing my pie," Waggoner said. He crouched down beside the goblin Drago had disemboweled, felt briefly for a pulse, and shook his head. Then he stood, putting his sword away, and glared down at Drago. "Remind me again. This is the part where we take whoever jumps you in for questioning?"

"Good luck with that," Drago said, trying and failing to sound unconcerned. "They don't seem all that chatty." Which, now he came to think about it, struck him as odd. The only one who'd spoken at all was the woman with the crossbow, and then only in response to Raegan's command to surrender.

"On the bright side," Raegan said, "whoever sent them seems to know where you live. Maybe they'll have another go."

"There is that," Waggoner agreed, apparently cheered by the prospect, and wandered off to interview the few witnesses who hadn't immediately found other, urgent business as soon as the watch appeared.

"So what went wrong?" Raegan asked. "It's not like you to walk into an ambush."

"I didn't." Drago strolled over to the nearest corpse, the one missing a head, and began rummaging through its pockets. They were all empty, which in his experience was highly unusual. Everyone had a coin or two about them, and a few personal possessions.

"Professionals," Raegan said, coming to the same conclusion. "Nothing to identify them if they got caught."

"Or who they were working for," Drago agreed. "But whoever it was, they could afford sorcery."

"Right." Raegan nodded. "That's how they sneaked up on you." He pulled a small leather bag from inside the shirt of the eviscerated goblin, tugging the string it was attached to over the corpse's head. He loosened the drawstring, glanced inside, and closed it again hastily. "I'll get our mages to take a look at this, find out what kind of enchantment they were using."

Drago shrugged. "Looked like basic shadow weaving to me. Apprentice stuff. Half the spell slingers in the city could throw something like that together."

"Can't hurt to try." Raegan tucked the bag inside a pouch on his sword belt, and wiped his fingers fastidiously on a moderately clean section of the corpse's shirt. "You going to put that thing away now, or am I going to have to do you for carrying a blade in public?"

"What?" Drago became aware that he still had his sword in his hand, and that his attackers' blood was beginning to congeal on it; which would do the fine steel no good at all. "Oh, right." He flicked the worst of it off, and wiped the rest against his sleeve—his shirt was so spattered with other people's ichor, one more stain wasn't going to make that much difference. Raegan watched impassively as he slipped the weapon back into its scabbard.

"Any idea how they knew where you live?"

Drago shook his head. "Don't recognize any of them. They must have been briefed."

"Which leaves us right back where we were before." Raegan sighed. "With no idea of why or by who."

"Doesn't make any sense to me, either," Drago admitted. The whole point of setting himself up to look like he'd be willing to take on whatever job the dead bounty hunters had agreed to had been to flush out whoever had hired them; but no one had come forward with a proposition. Maybe he'd jumped to the wrong conclusion, and their deaths hadn't been connected. Or maybe Raegan had been right to begin with, and someone was just pursuing a personal vendetta against the bounty hunters of Fairhaven. He sighed. "Coming in for a drink?"

"I'll pass," Raegan said, with a glance in the direction of Waggoner, who was just dropping a couple of copper coins into the hand of a convenient local urchin. The lad nodded, and ran off in the direction of the nearest watch house. "Got a lot of cleaning up to do."

"You know where I am," Drago said, making momentary eye contact with the sergeant, before returning his attention to Raegan. "If you want a statement." At least Waggoner wouldn't be able to cast any doubt on his claim of self-defense this time, he thought, with a faint sense of satisfaction.

Raegan shrugged. "Tomorrow will do," he said, with another glance in the direction of his deputy, who was now busily engaged in fending off the growing crowd of curious onlookers. "Unless you'd rather talk to George." He noted Drago's expression with a wintery smile. "Didn't think so."

"See you tomorrow, then," Drago said, with a final glance at the trio of corpses, before heading back home for bed.

CHAPTER SIX
"I don't really do trees."

Inevitably, the first person Drago saw as he slammed the front door behind him was Mrs. Cravatt, emerging from her parlor with the air of a wyvern spotting an unwary shepherd standing between it and a fair-sized flock. She looked him up and down, and opened her mouth to speak.

"I know," Drago said, before she could begin her unvarying oration. "Get it in cold water right away."

"You should." His landlady sniffed disapprovingly. "But that's not what I was going to say. You've got a visitor."

"Who?" Drago asked. It was almost unprecedented for Edna Cravatt to allow strangers on the premises at all, let alone leave them unsupervised. He craned his neck around the parlor door, half expecting to see someone in the room behind her.

"A gentleman," she said, in the overly elaborate diction she habitually adopted when dealing with someone further up the social scale, presumably in case they overheard, and might mistake her for someone of equal status. "I sent him up to your room." Noting his expression of incredulity, and the direction of his gaze, her expression hardened. "I'm a respectable widow. Got my reputation to consider."

Not to mention her purse, Drago thought. Letting someone into a tenant's room while they were out wouldn't come cheap. He nodded.

"No one around here would ever consider the possibility of impropriety involving you," he assured her, straight-faced. Not unless the gentleman in question was blind, at any rate.

47

Mrs. Cravatt emitted another sniff. "I should think not," she said, mollified, taking the remark at face value.

Since neither of them had anything else to say, Drago turned and made for the stairs.

"Cold water," his landlady said as his foot hit the first tread, unable to resist snatching the last word, and slamming the parlor door behind her before he had a chance to respond.

Drago made his way up to his room as quietly as he could, his hand on the hilt of his sword. It crossed his mind to turn round and tell Raegan about this unexpected development first, but he dismissed the thought almost as quickly as it came. There was so much going on outside by now that if he left the house to talk to the watchman it was bound to be noticed, possibly even by his visitor if he'd been standing near the window, and Raegan was bound to insist on providing some sort of backup, which was just as likely to complicate things as to help. Besides, he was used to watching his own back—just as well, as things had turned out.

He shrugged, philosophically. He'd just seen off three sorcery-assisted assailants entirely by himself: a man on his own on Drago's home ground shouldn't be that much of a problem.

Unless his visitor was the sorcerer who'd given the goblins their shadow-weaving charms, of course. For a moment he hesitated, wishing he'd thought to ask his landlady for more details about whoever was waiting for him, like whether or not they were wearing a pointy hat, but most of the hedge wizards he knew didn't go in for that sort of thing anyway. Besides, Mrs. Cravatt distrusted magic and all who wielded it, almost as much as she did people who read books, and was bound to have said something about it if the man was an obvious spell chucker.

Only one way to find out. Pushing the door open, he strolled into his garret, affecting complete unconcern.

His visitor raised an elegant eyebrow. "Oh my," he said, "what in the trees happened to you?"

"Guess," Drago replied, making straight for the wash stand. He poured half the jug into the basin, cleaning his face and hands with brisk efficiency, while keeping a wary eye on the elf lounging on his bed. A little over five feet tall, about average for one of his race, he just about fitted the available space, with one elbow propped up on the pillow; the previous tenant of the attic had apparently been a goblin, who'd disappeared one night leaving his furniture behind, to be seized by Mrs. Cravatt in lieu of several weeks' worth of unpaid rent. Quite how his predecessor had managed to get away with that, Drago remained unsure, other than concluding that the fellow must have been exceptionally charming and perhaps there were some mysteries in life best left undisturbed.

The bed was absurdly large for a gnome, but he didn't mind that—he liked to sprawl, and the extra room came in handy on the rare occasions he had company overnight.

"I'd rather not," the elf said, exuding the faint air of smugness which made humans, gnomes and goblins want to punch most of the ones they met in the face within minutes. "Client confidentiality, and all that. Wouldn't want to get off on the wrong foot by seeming to pry into your . . ." a perceptible pause, while he searched for the right phrase, "other business commitments."

"You're here about a job," Drago said, stripping off his shirt and dunking it in the basin, watching the water turn the shade of beet soup with detached interest.

"I might be. If you're as proficient as you seem." The elf pivoted smoothly to a vertical sitting position, avoiding cracking his head on a low beam by a disappointing fraction of an inch. His clothing was utilitarian, but of a quality no one in this part of town could afford even by pawning everything they owned. The fact that he'd got this far without so much as a visible mark on his immaculate jacket, the leather so soft that it folded like linen in the crook of his elbows, was a silent warning to Drago not to underestimate him. The ornate chasing on the hilt of his sword looked more ornamental than functional, but that was no guarantee that he didn't know how to use the blade attached to it.

"You're hardly in a position to call my proficiency into question," Drago said, drawing the obvious conclusion about his recent encounter with the goblins. "You were followed here."

"I know." His uninvited visitor smiled, in a manner calculated to make the face-punching impulse redouble, and glanced toward the window in the attic's gable end opposite the door. "I watched you deal with them from here. Quite impressive."

"You brought three hired killers to my door, and let me walk right into them?" Drago tried to keep his voice calm, but was far from certain he was succeeding. Unbidden, his hand brushed the hilt of his sword, and he moved it away with a brief mental effort. No point antagonizing the fellow until he knew what he wanted. "What were you thinking?"

The elf shrugged, a gesture so elegant it was almost like watching liquid flow and resolidify. Amusement danced in his sea-green eyes. "That you'd save me a little inconvenience when I leave."

"If you leave," Drago said without thinking, his hand drifting back to the sword hilt. This time he kept it there.

His guest smiled again, seeming more amused than ever. "I'll go as soon as our business is concluded," he said, one hand drifting inside his partially unbuttoned jacket. The shirt inside was of a lighter shade of grey, like a seagull's wing, in contrast to the charcoal hues of his jacket, breeks and boots. Drago tensed, but the hand emerged holding nothing more threatening than a purse. "I trust this will go some way towards compensating you for picking the fleas off my back."

"Some way," Drago conceded, taking the small leather bag. It was heavy, and chinked, and when he loosened the drawstring he saw a rich yellow gleam, like freshly churned butter. He was holding more money than he'd ever managed to squander in his life. He shrugged, and chucked it casually onto the nightstand, trying not to let his surprise show on his face, and certain he wasn't succeeding. Whoever the elf was, he was clearly nobody's fool.

"I take it I have your attention then," his visitor said.

"Most of it." Drago drew his sword slowly, keeping the point and the cutting edge well away from the elf, who followed every movement with the calm deliberation of a cat outside a mouse hole. Taking a small cloth and a phial of oil from his belt pouch, Drago began to clean the recently sullied blade. "Do you have a name?"

"Yes." The elf smiled, moving another conversational pawn, but didn't elaborate.

"I take it you know mine," Drago said, letting the observation hang.

The elf nodded. "Drago Appleroot. Bounty hunter, hardly ever left the city. Could be an advantage."

"How so?" Drago asked.

"No one would recognize you."

"Recognize me where?"

"Where your target would be." The elf paused. "All I'm prepared to say at this point is that he's upstream."

"And all I'm prepared to say at this point is 'piss off,'" Drago said, hoping he wasn't overplaying his hand. The elf's eyebrow rose again. He probably practiced in front of a mirror. "I don't work for anyone who won't even give me a name."

The elf shrugged. "You can take Greenleaf, if it makes you feel any better."

It didn't, really, but Drago nodded, pretending to accept the obvious lie. Unless it was true, and a double bluff: the name was common among elves from the forest kingdom far up the Geltwash, and quite often heard in the streets of Fairhaven as well, particularly around the quays where the riverboats docked.

"So you're from the Sylvan Marches. Is that where the job is?"

For the first time Greenleaf, if that was really his name, looked faintly surprised. Then he nodded. "What do you know about the Marches?"

Drago shrugged. "Lots of trees, they tell me. I don't really do trees."

"You should. Clean air, silence, solitude—" Greenleaf broke off, looking faintly embarrassed. "As you can tell, I don't really do cities. Unless it can't be helped."

"Things can always be helped," Drago said. "If they're not how you like them, you change them. One way or another." He examined the blade he'd been cleaning carefully, then returned it to its scabbard. He might have been imagining it, but Greenleaf's hand seemed to move a fraction of an inch further from the hilt of his own sword, and his posture become a little less tense.

"Which is where you come in. Or someone like you."

Drago shrugged again. "Damn few of those left in Fairhaven, so I hear."

Greenleaf nodded. "The assignment is not without risk."

"Never had one that was." Drago started rummaging for a clean shirt, although by now he didn't really see the point of getting dressed again. The adrenaline comedown after the fight outside was starting to kick in, and what he really wanted to do was sleep. No chance of that while Greenleaf was still occupying most of the bed, though.

"No doubt." Greenleaf nodded again. "But this one will be exceptionally hazardous."

"I got that impression from the way everyone you've spoken to about it so far's turned up dead," Drago said, before another thought struck him. "Or has someone else had better luck than the others?"

"Not yet," Greenleaf admitted. "But you seem a far better choice in any case. Shame you keep so low a profile. I could have saved a lot of time and a considerable amount of money by coming to you first."

"Then why didn't you?" Drago asked, hoping he didn't sound too eager. Greenleaf had to believe he was willing to go along with whatever this assignment was, but the more persuasion he apparently needed, the more the elf would open up in an attempt to convince him. At least, that was the theory. He'd set himself up as bait, and the bear was beginning to sniff the goat at last. Which didn't answer the question of who the goblins outside had been, or why they'd jumped him, but with any luck that would become clear too.

"You didn't appear to be interested in the kind of contract we're offering," Greenleaf said, a spark of doubt entering his voice. "And, to be honest, I'm not entirely sure that you would be now. But a couple of recent incidents suggest that perhaps we were mistaken."

"We?" Drago asked.

The elf nodded. "The people I work with."

"If you're answerable to someone, I want to talk to them," Drago said, standing dismissively, and glancing pointedly at the door. "I don't negotiate with messenger boys."

"I said work with, not for." For the first time a flash of irritation entered Greenleaf's voice, before being hurriedly suppressed. Good. Annoyed, he might let his guard down more than he'd intended. That had worked in Drago's favor many times, in both verbal and physical confrontations. "I'm fully authorized to make any agreement I see fit."

"Authorized by who?" Drago asked, in a politely reasonable tone that reeked of skepticism.

Greenleaf sighed. "None of the others asked. All they were interested in was the money."

"And look how well that ended for them," Drago pointed out. "If I take your job I want to know everything about it. Who, why, exactly what the risks are. Then I'll decide if you're paying me enough to chance my neck on it."

"Fair enough." The elf's smile became marginally more genial, and a little more genuine. He reached inside his jacket again, and produced a small silver medallion. An oak tree, more elegant and symmetrical than any found in nature, was embossed on it; the image seemed vaguely familiar, and after a moment Drago recognized it. He'd seen the same symbol many times before, pressed into the wax of the excise seals on crates being unloaded from riverboats newly arrived down the Geltwash. "I represent his Royal Highness Lamiel Stargleam, monarch of the Kingdom of the Sylvan Marches."

So, Drago thought, his guess had been right. He worked at keeping his face neutral. "And how can I help so exalted a personage as His Royal Highness?"

"A little less sarcasm would be a start," Greenleaf said, looking genuinely amused for the first time since the conversation started, which made Drago feel marginally less like hitting the elf than he had done since entering the room.

"Just leave that bit out of your report," Drago suggested. "So how many other agents does he have in Fairhaven?" Not that he cared, but it was information that Raegan would be interested in.

"Enough," Greenleaf said, "but that's beside the point right now. I'm the one handling this. If you want the job, you deal directly with me, and only me."

"I haven't said I do, yet," Drago said. "And I won't, until I'm sure I won't be getting out of my depth."

"Hm." The elf looked him up and down, comparing their relative statures. Drago waited for a disparaging remark about his height, but Greenleaf simply nodded again. "Fair enough. What do you know about the Lost Queen?"

"She's still missing," Drago said, "which means she's dead by now. Couldn't tell you how, or who did it, because I couldn't care less." He watched the elf for a reaction, but saw nothing beyond a simple nod of agreement.

"That's pretty much all anybody knows," Greenleaf conceded, "at least this far from the Marches. But we know who did it, and the king wants revenge."

"Hasn't he got an army for that sort of thing?" Drago asked. "Or people like you?"

"Yes, and yes," Greenleaf agreed, his tone becoming more businesslike. "But neither can get the job done in this instance."

"Then I don't see what I could do," Drago said, becoming interested in spite of himself. He pulled up a stool, and sat down.

"I'll need to sketch in a bit of background," Greenleaf said. "About the history of the Marches, and how the queen was killed." He stiffened, at a faint sound in the passageway outside, and his hand went to the hilt of his sword.

Drago smiled. It had taken even less time than he'd expected. He raised his voice. "Come in, Mrs. Cravatt."

The door opened, revealing his landlady, holding a tray with a couple of grubby tankards on it. She smiled, mainly at Greenleaf, and walked in.

"I thought you might be in need of some refreshment," she said, throttling every vowel to within an inch of its life.

"Very thoughtful," Greenleaf said, taking the nearest, and keeping it well away from his face.

"Mrs. Cravatt always takes a keen interest in the welfare of her tenants," Drago assured him, straight-faced, "especially when they have guests."

"The hospitality of the citizens of Fairhaven is legendary," Greenleaf said, in similar tones, although Drago suspected that he meant in the sense of entirely without foundation. "Thank you for your consideration."

"Indeed." Since the remaining tankard showed no sign of being moved in his direction without prompting, Drago stood up and helped himself to it. Mrs. Cravatt flinched a little, suddenly reminded of his presence, but failed to drop the tray as he'd half expected. "Now, if you'll excuse us, Mr. Greenleaf and I have a lot to discuss."

"Of course." His landlady looked at him as though she would like to consider his neck another vowel, and beat a dignified retreat from the room.

"If you wouldn't mind leaving the door open?" Greenleaf asked, as she passed through it. "I'm finding it a little stuffy in here."

"Of course." She descended the stairs, a faintly peeved sniff echoing back from the landing below.

"Now." Greenleaf placed his tankard, untouched, on the night stand. "Where were we?"

Drago drank and swallowed. "You were about to give me a history lesson," he said.

✧ ✧ ✧

"You have to understand," Greenleaf began, "that the Sylvan Marches is a prosperous place. And that means we have enemies. Especially in the Barrens."

"You've lost me already," Drago admitted. "Which barons? Did one of them assassinate the queen?"

Greenleaf sighed, almost inaudibly. "The Barrens are a place," he explained. "A wilderness area on our southern borders. Infested with bandits, who raid pretty much at will."

Drago nodded, to show he was keeping up, and took a gulp of his ale. Mrs. Cravatt had got the good stuff out for their distinguished visitor, or at least the best she could afford, and he meant to make the most of it. "And they killed the queen."

"I'm coming to that." Greenleaf sighed again, took a sip of his own ale, and hastily put down the mug. "The bandits are goblins, with no love lost for elves. It's not just raiding for loot or supplies with them, it's sheer wanton destruction as often as not."

"I see." Drago didn't really. In his experience goblins didn't bear the elves any particular malice—no more than anyone else did, anyway. "It's a blood feud kind of thing." He took a thoughtful sip. "What do they think their grievance is?"

Greenleaf looked at him appraisingly. "You're quick on the uptake," he conceded. "They claim the Barrens are rightfully theirs, although they've been a province of the Marches for nearly a century."

"And before that?" Drago asked.

Greenleaf shrugged. "They were just there. The old king sent a few troops in to tidy the borders up a bit, and they've been ours ever since."

"I see." At least Drago thought he did. Minor kingdoms were like that, grabbing whatever territories they could, before their neighbors had the same idea. "And the people already living there were fine with that?"

"Pretty much," Greenleaf said. "They didn't fight for long, anyway, and even then it was only the goblins. There were already a few elvish settlers there, and they were happy enough to be part of a civilized country again."

"Hm." Drago took a couple of thoughtful swallows. "Any humans or gnomes about?"

"Not back then," Greenleaf said. "But gnomes started moving in to work the mines after they opened, about twenty years ago."

"Mines?" Drago asked. That made sense. Gnomes were natural burrowers, with an innate affinity for tunnels and caves, and in high demand for jobs requiring skill with a shovel. Most of the ones outside cities like Fairhaven, where all kinds of species lived and worked together, still preferred to dwell in underground warrens of quite staggering complexity. Drago had visited the nearest a couple of times at the behest of relatives, but found it an unsettling experience, where his unease at not being able to see the sky for days at a time was seen as charmingly eccentric or faintly pitiable, depending on whom he was talking to. "What kind?"

"Gold," Greenleaf said, underlining the gravity of the revelation with a second sip of ale, which he quite clearly immediately regretted. "The vein was discovered by accident, when a hunter missed the boar he was aiming at, and went to retrieve the arrow. He pulled it out of the ground, and noticed a fleck of something shining on the head."

"And after that, the goblins decided they wanted their country back," Drago finished.

"Pretty much," Greenleaf agreed. "The bandits became more organized, the garrisons were strengthened, and the fighting's been going on for a couple of decades. The army holds the mines and the larger villages, but the Barrens are impossible to hold down completely; the terrain's too broken for large scale troop movements, and the goblins just fade into the hillsides after every raid."

"I'm beginning to see your problem," Drago said. "But surely the occasional skirmish with bandits is just a mild inconvenience with a mine full of gold at stake."

"To begin with," Greenleaf conceded. "But then they started to get more organized, more sophisticated in their tactics and planning."

"They found a leader," Drago concluded.

"They did." Greenleaf nodded seriously. "And a very effective one. Gorash Grover. Heard of him?"

Drago shook his head. "Don't think so." But then the only interest Fairhaven had in the Sylvan Marches, or any of the other upstream kingdoms come to that, was the amount of trade coming down the river. Parochial gossip didn't travel as well as timber or wine.

Greenleaf smiled thinly. "Then take my word for it, he's extremely effective. Not just a good general, but an orator, a rabble-rouser. His followers would cheerfully die for him." He glanced sardonically at Drago's shirt, still seeping blood into its bowl of water. "In fact, three of them just did."

"The ones who were after you," Drago said.

Greenleaf shook his head. "Not quite. They were after whoever I was going to meet." He nodded affably in Drago's direction. "It seems your reputation precedes you, Master Appleroot. None of the others were attacked until after our business had been concluded."

Drago felt a faint chill between his shoulder blades, where the target he'd imagined back in The Dancing Footpad had been centered. It was unlikely that Gorash would have had a mere trio of operatives opposing Greenleaf and his friends in a city the size of Fairhaven. He'd have to watch his step even more carefully than he'd anticipated until this affair was over.

"It still hasn't been," he said. He probably had more than enough information for Raegan by now, but his own curiosity was beginning to take over. "How did Gorash assassinate the queen? Seems like a pretty neat trick for a backwoods bandit."

Greenleaf shrugged. "Treachery, of course. And, possibly, her own naivety."

Drago nodded. "Not an ideal trait in a monarch. What happened, exactly?"

"Well," Greenleaf began, with the air of someone about to commence a long story, "the king died. Not Lamiel, obviously. His father. Ariella, the present king's older sister, inherited the throne. To everyone's relief, especially her brother's."

"No argument over the succession, then?" Drago asked. Not that he cared, but he had a nasty suspicious mind, a definite asset in his profession, and it wouldn't be the first time someone committed sororicide to grab a crown. Having a notorious bandit around to take the blame would only make that easier.

"None at all. Lamiel stepped up, but his heart's not really in it; he much preferred being the spare to the heir, where he had time to patronize the arts, that sort of thing, instead of making all the big decisions. If you ask me, no one misses his sister more than he does."

"Right." Either that was true, or Greenleaf genuinely believed it. Either way, it seemed the bandits were definitely to blame for his sister's demise. "So, we're back to my original question. How did she die?"

Greenleaf shrugged. "Quickly, one hopes. But with these savages, one never can tell." He sighed. "Everyone advised her against it, but when a queen makes up her mind, what can you do?"

Drago hid his impatience behind the draining of his tankard. "Made up her mind to do what?"

"Negotiate. Try and make peace with the goblins. She offered Gorash safe conduct, a face-to-face meeting on neutral ground."

"And the moment they're alone together . . ." Drago mimed an extravagant throat-slitting.

Greenleaf shook his head, with a faint trace of puzzlement. "That's just the thing. It seemed to be working at first. They were a bit wary of one another to begin with, but they seemed to be getting on well enough. That meeting led to others, and after a few months there was even a draft treaty prepared. The queen travelled to the Barrens to sign it, and that was the last anyone ever saw of her."

"So you can't be sure she's actually dead?" Drago asked.

"We're sure." Greenleaf's voice was grim. "Her escorts were ambushed almost as soon as they crossed the border. No one else knew they were coming. Just Gorash and his rabble."

"So let me get this straight," Drago said slowly. "You want me to travel to the Barrens, find a seasoned guerilla fighter who's known every inch of the terrain since he was a child, and has a small army of ruthless killers who idolize him standing between the two of us, and kill him in retaliation for murdering your queen."

"That about sums it up," Greenleaf agreed, pushing his tankard of ale across to the gnome. "So, what do you think?"

Drago's laughter was so loud, it disturbed the watchmen in the street outside.

CHAPTER SEVEN

"They've got magic, and they're not afraid to use it."

"And he really seemed surprised when I turned him down," Drago finished, concluding his narrative and a herring sausage in a bun at almost exactly the same moment.

Raegan nodded. "Not something he's used to, I imagine." He glanced around the bustling marketplace, relieved to find that none of the shoppers or stallholders surrounding them seemed to be listening. "But I'd keep watching your back for a while if I were you. At least until Gorash's people get the message."

Drago shrugged, his attention caught by a clothing stall, and stopped to browse through a pile of gnome-sized shirts. He'd visited a cordwainer's shop earlier that morning, with a couple of coins from the purse Greenleaf had given him, and walked out with the new boots he'd been promising himself. They were comfortable, and dry, and made everything else he owned seem a great deal shabbier than they had before donning the new footgear. But he could afford a few new clothes now, especially with the fee Raegan had channeled through the Tradesman's Association, so that was a problem easily solved. "I'm sure they'll find out soon enough," he said.

"Maybe." Raegan seemed less sure, but then he had a lot on his mind. The city council wouldn't be at all happy to hear that the parochial squabbles of a petty kingdom leagues up the river were spilling over onto the streets of Fairhaven, and the watch would be expected to clean up the mess. True, that would be a problem for his

59

colleagues all over the city, but as he was the one drawing attention to it, he'd probably be expected to propose a solution too: if only for the councilors to ignore it, and come up with a less effective strategy themselves. "But I'd feel a lot happier if you'd take this."

"Take what?" Drago paused for a moment, to debate payment with the stall holder, and exchange a few coppers for a shirt that looked as if it might fit. Raegan waited patiently for him to finish, before handing over a small leather bag, containing something about the size and shape of a plum stone. Knowing better than to open it, Drago slipped the bag into his pocket.

"You were right about the shadow-weaving charms those goblins had last night—too common to get us anywhere. But our sorcerers knocked up some counter-charms for the lads on the beat, in case they run into any more skulking about." Raegan shrugged. "That one seems to have fallen into my pocket, and I only need one, so . . ."

"Thanks." Drago nodded his appreciation. "But I don't suppose I'll come to much harm today. Other than terminal boredom."

"We need your statement," Raegan reminded him. "Anything you can remember that might help us work out how many troublemakers the Marches have dumped on us."

"Fair enough." Drago sighed, accepting the inevitable, and led the way toward the watch house.

As he'd expected, the interview was long and exhaustive, stretching well into the afternoon. Something he hadn't expected, however, was that it took place in Raegan's private office, away from the bustle of the main watch house where Waggoner had interviewed him before, and was conducted by the captain himself as well as his deputy. Two other people were squeezed into the relatively small space, besides Raegan and Waggoner: a corpulent goblin whose uniform and additional trappings clearly identified him as one of the magical support staff, and a human woman whose clothing marked her out as a member of the nobility, and who said very little in a manner the watchmen clearly found faintly unnerving. Drago hadn't recognized the name she gave, but assumed it wasn't her real one anyway; if she wasn't actually a member of the city council she was undoubtedly there to report back to them, and he knew they preferred to maintain the polite fiction that information only reached them through official channels.

To his private amusement, his diminutive stature meant that he was the only person there who didn't feel uncomfortable in the overcrowded room; perched on the stool someone had found for him, he was almost level with the faces of everyone else present, an interesting novelty in itself. Raegan had given up his seat behind the desk for the silent woman, who had introduced herself as Lady Selina something or other, and promptly bagged the only other chair for himself; Waggoner and Vethik, the goblin mage, were perched on slightly lower stools, though apparently less comfortably than Drago, judging by the amount of fidgeting they both did.

"You're sure there's nothing else you can tell us?" Waggoner asked at last, laying down his pen with an air of faint relief, and cracking his knuckles. He'd been a good deal more polite than he had while taking Drago's statement about Fallowfield's death; though how much of that was due to his having witnessed the fight with the goblin assassins himself, and being certain that this time at least the gnome had nothing to hide, and how much was about trying to favorably impress the agent of the council, Drago wasn't sure. Come to that, he didn't particularly care, either.

"Nothing springs to mind," Drago agreed. He made a brief show of careful ratiocination, then shook his head. "Nope. That's it."

"It's a shame you turned Master Greenleaf down so firmly," Lady Selina said, her tone of mild disappointment more appropriate to the discovery of a crease in a favorite pair of gloves. "If you'd accepted his commission, you might have discovered more about his network."

"With respect, your Ladyship, I beg to differ." Raegan sounded distinctly uncomfortable with the formal language, used to expressing himself in a far more direct manner. "He seems to have made it pretty clear that Drago would only be dealing with him."

"True." Selina inclined her head. "But Master Appleroot seems admirably resourceful. I'm sure he could have picked up more information than Greenleaf intended to reveal."

"If he didn't just end up feeding the fish," Waggoner said, forthright as always. "The Marchers'd top him the minute they realized he was reporting back to us."

"Assuming Gorash's lot didn't get to him first," Raegan added, his own formality beginning to slip.

"I think that would be a risk worth taking," Selina said.

"Well, I don't," Drago put in, a little more vehemently than he'd intended. "I nearly got killed just because Greenleaf was talking to me, and I'm not about to stick my neck out any further." The official line was that the elf had approached him with a bounty offer, like any other client, which was all the council needed to know. The trap he'd helped the watchmen to lay, with Wethers's help, wasn't something Lady Selina needed to hear about—although he couldn't help suspecting that she was already pretty sure of what had really been going on.

The woman shrugged. "Too late now, in any case," she said, with a trace of regret. "If you went back and told him you'd changed your mind, he'd be bound to suspect something."

"I'm more worried about the Goblin faction," Raegan said, belatedly adding "begging your pardon, ma'am," as he remembered whom he was talking to. "They've got magic, and they're not afraid to use it."

Vethik snorted derisively, reminding everyone of his presence. "Hedge wards and cantrips," he said dismissively. "Nothing we don't see on the streets every day. Even your regular arm-breakers can deal with that sort of thing without too much trouble."

"But we can't be sure that's all they've got," Raegan said. "They're clearly well resourced, and have some very capable people working for them."

"They don't sound all that capable to me," Selina said, casting a dubious eye in Drago's direction, "if one gnome was enough to take out three of them."

"One very lucky gnome," Drago corrected, "with two officers of the watch turning up in the nick of time." True, the brawl had been over before they could get physically involved, but Raegan's warning shout had probably distracted the markswoman with the crossbow at a critical moment, and it wouldn't hurt to spread the credit around a bit.

"Of course." Selina's voice was freighted with skepticism. "How very fortunate you both happened to be passing." The two watchmen exchanged an uneasy glance, but she let the matter go, apparently content just to have made her point. She turned to Vethik. "Could they have anything more dangerous?"

The goblin shrugged. "Of course they could, if they have the right contacts, or a mage of their own. And no, I'm not prepared to make any wild guesses as to what that might be without a shred of corroborating evidence. All I can tell you for certain is that they've used simple enchantments of concealment, which are widely available from any moderately disreputable sorcerer with scant regard for the city ordinances."

Waggoner muttered something which sounded suspiciously like "Most of them, then," before subsiding at a glare from Raegan.

"Would it be worth interviewing any of these disreputable mages?" Selina asked. "You must know who they are."

"I can think of a few names," Raegan admitted, "but I doubt it would do much good. If they were involved they'd just lie about it, and probably tip off their clients into the bargain. But we can shake a few trees and see what drops out."

Waggoner nodded. "Chances are we'd get someone for something, even if it wasn't what we were looking for," he agreed. "I'll get a few of the lads knocking on doors."

"Good." Lady Selina stood, with sudden decisiveness, and began edging out of the room, her elbow glancing from Vethik's forehead on the way. Just as she reached the door, it swung open, held by an astonishingly large man, looking more like a shaved troll than anything human, whose livery and well-worn scabbard positively screamed "high-priced bodyguard." Selina nodded an affable farewell. "I'll await further news with interest." Her gaze rested on Drago an instant longer than any of the others. "If you do change your mind, Master Appleroot, you'll find Greenleaf at the Clothiers' Guildhall most afternoons, haggling over textiles."

"I'll bear that in mind," Drago lied, pretending not to be surprised that she knew that. The aristocrat swept out of the room, her minder clearing a path for her through the crowded watch house like a polite but relentless avalanche, and disappeared into the street.

Everyone in Raegan's office suddenly relaxed.

"Right." Raegan stood too, projecting an air of decisiveness, and nodded at his subordinates. "George, round up a few of the lads and start kicking doors down. Take a spell chucker with you, in case any of the pointy hats decide to play silly buggers. Vethik, start checking the records. Anything recent that might smell of prohibited spell use, let me know."

The goblin scowled. "Get a clerk to do it. I didn't spend six years studying for a doctorate in thaumaturgy to go rummaging about in filing cabinets."

"Which is why you're the perfect choice," Raegan said diplomatically, while Waggoner made disparaging hand gestures behind the mage's oblivious back. "There's no one else this side of the university who'd know what to look for, and precious few of those with the investigative skill to recognize it even if they saw it."

"I suppose you're right." Vethik nodded, a trifle smugly, before the truculence returned to his voice. "But don't expect me to make a habit of it."

"Perish the thought," Raegan said, as the goblin mage disappeared through the still-open door into the swirl of activity beyond.

"Tosser," Waggoner opined, making the appropriate gesture again.

"But at least you have the courage to admit it," Vethik's voice floated back, and Drago suppressed a grin.

"And what about you?" Waggoner asked, turning to the gnome.

"Me?" Drago hopped down from the stool. He'd answered all the questions anyone could think of asking, and received his fee. No reason at all to stick around so far as he could see. "I'm off to the Footpad. Have fun."

"You too." Raegan waved a slightly distracted farewell. "But watch your back. At least until we're sure the dust has settled."

CHAPTER EIGHT
"That ought to learn him."

A few hours of food and drink at The Dancing Footpad, followed by an almost honest dice game in the back room of The Strumpet in which he retained nearly all the money he went in with, went a long way toward restoring Drago's good humor. He'd even found the time to complete his clothes shopping on the short walk between taverns, and had bought a new knapsack to carry his booty home in. His old boots he'd stuffed in the bottom, with the vague idea of getting them repaired in case they came in useful one day; the additional weight had been negligible, but the heels kept bumping uncomfortably against his spine as he made his way home.

The streets were still crowded as he left The Strumpet, mostly with humans, but with a few goblins and gnomes visible among them; elves tended to stay in their own parts of the city after dark, the occasional exception drawing curious or hostile glances, which they ignored with their usual supercilious air. Unwilling to weave his way through a forest of obstructing legs, Drago took to the labyrinth of narrow spaces between buildings through which he'd pursued Fallowfield, making for Mrs. Cravatt's lodging house as directly as the haphazard network allowed. Night was falling in earnest by this time, but his low light vision proved as reliable as ever, and he made good progress, unimpeded by the detritus which always seemed to settle in the unregarded corners of the city. The sounds of activity from the streets and buildings were muffled here, the close air a degree or two warmer than in the thoroughfares, and he began to feel a degree of peace and seclusion rare in a place like Fairhaven.

Not that he was entirely alone. There was enough squeaking and rustling in the shadows and garbage drifts to turn his mind to thoughts of an early supper, and the occasional cat or dog seemed to have had the same idea. From time to time he caught a glimpse of another gnome, using the same network of shortcuts, or carrying a ratting net and basket, but never close enough to exchange greetings with. Most of the windows he passed were shuttered, leaking lantern or candlelight, the few exceptions too high to look into even if he'd been interested in doing so. The handful of doors here were gnome sized, and few of them appeared to be in use.

As he approached the gap he'd been heading for, giving on to an alley leading to the street where he lived, he slowed a little. Raegan's warning about Gorash's minions not having got the message that he wasn't interested in going after their leader yet was still fresh in his mind, and he reached into his pocket, fumbling for the bag the watchman had given him.

It felt warm to the touch, and he closed his hand around it, a prickle of apprehension at the nape of his neck. Immediately he tightened his grip, a clump of shadow in a doorway opposite the passageway he was about to step out of dissipated like mist in the sun, and a goblin appeared, watchful eyes darting up and down the alley, and lingering a suspicious moment every time they passed the gap in the buildings down which Drago was lurking. He was dressed like the assassins last night, in dark clothing, and carried a sword, drawn and ready for use.

Drago let go of the charm in his pocket, but the effect still lingered; his would-be ambusher remaining perfectly visible. He rested his hand on the hilt of his own sword, and stepped out into the alley with a friendly smile.

"Aren't you getting bored yet?" he asked. "I might not be home for hours."

The effect was immediate. The goblin charged at him, his sword raised ready to strike. Drago sighed, turned on his heel to duck under the swing, and elbowed him in the ribs. A second's thought would have told his assailant that if Drago was confident enough to speak to him, and astute enough to have penetrated his magical concealment, it would have been far more prudent to listen to whatever he had to say. But then, in Drago's experience, prudence wasn't particularly high on the list of qualities required of hired muscle.

Grabbing the hilt behind the goblin's hand, Drago turned again, putting his other hand on the back of the blade and levering it upward, breaking his assailant's grip. With the goblin's sword securely in his possession, he snuggled the hilt more comfortably against his palm, and curled his fingers around it. The weapon was clumsy, the balance point too far forward, but then with weapons you tended to get what you paid for. His own had cost far more than he could afford at the time, but it had kept him alive, and in that regard alone had more than repaid his initial investment. As the goblin straightened up again, Drago rested the point against the fellow's codpiece; if he'd been taller, or his assailant shorter, he'd probably have gone for the hollow of the throat, which tended to get people's attention nicely, but when you were pushing two foot nine you often had to improvise, and threatening the family jewels was generally equally effective. In the rare cases it wasn't, you weren't far from the femoral artery either.

"Two things," Drago said reasonably. "I'm not interested in Greenleaf's proposition, so you people can sod off back to the Barrens, or wherever it is you're from, and stop making a mess of my shirts. My laundry bills are getting too high as it is."

"And the other thing?" The goblin glared down at him, but made no further move to attack. Something edged and pointy in the vicinity of the groin tends to have that effect.

"Thank you," Drago said, with a pleasant smile.

The goblin's brow furrowed. "Thanks for what?" he asked after a moment, curiosity winning out over truculence.

"For all the extra work coming my way. You people have taken most of my competitors out of the market."

"Don't expect to live long enough to get the benefit," the goblin said, anger trumping common sense as it so often did. "There are plenty more where I came from."

Drago sighed. "And just what part of 'I have no intention of accepting a contract on your boss' is failing to get through?" he asked patiently.

"The part where you're lying through your teeth," the goblin said.

"We've seen you laying in supplies. We know you're working for Stargleam's thugs."

"This?" Drago indicated the knapsack on his shoulders. "I just bought some new shirts. People keep bleeding on the old ones." He lowered the confiscated blade. "Now bugger off. I've got better things to do with my time than listen to people talking bollocks."

He took a step back, and pitched the sword down the gap between buildings behind him. The goblin might be able to retrieve it without getting his shoulders wedged, but it would take him a long time—long enough for Drago to get home and put his feet up, anyway. If the goblin wanted to hang around outside Mrs. Cravatt's all night after that, good luck to him. Raegan had promised to send a couple of watchmen past on a regular basis, and if his landlady spotted the lurker first, he'd probably be glad to see them.

"Then listen to this," the goblin said, his tone changing to one of gleeful malice. He spat out something in a guttural tongue that seemed to consist entirely of consonants and glottal stops. Drago had only heard the like a few times before, from mages he'd been hired to apprehend, and it had never presaged anything good. The goblin held up a small stone which he'd taken from his pocket, and threw it at Drago.

Drago drew his sword, and leapt aside, the speed of his gnomish reflexes taking him well clear of the object, which landed in the filth coating the alleyway with a faint squishing sound. For a second or two nothing seemed to happen, then the mud and ordure began to flow toward it, like a slow, viscid river. The goblin continued to chant, the same syllables repeating over and over, the harsh sounds raising the hairs on Drago's neck. The air became thick, crackling like a summer heat haze before the thunder breaks.

The filth reared up, forming a crude humanoid figure half again as tall as Drago, like something molded by a child from the riverside clay. Arms and legs extended, and a face, scowling in a parody of malice, grew from between the thing's shoulders.

It's not alive, Drago told himself, it's just a pile of crap with attitude. How dangerous can that be?

The sort of question that always tempts fate. Uttering a gurgling ululation rank with the smell of a thousand cesspits, the shambling monstrosity lashed out at him with one of its arms. Drago dodged the attack, the thing's still-forming fist pulverizing the bricks in the wall behind him, and smashing a new window in the rear of a tavern facing the main street beyond. Shrieks, shouts and curses echoed through the aperture, but no one seemed inclined to investigate, for which Drago could hardly blame them.

Drawing his sword, he hacked at the thing's arm as its next punch sailed past him, dodging out of the way with barely an inch to spare. It was hellish fast, almost as quick as he was, which was both unexpected and deeply worrying in a creature that size; although creature wasn't quite the right word. It wasn't alive in any real sense, just a construct for channeling magical energy and the malice of the goblin controlling it.

The blade sheared through the mass of filth, meeting barely any resistance, and emerged from the other side with a faint glopping sound. The muck simply flowed together in the wake of the cut, showing no sign at all of its passage.

This wasn't good. The crap golem turned to follow Drago as he dived to the left, putting a rain barrel between him and it, and lashed out again. Its movements were fluid, unconstrained by the rigidity of muscle and bone, and it wouldn't tire. Drago rolled in the nick of time, feeling the heels of his old boots dig painfully into his back as he landed on the rucksack, and swore, stagnant water and chips of sodden wood from the shattered barrel sousing him as he regained his feet.

The goblin sneered, a spiteful grin on his face, but kept on chanting, still the same few syllables over and over again; something short and easy to memorize. It must be the constant repetition, maintaining the spell, which kept the construct animated.

Fine, then, if he couldn't take out the crap monster he'd just have to deal with the puppeteer instead, and hope that would get rid of the problem. Which was fine in theory, but with five feet of ambulatory excrement standing between him and the goblin, easier said than done. The alley was narrow, and the foul abomination almost filled it, walling him off from his prey.

There was only one thing for it. He turned, as though making a dash for the other end of the alley, from which a faint glimmer of lantern light and the murmur of people going about their business drifted; the life of the city continuing unimpeded, oblivious to the life-or-death struggle occurring so close to hand.

The bluff worked: the accretion of mud and filth half strode, half flowed toward him, reaching out with soft, thick fingers, which stretched and flexed in their eagerness. As the semi-liquescent hand closed on his knapsack, Drago slipped out of the shoulder straps and turned, ducking low to dive between the thing's legs, striking out at where a live opponent would have had a hamstring. His blade simply slithered through the muck, as it had before, and with the same lack of discernible effect: precisely what he'd been expecting, but it was worth a try. He rolled to his feet, cursing at the coating of slime beslubbering his newly laundered jacket, and charged at the goblin.

The goblin's eyes widened with shock, but he kept on chanting, the hard-edged syllables still falling from his lips, though in a somewhat higher register. He took a couple of steps backward, chanting even louder and more urgently than before.

"You'd better have enough in your purse to pay for this mess!" Drago snarled, forgetting for a moment that none of his assailants the previous night had been carrying anything with them. But he never completed the strike. As his blade hissed toward the cowering goblin, something glutenous and foul-smelling wrapped itself around his chest, yanking him backward. He flailed wildly, trying to cut and stab behind him, but nothing connected, the animated filth simply closing seamlessly behind his sword as it had before.

The muck around him grew thicker, entangling his limbs, constricting his chest, and climbing higher with every panicked heartbeat. Moist, sticky foulness began to trickle inside his shirt and britches, flooding his new boots, and with a thrill of horror he felt it begin to flow across his face. It was in his ears too, muffling the chanting of the goblin, but not enough to hide the vindictive note now suffusing the unending repetition.

Drago took a last deep breath, almost gagging at the smell, and screwed his eyes closed as the spreading filth engulfed his nose and mouth, seeping into his nostrils. He felt a growing pressure against his eyelids, saw flashes of light and deeper darkness, and felt his chest begin to burn with the desperate need to inhale. Which would mean certain death, as the viscid slime enclosing him forced itself into his lungs, choking and drowning him in ordure.

Abruptly the pressure eased, and he plummeted to the ground, coughing and blinking his eyes clear, drawing deep, reviving draughts of stinking air into his abused lungs. The construct had suddenly fallen apart, becoming nothing more than a fetid heap of filth, already subliming back into the well-trodden dirt of the alleyway.

Somehow he'd managed to retain his grip on his sword, and he staggered to his feet, glaring round for the goblin.

"Where are you, you troll-shagging bastard?" he roared, more angry than he could remember ever having been in his life. He'd been close to death before, of course, that went with the job, but always in a straight-up fight where you could see what was coming at you. Every time he'd been on the wrong end of sorcery up until now, its wielder had intended only to hinder him long enough to flee.

"Over here, and I'll thank you to mind your language." Mrs. Cravatt wrinkled her nose, and aimed a kick at the now prostrate goblin, in response to a muffled groan and a myoclonic twitch. "And if you've any idea at all about setting foot in my house in that condition, I'm telling you now, you'll soon have another think coming."

"What happened to him?" Drago asked, excavating a plug of muck from his ear to hear the reply better, and instantly regretting it. When affronted, Mrs. Cravatt's voice tended to take on the quality of a stiletto straight to the brain.

"Me." His landlady nodded with evident pride at a job well done. "Lucky for you I came out to empty the chamber pots when I did." She brandished the piece of heavy earthenware in her hand; judging by the state of the goblin, Drago noted with a fair degree of vindictive satisfaction, it hadn't been empty when she hit him with it. "And there you were, wallowing about in that—stuff—and him capering around egging it on. So I told him, this is a respectable neighborhood, and we don't put up carryings-on like that around here. And he wouldn't stop, so I belted him one with the gazunder." She kicked the recumbent goblin again, for good measure. "That ought to learn him."

"Quite so." Drago got in a kick of his own, and bent down to retrieve his knapsack. As he'd expected, the filth had seeped inside, ruining his new shirts. "Might I trouble you to send a couple of messages for me? I'll pay you back, as soon as I've had a chance to wash the contents of my purse." Right now it was more like a bag of muck with coins embedded in it.

"You might do." Mrs. Cravatt sniffed suspiciously, then instantly regretted it. "If you move downwind. What are they?" She beckoned to a flock of the neighborhood urchins, who'd appeared at the mouth of the alley, drawn by whatever mysterious force invariably brings a huddle of spectators to someone else's misfortune.

"Let Captain Raegan at the watch house know someone he's interested in talking to has been detained by a—" he hesitated for a moment—"public-spirited citizen."

Mrs. Cravatt frowned. "Don't know about that. That lot are all bent as coat hangers. Better just dump this one in a canal. Least said, soonest mended."

"There may be a reward," Drago said. "Or, at the very least, he'll feel he owes you a favor."

"Oh, right." She flipped a penny at the nearest urchin. "You heard him. Make sure you get the big shouty one, don't get fobbed off with the stroppy sergeant." She watched the girl run off, and turned back to Drago. "Who else?"

"Greta at the laundry. Apologies for the short notice, can she do me a bulk wash as soon as possible. I'll pay double, and if she needs an enchantment I'll pay market rate for that too."

"I should think so, all the extra work she's having to fit in for you." Mrs. Cravatt hesitated on the verge of another sniff, thought better of it, and dispatched another messenger. "Anything else?"

"Yes." Drago nodded decisively. "One more, to Master Greenleaf, care of the Haberdasher's Guild. I've been considering his proposition, and would like to discuss the matter further." He wiped another layer of dirt from his face, and dropped it on the semi-conscious goblin, who he felt deserved it. "And if you could start boiling some water for a bath before I get back, I'd be very grateful."

His landlady's eyes narrowed. "Two shillings grateful?"

"At least," Drago said, turning in the direction of the waterfront.

"And where are you off to now, may I ask?"

Drago sighed. "The river," he said. If he waded in up to his neck for a few minutes, he might just be clean enough for the bath to make a difference when he came out. But he wasn't counting on it.

CHAPTER NINE

"She's not like that at all."

"Are you sure that's a good idea?" Raegan asked, over a late breakfast at The Blind Watchman, a tavern favored by off-duty members of the City Watch and the less dangerous of the local scofflaws in roughly equal numbers, both of whom found it useful to mingle with their professional adversaries on reasonably neutral ground. The watch heard a lot they found of interest, usually about the affairs of people they were a good deal more interested in than their drinking companions, and the local cutpurses and dolly-mops gleaned a reasonable idea of where the local patrols were least likely to be, which suited everyone fine. An arrangement which contributed not a little to the opinion Mrs. Cravatt, and a great many of her fellow citizens, had of the watch and its personnel, but so far as Raegan was concerned a little gossip was a small price to pay to keep the streets more or less safe for the law-abiding among Fairhaven's residents; he was certain there were a few out there somewhere.

"No. It's probably a bloody awful one," Drago admitted, around a mouthful of sausage. "But if they're going to keep coming after me anyway, I might as well get paid for it."

"True." Raegan still sounded doubtful, but then he'd been up all night, which hadn't improved his disposition. "That one you brought in last night . . ."

"Edna Cravatt brought in," Drago said, trying not to think too hard about that. He hadn't slept particularly well himself, and when he had,

73

his dreams had been far from restful. A fresh thought occurred to him, and he added, "I might have mentioned something to her about a reward."

"Oh." Raegan nodded. "That's why she's been hanging around all morning." He sighed, which turned into a yawn. "I'll get George to bung her a few shillings when I get back. Might even turn out to be worth it."

"Might at that," Drago agreed. "Not much goes on around here she doesn't know about." He took a swig of his ale, which, like the food, wasn't as good as the Footpad provided, but at least was being paid for by somebody else. "Has the troll shagger said anything yet?"

"Quite a lot." Raegan grinned, and took a bite of his bannock, the next sentence being delivered among a shower of crumbs. "Mostly adjectives, and unfounded speculation about your ancestry. But nothing of any use. And talking of which . . ." He broke off to wave at Vethik, who was glancing round the taproom with an air of impatient distaste from just outside the door, beneath the sign showing a member of the watch holding a bulging purse and ostentatiously not noticing the burglar shinning up a ladder a few feet behind him. Vethik preferred to patronize more salubrious establishments, and didn't mind making that obvious.

Catching sight of Raegan, the portly goblin mage sighed heavily, and rolled across the threshold. Once inside he began to make his way through the crowd of other patrons toward the table Drago and Raegan were seated at, Raegan on one of the chairs, Drago on a higher stool so he could eat unimpeded.

"There you are," he said, pulling up a chair of his own, and regarding the food before them with undisguised suspicion. He dropped the stone the assassin had thrown at Drago in the alley on the tabletop. "Don't worry, I've had it cleaned."

"Glad to hear it," Raegan said. "What can you tell me about it?"

Vethik shrugged. "Clever bit of work. Talisman of summoning, invokes a low-grade elemental, but nothing with the intelligence to be self-directed."

"Which is why the troll shagger never stopped chanting, I suppose," Drago put in, to show he was paying attention.

"Maybe. Or perhaps he just liked the sound of his own voice." Vethik glared at the gnome, nettled by the interruption. "A surprising number of people do."

"Please, go on," Drago said, chewing and swallowing a little more loudly than was strictly necessary.

"I can't tell you for certain who made it, but I followed your suggestion and took a look at the files. Does the name Elenath Swiftwind ring any bells?"

"Quickfart?" Raegan nodded. "Wasn't he the one those river pirates had brewing up waterspouts for them a couple of years back?" Vethik nodded a confirmation, and the captain went on reflectively. "It's his style, all right, but he's an elf."

"And in jail," Drago added. "Isn't he?"

Raegan shook his head. "Not as such, no. Turned council's evidence, dropped everyone else in it, and walked. Well, limped, after his old associates realized he'd grassed them up and sent the boys round for a chat about it, but he's still around. I'll get George to pull him in for a little talk."

"There's no need," Vethik said. "He's on Sergeant Waggoner's list already." He turned a scornful glance in Drago's direction. "And the fact that he's an elf doesn't mean he wouldn't sell an enchantment to the agents of a goblin bandit. This is Fairhaven, not the arse-end of nowhere. People get along with each other." He watched Raegan and Drago mirror one another's expressions of incredulity. "So long as they're making money out of it, anyway."

"Fair point," Raegan agreed. "So let's see what Quickfart has to say for himself, shall we?"

"I never meant any harm, Mister Raegan, you must be aware of that. The path of a mage is one of pure intellectual enquiry. The uses the fruits of my endeavors may be put to, however reprehensible, is not my responsibility." Swiftwind talked like a typical elf, but the arrogance Drago normally associated with his species was markedly absent. He looked sweatily nervous, and, in the close confines of Raegan's office, it had rapidly become apparent that, under stress, his nickname was well merited.

"I don't have time for this, Quickfart. Or the nose." Raegan leaned across his desk, managing to loom in a manner that even Clement Wethers would have been hard to equal. "Foreign agents have been murdering Fairhaven citizens, and the council aren't at all happy about that. Specifically, they're not happy with me, because we didn't stop it happening, which means I'm not happy with you, because you're an accessory. Are you following this?"

"Absolutely." The sweaty elf nodded, his ill-fitting conjurer's robes rippling with another nervous effusion. "This entire situation must be extremely unsatisfactory from your point of view."

"So the way I see it, there are two possible ways for me to make the council happy. Tell them I've got someone in custody with information about the goblin bandits' agents, and turn him over to their people for an intensive interview about the matter—" he broke off for a moment, until silence fell again in the office and the air cleared a little—"or tell them I've got an informant associated with the group who's happy to cooperate in keeping us abreast of whatever they're up to."

"Well, of course I'm happy to cooperate." Swiftwind forced a pallid smile of patent insincerity to his face. "What loyal citizen of the city wouldn't be?" Then his expression changed again, to one of undisguised alarm. "But these people are not to be trifled with. If they got so much of an inkling that I was informing on them, I'd be dead in a heartbeat."

"Then don't give them one," Drago put in, from his post leaning against the door; it looked appropriately intimidating, and at least there was a draft of relatively fresher air around the jamb. "And if you get any ideas about just telling Captain Raegan what you think he wants to hear, or holding out on him, I'll beat them to it. I've almost died twice because of the enchantments you've sold these ratbags, and I'm not in a forgiving mood."

"I think the significant word there is 'almost,'" Swiftwind said, with a desperate attempt at an ingratiating smile. "Which is a sterling testament to your skill and professionalism."

"Or maybe they should be asking you for a refund," Drago said, unable to resist another dig. "I would in their position." A possibility which had clearly not occurred to Swiftwind, judging by the sudden change in his expression. "Perhaps I should suggest it the next time they come after me."

"Maybe we should let them," Raegan suggested, with a wintery smile. "The rate you're getting through them, we might just solve the problem that way." He turned back to the odiferous mage. "So, names, places. Who do you deal with, and where can we find them?"

"You can't." Swiftwind squirmed, looking too uncomfortable to be lying. "They come to my workshop. Only place I ever see one of them."

"One of them?" Drago asked, already sure of the answer. It was pennies to pancakes Gorash's agents would operate in the same way as Stargleam's, and the mage would only have had contact with the opposition's equivalent of Greenleaf.

Swiftwind nodded, a little too fervently, eager to show he was cooperating. "Just the one," he confirmed. "She said it was safer that way." Safer for the goblin's network, anyway. Drago wouldn't have trusted the elf's discretion either. "Just used to turn up out of the blue. Well, black, really. She only came at night."

"I don't suppose this lady of the night gave a name, at all?" Raegan asked sarcastically.

Swiftwind flushed, his expression growing truculent. "She's not like that at all," he said vehemently. "She's a proper lady, and insinuations like that simply prove you're no gentleman."

Drago and Raegan exchanged surprised glances. It sounded as though the seedy mage had some finer feelings after all, had perhaps even been smitten by his client; if so, that could be useful. Subtly nurturing his romantic hopes might lead to a closer connection, and more useful information. On the other hand, it might divide his loyalties, rendering him useless as an asset. Or possibly get him killed. Not that any woman in her right mind would be likely to take a shine to Swiftwind, whatever her species.

Then a disturbing thought occurred to Drago, the narrowing of Raegan's eyes betraying that the same one had struck him at almost exactly the same moment. They'd have to get Swiftwind to take a look at the would-be assassin who'd tried to shoot him a couple of nights ago—all three of them were still laid out in the cellar of the watch house, where the cool damp air helped the preserving spells last a little longer.

"And does this paragon of virtue have a name?" Raegan asked.

"Hyacinth," Swiftwind said, with a faintly dreamy lilt to his voice. "Although I don't suppose for a moment it's her real one."

"How did she first get in contact with you?" Drago asked.

"The usual way. Just turned up at my workshop, like most clients do. She said she'd heard I was unusually skilled in certain areas, and I said I was pretty good at magic too. Just a little pleasantry to break the ice, as it were."

"And she found that amusing, did she?" Raegan asked, the edge of sarcasm back in his voice.

Swiftwind nodded. "She has a most mellifluous laugh. That was the first time I ever heard it."

Drago and Raegan exchanged glances again, and Drago felt an unexpected pang of sympathy for the shabby sorcerer. She had to have been playing him; and only someone who really wanted to be fooled could have failed to see it.

Before he could formulate another question, a loud rapping shivered the door timbers a foot or so above his head, and it burst open, almost crushing him against the wall.

"Guv." Waggoner ignored the aggrieved gnome, addressing his superior directly. "He's topped himself."

"What?" Raegan rose from his chair as though suddenly discovering it was on fire, and made for the door, ignoring Drago and Swiftwind alike. On the threshold, he turned and glared at the startled mage. "Don't move. If you so much as scratch your arse before I get back I'll have you charged with accessory to murder. Got it?"

"Got it," Swiftwind confirmed, underlining the point with a fresh burst of flatulence.

"Good." The two watchmen disappeared at a run, leaving Drago trotting ever farther behind in their wake.

"Lady Selina won't be at all pleased," Drago commented, finally catching up with Raegan and Waggoner in the cells. Fortunately most of them were empty at this time of the day, the few occupied exceptions at the other end of the corridor, as Raegan had given strict instructions to keep the suspect as far away from the rest of the prisoners as possible.

"Screw Lady Selina." Raegan kicked out irritably at the door of the cell, ignoring his subordinate's muttered "in your dreams." "*I'm* not pleased. Who found him?"

"I did," Waggoner admitted. "He'd had a couple of hours to cool down, so I thought I'd have another go at him while you were talking to Quickfart. Walked in, and found him like that." He indicated the erstwhile assassin, who was hanging from the bars of the narrow window, the single blanket from the bed twisted around his neck.

"And you're sure the door was locked?" Vethik asked, standing on the bed to reach the knot. The corpse was about the same height as the corpulent sorcerer, its feet dangling grotesquely, like a puppet hung up at the end of its performance. He muttered something, the knot came undone, and the cadaver slithered to the floor like a sack of grain.

"Of course I'm bloody sure," Waggoner said. "Why wouldn't I be?"

"Because in most cases of suicide, the victim's neck breaks after the noose has been tied, not before." Vethik hopped down to the floor, using the dead goblin as a convenient step.

"You're sure about that?" Raegan asked sharply.

Vethik shook his head. "No, I'm just taking a wild guess, completely ignoring all the evidence in front of me. What do you think?"

"I'm sorry, doctor." Raegan reined in his temper with a visible effort, resorting to flattery to mollify the mage. "It's just that every time we seem to be getting somewhere with this case, our leads turn up dead. And here, like this, is just bloody embarrassing!"

"Yes, I'm sure it is," Vethik said, unhelpfully.

"Can you tell us how he died?" Drago asked.

Vethik glanced in the gnome's direction, apparently noticing him for the first time, before returning his attention immediately to Raegan. "Judging by the pattern of bruising, and the fibers under his fingernails, I'd say the blanket did it."

Raegan took a very deep breath, released it slowly, and repeated the operation several times. "All by itself, I suppose."

"No, it had a bit of help." The corpulent mage stooped, peering at the floor, then gestured to Drago. "You're a lot lower down than I am, make yourself useful. Take a look under the bed."

Biting back the stinging retort he was sure was just about to occur to him, Drago stooped and took a cursory glance beneath the narrow padded bench. On the verge of standing again, he spotted something small, lying in the shadows, up against the wall. Swearing under his breath, he got down on his stomach, wriggled his head and shoulders under the bed, and reached out for it.

"Is that what you're looking for?" he asked, regaining his feet, and holding out the object he'd discovered. To his complete lack of surprise it was a stone, scored with intricate markings which made his eyes hurt if he looked at them too hard, and surprisingly heavy for its size. Almost identical, in other words, to the talisman the now-dead assassin had used in an attempt to kill him.

Vethik nodded, with an air of self-satisfaction which would have done credit to an elf. "Exactly what I would have expected to find," he said. "They waited until he'd fallen asleep, then lobbed that in through the window."

"Who did?" Waggoner interrupted, looking as though he didn't care particularly so long as it was someone he could hit.

"Whoever wanted him dead, of course," Vethik said, the unhelpfulness of his answer at least being mitigated by some accuracy this time.

"Another of Gorash's mob," Raegan said. "Making sure he kept his mouth shut." He glanced at Drago. "Maybe you leaving town for a while isn't such a bad idea."

"It couldn't be much more dangerous," Drago agreed. He still wasn't sure if he could go through with actually assassinating someone, if he even managed to find the bandit chief, but at the moment taking out Gorash was beginning to look less like cold-blooded murder and more like self-defense. If they'd turn on their own like this, his people were even more ruthless than he'd anticipated, and there was no telling how many more of them there were at large in the city. If he wasn't going to be looking over his shoulder for the foreseeable future, he was going to have to take the fight to their boss, and that was all there was to it.

"Unless you feel like being the bait again," Waggoner chipped in hopefully. "That'd make it a lot easier to find them."

"Think I'll pass," Drago said, as insouciantly as he could. "I'm off to talk to an elf about some linen."

"And I'm off to talk to one about this." Raegan hefted the recovered talisman, his face grimmer than Drago could recall having seen it in a long time. "And if the flatulent little scrote doesn't deliver, he's on his way to Her Ladyship's so fast his feet won't touch."

CHAPTER TEN

"I'll so miss our little chats."

To everyone's relief, however, Swiftwind turned out to have enough sense to admit that the talisman had been his handiwork as soon as Raegan confronted him with it. Rather less welcome was his admission that it, and the one used to attack Drago, had been part of an order for half a dozen, leaving another four still unaccounted for somewhere in the city: unless a few of them had already been used on other victims, who hadn't come to light yet. This in turn had prompted Vethik to take another look at Torvin's body; now he had reason to suspect thaumaturgy might have played a part in his excessively violent demise, but he wasn't prepared to speculate before completing his tests.

Drago left the watch house just after the mage had grumbled off to begin work in his private sanctum; he had no desire to witness a long overdue autopsy, however much amusement he'd derive from Vethik's annoyance at his presence, and Raegan had already promised to let him know the results if they seemed interesting.

"You've still got Quickfart's contact to follow up on," Drago consoled him as they parted, but Raegan shook his head ruefully.

"She's the one who tried to shoot you. I got him to take a look at the bodies." He sighed. "I almost felt sorry for the insanitary little scrote. I thought he was going to cry."

"He'd have felt a lot worse if you handed him over to the council's enforcers," Drago said, and Raegan nodded.

"There is that, I suppose. If Her Ladyship tries to poach him I'll tell her he's better off where he is, under observation, in case another of Gorash's goons decides they need some magical backup."

"I wouldn't hold your breath," Drago advised. "They're bound to know he's been compromised. They'll go somewhere else."

"Unless they decide he's a potential liability," Raegan said. He shrugged. "And if you won't be the bait again . . ."

"Good luck with that," Drago said. Personally, he couldn't see any point in trying to take out Swiftwind, who'd already told the watch everything he knew and a good deal he could only guess at, but the murky world of covert political action was new territory for him. He was used to taking down scofflaws like Fallowfield, who were easy to find and relatively easy to handle, with a guaranteed payday at the end of it.

"You're the one needing the luck," Raegan said, with more confidence than he probably felt.

"I'm happy to share it," Drago said. "I take it you've got eyes on Greenleaf, as he's the only other bugger we know in either faction?" If so, he'd have to move even more carefully in approaching the elf; Greenleaf was no fool, and if he caught sight of a lurking watchman in the vicinity of their meeting, he'd be bound to assume Drago was working with the city authorities now. Which, now he came to think of it, wasn't far from the truth. Shame he wasn't getting paid for it.

"I wish." Raegan shook his head. "Her Ladyship says to keep him at arm's length. Either the council have their own people on it, or she doesn't want him to know you've been talking to us."

"Probably both," Drago said, trying to sound unconcerned. "Be seeing you."

"Try not to end up in the river," Raegan said, actually sounding as though he meant it.

The Haberdasher's Guild was in the mercantile quarter, a couple of islands farther upstream, and on the opposite bank of the river. Drago took his time on the journey, leaving the Wharfside district over the main bridge to the North, dodging a steady stream of carts and sweating stevedores moving in both directions as he crossed the carriageway, and pausing to watch the skiffs and cargo barges passing underneath along the almost equally crowded canal. He loitered a number of times after that, purchasing a sausage in a bun from a street vendor, browsing a few market stalls which appeared to catch his interest, and ducking once into a convenient alley to relieve himself. Every time he paused in his journey he glanced around with apparent casualness, but if he was being followed or observed, he could see no sign of it.

Which didn't mean no one was there, of course. He'd trailed enough people himself to be aware of how easy it was to blend into the crowds along the main thoroughfares. Nevertheless, sooner or later he'd have to take a chance. Moving as casually as he could, he took to one of the narrow gaps between buildings none of the larger races could conveniently traverse. Now, if someone was after him, they'd have to tip their hand by attempting to follow, and he was confident he could outpace a goblin, elf or human easily in these cramped conditions.

Unless they knew this part of the city better than he did, which was quite likely so far from his home turf, and were able to cut him off . . .

He dismissed the thought; there was nothing to be gained by spooking himself, and he'd either be safe or he wouldn't. A couple more twists and turns, and he found himself back on the streets, a narrow lane running alongside one of the minor canals this time. There were fewer people about here, and a couple of heads turned, registering the presence of a stranger, but no one seemed concerned enough to challenge him. Good. If he stood out, so would anyone following him, and he'd get a clear heads-up from the body language of the locals.

A couple of dozen yards ahead, a ramshackle wooden staircase descended toward the water. As he approached it, a pair of humans trotted up from the landing stage at the bottom, making the timbers shake, linked arms, and ambled off in the opposite direction, their attention so clearly on one another that they probably wouldn't have noticed the approaching gnome unless they tripped over him.

Drago descended a little more cautiously, the treads of the stairway flexing beneath his feet. As he'd expected, a couple of skiffs were tied up there, wallowing gently in the wash of the larger vessels being poled down the narrow waterway by their crews, or propelled with rather more splashing and profanity by rear-mounted paddle wheels turned by trudging convicts.

"Where to, guvnor?" The nearest boatman unfastened his painter at the first sight of a potential customer. The other shrugged, content to go on munching his docky while he flirted with a deckhand on a passing barge.

"Woolen Wharf," Drago said, stepping aboard, and adjusting his balance instinctively as the boat rocked. Pretty much anyone native to Fairhaven had that particular knack.

"No problem." The boatman pushed off from the landing stage with practiced ease, and began pulling away with smooth strokes of the oars. "Shouldn't take long. Tide's coming in."

"Good." Drago kept an eye on the receding shoreline. No one seemed remotely interested in his departure, but he didn't feel entirely at ease until the little boat was well out into the main channel, the mast and sail had been raised, and they were scudding across the water toward the far bank.

The docks in the mercantile quarter were occupied almost entirely by riverboats, all but the smallest seagoing vessels having too deep a draught to navigate this far upriver, but the traffic was constant, and the skiff bearing Drago across the water had to weave and tack several times to avoid a collision. As well as the riverboats, and innumerable small craft like his own, this portion of the Geltwash was crowded with barges, transferring cargoes between the riverboat staithes and the ocean-going wharves downstream. Nevertheless, the boatman managed to bring the little skiff alongside a landing stage almost identical to the one they'd set out from without mishap.

"Mind how you go," he said cheerfully, pocketing the coins Drago had given him, and already extending a welcoming smile to a prosperous-looking merchant and her amanuensis descending the steps toward them. The most superfluous advice Drago had received in a long time, but he nodded affably in response, and began climbing the treads toward the street. As usual, they'd been spaced for a human stride, but he climbed them quickly, springing from one step to another as easily as ascending the stairs to his room at Mrs. Cravatt's.

Finding the Clothiers' Guildhall turned out to be simple enough, despite his relative unfamiliarity with this part of the city. As its name implied, the Woolen Wharf was where the vast majority of fleeces and fabrics arrived in Fairhaven from farther upstream, and the Clothiers had built their guildhall where they could inspect the incoming cargoes and haggle over their worth with the minimum of delay and inconvenience. Though the building was no taller than the warehouses which surrounded it, and perhaps a little more modest in the amount of space it took up, no expense had been spared on its ornamentation: eloquent testimony to the wealth of the guild and its members, and therefore their importance in the eyes of the city. Not to mention themselves, which was probably the real point.

Drago refused to be impressed by anything other than good food and fighting skill, so he plodded up to the doors without a glance in the direction of the ornately carved figures of various races apparently propping the place up, other than to note that they all seemed surprisingly underdressed considering the commodity being bought and sold there.

"That's far enough, shortarse." A big human, in a garish livery which made him resemble nothing so much as an overstuffed sofa, stuck out an officious hand to bar his progress through the open door. Well-dressed gentlemen and ladies of several species were filing in and out, including a couple of gnomes who glanced at Drago with barely concealed contempt, all ignoring the doorman as though he was little more than another superfluous embellishment to the fabric of the building. Perhaps, to them, he was. "The likes of you go round the back."

"The likes of me go wherever they damn well please," Drago said evenly. "Now go and find Master Greenleaf of the Sylvan Marches, and tell him Drago Appleroot would like a word." He shifted his weight in a seemingly casual manner, which wasn't lost on his suddenly far less confident interlocutor. Doing this just so happened to leave his hand resting lightly on his scabbard, where it could pull backwards away from the blade if he needed to draw his sword quickly. Taking the sheath back as he drew the weapon forward would drastically cut the time needed to ready the weapon. Not that he would; the man barring his way was all bluster, clearly recognized a seasoned fighter when he saw one, and instantly became more deferential.

"Do you have an appointment?" the man asked, trying to back away without seeming to, and failing dismally.

"I wasn't aware I needed one," Drago said, masking a smile. "But I'm sure he'll see me." He allowed a peremptory edge to creep into his voice. "And I don't have all day."

"Of course not." The doorman didn't quite call him sir, but the impulse was undoubtedly there.

"Good." Drago strode past him into the cool shadows of the entrance hall. Wood-paneled walls, an ornate staircase, even more encrusted with carvings than the exterior of the building, and a series of closed doors met his eyes, along with curious glances from the dozen or so people passing through it on business of their own. He dug a copper coin from his purse, of a denomination just the right side of insultingly low, and lobbed it at the liveried functionary, who caught it by reflex. "Then get moving."

The doorman did, leaving Drago to muse on just how easy it was to get people to do what you wanted by acting as if they didn't really have a choice.

"This is an unexpected surprise." Greenleaf descended the stairs a moment or two later with a welcoming smile, the doorman hovering a couple of paces behind until they reached the floor, whereupon he bolted for his place by the entrance, leaving the elf to talk to Drago alone. If he was curious about what business so ill-matched a pair might have together he gave no sign of it, but Greenleaf ushered the bounty hunter into a comfortably furnished side room and closed the door before saying anything else nevertheless. "May I ask what you're doing here?"

"I sent you a message," Drago said, wondering for a moment if his faith in Mrs. Cravatt's ability to disburse funds on his behalf had been a little on the optimistic side. But Greenleaf nodded, settling himself comfortably in a well-padded chair, before favoring Drago with a quizzical tilt of his head. The gnome remained standing; all the seats he could see would have required clambering into, and were so thickly upholstered that he would have had to fight his way out again. Not at all a good place to be, if things turned out badly.

"So you did. You're reconsidering my proposition." The tone was light, but the eyes fixed on him were hard and calculating. "May I ask why?"

"Because Gorash's rabble keep trying to kill me," Drago said. "And if I am going to die because they think I'm working for you, I might as well spend as much of your money as I can in the meantime."

The elf permitted himself a slight chuckle, which sounded genuinely amused. "Not quite the answer I was expecting, to be honest. But I can see why you might think that."

"Then what were you expecting?" Drago asked.

Greenleaf shrugged. "Honestly? Lies and evasions, intended to obscure your real objective."

"Which would be?" Drago wondered why no one connected with this business could ever say what they meant. Whatever you might think about Clement Wethers, and plenty of people thought a great deal, there was never any of this dancing around the point with him. It was just "That little toe rag's getting too cocky by half. Go and give him a slap," followed swiftly by the agreement of a fee.

"I'm sure the city authorities are well aware by now that my people are looking for someone like you to do the job we discussed, and that our previous choices have been prevented from completing their commissions," Greenleaf said. "In their place, I'd want someone reporting back to me about their activities. Who better than a local bounty hunter I'd already approached, having a sudden change of mind after an initial refusal?"

"Pretty much anyone?" Drago countered. He locked eyes with the elf for a moment, knowing Greenleaf would be the first to blink. Having eyes adapted to low light levels was a big help in that regard. "The only reason I'm doing this is because it's Gorash or me now, and it's not going to be me if I can help it. Blame his own people for not letting it drop after I turned you down."

"Of course. And Lady Selina suggesting you change your mind never even entered into it." The elf's smile was open, friendly, and about as trustworthy as a come-on from a lamia.

"Who?" Drago asked, being careful not to overplay his hand. Greenleaf was just guessing, he was certain of that, and if he wasn't, there was nothing he could do about it anyway. He'd heard enough lies and excuses in his line of work to know that the more you say, the less convincing it sounds.

"Never mind. It's not important." Greenleaf seemed willing to let it go, anyway. "Let's just say I believe you. How soon can you start?"

"Tomorrow," Drago said. He had a few things to take care of before he left, like leaving Mrs. Cravatt enough money to ensure that she didn't let his room out to somebody else before enough time had elapsed for her to be reasonably certain he was dead, and stuffing some potentially useful belongings into his knapsack. He noted Greenleaf's reaction, the evident suspicion on the elf's face receding noticeably as he assessed the implications of his timetable. If he was really intending to try and discover the extent of Greenleaf's network, he would be making excuses to remain in the city for as long as possible, not planning to leave the following day. "No point hanging about. The sooner I'm gone, the less chance they have to take another crack at me."

"That would certainly suit us," Greenleaf said. He paused. "Have you made travel plans?"

"Not as such," Drago said. He had an idea about leaving the city, but no desire to share it with anyone. "But I'll be gone by tomorrow night, you can count on that."

"And your fee?" Greenleaf asked.

"Your original offer sounds fair," Drago said. "I'll take the down payment now."

Greenleaf's eyebrow rose. "And what makes you think I have that kind of money on me at the moment?"

Drago waved an expansive arm, taking in their surroundings, and the rest of the guildhall beyond. "You're here, aren't you? How else are you going to do business?"

Once again, the elf permitted himself a brief chuckle. "Oh, I do hope you don't get yourself killed. I'll so miss our little chats." He pulled a bulging purse from inside his intricately brocaded doublet, and counted out the ridiculously high sum he'd offered on the eventful evening he'd visited Drago at home. There seemed to be plenty left, and the gnome wondered briefly if he should have held out for more, but the deal had been struck and that was all there was to it.

"I'll try not to disappoint you," he said instead.

CHAPTER ELEVEN
"It's a lot iffy."

"Well, aren't you full of surprises," Lady Selina said, as Drago stepped aboard the hired skiff he'd found bobbing at the same landing stage he'd arrived at on his journey to the mercantile quarter. His conversation with Greenleaf hadn't lasted more than a few minutes, and he'd set out to return home and prepare for his journey as soon as it was concluded.

"I might say the same," he rejoined. The last time he'd seen her, Selina had been dressed in a manner befitting her station, and accompanied by the sort of bodyguard most people of high standing trailed around like lapdogs. Now she was alone, in the rough working clothes of a professional boat handler, the strands of hair escaping from her red-knitted cap hanging as lank and greasy as though they hadn't been washed since the last time she fell in the river. Her movements were quick and assured as she unhitched the painter and pushed off, matching her appearance; only her hands, which lacked the calluses that went with a lifetime of handling rope and oars, would have betrayed the deception to someone sufficiently observant. Drago was, but strongly suspected that very few of the other passengers in the boat that day, if there had actually been any, would have noticed anything at all unusual about the ferrywoman conveying them across the Geltwash.

"I thought we could talk here without interruption," Lady Selina said, raising the sail and sending the little craft scudding across the water, tacking widely to avoid a riverboat laden with timber. "Or being overheard."

"Talk about what?" Drago asked.

"Greenleaf and his network," Selina said. "I'm pleased you reconsidered after our last little talk."

"I'm sorry to disappoint you," Drago said, "but that's not the reason I've taken the contract. I'm just tired of the other lot trying to kill me, so I'm going after Gorash."

"Tall order," Selina said, with a trace of a smile. "Do you really think you can kill him in cold blood?"

"If I have to," Drago said, suppressing a shiver of doubt as he spoke. "But I'm hoping he'll just call off the dogs if I talk to him nicely."

"Because murderous bandits are so well known for their obliging natures," Selina said, with evident amusement. She seemed to be enjoying the conversation, unless it was handling the boat that she found so congenial. People of her rank normally had servants for that sort of thing.

Drago shrugged. "Worth a try. And if he doesn't, it's him or me."

"Self-defense again, as Captain Raegan would say."

"I suppose so, yes," Drago agreed, looking for an excuse to change the subject. He narrowed his eyes against the glitter of the sun on the water, and relished the cool breeze against his face. "How did you know where to find me?"

"Lucky guess," Lady Selina said, and laughed at his resulting expression. "Well, not that lucky. I was the one who told you where to find Greenleaf, and that was the nearest landing stage to the guildhall."

"And you've just been hanging around there on the off-chance I'd want to talk to him again."

"Of course not." She went hard about without warning, noticing his reflexive duck under the swinging boom with evident approval, scudding across the wake of a riverboat heading upstream with a cargo of barrels lashed to its deck. What was in them Drago had no idea, but strongly suspected some kind of foodstuff; which reminded him in turn that it had been some hours since his breakfast with Raegan. "You sent him a message, remember? I was pretty sure you wouldn't be far behind."

"So you went to all this trouble just for me. I'm flattered." His boot bumped against something under the seat, and he groped for it, never taking his eyes off the woman at the tiller. There was clearly far more to her than met the eye, and in his experience that generally meant things were about to get complicated.

"Not just for you." Drago's hand grasped cloth, and he found himself pulling out a docky bag, bread and cheese and a gurgling bottle wrapped in a knotted rag. Selina grinned. "Trust a gnome to find the food. Help yourself." Never one to turn down a free meal, Drago did so, while she continued. "We've been keeping an eye on Master Greenleaf for a while now, but he's bright enough to assume he's under observation even if he can't be sure about that. So his associates are proving hard to identify."

"You must have some idea, though," Drago said, round a plug of bread and cheese. He chased it down with a pull at the bottle, which contained a rather better vintage than a boatswoman would normally have access to without breaking into a warehouse, and swallowed.

"We're narrowing it down," Selina said. "But you could make things a lot easier for us." They were almost midway across the river by now, and a good deal farther downstream, in spite of the still incoming tide retarding their progress. "If you ask him for a bit of help with your travel arrangements, or getting supplies together, that kind of thing, it'll make it a lot easier for us to identify his associates."

"I've already told him I'm sorting all that out for myself." Drago finished the last of the cheese, and followed it with the rest of the wine to clear his palate. He preferred ale, truth to tell, but it wouldn't be polite to say so.

"I see." The counterfeit boatswoman nodded, masking her disappointment. "And may I ask what arrangements you're making?"

"I'd rather you didn't," Drago said, more because he wasn't entirely sure than out of any sense of discretion.

"And you'll be seeing him again before you set out on your travels?" Selina asked.

"I doubt it," Drago said. "I'm leaving tomorrow."

"I see." If the woman was disappointed, she hid it well. "Then all I can do is wish you the best of luck."

"And the same to you," Drago said. He was, after all, a lifelong Fairhavener, and he supposed someone ought to be looking out for the city's interests.

"Can we assist you in any way?" Selina asked, lowering the sail, and beginning to pole the little boat into a narrow cut between the wharves and warehouses dominating the riverbank. Most of the vessels surrounding them now were noticeably bigger than the ones at the start of their journey, ocean-going ships, with only a handful of riverboats tied up in the smaller basins, ready to transship their cargoes with the minimum of delay.

"Thank you for the offer," Drago said, wondering what the catch would be if he said *yes*, and determined not to find out, "but you'd probably better not. If I was Greenleaf I'd be keeping an eye on me, and he's definitely got one out for you. He mentioned your name."

"Flatteringly, I hope," Selina said, steering the boat to a small landing stage halfway along the narrow canal. Nothing larger than the skiff was moored there, or, for that matter, could have found its way along the confined waterway to reach it. "I'm sure you can find your way from here."

"I'm sure I can," Drago said. Now that they were back in the Wharfside, he knew every inch of the area surrounding them. He was only ten minutes walk from the Footpad, and about twice that from Mrs. Cravatt's. Reluctantly, he pushed all thoughts of his favorite inn to the back of his mind. He had a lot to get done before he could think about eating again. Which reminded him. His hand hovered uncertainly over his purse. "What do I owe you for the ride?" Neither could be entirely certain they were unobserved, and failing to pay his fare would be certain to arouse suspicion in the mind of anyone watching.

"Sixpence should cover it." He wasn't sure, but he thought he detected a hint of amusement in the woman's voice. "And tuppence for my lunch." She watched him dig the coins out of his purse with a sardonic smile. "No tip?"

"Watch your back," Drago advised, as he trotted up the steps to the street above.

"Well, yeah, I can talk to some people. Not making any promises, mind." Clement Wethers, in defiance of all previous expectation, leaned back in his chair instead of forward across his desk. "All sounds a bit iffy, though, if you ask me."

"It's not. It's a lot iffy," Drago told him. Events were spiraling out of control, a sensation he never liked, and none of the outcomes he could see were particularly good. That said, the ones with him dead in them were particularly unappealing.

The worst thing about it was that he had no one to blame for the situation apart from himself. If he hadn't offered to act as bait for Raegan, seeing nothing more than the chance to earn some quick cash and get under Waggoner's skin, Greenleaf would never have approached him, and Gorash's minions wouldn't have made him a target.

"Well, leave it with me," Wethers said. If anyone in the Wharfside district had the connections Drago needed to follow through on his nebulous plan for leaving the city unnoticed by goblin assassins or elvish fixers alike, it would be the chairman of the Tradesman's Association. He would have felt a lot happier if he could have believed that Selina, or someone connected to her, would be equally easy to evade, but somehow he doubted that.

"Thanks." He slipped off the oversized chair, and paused in the doorway of Wethers's office. "I appreciate it."

"Always happy to help," Wethers assured him. "You know me."

"Indeed I do," Drago agreed, trying not to think about what a favor of this magnitude was liable to end up costing him in the long run. Chances still were he'd end up dead, and not have to worry about it anyway, but he preferred not to think about that either.

"You're going to be away for how long?" Mrs. Cravatt asked, her eyes darting around his attic room as though already contemplating how much to charge a new tenant.

"I don't know." Drago pulled a couple of Greenleaf's gold pieces out of his purse, noting with some amusement the way her attention suddenly became riveted on his hand. "But this should cover the rent until I get back." And then some. If he wasn't back in Fairhaven by the time that amount of money ran out, he wouldn't be coming back at all.

"I'll keep everything nice and tidy for you," his landlady promised, no doubt meaning she'd rifle the place for any unsecured valuables under the pretext of cleaning the moment his back was turned.

"No need to put yourself out on my account," Drago assured her, beginning to sort out some cleanish clothes as he spoke. His new knapsack was looking a trifle the worse for wear after its encounter with Fairhaven's streets, but was less aromatic than he'd feared, so he began packing some possessions carefully, maximizing the usable space. "Captain Raegan'll be dropping by from time to time, to air the place out." And to check for any messages he might want to send back without attracting any official attention. To be honest, he didn't think it was all that likely that he'd need to, but you never knew, and it was kind of reassuring to know that he could if required. Besides, with the possibility of an unanticipated visit from the watch at any time, the chances of finding most of his belongings where he'd left them would be substantially improved.

"It's no trouble." His landlady emitted a familiar sniff, but without the usual overtones of disapproval. "I'll just go and make you a bap for the trip. Can't have you going hungry."

"No fear of that," Drago assured her. He wasn't going to make the same mistake as his predecessors, by gathering supplies before leaving, which had attracted the attention of Gorash's assassins, but he wasn't planning to starve either. There were bound to be plenty of inns between here and the Sylvan Marches, and his purse ought to last the distance if he was reasonably frugal. If the worst came to the worst, he supposed, he could eke out his cash reserves by foraging along the way, underestimating the difficulty of such a course with the casual optimism of the lifelong urbanite. Squirrels, for instance. He'd seen pictures of those, and they looked a lot like rats—they couldn't be much harder to catch. Easier, probably, if they were crawling laboriously up a tree trunk.

"Well, you'll be glad of it later," Mrs. Cravatt said, and clattered off down the stairs, getting the last word in while she still could.

CHAPTER TWELVE
"It all spends the same."

As it turned out, Mrs. Cravatt was going to be right about him being grateful for the filled bread roll, even if both it and the cold bacon within were a little on the elderly side. Drago left his lodgings as dusk began to fall, making his way to the Tradesmans' hall through the narrow network of passageways only a gnome could have comfortably traversed, to minimize the chances of being spotted. Though he checked behind him at frequent intervals, particularly after crossing a proper thoroughfare, he saw no one, and nothing stirred in response to his hurrying feet beyond the occasional startled rat.

"This way." A human urchin he vaguely recognized, who hung around the Tradesmans' hall in the hope of being given messages to run, and occasional scraps from the kitchen, gestured to him as he emerged onto the street. Drago followed the lass, hanging back to make it less obvious that she was his guide, to the rear door of a warehouse close to the riverboat basin adjoining the landing stage Lady Selina had dropped him at. Probably a coincidence, but you never quite knew, and Drago felt a creeping sense of unease, until a large shadow detached itself from the doorway, looming over them both in a manner which was quite unmistakable.

"Well done." Clement Wethers dropped a couple of coins into the girl's outstretched hand. "Now sling your hook." He watched with narrowed eyes until the child had disappeared into the maze of darkened alleyways. "Anyone follow you?"

"If they did, they're better at it than me," Drago admitted. He was as certain as he could be that he'd successfully evaded anyone trying to keep an eye on him; but he was learning not to take anything for granted these days.

"Good enough." Wethers ushered him inside, with a quick glance at their surroundings, although his human eyes couldn't have seen much in the gathering gloom; but Drago's sharper night vision didn't spot any sudden flurries of movement which might have betrayed a hidden watcher either.

The warehouse was unremarkable, like most of the others Drago had ever been in: cavernous, cheaply built, smelling faintly of damp and old sacking. Shelves clambered up the walls, stuffed with small boxes and bundles, while stacks of crates and barrels covered most of the floor, casting shadows in the flickering light of a lantern hanging from the ceiling. Only one of the dozen or so up there had been lit, casting a small circle of light over a clearing in the boxes, its fellows dangling like roosting bats in the gloom.

"This him?" An elf stepped forward to greet Wethers, with a dismissive glance in Drago's direction. She was dressed in simple working clothes, topped off with a fraying blue coat, which marked her out as the captain of a riverboat; though not a particularly prosperous one, judging by the hard wear it had obviously seen.

"Yeah." Wethers waved a hand between them. "Drago, Marieth."

"Captain Clearspring will do," the elf said, coming completely into the circle of lantern light. Though she still had a trace of the elvish hauteur common to her species, her tone was devoid of the arrogance Drago had been expecting; and her complexion was so rough and wind-reddened that only her slender build and the points at the tips of her ears marked her out as non-human.

"Then Master Appleroot will do nicely for me," Drago said, with an exaggerated bow.

To his surprise, the elven woman laughed.

"I like him," she said to Wethers. "Where did you find him?"

"In my office," Wethers said. "When Drago wants something, he doesn't hang about."

"Sounds like I'll need to keep an eye on him, then." Captain Clearspring looked down at the gnome speculatively. "Why are you so keen to skip town?"

"Because people keep trying to kill me," Drago said. The woman was clearly no fool, and there was no point in lying unnecessarily. "And there are some other people I'd rather avoid too."

"Not sure you'd find the Marches much of an improvement," Clearspring said. "I was glad enough to get out of them, and I'm an elf."

"I was told there are jobs for gnomes there," Drago said, and the elven woman nodded.

"In the Barrens, at least. But you don't look like a miner to me." Her eyes narrowed. "You look more like trouble waiting for someone to happen to."

"I can take care of myself if I have to," Drago said, matter-of-factly.

"I'm sure you can." Her tone became businesslike. "Clement says you've got the money. How much do you think passage to the Marches is worth?"

Drago shrugged. "Couple of sovs?" he suggested. Two of the gold coins embossed with the image of the last monarch of the region, who'd been replaced by the city council in mysteriously fatal circumstances over a century before, would have got him a long way upriver under most circumstances. But these circumstances were highly unusual, and Clearspring knew it.

"Five," she shot back. "Take it or leave it."

"Three," Drago responded, knowing how the game was played.

But Clearspring shook her head. "I'm not haggling. You look like trouble, and I can do without that. Five sovereigns might make it worth my while to take the chance. Even then, if I think you're putting my boat or my people at risk, you're going over the side. Do we have a deal?"

"We do." Drago smiled at Wethers. "I like her too. Where did you meet? I'm guessing not at the temple."

"We know some of the same people." Wethers's tone made it clear that further enquiries would not be welcome. "I told you I'd ask around."

"And I appreciate it." Drago turned back to Clearspring, and dug five gold coins from his purse. "There. Five sovs."

The riverboat captain's face darkened. "That's Marcher currency. Where did you get that?"

"Does it matter? Gold's gold." Drago studied her face, which had taken on an unexpectedly harder edge. After a moment she nodded.

"Fair point. It all spends the same." But she still didn't look happy.

"I'll leave you to it, then," Wethers said, and Drago nodded, relieved at the diversion.

"See you when I get back."

"You'd better," Wethers said, though whether he meant to remind the gnome that he owed him a significant favor, or was really expressing concern for his safety, Drago couldn't quite tell.

A draft of cold air, and the muffled bang of the door, announced Wethers's departure. As he left, two humans dressed like their skipper, apart from the blue coat marking her position of authority, slipped into the warehouse. Clearspring scowled at them. "You took your time."

"Sorry, skipper," the man said, not really sounding it. He was tall, almost a head higher than Clearspring, and muscular with it; his companion wasn't particularly large for a human woman, about the same size as the elf, but broad and stocky. Of the two, she'd be the most dangerous in a brawl, strongly centered, and with the strength to capitalize on that. "Took us a while to get the cargo stowed. Where's the rest of it?"

"Right there." Clearspring jerked her head in Drago's direction. Both sailors looked surprised.

"Just him?" the woman asked.

"Just him." The elf turned back to Drago. "Well, jump in, then. We haven't got all night."

"Jump in where?" Drago asked, following her gaze, and finding himself looking at an empty barrel, its lid propped up against the curving wooden sides. He shook his head. "You have got to be kidding me."

"Fine, have it your way." Clearspring shrugged. "Walk down to the boat in plain sight. If you're that sure none of the people trying to kill you are anywhere around."

"Kill him?" The man looked at Drago with renewed interest, as though the evening was becoming more entertaining than he'd bargained for.

The woman just stared, in sullen hostility. "What've you got us into this time, Skip?"

"Nothing." Neither of her crew appeared to believe her. "We're going to the Marches anyway, he wants passage there. We get paid for taking him, everybody wins."

"Unless whoever's after him jumps us on the way," the man objected.

"Which is why we keep him hidden until we're well upstream," Clearspring said. She glanced at Drago. "Unless you're willing to pay double for the extra risk?"

"Fine." Drago clambered into the barrel, and crouched down. It seemed quite roomy, all things considered, and, not for the first time, he was grateful for his stature. The wood smelled faintly of apples, and he inhaled appreciatively.

"Comfortable?" Clearspring asked.

"Not particularly."

"Tough." She dropped the lid in place, tapping it home with an expert hand. Some of the staves turned out to be warped with age, admitting a few glimmers of light, and a modicum of fresh air. Drago put an experimental eye to the nearest, but his field of vision was so restricted he might just as well not have bothered; nothing could be seen except shadows, and occasional flickers of movement.

After a moment or two the barrel shifted, accompanied by grunting and muffled curses from the deckhands, swayed uncomfortably for a moment, then came to rest with a jar and a muffled bump. After that a slight rocking motion began, accompanied by a faint regular squeaking. From that, and the occasional semi-audible comment from one of the three people walking alongside, he inferred that the barrel had been hoisted onto a handcart, which was now being wheeled to the docks.

After just long enough for Drago to become numbed to the continuing discomfort, there were some more abrupt shifts, a sudden falling sensation, and a loud thud, which shook the wooden container. Disconcerted, he scrambled to the crack and peered through it again, seeing nothing; even his exceptional low-light vision was unable to make out anything but shadows and darkness.

"Stay quiet," Clearspring instructed in an undertone, which echoed slightly, then silence fell, broken only by the faint sound of retreating footsteps. A moment later there was a muffled, reverberating bang, and the darkness outside the barrel intensified.

"Great." Drago pushed against the lid, finding, to his complete lack of surprise, that it failed to move.

He considered his options. He could probably break out, given time, but that would make a lot of noise. At the very least Clearspring would object to that, quite possibly refusing to go through with the deal, and he didn't exactly have a lot of alternatives. If the elf and her crew had meant him any harm they'd have made their move by now; the fact that they seemed to have stowed the barrel in the hold of her boat would indicate that she intended going through with their deal, at least for now. Better to wait, and see what happened.

In the meantime, he might as well eat the bacon bap.

CHAPTER THIRTEEN
"Is she always that friendly?"

Eventually, to his own vague surprise, Drago fell asleep; something he only became aware of when he was jerked out of an unpleasant dream of being attacked by a swarm of rats, which merged into a large, vaguely humanoid form that flowed around him like liquid and began crushing and suffocating him at the same time. Two or three heavy blows shook the barrel, and he struck out by reflex, only remembering where he was as his elbow thudded into the surrounding wood. The impact jarred up his arm, leaving it tingling, and making him feel sick to his stomach.

"Rise and shine." The lid of the barrel disappeared, revealing the grinning face of the male human sailor. "Skipper says it's safe to come up on deck now, if you feel like it."

"Why not?" Drago responded, trying to stand, and belatedly discovering that every joint he possessed seemed to have locked solid during the night. After a moment, the sailor reached down a helping hand, which, after a moment of his own, Drago decided to accept.

"Have you really been sleeping?" the man sounded amused and impressed, in roughly equal measure, as he half helped, half lifted Drago out of the barrel.

Drago nodded. "I've had a busy few days," he said, trying to ignore the audible crackling as he unkinked his neck, and looking at his surroundings with interest. As he'd surmised, he was in the hold of the riverboat, which seemed full of neatly stacked boxes and barrels. A few smaller packages were stowed in nets fastened to the inside of the hull. Fore and aft, bulkheads ran the full width of the boat, more narrowly nearer the bow; here a small door gave access to the fo'c's'le, just below a pair of hammocks, in both of which rested a small bundle of personal possessions. Drago assumed that this was where the crew slept. About half the ceiling area was occupied by a cargo hatch, covered with a wooden lid. Forrard of that, where the hull began to curve inwards, a ladder led up to a smaller hatch, half uncovered, through which thin gray daylight was dribbling into the crowded space.

"You and me both," the man said, in a reasonably friendly manner. "But with less of the life threatening here," he added, after a moment's thought. He turned to the ladder. "Coming?"

"Might as well," Drago said.

The first thing which struck Drago as his head emerged from the hatch was a strange smell, which sliced its way into his sinuses and made him sneeze. Only after some time had gone by did it begin to dawn on him that this was fresh air, unfreighted with the familiar odors of Fairhaven, and therefore not to be trusted. The second was that there were no buildings looming over him, just the broad expanse of the Geltwash all around the boat, a rippling greenish blue, in stark contrast to the grayish sea water and brownish sludge of the city canals. About three hundred yards to the right, open fields studded with trees and the occasional barn or farmhouse scudded past, full of swaying stalks of grain almost as tall as Drago, the broad-leaved tops of some root vegetable he didn't recognize, or grazing livestock.

The opposite bank was almost three times farther away, but the landscape there seemed much the same: broad, flat and cultivated almost to the horizon, where a faint gray line could have been either a bank of cloud or low-lying hills. Pretty much every farm or hamlet they passed seemed to have a wharf or a landing stage, at which a couple of dinghies bobbed; occasionally they were joined by a riverboat like the one he stood on, loading crops to be conveyed to the city to satisfy the insatiable appetite of its inhabitants. Though he'd always known intellectually that Fairhaven was supported by an agricultural hinterland, it had never occurred to Drago that it was so large, or so apparently prosperous.

From his vantage point on the deck, Drago could see roughly a dozen other vessels, unremarkable riverboats for the most part, strung out along the river ahead and behind the one he was standing on. All the boats on this side of the water were heading in the same direction, bow waves creaming as their spread sails sent them slicing through the downstream current, the ones following the other bank making for the estuary and the waiting wharves of Fairhaven.

Reminded of his home, Drago glanced aft, where the human woman glared sullenly at him from her post at the tiller. Beyond her, he could see only a bend in the river, and still more of the ubiquitous farmland.

"Getting homesick already?" Clearspring asked, noting the direction of his gaze, and ignoring the answering shake of his head. "Wait until we reach the next bend." Sure enough, a moment later the woman at the tiller moved it across, the riverboat turned to follow the curve of the bank, and a longer view down the river appeared behind her. In the far distance, beyond the meander, a low ridge line of roofs and towers briefly appeared, before being occulted again almost at once.

"I didn't realize we'd come so far," Drago said.

"That's what happens when you sleep in," the deckhand said. He turned to Clearspring. "Snoring his head off when I opened the barrel."

"Well it wasn't like I had anything else to do," Drago pointed out. "Did I miss breakfast?"

"Of course you did. Tide turned well before sunup." Clearspring indicated the sun, now well above the horizon, with an impatient wave, presumably in case Drago hadn't seen it before and didn't know what it was.

"You left in the dark?" Drago asked. It was possible to sail at night, he'd heard, but only a skipper in a real hurry would risk it, and it seemed a strange thing to do if Clearspring wanted to avoid attracting any attention.

"Course not." The deckhand seemed highly amused at the idea. "We left at first light, though, to get as much out of it as we could before it starts ebbing again."

"And we didn't get nearly enough for my liking." Clearspring spat over the rail, the blob of saliva gliding smoothly astern in the rippling water. "It's on the turn already, so it's only just balancing the current. We'll be losing way before long."

"Not so much as you'd notice," the deckhand said. He glanced down at Drago again, and grinned. "No one can read the water like the skipper here. The *Rippling Light*'s the fastest boat on the Geltwash."

"Not quite," Clearspring allowed, with a tolerant smile at the deckhand, "but we can move when we have to." She glanced back at Drago. "Go with Greel if you're hungry. He'll find you something to eat."

"Anything for you, Skip?" the deckhand asked.

Clearspring shook her head. "I'm fine." She leaned on the rail, the conversation apparently at an end, then added "See if Hannie wants a bite too. Then take the tiller, give her a break."

"Will do." Greel, who somehow seemed more of a person now that Drago knew his name, beckoned the gnome across to a small superstructure, set aft of the main hatch. It was divided into two, widthwise—a roughly square room facing the bow, with a table, a bunk, and a couple of chairs, and a small galley, which seemed well equipped to Drago's inexperienced eye, behind it. The table held a couple of mugs, an unwashed plate, and a peculiar-looking map, in which the outline of the river was extensively annotated, and most of the landscape surrounding it left blank. "Know how to cook?"

"More or less," Drago said. The principle seemed simple enough, although he normally had enough cash in his purse not to have to put any of it into practice. One of the many reasons he never left the city if he could help it. "Put something on the stove. If it's runny it's raw, if it's black it's overdone."

"Hm." Greel looked at him for a moment as if wondering whether or not he was joking, before deciding correctly that he wasn't. "Go and ask Hannie if she wants something. I'll handle the food."

"Right." Drago made his way along the deck, compensating automatically for the minute shifts underfoot, which seemed much less pronounced than on the smaller boats he was used to. Hannie watched his approach without noticeable enthusiasm, her usual scowl remaining glued to her face. "Do you want something to eat?"

"Wouldn't say no," she conceded, a trifle warily. She leaned into the tiller a little, adjusting the boat's course by a minute fraction. "Hungry work, this."

"Looks it," Drago agreed. He turned to wave affirmatively at Greel, who disappeared into the galley. "Been on the river long?"

"Long enough," Hannie said. "Born on the water, hope to die on it too." She looked down at him narrowly, a little more of her previous wariness coming to the surface again. "But not yet awhile."

"Me neither," Drago agreed, with his friendliest smile.

"I know. Skipper said. That's why you're here."

"Something like that," Drago agreed. The full story was too complicated to precis, even if he felt like sharing it, which, under the circumstances, would probably not be a good idea. He decided to change the subject. "How long have you been crewing for her?"

"Couple of years," Hannie said, looking faintly surprised that he knew how to make conversation. "Greel's been with her a bit longer."

"Sounds like she gets on well with humans," Drago commented. That struck him as a little unusual, and in his profession the unusual was generally not to be trusted. Most of the elves he'd encountered would have alienated human underlings to the point of resignation, if not altercation, within a couple of months, never mind years.

"Pretty much everyone," Hannie conceded. "Just elves she has a problem with, generally."

"Why's that?" Drago asked, but Hannie just shrugged, and adjusted the position of the tiller another inch or two.

"You'd have to ask her," she said, the shutters coming down again.

"Maybe I will," Drago said, turning away in response to the appetizing aroma of hot bacon. Greel was approaching, two fresh filled baps in his hands, and a trace of grease around his mouth mute testament to the ephemerality of a third.

"There you go," the deckhand said, handing the hot snack to Drago, and turning to Hannie, who took the second gratefully. "Skip wants a hand taking in the sail when you've finished that."

"Murfle furg." She swallowed an overlarge mouthful, and relinquished the tiller. "I'll get right on it."

"Good." Greel took her place, and watched his crewmate bite, chew and swallow with all the finesse of a troll at a smorgasbord. "Been getting acquainted with our passenger?"

"Sort of." Hannie swallowed the last mouthful of her second breakfast, belched loudly, and trotted across the deck to where

Clearspring was doing something Drago didn't quite grasp to a tangle of ropes.

"Is she always that friendly?" Drago asked, taking a bite of his own bacon butty. The contrast with Edna Cravatt's parting gift could hardly have been stronger.

Greel grinned. "Which one do you mean?"

Drago shrugged, his eye on both the two women. They worked well together, so far as he could see, adjusting the sail with an easy rapport and a minimum of conversation. "Either of them."

"No." Greel shook his head, leaning into the tiller, and sending the boat curving neatly around the next bend in the river. The boom swung over, Clearspring and Hannie avoiding it with ease of long habit. "You must be quite the charmer."

"It's been said before," Drago lied, and returned his attention to his bap.

Drago began to get bored as the day wore on, despite incremental changes in the landscape along the river banks. As the *Rippling Light* continued to forge its way upstream, the intensively farmed hinterland surrounding Fairhaven began to give way to patches of moorland and scrub, the fields interspersing them becoming centered on increasingly isolated farmsteads and villages. Smaller craft on local errands, laden with sacks and farm tools, or conveying people between the scattered communities, began to be more common too, sharing the river with the bustling cargo boats. Leaning on the rail, Drago exchanged waves with a few children, but for the most part the adults aboard the little vessels ignored the rest of the river traffic, beyond shouted greetings between neighbors; for them, Drago realized, their tiny patch of the Geltwash was all there was, the bigger boats passing them by of no more significance than the clouds above their heads. Once they passed a crudely made raft, decorated with bunting and crowded with a wedding party, humans, goblins and gnomes in what out here were probably their best clothes singing, drinking, and in a few cases dancing with apparent indifference to the danger of capsizing the whole affair. Drago tried to spot the couple at the center of it all, but gave up after a minute or two, unable even to determine their species among so mixed a crowd. Maybe they weren't even there at all, having sneaked off on their honeymoon while their families and friends continued to party, or perhaps these were just some of the guests, making their way downstream to the main event at one of the scattered riverside communities the sturdy little boat had already passed.

As the raft moved astern, Drago found his vague sense of dissatisfaction intensifying. Everyone else seemed to have a purpose, a direction in life, and in most cases someone to share it with.

"Is there anything I can do?" he asked at last, and Clearspring shrugged.

"I don't know. Is there?" She looked pointedly at the billowing canvas above their heads, and the bewildering array of ropes attached to it. "Do you know how to take in a sail?"

"Not on something this size," Drago said. He could handle a dinghy tolerably well if he had to, like pretty much any native of Fairhaven, but generally didn't; that was what the ferrymen were for.

"And you can't cook, either, Greel says." She spat over the side, considered the result, and scowled. "Can you catch fish?"

"I don't know," Drago said, "I've never tried."

"Really?" Clearspring looked at him with something like astonishment for a moment, before her expression became once again studiedly neutral. "I thought everyone living by the river knew how to fish."

"Well, I don't. Live by the river, I mean."

"But you live in Fairhaven. The whole city's by the river." For a moment he wondered if she was joking with him, but her expression seemed earnest enough. And why would she understand? She'd live on her boat while it was docked in Fairhaven, and had probably never seen anything farther from the waterfront than a street or two.

"Well, it is and it isn't," he explained. "And most people just buy their food. If you want fish, you go to the fish market, and if you can't be bothered to go all that way you just buy it from the stall of someone in your district who could. Much more convenient." Not to mention the Fisherman's Guild, who took a dim view of anyone else helping themselves from what they regarded as their personal ocean, and whose displeasure could easily keep one of his less scrupulous competitors gainfully employed if the fishermen didn't simply take matters into their own fists.

"Take your word for it," Clearspring said, "but we're not in

Fairhaven now. If you want something to do, get Greel to show you how to cast a line. I'm not paying for my supper if I don't have to."

"Fair enough," Drago said, wandering off to find the deckhand, who was still at the tiller, and seemed happy enough at the chance for a bit of conversation.

"It's quite simple," he assured Drago. "All you need is a line and some bait." He raised his voice. "Hannie! Can you bring the fishing gear over?" He waited while the other deckhand finished whatever she was doing, which, like most things on the riverboat, seemed to involve pulling on or slackening off ropes before tying them in a complicated knot; once that was completed to her satisfaction she wandered over with a long line, into which hooks had been set at intervals, and a bucket which smelled pungent enough to remind Drago of home. "All you do is, you put some of that bait on your hooks."

"Bait. Right." Both sailors were looking at him with an air of expectant amusement, although Drago couldn't really see why. It seemed simple enough. "What is it?"

"Fish guts," Hannie said, matter-of-factly. So that was it.

"Right. I should have guessed." He plunged a hand in, grabbing a sticky, slippery fistful, and lifted it out carefully. It looked and smelled pretty disgusting, but he'd seen and smelled a lot worse in his time, often accompanied by loud noises, and he kept his tone mildly curious. "This about right?" He fumbled with the nearest of the hooks, trying to wrap the noisome bundle around it, wary of the sharp, barbed point.

"Too much," Greel said, his tone equally even, but not quite managing to conceal his surprise. "You just want enough to get them to bite. Piece about the size of your thumb ought to do it." He held out a battered clasp knife, which Drago took in his free hand, and opened with his teeth. After waiting for the gnome to cut off a piece of offal about the right size, he went on. "Put that on the point of the hook, but watch your fingers."

"Got it." Drago followed the instruction. "And the rest the same?"

Greel nodded. Once the remaining hooks were baited, he pointed to the rail. "Now chuck it over the side. Make sure you've still got the other end, mind."

"Right." Drago complied. "Now what?"

"Now you wait."

"How long?" Drago asked.

Greel chuckled. "Long as it takes. Couple of hours should do it. Maybe. Or a couple of minutes. You never can tell with fish. But you'll know when you've got one."

"How?" Drago asked, an instant before feeling a sharp tug on the line. "Oh. Right."

"Now bring it in slowly," Greel instructed, watching with interest from his post by the tiller. "And mind your fingers on the hooks."

"Slowly it is." Drago hauled the line in, while the two deckhands nodded approval. Something was thrashing in the water, raising splashes which caught the sun in glittering motes, through which he could catch a glimpse of shimmering scales. "Now what?"

"Bring it in to the side," Hannie said, taking a knife from her belt. "Carefully. If you let the line get too taut it'll just snap." Warned in the nick of time, Drago let a little of the line out again, just as the fish on the other end pulled hard in the other direction. It felt a bit like brawling, he thought, sensing the flow of energy between him and an opponent, letting instinct guide his reactions. To his vague surprise, he found he was enjoying himself.

"That's good," Greel assured him, as he took up the slack, bringing the struggling fish closer to the boat. The splashing became more pronounced, lapping against the planks of the hull. "Now haul it in."

Drago leaned back, taking the weight of the fish, which was almost as long as his arm. He'd never seen a living one before, and the speed and vigor with which it thrashed as it left the water took him by surprise. An awful lot of it seemed to be mouth, too, which would have seemed vaguely intimidating if it hadn't been choked by the metal hook.

"That's it! Good!" Hannie seemed more animated than he'd ever seen her, even going so far as to throw an encouraging smile in his direction. "Just a little further." She leaned over the rail, her knife at the ready.

Drago hauled on the line again, feeling the tension building in his lower back, and a growing sense of elation. The fish was entirely out of the water now, almost level with the rail.

"Got it!" Hannie leaned a little farther, seeming for a second in danger of overbalancing, then stood upright, scooping the fish onto the deck. Drago almost staggered with the sudden lack of tension in the fishing line, then regained his balance in time to see her plunge her knife into the flailing fish, severing its head with one quick twist. She grinned at Drago again. "Nice one." Another smooth motion with her knife blade, and the fish's guts joined the head on a quick trip over the side. "Now see if you can get a couple more."

"Two more coming up," Drago said, with newfound confidence, and returned the line to the water, where it remained until close to sunset without a trace of another bite.

CHAPTER FOURTEEN
"Can get a bit verbal."

"Is that it?" Clearspring asked, looking at his day's catch in a manner Drago thought of as distinctly elf-like. Then she shrugged, in grudging approval. "Not bad for a beginner, though."

"Not enough to go round either," Greel said, sounding hopeful and disappointed at the same time. "Especially when one of us is a gnome." He glanced at Drago. "No offense."

"None taken," Drago assured him. His people's fondness for food was well enough known to have become a standing joke throughout the known world, and if it amused the other races as much as it seemed to, then he had no objection to playing up to their preconceptions. Being underestimated had saved his life on more than one occasion. Besides, he seemed to have won a measure of acceptance from her crew, even if Clearspring remained elvishly aloof, and it wouldn't be prudent to squander that. "So what'll we do?"

Clearspring squinted ahead down the darkening river. The sun hadn't quite disappeared yet, but the shadows were gathering, and night would be falling in earnest soon. Fewer boats were abroad on the river this late in the day, the only ones visible now no more than distant sails scudding for shelter, or looming shapes nestled against the bank, already moored for the night.

She sighed, eyeing the bleak heathland on either side of the water with little sign of enthusiasm. "If you'd caught a couple more I'd be looking for somewhere to tie up for the evening by now. As it is, we'll have to crack on for a bit. Naught's Landing's not far from here, and we ought to make it by dark."

"Sounds good to me, Skip," Greel agreed, and Hannie nodded concurrence from her post at the tiller. "Been a while since we put in there."

"Not long enough," Clearspring said, "but it can't be helped." She dropped the cleaned fish into a nearby chest, on the lid of which a ward of preservation had been carved by someone whose forte had clearly been spell casting rather than woodwork. Then she disappeared into the cabin on the deck.

"What was that all about?" Drago asked. "Is she expecting trouble?"

"Not really." Greel shrugged. "No more than usual, anyway. But you get boats from the Marches putting in there sometimes. Can get a bit verbal."

"Sounds interesting," Drago said, trying to sound as if he didn't mean it. But he did. If there was a crew from the Marches there, he might hear some news of his quarry. "How soon will we get there?"

"Maybe an hour," Hannie said. "Give or take."

In the event, it turned out to be more take than give, and night was falling in earnest before the riverside settlement came into view. Drago was the first to spot it, his dark-adapted eyes giving him a clear advantage in that regard, and he watched from the deck with considerable interest as Clearspring and her crew brought the *Rippling Light* alongside a crude but sturdy wharf apparently constructed from felled tree trunks, already occupied by a couple of similar boats. A small wood surrounded the settlement, the raw material it provided presumably having been the main attraction for the people who'd decided to live there.

Clearspring nodded when Drago verbalized the thought. "That's right. Plenty to build with. But that's not the main reason. It's the nearest decent-sized piece of woodland to Fairhaven."

Drago remained puzzled for a moment; buildings in the city tended to be made of brick, and had been since the last big fire leveled most of the right bank about thirty years ago. What lumber was needed, mainly by the boatyards, arrived from the forests a long way upstream, where the supply was essentially inexhaustible. Most of the buildings he could see ashore were made of logs or crudely sawn planks, but he didn't imagine much of the local timber would be worth exporting.

As Hannie lobbed the mooring lines to a couple of people on the quay, who immediately began hauling the boat in, making the lines fast to bollards that were little more than cursorily finished logs, a faint odor of woodsmoke drifted across the water to his nostrils. The smell seemed to be everywhere, but there surely couldn't be that many cooking fires in a village as small as this one. Then he understood.

"Charcoal," he said. Now he knew what he was looking for, he was able to make out the faint wisps of smoke rising above the trees in the distance, fainter threads of darkness against the enclosing sky. Producing something every smithy in Fairhaven depended on.

Clearspring nodded again. "Biggest producer on the lower reaches. Good quality too, I'm told. Not that that makes much difference to me. Cargo's cargo." The boat bumped gently against the quayside.

Drago grinned. "And passengers are passengers?"

"Not to me." Clearspring shook her head. "Passengers are cargo too. Just noisier, mobile and more trouble."

"I'll do my best not to be," Drago said.

Clearspring favored him with a momentary, wintery smile. "Too late. Although, to be fair, a sack of charcoal can't catch fish."

"Neither can I, apparently," Drago said.

"That's just how it goes. One day you get all you can eat, the next nothing. Bit like life." She shook herself out of the pensive mood which seemed to have settled on her with the gathering darkness. "And talking of something to eat . . ." She vaulted over the rail with inhuman grace, landing on the echoing planks of the wharf with barely a sound. "Coming?"

"You have to ask?" Drago said, his boots landing beside hers with a noticeably louder thud. Satisfied with the security of the knots holding the vessel fast, Hannie and Greel clambered over the rail to join them. He glanced from one to the other with an air of puzzlement. "Who's watching the boat?"

"Him." Clearspring indicated a young human man seated on a barrel at the end of the dock, swathed in a cloak and munching a chicken leg. "And he knows if anything happens to her, or anything goes missing, he takes a swim. Isn't that right, Roger?"

Startled at being addressed by name, the young man glanced up, his face curdling into a scowl as he recognized his interlocutor. "Oh, it's you. Wasn't expecting to see you back so soon." His tone added *or at all*, and the clear implication that it would have been his preferred option.

"Not my choice, believe me." Clearspring spat into the water beside the wharf. "Ran out of daylight and wind."

"Not like you, running out of wind. Quite long on it, as I recall. 'Specially when you've had a few." He let his cloak fall open a little, revealing a glimpse of a sword. Its hilt was worn, and the leather of its scabbard scuffed; strong indications to Drago that its owner not only knew how to use it, but was willing to if he felt the need. He took a step back, into the shadows, where his face would be harder to see or remember; the man reminded him a little too strongly of a young George Waggoner.

"We're just after something to eat," Greel said, keeping his voice low and reasonable, jumping into the conversation an instant before Clearspring could reply. "Then we're getting our heads down till dawn. After that we're out of here. Right, Skip?"

"Right." Clearspring swallowed whatever she was about to say, and moved off, with a final glare at the young man. As they walked off the end of the dock, onto a shoreline of rutted mud, Drago was pretty sure he could hear both Hannie and Greel exhale with releasing tension.

"Local watch?" he asked.

Hannie shrugged. "Not exactly. But the closest you'll find out here. You see anyone wearing one of those cloaks, watch your step. They're there to keep things working smoothly for the locals. Anyone else, not so much."

"Not so different from the watch, then," Drago said, and Hannie laughed, although he hadn't really been joking. The watchmen he knew back in Fairhaven were definitely there to enforce the law, and generally did so regardless of whether felon or victim had been native to the city or not, but the way they went about it tended to treat the relevant statutes as guidelines rather than hard and fast rules.

He glanced back at Roger, now a shapeless mass in the gathering darkness, his outline obscured by the cloak—to anyone but a gnome he'd be almost invisible in the gloom, sitting well back from the line of lanterns delineating the edge of the quay. A faint pale smudge in the distance might have been a boat forging on in the darkness, desperate to get to Fairhaven with a perishable cargo, but it was hard to tell, and none of his business anyway. He had far more important things to think about.

"So," he said, "where are we going to eat?"

"This way," Clearspring said, without noticeable enthusiasm. "We're not exactly spoilt for choice."

Which Drago didn't find particularly surprising. A village this size could support only a couple of taverns, if that; transients would sleep on their boats, and all the locals would have homes, so there'd be no need for an inn. But the need for food, and something to drink with it, was universal, and someone was bound to have stepped forward to fulfill it.

The contrast with Fairhaven was marked, and intriguing; the only place he'd ever been outside the city before was the gnomish delving where his relatives lived, almost a day's coach travel down the post road inland, and the warren of tunnels there was so different from the tangle of streets he'd grown up in that comparisons were almost meaningless. Here, however, he could see buildings, smaller and shabbier than he was used to; other than the sheds around the wharf, only a few of them were more than a single story in height. Judging by their size, the majority of the people living in the houses were human, but he was used to that; what seemed strange, if not downright disconcerting, was the amount of distance between them. A few were even surrounded by fenced-off yards, with neatly weeded beds of vegetables, and in some cases flowers, although he couldn't see why anyone would waste the space growing those on purpose.

"Is that it?" he asked, spotting an exceptionally large building a little way farther down the street, from which lamplight was leaking around the first-floor shutters. Unlike most, it had a second story, the glazed windows of which were curtained, and mostly lit.

Hannie shook her head. "That's the store," she said. "You want anything around here, that's where you go."

Greel nodded, indicating a sign which read Foley's Emporium in large, ornate letters, and added "Dry Goods. Hardware. Boots and Haberdashery" in smaller ones underneath. "They don't cheat you much," he agreed, "and there isn't anywhere else anyway."

"Can't think of anything I need," Drago said, and Clearspring smiled mirthlessly.

"Then you must be unusually contented," she said, turning a corner. "Just down here."

Their destination was immediately obvious, a large, single-story building, of clapboard construction, from which the hum of conversation was audible even at this distance. There was no sign above it; clearly everyone was expected to know it was there, and what they'd find inside. Light was spilling out into the street, through a large gap in the longer wall, above which a tarpaulin had been tied back out of the way; if the place ever closed, which Drago doubted, or the weather grew inclement, it could be let down to cover the gap, or extended into an awning to create more room.

"Would Foley own this as well, by any chance?" Drago asked, and Greel nodded.

"This, and the warehouse by the docks. Who do you think pays Roger and his mates?"

"I wasn't thinking about that," Drago said, which was true; any community like this would have a Foley-shaped hole at its center, and someone would have filled it, as surely as water ran downhill. He didn't see any reason to care who that was.

"Come on, then," Clearspring said, leading the way inside.

CHAPTER FIFTEEN

"Remind me not to say anything nice about your hair."

Drago hung back a little as they entered the building, letting the taller elf and humans screen him while he got the measure of the place. As he'd expected, most of the clientele were human, and presumably local, seated on benches at the long tables running the length of the room, spooning down food from wooden plates. The majority were plainly dressed in home-sewn garments, the more prosperous easily distinguished by their store-bought clothes. Nearly everyone, men and women alike, wore sturdy britches, and leather vests were popular among those who could afford or make them; from the burrs and scraps of twig adhering to garments and hair, Drago inferred that they worked in the woods, felling timber for construction materials and the charcoal fires. The charcoal burners themselves were easy to pick out, from the grey ash ingrained in their clothing and skin, and the odor of woodsmoke which clung about them. Most kept to themselves, at one end of the table nearest the entrance, although a few were laughing and joking with friends and relatives among the villagers. Not all the locals would be here, of course, many of those eating and drinking would have wives or husbands waiting in one of the huts they'd passed, but Drago was willing to bet that the vast majority would be in here several times a week.

The most noticeable exception was a small group of goblins seated about halfway down the farthest table, laughing and talking among themselves, and with their immediate neighbors. Both groups were dressed like Clearspring and her deckhands, and only a few seconds of listening to their chatter was enough to confirm Drago's immediate guess that these were the crews of the two boats they'd found already tied up at the wharf on their arrival.

"Look who's here!" The goblin skipper glanced in their direction, and waved a hand in greeting. "Marieth!"

"Sleer." Clearspring nodded at him as affably as an elf could be expected to manage, and turned her head a little to meet the gaze of his human counterpart. "Hathead."

The man nodded back, a little curtly. "Clearspring."

"What's the matter with him?" Drago asked, keeping his voice low.

Hannie shrugged. "Nothing. Sore loser. He'll get over it."

"We beat him to a contract last year," Greel amplified. "Told the shipper we could get it to Fairhaven a day earlier than he could."

"And did you?" Drago asked.

"Nearly. I told you, the *Light*'s a fast boat. But it didn't matter anyway."

"Skipper just changed the date on the paperwork," Hannie added, oblivious to a glare from Clearspring. A young man was rising from a nearby bench, and her attention was entirely on him.

"Hannie!"

"Clem!"

The young man swept her into an enthusiastic embrace which momentarily staggered her, his voice rising with surprise and delight. "When did you blow in?"

"Just got here." She regained her balance, and indicated the serving counter at the far end of the room. "Wanted something to eat."

"Got plenty of that over here." He urged her in the direction of the table, where a few of his friends were clustered around a substantial meal. After a token show of reluctance she followed him, with a backward grin at her shipmates. "How long are you here for?"

"Just for the night." Her grin widened, and her arm went round his waist for a moment, before heading south to collect a handful of buttock. "So let's not waste it, eh?"

"And that's the last we'll see of her before dawn," Greel said, following Clearspring to the far end of the room, where she was already making a selection from the food on offer.

Drago strode after him, conscious of standing out among so many humans, and determined not to show his unease. "She must be happy about that," he said, keeping his voice conversational, and glancing casually around. No one was taking more than a passing interest in his presence, so far as he could see, but after his experiences in the back alleys of Fairhaven he wasn't about to trust to that. "Putting in where her sweetheart lives. Especially as it wasn't planned."

Greel laughed. "I don't think she even knows what a sweetheart is. She's got a lad like that in every settlement on both banks, and at least three on the go in Fairhaven."

"So long as she's back at sunup, I don't care if she's got them taking turns." Clearspring turned away from the counter, holding a wooden bowl of pottage, and a wooden spoon to eat it with. "What are you having?"

"The same," Drago said, to save time. He was hungry, and couldn't see much of what was on the counter without jumping up to look anyway, which he was damned if he was going to do. Apart from being undignified, it would attract too much attention.

"Bread and cheese," Greel said, pointing to something out of Drago's eye line, "and something to wash it down." He glanced at Drago. "Best ale on the lower reaches, they do here."

"That we do," the man behind the counter agreed cheerfully, handing Greel a tray, on which the food and drinks were balanced. To Drago's immense lack of surprise, it, the bowl, Greel's trencher, and the ale mugs were all made of wood. "That'll be six shillings and eightpence."

"He's paying," Clearspring said, with a glance down at Drago, and began scanning the room for somewhere to sit. Drago sighed, pulled out his purse, and began to count out the change.

"Marieth! Over here!" Sleer gestured an invitation. Captain Hathead and his crew had evidently finished their meal, and were getting up to go. "Plenty of room!"

"Isn't that handy?" Greel asked, with a trace of sarcasm. Clearly the lingering animosity between the two crews wasn't entirely one-sided. Nevertheless, he waved a cheery farewell as the human sailors filed out, which a couple of them, somewhat sheepishly, returned. He lowered his voice as they made their way over to the vacated bench. "I was lying about the ale, by the way. Tastes like troll piss. But the hicks here are proud of it, and a bit of flattery usually means more food for your money."

"Thanks for the warning." Drago clambered up onto the bench, which, as he'd expected, was too low and too far from the table for him to eat comfortably sitting down. After a moment he raised his knees and knelt on the narrow plank; which wasn't exactly comfortable either, but better than having to reach up and across for every spoonful. He took a cautious sip of the ale, and found it wasn't quite as bad as Greel had intimated, even though it wouldn't have passed muster in any but the cheapest of taverns back in Fairhaven.

"Taken on a new deckhand, have you?" Sleer asked Clearspring after a moment, with a glance at Drago, as the elf plied her spoon in silence.

She shook her head. "Passenger. On his way upriver."

"Long way to the mountains," Sleer said, making the obvious deduction. The Geltwash started in the spinal range at the heart of the continent, meandering almost a thousand miles to the sea, and the vast majority of gnomes lived in the city-sized delvings which riddled the highest peaks. He turned to Drago. "And you're dressed like a city boy. Heading home, or out to see the ancestral halls?"

"Neither," Drago said, choosing his words carefully. He had no objection to lying in principle, but in practice it was always better to shade the truth if he could. It was harder to get tripped up that way. "I heard there was work for gnomes in the Barrens."

"Did you now?" Sleer nodded, his voice still affable, but his posture betraying a sudden inner tension.

Drago shrugged, busying himself with the pottage, which wasn't nearly as bad as the ale, as if he hadn't noticed the goblin captain's change in demeanor. "Tell you the truth, things were getting a bit iffy where I was. Pissed off the wrong people, if you know what I mean. I just grabbed the first ride out of town I could get."

"Well, it's not like we haven't all been there." Sleer glanced meaningfully at Clearspring, who deliberately failed to react. "But if I were you I'd bypass the Barrens. Keep heading upstream until you're well past the Marches altogether. Go see those halls."

"Maybe I will," Drago said. He knew a veiled warning when he heard one, and this particular specimen had pretty much danced a striptease.

"Good lad." Sleer glanced up, and nudged Clearspring. "Friends of yours?"

"No." She followed his eye line, to where a trio of elves had just walked in. They were dressed like sailors too, though they carried themselves like aristocrats surrounded by peasants, and Drago remembered the sail he'd seen in the distance as they left the wharf. Evidently he'd been wrong about the skipper's intention to push on through the night. "Never seen them before."

"Marchers, though," Sleer said. He turned to his crew, with a smile almost devoid of humor. "Let's remind them of home." He cleared his throat and began to sing, the other goblins joining in with gusto. "*Oh Gorash is a reiver bold, he leads a gallant band, who fight for truth and justice, and to free our stolen land . . .*"

The elves stopped moving, conferred quietly among themselves for a moment, then walked to the counter to order food, ostentatiously ignoring the rest of the song. To Drago's quiet surprise, several of the humans in the immediate vicinity joined in enthusiastically with the chorus. Evidently the ballad was popular even this far from the Sylvan Marches.

"Who's that about, then?" Drago asked, as the song came to an end. "I haven't heard it in Fairhaven."

"I don't suppose you have," Sleer conceded. "Too wrapped up in your own concerns. But you'll hear it a lot on the river, 'specially higher up. Gorash is—"

"A murdering bandit." The elves had drifted over to the table, and stood looming over it, in a manner Clement Wethers would undoubtedly have approved of, plates and mugs in their hands. "Who'll be caught and hanged as he deserves." Their captain, easily distinguished by the intricate embroidery on his vest, bowed formally to Clearspring. "Are these people bothering you, madam?"

"No." Clearspring chased the last of her food around the bowl, without looking up. "They're my friends."

"I see." The elf clearly didn't. "Perhaps if your crew aren't here—"

"We are," Greel said, standing slowly, and extending a hand. "Some of us, anyway. But thank you for your concern."

"I see." The elf captain glanced from Greel to Clearspring, then to Drago, refusing to take the human's proffered hand. Then he nodded curtly to Clearspring, his lip curling in clear disdain. "My apologies for the intrusion, madam. I'll leave you to your . . . friends. No doubt you find them more to your liking."

"No doubt I do," Clearspring agreed evenly, in the kind of calm, reasonable tone which, in Drago's experience, generally preceded someone drawing a knife. He let his hand drift a little closer to the hilt of his sword, without making it obvious, but none of the elves seemed to notice. They were already turning away, heading toward a bench being vacated by a group of charcoal burners.

"Typical trait," one of them said, in a voice clearly intended to be overheard, and Clearspring's fist bunched. She gathered herself to rise, but before she could move, Greel's hands were on her shoulders, exerting gentle downward pressure. After a moment she went with it, relaxing a little, but her jaw remained clenched.

"Typical twat," Sleer said, unleashing a chorus of raucous laughter from the goblins and Greel. After a moment, Clearspring's mouth relaxed into a tight smile.

"If I asked what that was all about, would I regret it?" Drago inquired, trying to sound as though he was still more interested in the contents of his bowl.

"Long story," Clearspring said, draining her ale mug, and looking faintly disappointed to find the bottom of it so soon. "Let's just say I don't like the way things are going back home, or the people who do."

"That thing he said sounded like an insult." Drago pushed his own, almost full, mug across to her. Not much of a loss, and the gesture might get her talking. Sure enough, she picked it up, took a thoughtful gulp, and replaced it with a nod of thanks.

"It was, to him. I think of it more as a compliment."

"You were still ready to punch his lights out," Drago said. "Remind me not to say anything nice about your hair."

"It wasn't the words, it was the intention," Clearspring said. "Trait's the short version for a phrase these people use. 'Traitor to the race.' Which is how they regard anyone who treats a non-elf as an equal."

"Nope." Drago chased the last of his pottage around the bowl, and licked the spoon. "You've lost me." He tried to picture Fairhaven if any of the people living there had the same attitude, and failed dismally. Even the snottiest elves would cheerfully do business with anyone regardless of race, and probably knew several non-elves socially in the bargain. The whole place would just fall apart, otherwise.

"That's because you're a Fairhavener," Greel said. "You're used to being somewhere lots of different people live together. In the Marches, it's pretty much all elves, and that breeds a certain attitude. As you saw."

"And it's always been like that," Sleer added. "There are some with a more open-minded attitude," he smiled at Clearspring, "but it doesn't pay for them to make it too obvious."

"No. That it doesn't." She finished Drago's drink and looked round hopefully, but one of the goblin sailors was already heading back to the table with a trayful of replacements. "When the old king died and his daughter took over, things looked like getting better. She expanded trade, encouraged travel and visitors, even tried talking to the goblins in the Barrens about their grievances."

"Then she vanished," Drago said. He grinned at the expressions of surprise suddenly directed at him. "We've heard that much in Fairhaven, at least."

"Then she vanished," Clearspring agreed. "And her idiot brother took over. And things went back to normal, if not worse."

"Sounds like you'd had enough," Drago said.

"More than enough. So I scraped the money I needed to buy the *Light* together, and the only time I ever set foot in the Marches now is if somebody pays me to. And even then only long enough to find a fresh cargo."

"Probably best," Sleer said. "And at least the brokers will talk to you. Try being a goblin and getting a reasonable deal out of them." He shrugged. "It's getting so bad half the skippers on the river won't even put in there anymore."

"Tell me about it." Clearspring seized on the newly arrived ale gratefully. One appeared in front of Drago too, and he took it with a nod of thanks, more to appear sociable than because he wanted it. Then again, free beer was free beer, and it was probably worth the price he'd paid. "Last time I was there I had to leave Hannie and Greel below decks until the deal was done."

Greel chuckled. "Worth it for the expressions on their faces when they realized you had a human crew." He turned to Drago to explain. "Most of them'll only trust their cargoes to an elvish boat."

"And more fool them," Sleer opined. "Cutting their own throats, they are." The prospect didn't seem to be distressing him unduly.

"How's that?" Drago asked. He was certainly getting a lot of new information, even if it wasn't entirely clear how it all fitted together yet, or if it would help him to find Gorash.

"Because there aren't enough boats on the Geltwash with entirely elven crews," Clearspring explained. Drago noticed she used the common name for the river instead of calling it the Silverroad, like most elves did. "They're throttling their own economy." She took another gulp of her ale. "And serve them right. They're about due for a smack in the face from the reality club."

"They'd have had one already if it wasn't for the goldmine in the Barrens," Greel said. "No wonder they're so desperate to keep it."

"Keep it?" Drago asked ingenuously. "Who's going to take it away?"

"Gorash," Sleer said. "The one that song's about. He's got a lot of friends, and they're causing all kinds of trouble up that way." He nodded judiciously at Drago. "Which is why I wouldn't recommend looking for work there. They're always raiding, after the gold, or supplies, or both."

"I'm surprised King Stargleam puts up with it," Drago said, some of the doubts he'd felt during his conversations with Greenleaf resurfacing. "Hasn't he got an army for that sort of thing?"

"He's got soldiers," Greel said, "but the bandits know the country. By the time word gets to the garrison, they've faded back into the hills. And most of the local commanders are too scared of being ambushed to send out patrols, so Gorash pretty much has the Barrens to himself."

"How nice for him," Drago said, taking another drink, and deciding that he might as well finish it now he'd started.

CHAPTER SIXTEEN
"Could do with one myself, as it happens."

Inevitably, more drinks followed, and the evening was well advanced by the time the two crews rose from the benches to return to their boats. To Drago's relief the elves had left long before, as soon as they'd finished their meal. Not that he'd been expecting any further trouble, but he'd kept an eye on them anyway out of professional habit, and the conviction born of experience that it was often the unexpected that tripped you up. As they passed out of the building into the cool of the night, he glanced in the direction of the table Hannie and her friend had been sitting at, but to his complete lack of surprise there was no sign of either.

In the usual way of indifferent ale, the flavor had seemed to improve the more he'd drunk, although he'd stopped some way short of intoxication. This was a new and strange environment, and he intended to keep his wits about him. Not all his companions had been as cautious, though, most of the goblins seeming a little unsteady on their feet even for sailors adjusting to their land legs. Clearspring, he strongly suspected, had finished the evening severely inebriated, but was too hardened a drinker to show it; her gait seemed steady enough, but Greel, who had drunk the least while appearing to keep up with the others, was walking a little too close for casual companionship, poised to step in if she stumbled and needed sudden support.

Remaining sober hadn't done anything to mitigate the other effects of consuming large quantities of a mildly alcoholic beverage, however, a fact he'd been reminded of almost as soon as he'd stood up, and which was growing ever more pressing as the ache in his bladder increased.

"Where do you go for a piss around here?" he asked, glancing around in perplexity. There were no welcoming alley mouths or doorways in the immediate vicinity, and even though none of his companions could see half as well in the dark as he could, there was enough starlight in the almost cloudless sky for him to feel self-conscious about simply unbuttoning his breeks in the middle of the street.

He glanced up at the heavens, feeling a momentary rush of vertigo. If he'd ever noticed the stars before, they'd been glimpsed through the narrow strips of sky visible between the rooftops of Fairhaven, pale and clustered in twos and threes. On the few occasions he'd been down by the estuary after dark, clouds or the famous sea fogs had obscured most of them. Now, uncountable motes of light blazed down on him, shimmering faintly, casting a pale blue glow over the scattered hamlet. For a moment he forgot everything, even his physical discomfort, lost in a haze of awestruck wonder.

"Off the dock, mostly," Sleer said, picking up his pace a little. "Could do with one myself, as it happens." The lanterns strung along the edge of the wharf were clearly visible a couple of hundred yards away, and Drago picked up his pace a little. "There's plenty of room the other side of Hathead's boat."

"Not anymore," Clearspring said, as their boot soles began to resound on the wooden decking. A mast was visible in the previously clear berth at the far end of the pilings, though the deck to which it was attached remained below eye level; heavily laden, the elven vessel was riding far lower in the water than any of the other three boats. A ladder ran down from the wharf edge, presumably left there when the crew returned.

"You sure?" Sleer kept his eyes fixed on the middle distance as he approached the lip of the planking, carefully not looking down at the gurgling river below. "I can't see a boat."

"Me neither." One of the goblin sailors joined him, unfastening his britches as he did so.

"Nor me." Drago was pretty sure this was a bad idea, but the pressure in his bladder was growing insistent, and if he didn't relieve it now, when would he? He glanced down, seeing a polished wooden deck about six feet below his boot toes, and beyond caring about the consequences. A shadow moved to his left, and Greel joined him, unbuttoning without a further word.

"Really not a good idea," Clearspring said, in the tone of someone not expecting to be listened to, and who would be mildly disappointed if anyone actually did.

"Too late," Greel said, and it was, a sudden gush of urine pattering on the deck below, accompanied by hoots of intoxicated laughter. Drago felt a sudden surge of relief, followed almost at once by one of caution as he rearranged his dignity.

"What the scut!" a furious voice bellowed from down below. One of the crew had evidently been left on watch, perhaps anticipating something like this. "You filthy animals!" Glancing down, Drago saw the elf running for the ladder, murder in his eye, and a long knife in his hand. Suddenly this all seemed a lot less funny. But just as the furious elf reached it, the ladder vanished, plucked out of his reach by Clearspring. "Put that back, you trait bitch!"

"Not till you ask nicely," Clearspring said, grinning vindictively. "Say please."

The other two elves were coming out onto the deck now, attracted by the commotion, grabbing improvised weapons as they came. Drago backed quietly into a deeper pool of shadow, reaching for the hilt of his sword, and considering his options. He could just withdraw, and leave them to it, but if anything happened to Clearspring he'd be stranded. On the other hand there was no telling how many more of Gorash's agents were on his trail, and if he waded in to finish this, the inevitable gossip about his fighting skill would be bound to reach their ears sooner or later. He'd tracked enough fugitives himself to know how easy it would be to deduce his whereabouts from rumors like that.

While he deliberated, the furious elf leapt for the edge of the dock, getting his forearms over it, and began to haul himself up, the knife still clutched in his fist.

Sleer clenched his. "Come on then," he bellowed. "Have a go if you think you're hard enough."

"Here. Take the bloody thing if you want it that much," Clearspring said, lunging down with the ladder, and taking the rising elf full in the face with the lowest rung. He lost his balance and fell back to the deck, with a howl, landing on his crewmates, and effectively winding all three of them. Clearspring tossed the ladder into the water. "Here. Catch." She listened to the splash in feigned surprise. "Oops. Butterfingers."

Drago waited expectantly. If they had any sense the elves would back down, realizing they couldn't get up onto the wharf now without turning their faces into footballs for the other crews, but he'd seen enough brawls to know that wasn't likely to happen. By this point, anger and adrenalin was going to override common sense, which in his experience wasn't all that common to begin with, and blood was going to be spilled. Preferably not by him, but his options were getting narrower by the minute . . .

"Oi! What's going on?" The clatter of boot heels on planking heralded the arrival of Roger, the not-quite watchman, his sword drawn, his voice heavy with the menace of a bully used to being listened to. He glanced at Clearspring, registering her presence, and his tone became freighted with sarcasm. "Captain Clearspring. This is a surprise."

"Evening, Roger." Either the alcohol in her system was insulating her from the full realization of just how much trouble they were potentially in, or she genuinely didn't care. Drago would have bet on the latter, but he was acutely aware of what a terrible gambler he was, so didn't pursue the thought. "What are you doing here?"

"Keeping the peace. So hold yours, if you know what's good for you." He looked down at the elves, who were disentangling themselves to an accompaniment of profanity which even Drago, who was used to the waterfront of Fairhaven, found inventively impressive. "Who started it?"

"They did." The captain stepped forward dramatically and pointed to the goblins and Greel, who immediately adopted expressions of bewildered innocence that made them look twice as guilty. "They attacked our boat."

"Attacked it how?" Roger looked down curiously. "I can't see any damage."

"They—they—" Words seemed to fail him. "It'll take weeks to get the stink out."

Roger sniffed the air, and an expression of dawning comprehension bloomed across his face. "You mean they pissed on your deck."

"That's all they had time to do before we challenged them. Apart from assaulting our duty watch. Look at his face!"

"That was self-defense," Clearspring said. "He came at me with a knife, and I had to fend him off. With a ladder."

"What ladder?" Roger asked. He glared at the elf. "I can see he's still holding the knife. Which he's about to drop, if he doesn't want me to take him in, isn't he?" He waited for a moment, while the blade clattered to the deck. "That's better." He turned back to Clearspring. "What ladder?"

"The one in the water over there." Greel pointed. "I'm sure they'll be able to fish it out without too much trouble. Thing is, we all had quite a bit to drink, and, you know, nature took its course, and by the time we got back we were feeling it. There wasn't a boat there when we left the wharf, and by the time we noticed one had put in while we were away, it was too late. So to speak."

"So you accidentally pissed all over a forty-foot boat none of you noticed was there." Roger nodded judiciously, keeping his face commendably straight. "I could see how that might happen. Did you apologize to these gentlemen?"

"We would have," Sleer said, "but they were too upset to listen."

"Right. Then we have an unfortunate misunderstanding, don't we?" Roger glanced down into the boat, at three faces clenched with silent fury, then back to the smirking visages of Clearspring, Greel and the goblins. "What I suggest is, everyone goes back to their own vessel, and stays there till the morning. Then at first light you all bugger off. Because if I have to get the magistrate involved, she'll impound them all pending further enquiries, then take half your cargo in fines. Sound reasonable?"

"Eminently," Clearspring said, the careful enunciation of the severely intoxicated bleeding into her voice. "You're a credit to the uniform, if you actually had one. And sorry about shoving you off the dock that time. I was tired and emotional."

"As a rat," Roger agreed. "But no harm done. My cut of the fine came in handy, as it happens." He turned, and led the way down the dock toward the other boats. Drago remained lurking in the shadows until he was sure the seething elves were going to stay put, and after a moment or two he followed the others.

"So Foley's a magistrate now?" Sleer asked. "How did that happen?"

Roger shrugged. "How do you think? She made herself one."

"Right. Should have guessed." Sleer clambered over the rail of his boat, followed by the rest of his crew, and raised a hand in farewell. "Night, Marieth. Sweet dreams."

"I wish." Clearspring led the way onto the deck of her own boat, and turned to Drago. "You can have Hannie's hammock tonight if you like. She won't be needing it."

"No thanks." Drago paused at the top of the ladder leading down into the depths of the hold. "I've got a bedroll with me. I'll sleep up here, in case our friends with the floating urinal get any ideas about paying you a visit in the small hours."

Clearspring regarded him appraisingly for a moment, suddenly seeming a lot more sober. "I would ask what you think you could do about it if they did, but I'm not sure I want to know." Then she turned, and disappeared into the deck cabin.

Drago lay awake for a long time, but nothing happened, and eventually he fell asleep still marveling at the sight of the stars.

CHAPTER SEVENTEEN
"Don't expect us to hang about afterwards."

Drago woke with the dawn, the first flush of sunlight casting a red glow across the deck, and felt a momentary surge of disorientation which propelled him to his feet, his hand closed around the hilt of the knife he'd kept tucked beneath the knapsack he'd been using as a pillow. Then he remembered where he was, breathed in the unwelcome draught of fresh air blowing in off the river, and sneezed.

"You can move pretty quick when you want to," Clearspring remarked, observing him from the doorway of the deck cabin. She had a steaming mug of something mulled in her hand, to chase away the morning chill, and the aroma tantalized Drago's empty stomach. "I was going to give you a shake and see if you wanted one of these, but I'm glad I didn't now."

"Probably wouldn't have ended well," Drago agreed, returning the knife to its scabbard inside his boot, and bending down to roll up his blanket. "But I wouldn't say no."

"Thought not." Clearspring strolled over and handed him a second mug. "I take it you didn't have to fend off any visitors after all."

"No," Drago said. He looked around, but the *Rippling Light* was the only boat still left at the wharf. Half a dozen sails were already visible out on the river, but if any of them belonged to Hathead, Sleer or the elves they were too far away to be sure. "Any chance of some breakfast?"

"Every chance." Greel stuck his head out of the galley. "Pancakes all right with you?"

Drago nodded, leaning on the rail. The river curved away ahead of them, trees lining the banks almost as far as he could see, before petering out into the same monotonous heathland he'd seen so much of the previous day. Smoke rose in several places along the banks, where other crews who'd simply moored for the night were preparing their own breakfasts, or the charcoal burners were plying their trade. "Pancakes are fine."

"Good. Cause that's all I've got." Greel grinned, and disappeared again. Drago sipped the drink Clearspring had given him, warming his hands around the mug, feeling curiously at ease despite the silence and the lack of people pressing close around him. The flavor was unfamiliar, but not unpleasant, with a spicy aftertaste; he could feel every swallow warming its way down to his stomach, from where it radiated out through the rest of his body.

"Morning!" A cheery hail from the dockside drew his attention shoreward, where Hannie was approaching. The settlement seemed more pleasant in daylight, the rising sun playing against the buildings, and highlighting the splashes of color in the makeshift gardens. Those closest to the eastern tree line were still in shade, dappled by the shifting blotches of sunshine which managed to wriggle their way through the obstructing leaves. The early risers, which seemed to be most of the villagers, were beginning to emerge from their houses, heading toward the woods with tools and bags, and for the first time Drago saw children among them, running and chattering with the careless abandon of those for whom the afternoon seems like a lifetime away.

"What time do you call this?" Clearspring demanded, as Hannie clambered over the rail. "You should have been back at first light."

"Well, I had to say goodbye properly, didn't I?" Hannie said, with a distinctly self-satisfied grin. "That's just manners. Anyway, Greel's still cooking." The grin widened. "Lucky that. I've worked up quite an appetite."

"He can cook just as well while we're under way," Clearspring said testily. "Get those mooring lines unhitched, and help me with the sail." She strode off to hoist it, while Hannie got to work, whistling cheerfully under her breath.

The next few days settled into a routine Drago almost began to find comfortable. As the landscape on the banks gradually changed from monotonous heathland interspersed with progressively larger clumps of woodland to sprawling forests separated by dwindling stretches of moor, life aboard the boat acquired a rhythm that was almost soothing. A good deal of his time was spent trailing the fishing line in the water, while the *Rippling Light*'s crew attended to more urgent matters, and although he never quite felt as proficient as he would have liked, Drago began to take a quiet pride in the steady supply of fish he began to bring aboard. As Greel had warned him, the size of the catch was never predictable, but, somehow, that made it even more satisfying.

In the quieter moments of their passage one or more of the crew would generally find time to chat with him, asking about life in Fairhaven with evidently genuine curiosity: how the people there could stand the crowding and the stench, how many foreigners he'd met from overseas, if the wizards there really were as skillful and learned as rumor had it. To which he answered with vague generalities, the occasional joke he then had to explain, and a faint sense of unease that so much he'd always taken for granted didn't really make much sense when you looked at it too closely. But then he supposed most people felt like that. The one topic he was careful to deflect, a fact he was sure hadn't gone unnoticed, was anything touching on how he earned a living. Clearspring had evidently inferred that it was something on the fringes of the law, which he supposed was technically true, and he made certain he said or did nothing to disabuse her of the notion.

In return, he learned a lot about life on the river; how to tie knots he'd never heard of, even living in a maritime city, how to handle tiller and sails, and how to spot the minute ripples on the water which indicated where the best wind could be found. At times, he even lost sight of the reason for his journey for a moment or two, before recalling himself to business with a silent admonition of his own carelessness. His life was still in danger, and would be until he found and challenged his quarry.

Some nights along the way they simply tied up to the bank, driving steel spikes deep into the ground to take the mooring lines, eating the fish he caught or foraging along the banks while the daylight lasted. Greel seemed to have a particular knack for finding herbs and setting snares, and Drago was surprised to discover how prominently rabbit featured in a riverboat crew's diet. Other nights were spent in riverside settlements like Naught's Landing. In some of these, Clearspring seemed as uneasy as she had been in the first village they'd stopped at, while in others she seemed affable and relaxed; it didn't take Drago long to realize that the better her mood, the lower the likelihood of meeting other elves while she was ashore.

The farther upriver they progressed, the less comfortable she seemed to become at the prospect of leaving the boat once they'd put in at a settlement, even electing on a couple of occasions to remain aboard for the night while Greel went in search of a drink, Drago of any information he could find, and Hannie of whichever young man of the village she was currently taking an interest in.

"She's always like this when we get near the Marches," Hannie confided one afternoon, coiling ropes, while Drago trailed the fishing line astern.

Drago pricked up his ears. "We're close to them, then?" he asked, trying to make the enquiry sound casual.

Hannie nodded. "Two more days, we'll be there. Then you'll need to decide where you want to get off."

Drago shrugged. "Close to the mines, I guess. Is there a wharf in the Barrens?"

Hannie laughed, Greel joining in from the tiller. "Not much point. They're inland." She pointed. "Just over the trees there, you see?"

Drago squinted. A line of hills rose out of the forest a long way ahead, hanging over them like a low, threatening thundercloud, their outlines blurred by distance. "Just about."

"But there's a wharf a little way inside the border of the Marches," Hannie said, "where they offload supplies for the mines, and take on the gold. We could always drop you there."

Greel nodded agreement. "There's a road, they tell me, if you're willing to risk using it. Gorash doesn't raid every convoy passing along it."

"Least he didn't the last time we heard," Hannie added.

Drago thought about that. If he presented himself as a miner looking for work, he might be able to slip in among a crowd of other people, and bide his time until he got a firm lead on the bandit's whereabouts. If he was really lucky the reivers would attack the group he was traveling with, and he could follow them back to their camp when they withdrew. "Where are we putting in tonight?" he asked.

"Birch Glade," Hannie said. "Skipper's not keen, but we picked up some letters for there on the way upstream, so we don't have a choice. Nice little town, if you ignore the pointears who think the rest of us are talking livestock."

"Sounds delightful," Drago said. "I can't wait."

In the event, Drago was pleasantly surprised. Birch Glade turned out to be a real town, at least by the standards of the riverbank, rather than the village he'd envisaged, with a tangle of wooden wharves reaching out into the waterway like a miniature model of one of the Fairhaven docks. Over a dozen boats were tied up there, and even before it came into sight, homes and warehouses were visible sprawling out along the bank for almost a mile. At first they were mostly farmsteads, carved out of the forest, then lumber mills and denser housing took over. Thousands of trees must have been felled to create a clearing large enough to encompass the town, and it was clearly growing bigger by the day. Drago had never seen or imagined anything like it, or stopped to wonder before where all the chairs and tables in Fairhaven had originally come from.

"Not the biggest," Clearspring said, when he asked if this was the principal source of timber along the river, "but a major one. There are logging towns along the banks for the next couple of hundred miles, but most of them are smaller than this. Why do you ask?"

Drago shrugged. "Just wondering if we're in the Marches yet."

"No." Clearspring shook her head. "We manage our woodlands more carefully than this. About the only thing Marchers do get right." She swept an arm across the panorama, taking in the town, the bustling industry, and the scattering of logging camps and hamlets on the far bank. "The people here keep this up, and there won't be anything worth felling in a generation or two." Then she shrugged. "Not my problem, though. Maybe they'll take up farming instead."

"Maybe." Drago found it hard to care either. "Do you call in here often?"

"If we have to," Clearspring said. "There's always timber to be hauled, and that's a good earner, but there's too many Marchers around for my liking. On the other hand, they're not exactly in the majority, so that can be entertaining."

Drago forbore from commenting. The implication wasn't lost on him; many of the elves in Birch Glade would be exiles like Clearspring, washing up at the closest community to their homeland, and feelings would run high between the two groups. The local watchmen would more than earn their salaries, he was sure.

"Hannie tells me we're only a couple of days from the mine wharf," he said, and Clearspring nodded. "Could you stand to let me off there?"

Clearspring shrugged. "It's your money. We'll drop you wherever you like. Just don't expect us to hang about afterwards."

"Fair enough." Drago watched as the town got closer, Greel leaning into the tiller to bring the boat in alongside the wharf. Men were already waiting there to grab the lines, moving with expert precision to haul the *Rippling Light* in alongside the quay, which seemed to Drago to be far more sophisticated in its construction than the one he'd seen at Naught's Landing. The whole dock, in fact, was bustling, making him feel faintly nostalgic for his hometown; pretty much the only thing missing was the smell. "Do you have much to unload here?"

"Not really." Clearspring waved away an enquiring shout from the operator of a hand-cranked derrick, who nodded, and swiveled his jib over to the cargo hatch of the boat in the neighboring berth instead. "Picked up a couple of mail pouches for here on our way upstream, or I'd just have kept going." Drago nodded; it was an interesting novelty to be berthed somewhere with a few hours of daylight still to go. "Most of the stuff in the hold's for the Delvings upstream, but we added a couple of crates of our own, with things we can always sell along the way. If I can get a good price for that here, and clear some space, we'll fill it with offcuts from the lumber mills. People always want firewood, and in the bigger towns they can't gather it for themselves."

Which meant a lucrative second line of business for the boatyards in Fairhaven, Drago reflected. He'd once made good money keeping thieves from the offcuts, until he realized how desperate most of them were, and had found other contracts to fill his time with. Beating up beggars hadn't sat well with him.

"Sounds like you're going to be busy," he said.

"I'm always busy," Clearspring said. "What are you going to do?"

Drago shrugged. "Take a look around town, I guess." And see if he could pick up any clues to Gorash's whereabouts. A place this size, this close to the Marches, would probably be swirling with rumors. "And see about finding a drink. Know anywhere good?"

"One or two places," Clearspring said. "Maybe I'll show you if I get finished in time. But you're paying."

"I always do," Drago said.

CHAPTER EIGHTEEN
"It's what you do with it that counts."

In the event, dusk was falling before Clearspring had finished transacting her business, and she and Drago went in search of the drink they'd discussed. Hannie had disappeared as usual, and Greel elected to remain behind on the boat to keep watch. The risk of pilferage was theoretically low, with so many people working on the docks with the boats in their eye line, but that only increased the chances that one of them might be less than honest—and everyone knew that "finding" the odd item that had been left lying around was a time-honored stevedore's perk to which no one would object. No one local, anyway.

"So, what did you make of it?" Clearspring asked, as they made their way into the heart of the town. Drago had spent the intervening hours walking the streets, sampling various foodstuffs from itinerant vendors, and watching the people. He hadn't seen more than a handful of other gnomes since boarding the riverboat, most of them travelers like himself, but the streets were full of humans, elves and goblins, who seemed to be getting along reasonably well with one another. The elves from the Marches were easy to pick out, by their tendency to cluster together and the contemptuous manner they adopted toward everyone else, but since nobody seemed to want to have any more to do with them than they could help, that didn't seem to matter very much. Certainly there was no more tension in the air than there generally was in his hometown, and that was fueled by a myriad of rivalries between districts, guilds, businesses, street gangs, watch houses and families, irrespective of the species of anyone involved.

"Bit quiet," Drago said, determined to seem as cosmopolitan as a Fairhavener ought to be anywhere less sophisticated, "but it seems nice enough."

"Yes, it does," Clearspring said, in the tone of someone who'd learned not to trust appearances a long time ago. She paused, to glance in the open window of a cobbler's shop; unlike the hamlets they'd stopped at in their journey up the river, Birch Glade was large enough to support specialized tradesmen, and every street had at least one or two businesses interspersed among the houses. Not seeing anything there she liked or needed, she moved on. "Not far now."

The tavern she'd been aiming for turned out to be on the next street, warm lamplight spilling from an open door, outside which a couple of patrons leaned, tankards in their hands. One human, one elf, both male, they watched Clearspring pass inside with obvious interest, and Drago with faint curiosity.

The by now familiar strains of "Reiver Bold" greeted them as they passed over the threshold, and Drago glanced around, finding to his surprise that a few of the elvish customers were joining in with the goblins and humans making up the bulk of the singers. Clearspring smiled and nodded to a couple of them, who returned the greeting and carried on singing with gusto.

"Didn't expect to hear elves singing that one," Drago said, rising on tiptoe to see over the bar. He'd been listening to versions of it at nearly every settlement they'd called at along the river, but almost always sung by goblins, and the occasional human.

"Didn't you?" Clearspring smiled tightly. "We're near the Marches now. I told you, not everyone likes the way things have been going there since the queen disappeared." She caught the bartender's eye. "Two ales. And the same for him." She nodded downward, in case the goblin in the grubby apron pushing a lump of stain that might once have been a rag around the countertop had missed Drago's presence. "He's paying."

"Of course he is," Drago said, resigned, pulling the right change from his purse. He picked up his drinks, and followed the riverboat captain across the crowded taproom, sticking as close to her as he could without his intentions appearing dishonorable to avoid having to weave around innumerable bodies almost twice his own height. For a moment he was incongruously reminded of the unusually cold winter a couple of years before, when ice had formed in a couple of the more sheltered inner harbors, and he'd sat on the dock watching a departing ship cleaving a channel through the frozen water, her tender bobbing behind her at the end of a cable. "So what do you think happened to her?"

"Who?" She found a couple of seats at a nearby table, next to the singing elves, who'd moved on to another ballad by now. She began humming along with this one too. "'*Tis fair to be a king, I trow, with all the king's delights. With wine and lace and feather beds to share with catamites . . .*"

"The queen." He took a mouthful of the ale, which turned out to be surprisingly good. Another advantage of spending the night somewhere almost civilized. He kept his voice casual. "I got talking to someone who thought Gorash killed her." Which was true, although the way he'd phrased it, Clearspring would no doubt assume it was someone he'd met exploring the town earlier that afternoon.

"Bollocks he did," a goblin at the next table cut in, genuine anger suffusing his voice. "What are you, a Marcher he cut off at the knees?" His fists were clenching, and Drago shifted his weight, silently cursing his oversized chair. Jumping down from it and getting properly balanced would take an appreciable fraction of a second, by which time the goblin, with his feet already on the floor, would be standing and swinging at him. He tightened his grip on the tankard of ale. It'd be a shame to waste the first decent drink he'd had since leaving home, but throwing it in the goblin's face would buy him enough time to take the initiative.

"Don't mind him. He's from the coast. Why would he know anything?" Clearspring said, leaning over to put one of the spare drinks on the other table in front of the goblin. Not hers, Drago noted. "Have this one on us." She turned back to Drago. "Would this happen to have been a Marcher you were talking to?"

"He said that was where he was from," Drago said truthfully. He had no reason to doubt Greenleaf's veracity, on that score at least.

"There you are, then," the goblin said, mollified by the unexpected acquisition of a free drink. "They're all lying bastards." He shot a quick glance at the elves around him. "The ones still living there, anyway. No offense."

"None taken," Clearspring assured him, "but if you want to get the next round in, that'd go down well as an apology."

"Fair enough." The goblin took an appreciative gulp, and turned to Drago. "Gorash was talking to her. First chance in a generation to get back what's rightfully ours. Why would he do something as stupid as killing her? If you ask me, it was that pukebag Stargleam. Topped his own sister to grab the throne."

But Clearspring was shaking her head dubiously. "Can't see it myself. That ballad pretty well sums him up. He was more than happy to hang around the palace spending her money on trinkets, whores and pretty boys, but he never showed any sign of wanting to rule. Too much like hard work."

"I agree." The nearest elf joined in, with a nod of the head. "Look up 'bone idle tosspot' in the dictionary, and you'll find his portrait. If he was going to have her killed it would have been over something that mattered to him, not the throne. Even his father did a better job, and he wasn't exactly the sharpest sword in the arsenal."

"Fair point." The goblin drained his tankard. "You'd know better than me, being from up that way. Same again all round?" Everyone nodded, and he rose, intent on heading for the bar. Then he turned back on the point of leaving, struck by an afterthought. "Whoever did it, though, she's definitely dead, right? Otherwise she's bound to have come back by now, the pig's breakfast he's making of everything." Then he disappeared into the crowd.

"You'd think so," Clearspring said, but the elf shook his head, and leaned in confidentially across the tabletop.

"I heard she's biding her time. Building an army to invade the Marches, and regain the kingdom."

Clearspring snorted derisively. "Building an army where, exactly? I've been along every inch of this river, from the Delvings to the sea, and I've never seen a trace of one, or spoken to anyone who had." She turned to Drago. "Unless your folk are hiding them in the caverns. Does that sound likely to you?"

"Not unless she's paying them a wagon load of rent," Drago said, to general amusement. The gnomish homelands were known to keep themselves to themselves, unless there was something in it for them, which probably explained why so many of their scions did so well in places like Fairhaven. Even then, he couldn't quite see it. For one thing, the queen's putative army would be spending most of their time shuffling along gnome-sized tunnels bent almost double, and he didn't think that would do much for their martial prowess.

"Maybe they're in the Wastes, then, or overseas," the elf persisted hopefully. "The Icelands, perhaps."

"Perhaps," Drago said tactfully, although that sounded even less likely. An invasion or a *coup d'état* relied on the element of surprise, which would be somewhat lacking if the invading army needed weeks to get where it was going. The more he heard the more likely his original conclusion, that the missing queen was lying at the bottom of the river or in a hastily dug hole somewhere, with a stomach full of elfbane or a back full of dagger, seemed to him. "You never can tell."

"No, you can't," the elf said, seeming to feel his point had been made.

After that, the evening proceeded convivially enough, ending with several more songs about the heroism, gallantry, and irresistible romantic allure of the elusive Gorash, which Drago might have been a little less cynical about if the bandit hadn't been so energetically trying to murder him by proxy, and the current king of the Sylvan Marches' complete lack of any such virtues. Or, indeed, positive qualities of any kind, unless some of the listeners felt that such a single-minded dedication to hedonism was somehow inherently admirable—which, so far as Drago could tell, no one did. The upshot of which was, by the time he and Clearspring left the tavern, he'd had a good deal more to drink than he'd intended, and night had fallen in earnest in the street outside.

"I'll say this for your friends," he said, taking a deep breath of cooler air as he hit the thoroughfare, and waited for his head to stop spinning in response, "they know how to have a good time."

"Friends?" Just like the evening in Naught's Landing, Clearspring seemed to be overriding the effects of intoxication by sheer willpower—a knack Drago was beginning to envy her. The streets of a strange town, close to the *de facto* fiefdom of someone who wanted him dead, was no place to suddenly discover that his reaction time was reduced, and his sense of balance mildly impaired, but he was beginning to suspect that both of these were precisely the case. "Never seen any of them before in my life."

Drago didn't quite know how to respond to that, so he didn't, opting instead for "Which way back to the wharf?"

"Stick with me," Clearspring advised, confirming his original guess by shaping each word with exaggerated care. She seemed steady enough on her feet, though, so Drago fell in beside her, lengthening his stride a little to keep up with her leisurely stroll. "I know a short cut."

"Good." The sooner they got back to the boat, the better, he thought. The shadows were thickening, and although they couldn't conceal much from his gnomish night vision, it was possible Gorash's agents here had access to the kind of shadow-weaving charms their counterparts in Fairhaven had been using. He should have asked Raegan or Vethik for a few of the counter-charms before he left.

Well, it was too late to worry about that. He'd just have to keep his eyes open, and hope for the best.

Almost as soon as the thought had crossed his mind, Clearspring headed down a dark alleyway between a couple of nondescript buildings, both shops of some kind, although with the shutters closed there was no clue as to what either of them sold. Names were written above the barred windows, but neither meant anything to him. The elf was striding out with confidence, despite the darkness between the walls, which must have been all but impenetrable to her. Drago could make out the usual detritus which seemed to spontaneously generate in the less travelled corners of most towns and cities, but nothing seemed to threaten any consequences worse than having to wipe their boots.

"Are you sure you know where—" he began, then fell silent as they came out into an area he thought he recognized from his earlier peregrinations. Tall warehouses stood all around them, men, elves and goblins still delivering and removing boxes, bundles and barrels on handcarts, or loading horse-drawn wagons, by the light of flaring sconces. A little farther down the street, and they could cut through to the waterfront.

"Course I do. Should be able to find my way back to my own sodding boat." Clearspring wove her way through the dense crush of constantly moving bodies and obstacles as though she were a windblown leaf surrounded by mist; Drago, with reflexes honed by a lifetime of passing unscathed through the streets of Fairhaven, followed with equal ease. In fact he even pulled a little way ahead of her, turning down a narrow passage between a couple of warehouses a pace or two before she did.

There were no lights here at all, the tall, windowless sides of the huge timber buildings looming on either side of them, making the narrow passageway seem even more constricted than it was. Still able to see as well as he ever did in the dark, Drago strode out confidently, until a clatter and a string of profanity behind him made him glance back. Clearspring was clutching her shin, and swearing with a vigor and fluency only possible to someone who spent their life on the water bawling at underlings. "Slow down, you sawn-off troll shagger! We can't all see in the pox-rotting dark!"

"Sorry," Drago said, almost meaning it. Wrapped up in his own thoughts, he had momentarily forgotten that the elf couldn't see in the dark as well as he could. Or at all, really. "It's not far. River's just at the end here." He could see it already, beyond the lip of the wharf onto which the warehouses faced, the surface writhing smooth and glossy in the faint glow of starlight seeping through the cloud overhead like a tub full of eels in the fish market back home. The thought made him feel uneasy.

"So you say," Clearspring grumbled. Then she turned her head, listening. "What's that?"

"Quiet," Drago said in an urgent undertone, fully prepared for an argument, but Clearspring was quick on the uptake, even inebriated, and didn't challenge the point. "Someone's coming."

"Who?" She matched his quiet tone, drawing a knife from somewhere beneath her shirt. Drago kept his hand hovering close to the hilt of his sword, but didn't take hold of it quite yet, content to wait and see what happened. Whoever was lurking further down the passageway wouldn't have the advantage he did in the dark, unless it was another gnome, and they seemed too tall for that.

"Goblins," he whispered after a moment. "Three of them."

"What are they up to?" Clearspring murmured, and Drago shrugged, before remembering she couldn't see him.

"Can't tell yet. But they don't want to attract any attention, that's for sure." All three of them were swathed in the same dark cloaks his would-be assassins had worn when they'd jumped him outside his lodgings, rendering them effectively invisible in the gloom of the narrow passageway, but at least these ones didn't seem to be employing sorcery. If they were Gorash's agents at all, of course. For all he knew they were innocent warehouse workers, sneaking off to relieve themselves down the nearest alley, or avoid some particularly onerous job until it had been given to someone else.

A metallic clink echoed in the night air, followed by shushing sounds from whomever of the trio was their leader. Crowbars appeared in their hands, followed a moment later by a muffled thudding and a splintering of wood, as they began to lever planks out of the wall nearest to where they stood.

"What's that?" Clearspring asked again, even more quietly than before. "What are they doing?"

"Breaking in," Drago whispered. He took hold of her arm, and began to urge her away, back in the direction they'd come. "I suggest we take the scenic route back to the boat." He wasn't being paid to protect whatever the thieves were after, and didn't see any point in confronting them. They might have some information he could use to help track down the bandit chief, but there wasn't any real reason to suspect that either—if Birch Glade really was a miniature analog of Fairhaven, there would be plenty of gainfully employed thieves around the docks with no allegiance to anyone or anything beyond their own purses and a handful of associates.

"Works for me," Clearspring agreed, slipping the dagger away in whatever recess of her clothing it had come from, much to Drago's silent relief. The idea of being next to someone waving a lethal weapon around while she couldn't see what she was doing with it was far from appealing. With his help, she made it back to the lit and bustling area without getting entangled in any more obstacles along the way, which suited Drago fine. The thieves were probably armed, and if they realized they'd been spotted, might have come after them. Not that it would have been a problem if they had; in the dark of the narrow passageway the advantage would have been entirely his, but he was a long way from Greta's laundry, and he wanted to keep his shirts as unsullied as possible.

"That must have been the shortest quickie on record," one of the dock workers greeted them as they emerged onto the street, grinning ribaldly as he spoke. He was a short man as humans went, about Clearspring's height, but broad with it, his arms bulging with muscle as he manhandled a laden handcart past the mouth of the passageway. He must have spotted them entering the gap between the buildings a couple of minutes before, and drawn the obvious but erroneous conclusion from their emergence at the same end. He nodded at Drago. "In more ways than one."

Drago hastily let go of the elf's arm, but fortunately Clearspring seemed to see the funny side, leering at the docker in a conspiratorial fashion.

"It's true what they say," she assured him, with the kind of straight face a professional card player would have sold their soul to acquire. "It's not the size, it's what you do with it that counts."

"Take your word for it, love." The docker picked up the handles of his barrow, and moved off, chuckling.

"Sorry about that," Drago said, wondering why he was apologizing.

Clearspring shrugged. "Not your fault," she said. "And he didn't mean anything by it. Just banter." She looked pensive for a moment. "If I thought he was really impugning my honor, I'd just have killed him." Another momentary pause, then a bark of laughter. "Oh, your face. If I'd realized you were that easy to wind up, I'd have had a lot more fun this trip."

"Nice one," Drago said, adopting an easygoing smile. In truth, the brief conversation had disturbed him. The docker would remember them now, and when the warehouse theft was discovered, the local watch would want a word with an elf and a gnome seen leaving the scene together. Possibly even consider them suspects, rather than witnesses. Either way, the resulting attention was far too likely to attract the notice of Gorash's people. He just had to hope that the *Rippling Light* would have resumed its journey by then.

Which reminded him. He glanced back down the passageway, just in time to see the last of the burglars slipping in through the hole they'd made in the wall. Everything seemed quiet and empty down there, and it briefly occurred to him that they could probably get back to the boat that way after all now, just slipping past the hole while the thieves were occupied. But on the other hand, why take the risk? It wasn't as if Clearspring was about to cast off before morning anyway, so they weren't in that much of a hurry to return. In fact . . .

"Is there anywhere around here we can get another drink?" he asked. "I think I could do with one after that."

"Most sensible thing you've said all evening," Clearspring agreed.

CHAPTER NINETEEN
"Does anyone know who this elf is?"

Docksides being the kind of places they were, it didn't take long to find an open bar not far from the waterfront. Though a good deal less prepossessing than the establishment they'd spent most of the evening in, the beer was passable, and they served basic but wholesome food which Drago took full advantage of, to Clearspring's evident amusement.

"I'm surprised you've got room for any food, after all that ale you've taken aboard," she said.

Drago shrugged, and continued ploughing his way through a plate of bread, cheese, and pickles. "Easy come, easy go," he said, having just returned from a trip outside to jettison what felt like the larger part of his cargo. The food should soak up most of the rest, and the tankard or two by which he'd topped it up. The near encounter with the warehouse thieves had been a salutary lesson in not letting his guard down, and he wasn't going to ignore it. "You know what they say," he said, his voice slightly muffled, "you don't buy ale, you just rent it."

Clearspring laughed. "True enough," she said. "Are you about done?"

"I am." Drago chewed and swallowed the last of his food, and chased it down with the dregs of his drink. As he hopped off the stool he'd been sitting on, he felt more centered and sure of himself, as sober and alert as he'd ever been. "Are you?"

"I guess." The elf stood too, swaying slightly for a moment before regaining her own balance, as sure-footed as if the floor had been the deck of her riverboat. Drago supposed that it didn't really matter whether the subtle shifts underfoot she was compensating for were real or subjective, if you did it as instinctively as that.

The watering hole had been crowded when they entered it, and was even more so now as they wove their way through an influx of off-duty stevedores celebrating the end of their shift, so they became separated on their way to the door. Drago, having had a great deal more practice at making his way through masses of intervening bodies, and a natural ability to take advantage of whichever smaller gaps opened up around him, reached the entrance first, and paused outside waiting for Clearspring to catch up with him. The street seemed busier than he remembered it, people running past the tavern with grim, purposeful expressions, or, just as often, excited and curious ones.

"What's going on?" Clearspring asked, elbowing her way into the open air a moment later.

Drago shrugged. "Haven't a clue."

"There's a fire," a passing goblin called back, evidently having overheard the exchange. "Along the waterfront."

"Where?" Clearspring called after her, but by that point the goblin had vanished among the scurrying throng. The elf's face became grim, any lingering trace of intoxication vanishing at once. "If it's anywhere near my boat—"

"Go," Drago said. If she started running, he'd never be able to keep up with her, so there didn't seem any point in even trying. "I'll see you back at the wharf."

"Damn right you will," Clearspring said, sprinting away in the same direction that the crowd was flowing. In a moment Drago had lost sight of her, and set out to follow, walking quickly among the hurrying humans, goblins and elves. He had to keep his wits about him, as few of them thought to look down, and he was forced to dodge out of the way of the most preoccupied with irritating frequency.

"Make way!" a peremptory voice bellowed, and the crowd flowed aside to let a party of watchmen through, double-timing it with buckets and axes in their hands, the sergeant in charge yelling encouragement to her subordinates.

With so much commotion going on around him it took Drago a moment or two to orient himself, and when he did, he was taken aback to realize he was approaching the front of the warehouse he'd seen the thieves breaking into earlier that evening. Smoke was billowing out of it, spinning away across the harbor toward the distant lantern lights of the logging camps on the opposite bank. That was a blessing, at least; if the prevailing wind had been in any other direction, the entire town would already have been at risk from drifting sparks. As it was, the watchmen swiftly organized the most able-bodied among the milling onlookers into an efficient pair of bucket chains, one passing pails of water toward the combusting building, while the other conveyed the empties back to the edge of the dock to be refilled. All along the wharf edge, boats were putting out into the middle of the river, as far from danger as possible; Drago narrowed his eyes against the stinging smoke, thinking for a moment that he could see the *Rippling Light* among them, her hastily slipped cables still trailing in the water, then the choking cloud drifted across him and he lost sight of everything until the wind shifted again.

"It's not going to be enough," one of the watchmen said, and the sergeant nodded in agreement, her eyes narrowed against the drifting smoke.

"That's well alight," she confirmed, as the first orange flames began licking around the door frame. A dull roaring sound began to make itself heard over the bleating of the crowd. "We'll need a damn sight more than buckets to put this one out." She turned, and began bellowing to the watchman at the head of the bucket chain. "Leave it, Gengiz, it's got too strong a hold. Start wetting down the neighboring ones!"

"Right, Sarge!" the burly goblin called back, and began hurling water against the side of the adjacent structure, from which steam immediately arose in response. Drago began to edge away. This wasn't boding well. He glanced inside the warehouse, through the open door, and was immediately reminded of the oven in the baker's shop in the next street to Mrs. Cravatt's. Though without the appetizing smell. Barring a miracle, it would only be a matter of time before the flames spread along the entire row of warehouses.

"Make way! Wizard coming through!" a fresh voice yelled, aiming for impressively authoritative, and missing in the direction of squeaky with excitement, before petering out in a paroxysm of coughing courtesy of a lungful of smoke. Drago turned. A young human with streaming eyes, in a scholastic robe which almost fitted him, was picking his way through the crowd. A few of the locals laughed, nudging each other in the ribs, clearly anticipating some unexpected additional entertainment.

"Sod off, Aris, I haven't got time for any of your cock-ups now. Things are bad enough already." The sergeant turned away, the young sorcerer already dismissed from her mind. He glared at her back, then started rummaging in his satchel regardless.

Better and better. Drago started looking for a way out of here, but the steadily growing crowd was hemming him in more tightly than ever.

"Who's in charge here?" A well-dressed elf, whose supercilious air and the muttered imprecations of many among the onlookers marked him out as a Marcher, elbowed his way through the bucket gang, and strutted toward the sergeant.

She returned a look of almost equal disdain, which was only emphasized by the professional politeness of her words. "That would be me." A fractional pause before the "Sir," which protocol demanded. "Sergeant Dickson of the Dock Watch." Another pause. "And you are?"

"Cloverbell Fennel. I own this building."

Dickson nodded. "Then I suggest you let us get on with our jobs, if you want any of it left standing."

"What I want, sergeant, is for you to arrest the arsonist responsible!" Fennel glared at her as though she were a kitchen maid who'd just let his morning infusion grow cold. "Right now!"

"Right now, I'm more concerned with preventing the rest of the docks from going up in flames." Dickson's voice was calm, reasonable, and, to Drago's ears at least, freighted with a menace the elf seemed deaf to. "*If* we find any evidence of arson, and *if* that doesn't point to an attempt to defraud debtors, we'll no doubt have time to discuss your suspicions. *After* we've got the bloody fire out. And anybody getting in my way while I do that is going to see the inside of a cell for obstructing the watch and endangering the public. Are we clear?" Another fractional pause. "Sir?"

"Oh, I think we're clear all right. We all know the authorities in this maggot-ridden midden are hand in glove with the bandits from the Barrens, don't we? Getting your bribes to look the other way while the king's goods are stolen or destroyed."

"I'm not aware of any such arrangement," Dickson said, not even pretending to add the honorific anymore. "Are you saying the contents of this warehouse belong to the king of the Marches?"

A few of the crowd began to sing the song Drago had heard earlier in the tavern, although the roar of the fire made it hard to hear them. Flames were visible on the roof of the warehouse now, and the bucket gangs redoubled their efforts to damp down the neighboring buildings, although the wisps of smoke rising from the blackening woodwork indicated they were buying scant time at best. More of the crowd were joining in the firefighting efforts, but from where Drago was standing, it looked ultimately futile. All his survival instincts were urging him to get away as swiftly as possible, but the conversation he was overhearing was just too good to walk away from. Perhaps Fennel had some pertinent information about the bandits, which he was definitely not going to be willing to share with a wandering gnome.

"Not personally," Fennel snapped, as though trying to explain the color of the sky to a particularly obtuse child. "It's a consignment of supplies to his troops. Boots and winter clothing for the garrison in the Barrens." Without which their ability to mount effective patrols once the year waned, and the cold mountain winds began to bite in earnest, would be severely impaired. It seemed the trio of goblins Drago had seen breaking in earlier had been Gorash's agents after all.

He glanced around, hoping to catch sight of them in the crowd, though what he'd do if he actually saw them wasn't entirely clear to him. He could hardly hope to follow them back to the Barrens undetected, but he supposed that if they were living locally he might be able to track them as far as their lodgings at least. If he kept them under observation after that he might be able to glean some information on the bandit chief's whereabouts, or even corner one of them to ask a few questions directly, but that was an even more tenuous hope, and would raise the risk of exposure to much higher levels than he was comfortable with. So perhaps it was fortunate that he didn't spot any of them after all.

"Stand back!" Aris the mage had completed his enchantment, holding up the small leather bag in which he'd combined the essence of his spell. The spectators not actively engaged in fighting the fire edged away from him, a little nervously. "I'm starting the invocation!"

Dickson spun on her heel, the elf forgotten, and strode toward him, her face grimly set, her hand held out for the charm. "I'm warning you, Aris, if you don't knock this off right now—"

But before she could grab the tiny object, Aris threw it, with surprising strength and accuracy, straight into the heart of the inferno, and began chanting something under his breath.

"That does it, you scrawny little cantrip monger, you're nicked!" She grabbed the young mage by the collar, almost hoisting him off his feet. "Now pipe down!"

But Aris continued to chant, his eyes apparently focused on something invisible in the far distance. Dickson shook him like a terrier with a rat, but it didn't seem to make much difference; Aris's mind was no longer connected to his physical body, or so it seemed, concerned only with focusing his will through whatever charm he'd created.

Drago felt a puff of wind on his cheek, a cool caress cutting through the furnace heat of the blazing warehouse. From where he was standing, there didn't seem any point in trying to stop Aris from doing whatever it was he was trying to do; despite the best efforts of the bucket wielders, the warehouses on either side of the burning one were beginning to smolder, and looked liable to burst into flame at any minute. But then he didn't live here; it sounded as though Dickson knew the young mage well enough to be wary of the results of his attempts at spell casting. And not without reason, if the muttering and apprehensive glances among the onlookers were anything to go by.

The wind was definitely picking up now, tugging at his hair and clothing. The crowd began to back away, the flames engulfing Fennel's warehouse flickering and flaring in the strengthening gusts. The firefighters nearest the conflagration dropped their buckets, retreating to a safer distance.

"What are you up to, you little snot?" Dickson demanded, but Aris just kept on chanting, and after a moment she simply dropped him, turning her mind to the immediate demands of public safety. If she couldn't shut him up, and break the spell, she'd just have to make sure no one got hurt by it. Drago supposed she could simply have cut the young man's throat, and shut the spell down that way, but a course of action that drastic would need far more justification than the (apparently) widespread belief that he was a congenital screw-up. "Everyone get back! Far as you can!" Instructions, which, to be fair, few of the people present seemed to need.

Drago backed away among the slowest of the onlookers, unable to tear his eyes away from the spectacle, making instinctively for the edge of the dock. If things went badly wrong he could always jump into the water: though he was an indifferent swimmer by Fairhaven standards, gnomes not being particularly noted for their buoyancy, he could manage well enough if the alternative was a messy and painful death. Something was definitely happening in and around the burning warehouse, the smoke and flames swirling around it in a circular vortex, drawing them up and away from the buildings on either side.

"Bugger me, Sarge, he's actually doing it," the goblin watchman muttered, and Dickson nodded, her face a picture of astonishment.

"You're right. He really is." Her voice rose in a yell of encouragement. "Come on, Aris! You can do it!" Then she turned back to her subordinate, shaking her head. "I can't believe I just said that."

"A—ris! A—ris!" The crowd took up the chant. The young mage showed no sign of having heard them, but the vortex of burning air around the warehouse seemed to increase in strength, rising higher, and narrowing, drawing the flames up, out, and into the air. A couple of loose boards ripped away from the roof and joined them, incinerating in an instant as they met the hovering flames. Now the entire conflagration seemed to be dancing and whirling above the town, like a sullen and miniature sun, more and more of the structure of the warehouse tearing loose and flying up to be engulfed by the furnace heat it contained.

"Stop him!" Fennel strode across to the two watchmen, and grabbed Dickson by the upper arm. "He's destroying the entire building!"

"And saving the rest of them," Dickson said. She put her other hand over the elf's, breaking his grip, and twisting his wrist away from her arm in what Drago recognized with quiet professional appreciation as an extremely painful lock. "And you're under arrest for assaulting an officer."

"Take your hands off me!" The elf drew himself up to his full height, bristling with indignation. "Have you any idea who I am?"

"Hang on a minute." Dickson drew in her breath, and turned to the nearest section of the crowd, who were edging a little closer again now the worst of the danger seemed past. "Does anyone know who this elf is?" she bellowed. "He seems to have forgotten!" She waited for the laughter and catcalls to die down, before turning back to the goblin watchman. "What a surprise, nobody does." She shoved the fuming elf in her subordinate's direction. "Here, take him in and make up some charges, before I forget I'm a lady and do something he regrets."

"My pleasure, ma'am." The goblin saluted smartly, grabbed Fennel by the arm and marched him off, still loudly protesting, much to the amusement of the bystanders.

Drago returned his attention to the swirling vortex of flame overhead, which by now was lighting the entire town in what might have passed for the warm light of dawn. Far out on the river the fleeing boats bobbed, basking in its glow, riding at anchor or simply drifting with the current, their crews preferring to make for the safety of the far bank without the effort of quanting or raising sail. Again, he tried to make out the *Rippling Light*, but at this distance there was little to distinguish one vessel from another.

A loud *crack!* from the direction of the warehouse snatched his attention back to the magical conflagration, just in time to see a substantial wall section break loose and whirl up into the levitating furnace, where it combusted immediately. Oohs and aahs rose from the crowd.

The end was clearly near now, the battered structure disintegrating faster and faster, each fresh piece flying upward to be immolated. Soon the site was completely clear, only the wide expanse of packed and slightly scorched earth standing between its neighbors showing any sign at all that a building had once stood there.

With no fresh fuel to sustain it, the levitating furnace eventually flickered and died, the preternatural wind which had borne it aloft dwindling away to nothing. An expectant hush fell.

"Heads!" Dickson bellowed, ducking an instant before a rain of ash descended, pattering into the river and covering everyone present in a patina of charcoal. Drago spat out a gob of blackened sputum.

"Did it work?" Aris asked, looking dazed, and a little surprised to find himself sitting down. He blinked twice, and staggered to his feet, only to be almost knocked off them again by a hearty slap on the back from the watch sergeant.

"It worked." Dickson looked almost as surprised as he did, but the tone of congratulation in her voice was sincere enough. "Well done, lad."

"I'm just glad I could help." Aris nodded, taking in the devastation around him with a fair simulacrum of professional detachment, although Drago could see elation bubbling just below the surface of his studiedly sober demeanor. "Could have got a bit nasty otherwise." He coughed. "Sorry. Throat's a bit dry."

"That shouldn't be too much of a problem," Dickson said, with a wry glance at the crowd, which was swarming in to offer congratulations of its own now the danger was past, cheering loudly and chanting the young mage's name with undiminished enthusiasm. "Looks like you won't have to pay for a drink in this town for at least a year."

"A—*ris!* A—*ris!*" Ignoring the mage's token protestations, the crowd scooped him up and carried him shoulder high in the direction of the nearest tavern.

Which seemed like a good idea to Drago as well. His throat was still lined with ash, and another ale or two seemed just the right thing to help shift it.

After all, it would take Clearspring and Greel a while yet to return to the wharf, so he had plenty of time before he could rejoin the boat: he might as well spend it wisely.

CHAPTER TWENTY
"That'd be a first."

The *Rippling Light* was later leaving the wharf the next morning than Clearspring had intended. Drago didn't find that particularly surprising, as she and Greel had spent half the previous night on the river and slept correspondingly late, but the main reason was that Hannie took even longer than usual to find the boat, which, like most of the others, hadn't returned to the berth she'd cast off from in the general exodus.

"What's the idea of shifting moorings on me?" she demanded, only partly mollified by the bacon bap Greel handed her as she passed the galley. He, Clearspring and Drago had already finished theirs, and been ready for departure for some time. Now they all glanced at one another in silent astonishment. "Thought it was funny, did you?"

"So you really haven't heard?" Greel asked, pausing on his way to loose the forrard mooring line.

Clearspring looked up from the aft one, already coiling it. "You can eat that at the tiller. We've already lost enough time as it is."

"Haven't heard what?" Hannie slouched over to the stern, managing to sound sulky even with her voice muffled by bread and pig flesh. Hung over, Drago decided. Quite badly, by her usual standards.

"See if you can guess," Greel said, with a wave at the void between buildings where Fennel's warehouse no longer stood.

Hannie stared vacantly at the waterfront for a moment, chewing with bovine placidity, and shook her head. "Nope. Not getting it."

"That'd be a first," Greel muttered, beginning to hoist the sail. The *Rippling Light* caught the breeze, began to pick up speed, and her steerswoman abruptly became a great deal more conscious of her duties.

"There was a fire last night," Drago said. "A big one. All the boats had to cast off in case it spread."

"Can't see much damage," Hannie said, glancing briefly back at the wharf for the last time, before returning her attention permanently to the river ahead. "Fire that big would have leveled it."

"Local spell-chucker put it out," Clearspring said. "Took down the building to do it, but saved the rest." A faintly vindictive grin flickered across her face. "Luckily the stuff inside belonged to Stargleam, so everybody's happy."

Drago thought of Cloverbell Fennel, who most certainly hadn't been. "Everybody?" he asked, in a tone of playful skepticism which had often proved surprisingly effective in getting people to tell him things they hadn't meant to.

"Everybody who counts," Clearspring said. "Birch Glade might have a lot of stuff coming through it on the way to the Marches, but they only deal with the Marchers for the money. Lot of folk there have relatives in the Barrens, if you get my drift."

Drago nodded. Perhaps he should have got off the boat there after all, and tried to pick up a lead on Gorash using his usual methods. The closer he got to the Barrens, the more unlikely his chances of ever being able to successfully pass for a miner were beginning to seem to him. It might have taken some time, but if, as Clearspring seemed to be hinting, there really were substantial numbers of sympathizers among the locals, he was fairly sure he would have found something before too long.

On the other hand, the news of the failure of the goblin warlord's agents to kill him back in Fairhaven must be making its way upriver by now, no more than a day or two behind the *Rippling Light*, probably trailed by follow-up reports about his disappearance. The sudden arrival of a single gnome in Birch Glade, asking questions, would be bound to attract potentially lethal attention there too.

No, the only way he was going to get to the Barrens without painting a target on his back was to do his best to look like a gnome who'd been going there anyway.

"You think that was Gorash's people we saw?" he asked, trying to sound surprised.

"You say you saw." Clearspring smiled thinly. "It was dark. No one had lights. I didn't see a thing."

"Didn't see all that much myself," Drago agreed untruthfully. "But it's still lucky we left before the watch got around to asking us any questions."

"That wasn't luck," Clearspring said, "that was good timing." She shrugged. "Besides, why would they care? Nobody local lost anything."

"Not sure the guy who owned the warehouse would see it like that," Drago said, picturing Fennel's face as he'd watched the building burn, and failing to feel much in the way of sympathy either.

Clearspring spat over the rail, and watched the result with evident approval. "He's not local," she said, "he's a Marcher who bought the place with Stargleam's money, and gets his orders direct from the palace. You really think they're going to leave military supplies in the hands of a local civilian?"

Drago hadn't actually thought about that, but it made sense now that she'd pointed it out. Something else didn't, though. "Why leave the stuff in Birch Glade anyway?" he asked. "Why not take it straight up the river to the Marches?"

Clearspring laughed. "They thought they were being clever," she said. "Ship the stuff in small batches, so no one could estimate the strength of the troops it was for, then consolidate it for final delivery. Never occurred to them that their enemies would work out what they were up to, and wait till it was all in one place. Probably didn't even bother to leave a guard."

Drago rather hoped they hadn't; he could still taste the ash that had descended on him when Aris's spell had run its course, and the thought that a portion of it might once have been part of a person was vaguely disquieting.

"When did you work it out?" he asked, more to distract himself from the idea of having ingested an accidental fragment of elf than because he was particularly interested in the answer.

Clearspring shook her head. "I didn't," she said. "I just kept my ears open. Half the town knew what was going on. No wonder Gorash decided to do something about it."

"Seems like a risky thing to do, though," Drago said, starting to lay out the fishing gear with a confidence he wouldn't have believed a week before. Clearspring watched his practiced handling of it with a grudging nod of approval. "Like Hannie said, that fire would have taken out half the waterfront if some local charm-lobber hadn't turned up. Might even have spread into the town itself. That would have lost him a lot of friends."

Clearspring shook her head. "Just because they sing songs about him being a noble-hearted hero, it doesn't actually make him one you know. He'd probably cut your throat just to see how sharp the blade is." She sighed. "Anyway, most of the folk around here would only have blamed Stargleam for having his stuff there in the first place."

"Even though they were happy to take his money?" Drago finished baiting the hooks, and trailed the line over the side, absently licking the congealed fish blood from his fingers as he did so.

"Way of the world." Clearspring hesitated, seeming uncharacteristically lost for words for a moment, then went on in a rush. "Listen, you've been a lot less trouble than I thought you'd be, so how about I save you a little? Forget the mines. Skip the whole Marches, and I'll take you on up to the Delvings instead. No extra fare."

"You'd do that?" Drago said, trying to sound as though he was considering the offer, which had blindsided him completely. It was tempting, there was no denying that, but he really had no desire to visit the land of his ancestors. He was too used to the cosmopolitan nature of Fairhaven to feel comfortable with the idea of being surrounded almost entirely by gnomes for the rest of his life, and although he was sure the caverns there were much more spacious than the burrows he knew closer to home they were sure to be correspondingly more crowded. Besides, if he accepted, he'd still be looking over his shoulder for Gorash's assassins for the foreseeable future, and he was already getting tired of that. Not just Gorash's either; as soon as the Marchers discovered he was reneging on their contract, they'd be sending someone after him too. "Getting worried you'll have to pay for your own drinks after you drop me off?"

"Offer's there," Clearspring said, turning away with a shrug. "Whether you take it is up to you."

"It's not too late to change your mind, you know," Greel said, as the *Rippling Light* pulled in to a landing stage on which a couple of elves stood, aiming drawn bows at Hannie and Greel. A couple more were running along the narrow jetty, arrows already nocked, presumably to cover Drago and Clearspring, who must have seemed like less immediate threats. An impression Drago was certainly not intending to disabuse them of. The sailor nodded in the direction of the soldiers, the tabards over their mail coats emblazoned with the oak tree crest Greenleaf had shown him back in Fairhaven. "These are the friendly ones."

"This is a restricted landing," one of the archers called, addressing Clearspring directly, despite both Drago and Greel being closer to his eye line. "What are you doing here?"

"Dropping a passenger," Clearspring said, at which Drago raised a hand in a friendly greeting; to his immense lack of surprise it was completely ignored. "Miner looking for work. Soon as he's ashore, we're gone."

"You'd better be. Traits aren't welcome here, any more than their cattle are."

Drago found himself glancing round for some livestock, before realizing the elf meant him and the humans. Greel tensed beside him, but kept a bland expression.

"And yet, even with such outstanding courtesy, no one wants to do business with you. Imagine that." Clearspring directed a glance of withering disdain at her interlocutor, and turned to Drago. "This one's polite for a Marcher. Most are worse. Are you sure you want to get off here?"

"I'm sure." Drago nodded. "I can't explain, but I need to do this. And I appreciate the thought."

She echoed the gesture. "I haven't asked, and I'm not about to. Because I really don't want to know. But fair winds and strong currents go with you." Then she nodded a final farewell. "You've been a lot less trouble than most, and you know how to stand your round. I'd take your fare again."

"Let's hope you get the chance to," Drago said, as the *Rippling Light* bumped the planks of the jetty, a little harder than he'd expected. The archers swayed as the vibration jarred through the decking supporting them, losing their balance, and a single arrow sailed over the masthead to vanish with a derisive-sounding *plop!*

"Oops. Sorry Skip." Hannie sounded anything but. "I just get a little nervous when nad-brained spunkbuckets point arrows at me."

"Hannie." The warning tone in Clearspring's voice was unmistakable. "One more word and they'll do a lot more than point. We're in the bloody Marches now, so mind your manners. And your sodding language."

"Sound advice." The senior archer spoke again, still directly to Clearspring. "Unload your passenger and go."

"With pleasure." She turned to Drago. "Now would be good. Before we die of old age."

"Or at least still have the option." He shouldered his knapsack, and climbed over the rail for the last time, feeling his boots impact on the planks of the landing stage with what sounded like emphatic finality. He was committed now, whatever misgivings he might feel about that.

Clearspring and Greel went straight for the sail, and Hannie leaned into the tiller, directing the boat away from the jetty. Drago stood and watched it recede until it had rejoined the steady traffic heading upstream, becoming just one more sail among many, but none of the *Rippling Light*'s crew turned to look back. Feeling vaguely deflated, he turned and walked along the landing stage, feeling the stares of the soldiers on his back the whole way, but none of them spoke again.

Well, that had been easier than he thought. Reaching the rutted mud of the river bank, Drago paused to look around him. Elven soldiers were everywhere, hurrying about on errands of their own, or huddled around cooking fires; appetizing as the aromas arising from them were, he felt little inclination to linger. Certainly none of the elves he could see looked as though they'd be willing to spare a bowl of broth for an itinerant gnome.

In some ways the camp struck him as similar to the riverside settlements he'd already seen: muddy, chaotic, and noisy. Even the wooden buildings bore a passing resemblance to the ones he'd seen in Birch Glade, lap-boarded planks nailed around a skeleton of beams, both hewn from the local woods. Instead of the profusion of randomly scattered structures, however, these were of uniform size and shape, about three times longer than they were wide, and arranged in a grid, creating arrow-straight lanes between them. The other main difference was the wall, about two and a half times the height of the average elf, enclosing the entire encampment on three sides, the fourth being occupied entirely by the riverbank.

A wider open space separated the two main blocks of wooden buildings, from which occasional carts drawn by plodding donkeys emerged, or into which others disappeared, so Drago made for that, encouraged by glimpses of a larger structure midway along the longest wall. As he'd surmised, this turned out to be a gatehouse: a steady trickle of carts was arriving through it, loaded with what looked like firewood, while others departed empty to collect more. None of the elven soldiers engaged in this activity seemed particularly enthusiastic about it, but, as he was beginning to expect by now, they all found it far more interesting than the presence of a gnome.

Moving at the kind of steady pace that seemed to encourage being regarded as invisible, and keeping well to one side of the roadway to avoid being trampled or run down, Drago approached the gateway. Staircases rose on either side of it, leading to a platform running around the wall about three feet from the top, and which seemed to pass through some kind of guardhouse perched over the gate itself. Turning his head, he could see similar structures at both ends of the wall, where it met the ones running riverwards at a right angle to it, and a couple of intermediate staircases rising to the platform. Given the number of soldiers he could see, and assuming they had an adequate supply of arrows, the camp could mount a formidable defense against anyone trying to attack it; even professional soldiers would have their work cut out, and any bandits making the attempt would simply be throwing their lives away.

Drago braced himself for a challenge as he passed through the gates, but once again the guards simply ignored him. Then again, why wouldn't they? Their job was to keep people out, not in, and he could hardly have been the first gnome to arrive at the wharf. In fact, judging by the size of some of the footprints he could see in the muddy earth just outside the stockade, he probably wasn't even the first to have passed through the gates that day.

He glanced around, getting his bearings. As he'd expected, a wide expanse of clear ground surrounded the walls, partly to provide the material for their construction, and partly to ensure their continued security. Nothing but stumps, scrub and thick, wiry grass could be seen extending out to well past the range of a bowshot; sneaking up on the place unobserved, and subsequently unperforated, would have been almost impossible, even at night.

From where he stood, wagon tracks meandered away in many different directions, and there was little discernible pattern to the movements of the donkey carts crisscrossing the elf-made heath. Drago briefly debated whether to turn back and ask the guards for directions, but if the ones he'd met at the wharf were anything to go by—and the crew of the *Rippling Light* certainly seemed to think they were—he didn't think they'd be all that helpful. Some of them might even think it was funny to send him off in the wrong direction entirely. So much open, empty space was a little disorientating for a city boy; he found himself wishing for a few cramped alleyways to walk down.

All right then, if he'd been in Fairhaven, how would he have found his way? You certainly didn't stop and ask for directions there, unless you wanted to advertise the fact that you were from a different district, and confident enough to handle the consequences.

The majority of the wheel ruts, and all the gnomish footprints, led straight from the gate behind him toward the distant line of the forest, disappearing into a notch among the trees which probably marked the beginning of a track. That would do for a start, especially as the line of hills looming over everything seemed to be in more or less the same direction.

Looking as untroubled and confident as he could, Drago set out to see where it led.

CHAPTER TWENTY-ONE
"Hmm."

Sure enough, after a few minutes' walking, Drago found himself among the trees, heading along a broad, flat cart track. Every now and then he had to step aside to avoid being trampled by kindling scavengers from the garrison, but the further he went, the less frequent these encounters became, until eventually they petered out altogether.

It felt strange to be surrounded by so many living things, but completely out of sight of any other people. An astonishing number of creatures rustled in the grass and undergrowth, scuttling away before he could get a good look at them. More birds than he had ever seen or heard in his life squawked, twittered and chirruped overhead, staring down at him from the branches like tiny gargoyles, or wheeling in the sky above the woods. None of them were species he recognized, but that wasn't surprising; the closest he'd ever come to some of them in Fairhaven had been as tiny migrating dots in the strips of sky between buildings.

Several years' accumulation of fallen leaves littered the ground beneath the trees, turning the earth underfoot into a wet, slippery mess, in which his boots slithered even more than they had done in the back alleys of home. Nevertheless, Drago kept to the margins of the track as it wove its way deeper into the woods, meandering like the river around knolls and sharp rises in the ground. Partly he did this so he could retreat into the shelter of the trees at the first sign of danger, but mainly because the ground between the cart ruts had been churned into a quagmire by the plodding of the animals which had drawn them. Every now and then a clear hoofprint showed in an unusually firm patch of mud, but for the most part there were few tracks to follow now. Presumably the other gnomes, in whose footsteps he followed, had done the same, or ridden in the cart.

Up ahead, the hills continued to glower at him in intermittent glimpses between the boughs, like thunderclouds which had sunk to earth under the weight of their rain, but it wasn't until nearly noon that he broke out of the trees entirely and got his first real look at them. They were bigger than he'd imagined, the highest peaks wreathed in wisps of cloud, and stained purple and brown by the bracken which enfolded them.

Impressed in spite of himself, Drago lurked just inside the tree line, trying to make out more detail. Dots on the nearer hills seemed to be moving, painfully slowly, across the near vertical slopes, and for a few moments he wished he'd had the foresight to buy a farseeing charm before boarding the riverboat; then he realized he was probably just looking at wandering sheep, grazing on whatever fodder they could find up there.

Which, in turn, made him think of mutton stew, then of how long it had been since he'd breakfasted. Too long, he decided, even if he hadn't been burning off all that energy slogging through the woodlands. Remaining just inside the trees, he shrugged off his knapsack and began rummaging inside it for some food. Greel had found some almost fresh bread and some cheese he seemed pleased to see the back of, even though it still seemed fine to Drago, to which Clearspring had added a bottle of ale by way of a parting gift, claiming it gave her gas anyway.

Though the meal was basic, he ate heartily enough, forcing himself to break off and return a lump of the bread to the knapsack before it was all consumed. It would be hours yet before he made it to the mining camp, even if he didn't turn out to be on the wrong road entirely. And now he'd finally seen a squirrel, trying to catch one for the pot he didn't actually possess anyway seemed like it would be a great deal more trouble than he'd fondly imagined.

Shading his eyes, he tried to follow the line of the road, which wound its way into the distance before vanishing among the hills. Failing to see anything remotely threatening, he returned the rucksack to his back, and prepared to set out again. Just as he did so he caught sight of a small black dot on the highway, emerging from behind a fold in the ground, before disappearing again behind the crest of a ridge.

"Hmm." It seemed he wasn't the only traveler on the road today after all. He waited a moment, but it didn't reappear, so he shrugged and began walking again, trying to remember any details that might give him a clue as to whom or what he was following. The trouble was, the glimpse had been so fleeting, and at such a distance, that he hadn't been able to make anything out at all. He couldn't even be sure whether it had been a single person or a small group, clustered so close together that they couldn't be told apart.

Once he was clear of the trees, the track grew less muddy, and the going a little firmer underfoot. Thick, wiry grass, like the stuff he'd seen outside the stockade, spread over everything as far as the eye could see, interspersed with patches of scrub. Here and there, outcrops of dull gray rock reared up as if tearing their way out through the matted blanket of roots, their sides and upper surfaces still swathed in the sward as though they were huddling into cloaks of the stuff to escape the wind which blew constantly across the desolate moor.

Drago shivered, and picked up his pace. The wind was blustery, and ruffled his clothes and hair, finding its way through every gap in his garments. Now and again bright sunshine elbowed the clouds aside, and the moorland seemed to glow around him, although it brought little warmth along with it. In the distance, an ever-changing patchwork of light and shade flowed across the hills, making individual crags and screes stand out with astonishing vividness for a moment, before fading back into the amorphous mass looming over the plain.

At least the going was a little easier here, with springy grass or other plants underfoot, some of them astonishingly delicate in color and shape, over a firm foundation of bedrock. The line of cart ruts he followed was showing bare stone in places now, sometimes broken into pebbles or patches of gravel by the inexorable processes of erosion. On the other hand, virtually none of the road was level anymore, rising steadily toward the hills, or dipping back into the clefts between ridges before beginning to climb once again.

Used to the relatively flat streets of a city built on the coastal plain,

Drago found the constant change of slope harder work than he'd bargained for, and before long his thighs and calf muscles were protesting in no uncertain terms. But every ridge crest was higher than the previous one, and when he paused to look back, he was astonished at how far he'd come. The stretch of woodland was below him now, the treetops a wide expanse of clotted green, through which the glittering thread of the river curled away in both directions. From up here he could just make out the scudding dots of the riverboat sails, hundreds of them, in two constantly moving lines, keeping commerce flowing through the heart of the continent. The garrison at which he'd disembarked was hidden by the trees, but he could make out a score of other villages and hamlets up and down the distant banks.

He wasn't here to admire the view, though. The sun was well on its way to the horizon, and it occurred to him that he had no idea how much farther he still had to go. Finishing the rest of the bread, as much as for the excuse to linger for a few more minutes that it afforded him than to ward off incipient hunger, he turned his face resolutely toward the hills again. They seemed somehow to be both larger and no nearer than they had before.

Well, there was nothing he could do about that. He must be getting close to his destination by now. The mines and the wharf which served them were sure to be within an easy day's travel of one another; camping out halfway simply wouldn't be an option in an area rife with bandits.

Which was another uncomfortable thought. The closer he got to the hills, the more wary he'd have to be. Keeping his eyes as much on the landscape surrounding him as on the road itself, he set off again, trying to quell his misgivings.

Another hour's steady walking brought Drago out of the moors and into the foothills themselves. The road carried on climbing just as steeply, but was now passing through gullies and ravines as often as it ran along ridge spines or ledges in the steeply sloping hillsides, and Drago's sense of wariness increased with every step. The trouble was, the more he tried to look out for movement in the forbidding landscape surrounding him the more he saw, and he had no idea what could be safely dismissed in this unfamiliar landscape. Accordingly he wasted a lot of time stopping at frequent intervals to make sure that what looked like stealthy movement in the heather was only a rabbit, not a goblin bushwhacker trying to sneak up on him, or that a sudden shadow flashing across his path had merely been cast by a high-flying raptor looking for a rabbit of its own to invite for dinner, before deciding to hell with it, and pressing on regardless. If anyone jumped out of the rocks with designs on his pack or his purse he'd just have to deal with it as he would have done back in Fairhaven.

Thus resolved he made much better progress, only stopping on one more occasion, to examine a place where someone had apparently paused for a little refreshment not too long before: a sheltered spot in the lee of an overhang just off the track, where the grass had been trampled flat and not yet sprung fully back. There were a few scattered crumbs on top of a boulder, where someone taller than a gnome could have comfortably sat, although he couldn't tell if it had been a goblin or an elf. Whoever it was, they hadn't left that long ago, though, as the crumbs hadn't been scavenged by any of the local wildlife yet, and a moist half-moon where a water bottle had rested was still damp to the touch. It seemed he was catching up with the traveler he'd glimpsed in the distance a few hours before.

Drago returned to the road and glanced around, hoping to find some other trace of the stranger's passing, but without any success; the thin veneer of vegetation had all but vanished now, leaving nothing but bare rock, pebbles and gravel. Giving up, he shouldered his pack again, and continued plodding doggedly uphill.

So used had he become to the monotony of his journey, he was almost taken by surprise when something happened to disturb it. Almost, but not quite; one sound he was more than familiar with was the clashing of blades, and the hoarse panting of people pitted in combat, with no breath left to threaten, scream, or engage in polite conversation. This was drifting his way on the breeze, and he tilted his head, trying to get an idea of how far away it was; back in the avenues and alleyways he knew so well, he'd be able to pinpoint it practically to the inch, but up here, with its unfamiliar echoes and acoustics, he couldn't be sure. Not far, though, on that he'd definitely bet.

The question was, what to do about it. Intervene, keep out of the way until the noise stopped, or try to get close enough to the fight to see where the bandits went when they broke off, and hope to follow them? Gorash's people had to be involved, he was certain of that. The real question was who they might be fighting.

So musing, he picked up his pace, hurrying along the road toward the sound of combat. He wouldn't be able to choose an option unless he knew what was happening anyway, and his body was already reacting even while his mind was dithering. His sword hissed from its scabbard without him even being fully aware of it.

Then he crested the next ridge, and there was no more time to think at all.

CHAPTER TWENTY-TWO
"Stinks like a midden."

Drago paused as he reached the top of the next downward slope, pressing himself against the rock face bordering the left-hand side of the track in an attempt to remain unnoticed while he tried to work out what was going on. The road descended into a gully here, the perfect place for an ambush, and that, it seemed, was precisely what the bandits had done. Three carts, each with a disgruntled-looking donkey between the shafts, had been halted, presumably by the small group of goblins with drawn bows still blocking the narrow track, and edging forward to cover the half dozen gnomes who'd been driving them. Most of the carters looked more irritated at the delay than particularly frightened.

Between the carts and where Drago stood watching, a vicious melee was filling the road, elven soldiers in the uniforms he'd seen back at the wharf hacking at goblins armed with short swords and shields. The two sides seemed about evenly matched, although the elves were outnumbered, several of them already lying dead or incapacitated on the unforgiving ground, struck through with green-fletched arrows. Evidently the archers had struck from cover, before emerging to halt the wagons.

"Get those covers off!" One of the goblin archers slackened off her string, returned the arrow to her quiver, and slung her bow across her back to free her hands. The others clearly regarded her as a leader, as the nearest two immediately followed her instructions, trotting across

173

to a wagon each, and flinging back the tarpaulins covering their loads. The goblin woman tore the sheeting from the leading cart. "What have you got?"

"Tools. Picks and that." The goblin at the rear cart shrugged dismissively, and spat in the dust, reminding Drago incongruously of Clearspring. "Sod all we can use."

"Food." The one in the middle looked a lot happier, rummaging among the boxes, barrels and sacks thus revealed. "Pork, flour, pickled fish . . ."

"Take it." The leader glanced into the bed of the leading wagon, then to the nearest gnome. "What's in here?"

"More food." The gnome shrugged. "Be sorry to see it go. Don't get much rat up at the mine."

"You're welcome to it." She turned to the middle cart, directing the others with the wave of a hand. "Let's get this one back, take anything you can carry off the lead one that's not something only a shortarse would eat. And get a move on, the others won't hold the guards off forever."

That was true, Drago reflected. Few of the goblins seemed to have been hurt so far, but that wasn't for the want of trying, the elven swords clashing against their steel, or biting deep into their shields. Even as he watched, one went down to a vicious sword thrust that burst clean through his body, and hit the ground, where he twitched for a minute and lay still.

"That's more like it!" The elf who'd struck the killing blow brought his sword back up into a guard position, and began to batter away at the defenses of the next goblin, who'd stepped in to the gap the fall of his comrade had opened up in their ranks. Unlike any of the other elves he wasn't in uniform, and didn't appear to be wearing mail, being dressed instead in gray leather that had seen a good deal more hard use than Greenleaf's jacket and breeks could ever have imagined, and a similarly hued cloak, which seemed more patch and stain than wool. He seemed a lot older than any of the others too, his hair iron gray, although his movements as he blocked, parried and struck were more fluid and assured than any of the soldiers surrounding him. This one, Drago thought, would be worth ten of them, and wasn't an elf he'd like to face unless he had to.

The question was, should he intervene, or carry on lurking in cover to see if he could follow the bandits when they moved away? If they were taking one of the carts they couldn't have been going far, surely?

Then, abruptly, the decision was taken out of his hands.

"One of them's getting away!" the goblin leader shouted, pointing at him. Three of the bandits immediately broke off from the melee with the soldiers, and came sprinting up the hill, brandishing their swords.

Drago reacted instinctively. The bandits would be secure in the knowledge that they had him outnumbered, and probably thought he was a terrified civilian. They'd be expecting him to bolt, or stay rooted to the spot in terror. They were also running up a fairly steep slope, after fighting for their lives for several minutes, so would be relatively slow to react to the realization that they were wrong in pretty much every assumption they were making.

With a yell that sent echoes bouncing from every rock face, Drago charged headlong down the hill toward them, brandishing his sword; which, by great good fortune, caught the westering sun, tinting it the shade of blood, and, with any luck, dazzling his opponents into the bargain. Almost before they had time to react he was among them, scoring a long gash across the ribs of the goblin in the center of the group as he passed between him and the one on the right. It would be a painful and disorientating wound rather than a critical one, but it produced a satisfactory amount of blood, which clearly disconcerted them all, buying him enough time to turn and slash at the leg of the goblin on his other side.

Who turned out to have impressive reflexes, bringing his shield down smartly enough to protect his leg, and pivoting on the spot to cut at Drago as the rotational movement pulled the gnome forward and off balance. It was an impressive move, and against an elf, goblin or human would probably have proven lethal, but habit made him strike at the height of the ribcage of an opponent roughly his own size: Drago ducked under it easily, kicking out at the back of the goblin's knee, and bringing his own blade around in an arc which would have decapitated him as he went down if it hadn't been for the shield. As it was, the bandit raised it just in time to deflect the blow. Continuing to spin, Drago kicked out, catching his opponent in the temple more by luck than judgment, and sending him crashing to the ground. He wasn't sure if he'd struck hard enough to land a killing blow, or merely stunned his attacker, but the reiver was definitely incapacitated either way, which worked fine for Drago.

"Think you're hard, do you?" one of the other goblins snarled, the one he hadn't hurt yet of course, as he circled looking for an opening. The one Drago had cut was moving too, in the opposite direction, the stain on his shirt growing visibly by the moment, but too charged up with adrenaline to be feeling the worst effects yet. If anything, he'd be the more dangerous of the two, angry and looking for revenge, and too deep in the endorphin rush of combat to be taken down by anything short of an all-out assault.

"Hard enough to take a pair of jessies like you," Drago said, hoping to provoke them into doing something rash he could take advantage of. Despite their aggressive posturing they were both hanging back, looking for an opening, probably hoping the other would move first; the ease with which he'd dispatched their companion had clearly come as an unpleasant surprise to them, and even though they'd probably overwhelm him with ease if they coordinated their attacks successfully, they didn't quite have the confidence to do that yet. Fine, then, he'd just have to take the initiative himself, before they recovered their nerve.

Without another word he lunged at the wounded goblin, going wide on the bandit's sword-hand side; hardly anyone brought a shield to a street brawl, and he was at a disadvantage in trying to get through one. Getting past a blade parry, on the other hand, was second nature to him, and with any luck the goblins had got so used to relying on their wooden shields for protection they'd be less practiced at defending with their weapons.

It almost worked. Taken by surprise, the bandit barely raised his blade in time, and Drago's sword skidded off the edge of the sharpened steel, almost taking his balance with it. Forewarned by instinct and experience, he jumped back in the nick of time, as the other goblin's sword slashed through the space formerly occupied by his extended arm, rebounding from the back of his own blade with a *clang!* which reverberated up his entire limb. Which, uncomfortable as it was, still seemed preferable to picking his right hand off the ground and trying to find a mage who could reattach it, something which hardly seemed likely around here. He gave ground slowly, as his opponents closed in, forcing him back downhill toward the fight still going on in the gully.

He was running out of options. They had the advantage of height as well as numbers now, and both were advancing with murder in their eyes. Not only that, the closer he got to the melee, the more likely it was that someone would take advantage of his distraction to get in a free hack at his back.

Then a piercing whistle ripped through the air, and the bandit leader removed two fingers from her mouth. "That's it!" she yelled. "We're leaving!"

Without another word the two bandits took a simultaneous step back, opening the distance between them and Drago, hesitating for a moment in case he was rash enough to follow up. Then they turned, lifting their limp comrade between them, each taking an arm across their neck and shoulder, and hurried off to rejoin the rest of the band.

Drago stood, watching them go, breathing heavily. The group engaging the elves pulled back in good order, staying between them and the cart full of foodstuffs as it was led away, now laden even more heavily with half the goods from the other one carrying provender, to prevent any attempt at recovery. None of the soldiers seemed inclined to follow up and press the attack, much to the audible disgust of the gray-haired elf.

"Get stuck in, you useless bunch of pansies! I've seen better fighters in a dame school playground!"

"Our orders are not to pursue." One of the soldiers, with a larger and more ornate plume on his helmet than any of the others, shook his head, as the last of the bandits disappeared round the next bend of the trail, still poised to renew the hostilities if necessary. "We've lost too many people that way."

"I'll just bet you have." The gray-haired elf flicked the blood and slivers of flesh his sword blade had acquired away with a casual ease that immediately confirmed Drago's initial impression of how dangerous he was, and resheathed it. His lip curled.

The officer's jaw tightened, but he could clearly read the signs too, and wasn't foolish enough to decide his honor was being impugned. "They know every inch of these hills, and split up as they retreat. If we try to follow them they'll just pick us off one by one." Drago wondered if that was true, but it didn't look as if he was going to get the chance to try anyway; following the bandits would mean getting past the elves and the goblin carters unnoticed, and that simply wasn't going to happen. "Anyway, we have wounded to attend to." Drago suspected this was as much a face-saving excuse for inaction as it was genuine concern for the officer's men, and it was clear from Gray Hair's expression that he thought the same, but would let it go for now. "And who the hell are you to be giving my men orders anyway? You turn up out of nowhere, attach yourself to my column, and then suddenly we're up to our elbows in bandits. Doing a little scouting for them, were you?"

"My name's Elerath, but I don't use it much. I generally go by Graymane. And I'm here because I've been hired to do a job, which I'll discuss with your captain when we get to the mines. Does that answer your questions?"

"It does." The officer nodded, with sudden wary respect. Whoever this Graymane was, his reputation in this part of the world clearly preceded him.

"Good. See to your wounded." Graymane waited until the officer was turning away, before adding "and if you accuse me of aiding or sympathizing with bandits again, I'll call you out. Is that clear?"

"Absolutely." The officer nodded, a trifle stiffly. "My apologies for any offense given by my words. The stress of combat and losing so many good comrades may have affected my judgment."

"Then you're not much of a soldier, are you?" Graymane asked. The officer flushed, but had the sense to turn away, and start bawling at his troops instead—Drago suspected they were in for a hard time for the next few hours.

"That was amazing," someone said, and Drago became aware that he'd become the center of interest for the gnomes, which was hardly surprising under the circumstances. One of the younger ones was staring at him with an expression which could only be described as awestruck wonderment. "Where did you learn to fight like that?"

"Trying to get to the bar in The Strumpet," Drago said, which was less of a joke than it sounded. He'd never had to draw a sword to get served there, but he had been forced to use his elbows several times, and on one occasion his teeth. He registered his interlocutor's expression of bafflement, and smiled. "It's a bar in Fairhaven. Can get a bit crowded."

"You're from Fairhaven?" The young gnome sounded as though he thought that was as outlandish as Drago claiming to have come from the moon. "What's it like there?"

"Crowded. Noisy. Stinks like a midden. Love every inch of it." And that was true, he reflected. He wasn't exactly homesick, he'd had too many novel experiences since leaving for that, but he did miss the bustle and the energy there. He stuck out a hand. "Drago Appleroot, by the way."

"Clovis Gravelseam." The young gnome shook it, a little warily, perhaps reflecting that a few moments ago the same hand had been grasping a sword and using it to deadly effect. He waved, taking in the rest of the group, and reeled off a litany of names so quickly that Drago was left with only the vaguest idea of which one belonged to which gnome. Fortunately the one in charge was easy to pick out by his belt-length beard and red conical hat, folded over at the top, and the fact that everyone else addressed him as Gaffer.

"Pleased to meet you all," Drago said, trusting that he'd be able to work out who was who if it became necessary. No one else seemed inclined to shake hands, but that didn't mean much. These were mountain gnomes, stockier than the inhabitants of the lowland burrows, and widely reputed to be more taciturn than the ones he knew.

"You're a long way from home, then," the Gaffer said, curiosity and suspicion not far from the surface of the remark.

Drago nodded. "I heard there was work for gnomes up this way. Thought I'd try my luck."

"Fancy yourself as a miner, do you?" The ripple of amusement around the group was unmistakable. "Not much call for that down your way, I'd have thought."

"You'd have thought right," Drago said. "Which is why I'm here, instead of there."

"Is it, now." The Gaffer was clearly unconvinced. "I'd have thought you could find something to suit a bit closer to hand than that."

Drago nodded. "Tell you the truth," he said, "I thought a river trip would be good for my health. If you get my meaning."

The Gaffer nodded too. "I think I do, and I'm not sure I want to. But we owe you for pitching in when you didn't have to, and that's worth a ride up to the diggings. After that, it's up to the boss."

"Fair enough," Drago agreed. He glanced around, wondering how the elves would take to acquiring an extra passenger, but most of them seemed too busy to even notice that another gnome had joined the party. The wounded soldiers were being assisted into the remaining wagons, where they perched uncomfortably on top of the remaining loads, and their able-bodied comrades were busy dragging the corpses of the less fortunate to the side of the road, presumably for later recovery. All the abandoned casualties were being stripped of their weapons, armor and personal effects, presumably to deny any lurking bandits the opportunity of looting them at their leisure; watching this procedure with a professionally cynical eye, Drago couldn't help noticing a number of small items disappearing into pockets and pouches instead of being bundled up with the recovered kit.

The exception was Graymane, who was examining the body of the goblin he'd killed in minute detail. Giving up, he gestured a passing soldier to take it to the far smaller heap of dead bandits, no more than three in number, with an impatient kick. "Shouldn't have killed him so thoroughly," he said. "He could have told us where their camp is."

"I wouldn't be so sure," the soldier said incautiously, before noticing Graymane looking at him and hastily adding, "begging your pardon, sir. We've never taken a live one yet."

"How very careless of you." Graymane turned away, and caught sight of Drago looking at him. They held one another's gaze for a moment, then the gray-haired elf nodded, almost imperceptibly, before turning his head to start conferring with the officer again.

Drago knew what that meant: later. He just had to hope that whatever discussion they had then remained on the right side of amicable. Graymane, whoever he was, was clearly not someone to trifle with.

CHAPTER TWENTY-THREE
"That rather depends on how you define adequate."

Dusk was falling by the time they reached the mine workings, which were like nothing Drago had ever seen before. He'd been expecting something akin to a gnomish burrow, a wide, high tunnel (at least by gnomish standards) striking into the heart of the hills, probably protected by richly decorated doors. What he found instead was another stockaded garrison, not unlike the one he'd seen at the wharf, except that instead of wood, the buildings and the walls enclosing them had been constructed from locally quarried stone.

The fortified camp squatted on the rim of a huge hole, at least a quarter of a mile across and a couple of hundred yards deep, part of the bottom of which had flooded, forming a small, shallow lake. Tiered terraces, linked by ramps, fell away into the depths, where a scattering of huts and storage sheds could be dimly seen in the shadows; rather better by Drago and his new friends than any of the elves accompanying them. This, presumably, was the source of the building materials, although there seemed to be a lot more hole than dressed stone anywhere in the vicinity.

"That's right," Clovis said, when he wondered aloud about that. "The locals have been quarrying here for generations. The old ones, I mean, not . . ." and he gestured quietly but eloquently at the elven soldiers all around them.

"That's how they found the gold in the first place," the Gaffer put in helpfully. The little group of gnomes had walked from the site of the skirmish, trailing behind the wagons conveying the wounded, seemingly invisible and inaudible to the elves, which seemed to suit everybody fine. "Just dug down into the seam while they were looking for building stone."

"At which point the Marchers suddenly decided the Barrens had really belonged to them all along?" Drago asked, and the older gnome shook his head.

"That's a matter between them and the goblins," he said sagely. "I couldn't possibly comment. But I do know who pays me to help dig it out."

"Point taken," Drago assured him.

Stout wooden gates thudded closed behind the limping convoy as the sun slipped below the rim of the surrounding hills, but the garrison remained brightly lit, sconces and braziers flaring in front of every structure. More elves hurried forward to help the wounded, leading them away, and Clovis regained the cart full of mining tools, reaching up to take hold of the donkey's bridle.

"S'all right, Gaffer," one of the gnomes, Della something if Drago remembered right, called from the back after a cursory inspection. She held up a bundle of candles. "Not much blood on 'em."

"Good. Don't want any of it rusting before we've even had a chance to use it." The Gaffer turned to Clovis. "You two get everything squared away. I'll take care of our new friend here."

"Who's this?" A new voice, feminine, tart, and no-nonsense asked behind them, and Drago turned in response. The speaker was a gnome, of course, dressed like all the others he could see in stout, utilitarian clothing. Gray eyes gazed at him with a hint of amusement.

Drago gazed back. She was stocky, well-muscled, and wore her hair stuffed up inside a cap like the Gaffer's, but which she'd allowed to remain rising to a point. So far as he could tell from the wisps of it escaping from under the brim, her hair was midnight black, with the faint sheen of polished slate. Her smile was welcoming, though faintly reserved.

"Drago Appleroot, at your service." He bowed formally, allowing himself a hint of a smile, to show that he was playing up to the occasion and wouldn't normally have bothered with such an elaborate display of etiquette.

"City boy," the Gaffer put in. "Found him in the hills on the way back here. Says he wants a job."

"Does he now." If anything her amusement seemed to increase. She turned back to Drago, and extended a hand. Her grip was firm, and calloused, fine particles of powdered rock ingrained among the seams. "Loma Claybed, but you can call me Boss or Ma'am. If I decide to take you on." She glanced up and down his full height, taking in every detail of his appearance. "Had much experience of mining, have you?"

"Not as such," Drago admitted breezily, "but I know one end of a pick from the other."

"Really." She reached out and tapped the hilt of his sword, and Drago flinched, forcing himself to override the reflexive urge to attack before she could grab it. Loma must have noticed the movement, and deduced the reason for it, because her expression hardened at once. "What about this?"

"He can use that all right," Clovis put in enthusiastically, glancing across from where he and Della were stacking the crates and bundles from the wagon. "He saw off three bandits with it single-handed!"

"Really?" Loma's voice was quietly skeptical. "Told you that himself, did he?"

"Didn't need to," the Gaffer said. "We all saw him."

"Did you now?" Loma's voice became a little more thoughtful, her glance at Drago a little more appraising. "Pretty impressive for someone who just wants to dig holes. Where did you learn to fight like that?"

For a second, Drago considered deflecting the question with a joke as he had with Clovis, but almost instantly decided against it. Loma was clearly no fool. Perhaps a little of the truth would be better.

"Fairhaven can be a dangerous place. I learned early, and found I had a knack for it."

"I see." Loma nodded thoughtfully. "In my experience, the quickest way to find trouble is to go looking for it."

"Mine too." Drago echoed the gesture. "But sometimes it comes looking for you instead."

"And did it?"

Drago hesitated. There were only two answers he could give at this point, and the wrong one would ruin everything. But the more Loma said, the more his initial impression of her astuteness was confirmed. Still not entirely sure he was making the right decision, he opted for honesty: or at least an approximation of it. "Yes. So I decided to avoid it if I could."

"Fair enough." Loma thought for a moment. "All right, I'll take a chance. Two weeks trial period, see how you go. But if you give me any reason to regret it, you're gone the next day. Are we good?"

"We're good," Drago assured her. "And you won't regret it."

"I'd better not. Gaffer'll find you somewhere to sleep, and I suppose you'd like something to eat as well?" Drago nodded. By now his stomach was beginning to forget what it was for. "Clovis, take Drago over to the mess hall while the Gaffer finds him a bunk."

"Right. Will do." The young gnome abandoned his stocktaking with an alacrity Drago found mildly disturbing, and hurried over to join them. It seemed he would have to do a lot more verbal deflection before the evening was out, if he wanted to avoid any more complications.

"I'll leave you to it, then." Loma turned away, then, struck by an afterthought, glanced back at Drago. "This trouble you're trying to avoid. It wouldn't involve a sudden need for money, would it?"

"Would it matter if it did?" Drago asked, happy to reinforce that impression without actually saying so.

Loma shook her head. "Not to me. But if you're tempted to supplement your wages with the odd nugget from the seam, forget it. According to the lofties, the gold belongs to their king, which makes pilfering any of it treason. For which they'll hang you."

"I don't need money that much," Drago said, with what he hoped was a carefree smile.

"No one does," Loma said, and strode off without a backward glance.

"She likes you," Clovis said, with what seemed to be a genuine mixture of surprise and relief, then gestured toward the sloping road leading down into the depths of the quarry. "Our quarters are this way." He stared at Drago's scabbarded blade, in a manner the bounty hunter found all too familiar. "Could you teach me how to handle a sword as well as you do?"

"No. That only comes with experience." Drago followed him toward the descending ramp, intending his tone to have ended the discussion. Clovis, however, seemed incapable of taking the hint.

"Could you teach me the basics, then?" he asked.

"I could." Drago nodded, looking down into the depths of the quarry, which stood out clearly in his gnomish night vision. On the next tier of terracing, several shafts had been driven horizontally into the stone, spilling light and warmth, a typical makeshift burrow. He found himself wondering which one was the mess hall, and whether they had any rat. "But I'm not going to."

"Oh." To his relief, Clovis simply seemed disappointed by his answer, rather than antagonized; he needed friends here if he was going to make any progress in his assignment. "Why's that, then?"

"Because you'd only learn enough to get yourself killed," Drago said, "and if you're not carrying a sword you're less likely to get into a fight in the first place." The two gnomes began to descend the gently sloping track.

"Do you get into lots, then?" Clovis asked, and Drago shrugged.

"Only if I can't avoid them." Then he stopped walking, and held up a hand. "Hang on a minute."

"What for?" Clovis turned back, his expression curious, and Drago gestured for silence.

"Someone's coming," he said, and shrank back against the steeply sloping side of the quarry. They'd already descended the best part of a yard, leaving the ground above almost at the level of his nose and eyes; here in the shadows, away from the flaring torches, the top of his head would be invisible to elven eyes unless they were searching very carefully for eavesdroppers. At least he hoped so.

"Who?" Clovis asked, scuttling across to join him, and peering over the lip of the ground in turn.

"Graymane." Drago spoke in an undertone, curtly gesturing to his companion to be quiet. "I want to know what he's doing here."

Clovis looked puzzled, but to Drago's relief seemed to have enough sense not to ask any more questions, at least for now.

The gray-clad elf seemed to be waiting for someone, with a palpable air of impatience. After a moment he glanced away to the left, where a flurry of movement just outside the circle of firelight he stood in resolved itself into a trio of elves: the officer from the ill-fated convoy, another identically dressed, and therefore presumably of equal status, and a third, who they flanked, a deferential pace behind. From the even larger plume on his helmet, elaborate embroidery sprawling across his cloak, and distinctly fleshy jowls, Drago deduced that this was the garrison commander. From the scrunched-up letter in his hand, and the expression on his face, he was also able to deduce that whatever news Graymane had brought with him was distinctly unwelcome.

"What kept you?" Graymane asked, and the commander's jowls wobbled as his jaw clenched in response. Nonetheless, he nodded with every outward expression of courtesy he could muster.

"There's always something in a place like this," he said blandly. He nodded at the officer from the convoy. "And when Captain Meadowsweet handed me your letter, I felt the least I could do was read it with the attention it deserved."

"Given that it has the king's personal seal on it, I'd expect nothing less." Graymane nodded too, accepting the excuse at face value, and making it clear that he was only doing so because it suited him. "So you'll cooperate with me?"

"Of course." The effort of remaining polite was almost strangling the commander, unless it was the neckline of his mail shirt, which had clearly been used to accommodating a little less neck in former years. Drago found himself wondering if the grandly dressed elf was wearing a corset underneath his armor, or was simply relying on the linked steel rings to keep his belly in check. "Though I really don't see the need—"

"Don't you?" Graymane's voice grew quieter and more menacing; Drago had heard that tone before, generally not long before the shedding of blood. "I do." He turned to the elven officer who'd led the convoy. "How about you, Captain Meadowsweet? Do you see the need?" He turned his gaze on the other officer, who so far had said nothing. "Or you, madam. Or perhaps we should ask the soldiers you lead." He smote his forehead, in a pantomime of bewilderment. "Oh, I forgot. They're too busy picking rebel arrows out of themselves to have an opinion."

"I'm beginning to find your tone needlessly offensive," the commander said, drawing himself up with all the dignity he could muster. Which even Drago could see was entirely the wrong tack to take. Graymane clearly had scant respect for anyone's opinion but his own.

"And I'm beginning to find your obtuseness and incompetence appropriately offensive," Graymane shot back. "Are we clear about that, Oaktwig?" Drago wasn't entirely sure, but from what he remembered about elven manners, the use of somebody's family name without an attached title or honorific was a mortal insult. The two junior officers exchanged horrified glances.

"By the roots, sir, if you weren't the king's emissary—" Oaktwig grasped the hilt of his sword, his jaw jutting as belligerently as possible beneath its protective layer of fat.

"You'd bleed all over my sword. Fine. But I am, so we won't be dueling tonight. Do any of you have anything useful to say before I get to work?"

The second officer raised her hand, a little diffidently. "I haven't seen the letter myself. Am I to infer that you're here to assess our security and report back to the throne?"

"At last, an elf with a brain who attempts to use it. You are?"

"Rinora Moonshade. Captain of the second century."

"And in your opinion, Captain Moonshade, is security around here adequate?"

The officer looked distinctly uncomfortable, darting quick glances at the other two, who did their best to keep their own faces impassive.

"That rather depends on how you define adequate," she said at last.

"A good question." Graymane nodded judicially, like Clement Wethers preparing to send the boys round for a little chat about some minor inconvenience to the Tradesman's Association. "I'd define adequate as the rebels not being able to steal your supplies or intercept the gold you're digging out of here on the way to the wharf any time the inclination strikes them. With an ease which indicates to me that someone in this garrison is telling them exactly which shipments have the highest value, or contain items of particular use to them."

"You think we have a traitor in the camp?" Oaktwig was quivering so much with indignation that Drago kept expecting to see ripples spreading across his entire body. Perhaps he was wearing a corset then. "That's inconceivable! No elf would ever—"

"You'd be surprised what an elf would ever, for the right kind of bribe," Graymane said dryly, leading Drago to wonder if, against all appearances to the contrary, the grim-visaged elf possessed the rudiments of a sense of humor.

"Why would it have to be an elf?" Meadowsweet asked. "The place is crawling with shortarses. They've got much more in common with the gobs."

"And you trust them with sensitive information, do you?" Graymane asked.

"Of course we don't." Oaktwig bridled afresh at the insinuation. "Ghastly little rodents. We only keep them around because they can get twice as much ore out in half the time as elven miners. But no one actually speaks to them."

"They've still got eyes and ears," Graymane said, "but for now I'll accept your assurance, and focus my attention on the elves here." His eyes swept meaningfully across the trio in front of him. "All of them."

"You do that." Oaktwig's gaze was glacial. "I suppose I ought to wish you luck, but I can't see the point. If Gorash has agents in the camp, we'd all have had our throats cut long ago." Which, still listening from the shadows, Drago had to concede was a good point.

"Perhaps." Graymane still seemed unconvinced. "We'll talk again in the morning."

"At your convenience," Oaktwig said, in tones which strongly implied that it most certainly wouldn't be at his, and turned away, followed by his subordinates. From where Drago was standing, their voices drifted back on the wind.

"It depends on how you define adequate? For sap's sake, woman, what were you thinking?"

"I was thinking one of you might actually back me up for once . . ."

Graymane smiled briefly as the bickering voices faded into the distance, then turned his head, looking long and hard in Drago's direction. Drago grabbed Clovis by the arm, his fingers digging into the other gnome's bicep, silently signaling him to not move and remain quiet. Fortunately, the young miner took the hint.

After a moment Graymane relaxed, saying nothing, and turned away with a faintly quizzical expression on his face. Drago waited a few moments, then relaxed himself, stepping away from the rock face back into the middle of the downward-sloping path.

"Why were we listening to that?" Clovis asked, looking even more confused than before. "It had nothing to do with us anyway."

"But it might have done," Drago said, and fortunately Clovis seemed inclined to let it go at that.

Which was more than Drago could do. If Graymane was right, and Gorash had an agent inside the camp, then that just might be the opportunity he needed. If he could find out who it was before Graymane, he might be able to follow them to a meeting with the bandits, and get a solid lead on Gorash's whereabouts.

Then again, if the agent found out he was there his own life would be hanging by a thread, waiting only for the goblin bandit's instructions to kill him to catch up. The chances were he only had a couple of days left in which to act.

Well, best not to waste them, then. He knew exactly what his first move should be.

"Right," he said to Clovis. "Two things. Which one of these burrows has the food, and will there be any ale to go with it?"

CHAPTER TWENTY-FOUR
"Heard from the wife lately?"

As it turned out there was ale, of a reasonable quality, and food, in reasonable quantities, both of which Drago took full advantage of. The mess hall, as he'd expected, was an artificial cavern hewn out of the quarry wall, in which, for once, he found all the furnishings were the right size for the gnomes who used them. The light levels were dim by the standards of the other species, with only a handful of candles scattered around the wide chamber, but that was more than adequate for gnomish eyes; used to the harsher illumination most of the inhabitants of Fairhaven preferred, Drago found it quite restful.

The mess hall was relatively quiet, to his unspoken relief, with only a couple of dozen off-duty miners spooning up rat stew, or redistributing their wages through the time-honored route of games of chance, in which chance figured less than many of the players fondly imagined. Drago noted these with the interest of someone who hadn't rolled any dice in earnest for a lot longer than he was happy with, but overcame the temptation to join in. For now, he preferred to fade into the background, as much as an unfamiliar face could, content for Clovis to make more introductions to people whose names and faces blurred in his mind almost as soon as the ritual exchange of greetings was over.

"Do you know everybody around here?" he asked at last, and Clovis frowned thoughtfully, taking the query at face value.

"Not everyone," he said at last, "but I know most people by sight, and I've always been good with names." He shrugged, chewing on a particularly resilient piece of rat for a moment. "It's a gift."

One which Drago, if he was honest, rather envied. Back in Fairhaven you got used to the idea that you recognized your neighbors, the stallholders you did most of your business with, and the staff of the taverns you used on a regular basis. Some you knew by name, most you didn't. Apart from them, there were the ones most people avoided out of a sense of self-preservation, and whom Drago knew primarily as a source of income, and a handful of prominent citizens in every district whose attention could be seen as something of a mixed blessing. But for every one of these you'd encounter a dozen or more whose lives never intersected with yours in any way more meaningful than happening to walk down the same street at the same time.

Things seemed to be different in the smaller communities he'd visited briefly on his journey up the Geltwash, where pretty much everyone did seem to know everybody else, but he'd been an outsider in those places, never really making a connection with any of the locals. Here, however, everybody seemed to accept him, even if they didn't know him yet, simply because he was a fellow gnome in a small enclave surrounded by condescending elves, who in turn were surrounded by hostile goblins.

"There you are." The Gaffer was making his way over to their table. "Thought I'd find you here." He nodded to Drago. "Young Clovis keeping you entertained?"

"He's been filling me in on who's who and what's what," Drago agreed. Thanks to the young gnome's garrulity he was pretty sure he could find his way around most of the burrow, and a fair part of the mine workings to boot, putting names to most of the people he encountered even if he hadn't actually met them yet.

"Good lad. Found you a bunk. Not the most comfortable lodgings in the world, but it'll do, I imagine."

"I doubt it's any less comfortable than the deck of a riverboat," Drago said, and the older gnome nodded judiciously.

"Never slept on one, so I couldn't possibly comment. But I imagine you're right." He glanced at the empty bowl in front of Drago. "Finished your supper?"

"Pretty much," Drago said. He could probably have found room for another ale or two if there had been enough time, but now the edge of his hunger had been dulled, he found he was tired more than anything.

"Good. Whenever you're ready, then."

Knowing an implied instruction when he heard one, Drago stood, with a farewell wave to Clovis, and followed the older gnome out of the mess hall. He'd half expected to be led out into the open air again, but instead the Gaffer moved off in the opposite direction, toward the far wall, in which the mouth of a tunnel could be seen, leading into the depths of the hill.

It seemed that the gnomes here had constructed a fair-sized burrow over the years, which was hardly surprising given the decades the mine had been in operation. The walls and floor were smooth, showing little sign of tool marks, while the ceiling, as in most gnomish dwellings, had been raised into a curving arch, from the apex of which lanterns hung at intervals. Once they passed a lamplighter and his apprentice, lifting one down with the aid of a hooked staff, which blocked their way for a moment; the Gaffer seemed happy enough to wait, exchanging pleasantries, until they'd replaced the stub of candle with a fresh one and hoisted it back into place, before continuing on their way.

"Very cozy," Drago said, trying not to sound too impressed, although the corridors they passed through wouldn't have looked that out of place in one of the less prosperous parts of the delving his relatives lived in back on the coastal plain. "I thought a mine would be a bit more . . ." he searched for the right word for a moment, before settling on "basic."

"Oh, the mine's basic enough," the Gaffer assured him, leading the way past what looked like a series of kitchens and storerooms, some of which were deserted, while in others gnomes bustled about on mysterious business of their own, before taking a sharp left down a narrower corridor lined with wooden doors. All had been smoothed and varnished, and bore a different number incised carefully into the planks. "But there's no reason we can't be comfortable when we're not working." He stood aside to let a gnome hurry past, bearing a wine bottle and a faintly guilty expression. "How do, Harald. Heard from the wife lately?"

Harald colored visibly. "Got a letter last week," he said, with faintly strained casualness.

"That's nice." The Gaffer watched him go. "Enjoy your drink." He turned back to Drago. "Everyone knows he's carrying on with Etta Rootstock, and he knows we know, but nobody says anything. It's like that around here. No one keeps secrets for long."

"I'll bear that in mind," Drago said, as neutrally as he could.

The Gaffer nodded. "Just saying. Don't mean anything by it." Which struck Drago as disingenuous to say the least. He wondered how many more coded warnings he was liable to get from well-meaning strangers before this affair was concluded. But the point was well taken. In a community this close-knit, he was bound to attract attention; thanks to Clovis's enthusiastic descriptions of his fight with the bandits he was probably already the subject of gossip. Before he could pursue the thought any further, however, the Gaffer stopped outside one of the doors, bearing the number 138. "This is you."

For a moment Drago was at a loss, until the older gnome tripped the latch and pushed the door open, revealing a small room containing a bed, a table and a chair. He walked in, and turned round slowly. It was nowhere near as large as his attic room in Mrs. Cravatt's, but it would take four paces to cross, which made it spacious enough for his needs. "When you said a bunk, I thought you meant in a dormitory somewhere," he said.

"We like our privacy around here," the Gaffer said, with a faint smile. "Just ask Harald and Etta." He pulled the key from the outside of the door, and handed it to Drago. "Gazunder's in the usual place, slop bucket's at the end of the hall." Drago felt under the bed with his foot, heard a reassuring chink of china, and nodded. "Wash jug's full, which you'll probably be glad to hear after your journey." He indicated the jug and basin perched at one end of the small table. "Can you find your way back to the mess hall?"

"I think so," Drago said, dropping his knapsack on the bed. It sank into the mattress, with a faint rustling of straw, and he found himself trying to remember how long it had been since he last slept in a proper bed. The night before he left Fairhaven, almost a week and a half ago. He wondered if Mrs. Cravatt had kept her word, as well as his money, or had already sublet his room to a fresh tenant. Probably not, if she was expecting Raegan to drop by at irregular intervals. He found himself wondering how the watch captain was getting on in his investigation, if Lady Selina hadn't quietly cut him out by now, and whether Greenleaf was still stirring up mischief and dodging goblins. But none of that was his concern anymore. No doubt he'd find out when he returned home, if he ever did, and any speculation in the meantime would be pointless.

"Good." The Gaffer nodded. "See you at breakfast, then, and we'll put you to work."

Secure behind a locked door, and in a bed which yielded beneath his weight, Drago slept long and soundly, until a loud knocking on the wooden panel jerked him awake. Grasping the dagger from under his pillow he sat up, listening carefully. He'd blown out the candle before going to sleep, leaving the windowless room in almost total darkness, but faint lines of light limned the outline of the door, providing enough illumination for his gnomish night vision to pick out the main objects as clumps of solid-seeming shadow.

He listened for a moment, but no one fumbled with the latch, or attempted to pick the lock, so he relaxed a little. After a short while the knocking was repeated, sounding a little less loud and urgent without the intervening filter of sleep.

"Who is it?" he called, trying to sound a little more sleepy and less alert than he actually was.

"It's Clovis," a familiar voice called, slightly muffled through the intervening timber. "I thought you might have overslept."

"You thought right," Drago said, opening the door a crack, to admit more light and the inquisitive head of his new friend, and conceal the dagger he was still holding ready for a quick thrust up under the ribcage if he needed to. Reassured that no one was lurking in the by-now-bustling corridor with nefarious intent, and that his state of *deshabille* was attracting a few curious glances, particularly from the female passers-by, he retreated inside the room and struck a light. "Hang on a minute while I get my britches on."

"All right." Clovis hovered indecisively just outside the doorway until Drago emerged, locked the door behind him and tucked the key away securely in the belt pouch where he normally kept the cleaning kit for his sword. With a faint pang he'd decided to leave the weapon and its scabbard back in his room, tucked under the mattress; which would be the first place anyone searching the chamber would look, of course, but there weren't that many potential places of concealment in such a confined space, and at least it would be out of sight of any casual visitor. Not that he expected many of those. The lock seemed stout enough, although he'd apprehended enough burglars in his time not to place too much reliance on that; most locks could be picked a great deal more quickly and easily than their owners would have been comfortable knowing, particularly when privacy rather than security seemed to be the issue most concerning them, as was generally the case among gnomes. Gnomish delvings tended to be crowded, with a preponderance of well-travelled corridors, so breaking and entering without attracting the attention of witnesses was far more difficult than it would have been in a human-dominated city like Fairhaven with its plethora of hidden courts and alleyways. Clovis glanced in the direction of Drago's belt, with a faint air of disappointment. "Not wearing the sword today?"

"Why would I?" Drago asked. He tried to make his tone sound bantering. "Do you think I might need it?"

"Shouldn't have thought so." Once again, Clovis took the question at face value. "I can't see any bandits sneaking in without being spotted, and the lofties'd have them long before they got as far as the mine."

"My thoughts exactly," Drago said, suddenly acutely conscious of the dagger tucked inside the top of his boot. Being entirely without a weapon never sat well with him, and he felt its familiar weight as a reassuring presence.

The mess hall, when they reached it, was crowded, a couple of hundred miners chatting and eating at once, their voices and the clatter of their utensils redoubled and multiplied in the large, echoing space, making the noise level correspondingly high; Drago felt it as a constant pressure against his temples, as though a thunderstorm was brewing not far away.

"Are you all right?" Clovis asked, as they found seats in a relatively quiet corner, and Drago nodded, beginning to spoon porridge into his mouth.

"Just a bit tired still," he temporized, between mouthfuls. "It's been a long journey." A smear of weak sunlight was creeping in through the mouth of the cavern, and into the hall, making him feel a little more comfortable, and restless at the same time. The gnomes around him were used to spending days, even weeks, underground, but he'd spent his entire life living in a surface city; constant semi-darkness and musty air dulled his senses and left him feeling vaguely listless.

"I hope you've got enough energy to get some work done," Loma said, appearing at his elbow.

Drago turned and looked up at her, nodding as he did so. "Can't wait to get started," he assured her.

"Glad to hear it." She hastily suppressed the beginnings of a smile. "Let's hope your enthusiasm holds up when you've got a pick in your hands."

"I'll do my best," Drago assured her, with every appearance of sincerity he could muster.

"You'd better. I wasn't joking about turfing you out if you let me down." She turned her head a little, to address Clovis. "You seem to have hit it off with our new friend here, so how about you show him the rocks? I'll assign him to your gang for a while, at least until we see what he can do. All right?"

"Fine, Boss. I'll take care of him." Clovis looked as though all his birthdays had come at once. "Does the Gaffer know?"

"Already told him." Loma nodded, and turned away, with a final appraising look at Drago. "I'll be keeping an eye on you."

"I suppose I should be flattered," Drago said, returning to his porridge with what he hoped was an insouciant shrug. But Clovis shook his head.

"I don't think she meant it like that," he said.

CHAPTER TWENTY-FIVE
"There's always a flaw somewhere."

Their meal over, Drago followed Clovis out of the mess hall and into the open air, where he breathed in deeply, enjoying the sight of a sky overhead while he still could. The morning was chill, and the light still gray, but he found himself savoring the ruffling of his hair by the breeze. Most of the miners were heading down the ramps leading to the lower terraces, but Drago loitered, getting his first full sight of the quarry in the weak morning sunlight.

"Quite a sight, isn't it?" a voice asked behind him, and he turned, bringing up his hand in a casual-seeming gesture which would have blocked an incoming punch. Finding he was being addressed by the Gaffer, he continued the movement, and brushed the fringe of his hair from his eyes.

"It certainly is," he agreed. From up here, most of the complex was visible: not just the shafts driven into the side of the cliff face on the lowest level, and into which the gnomish miners were flocking, but the scattering of buildings on the floor of the quarry he'd noticed on the evening of his arrival. All were built of the gray stone hewn from the ground here: the closest ones, showing obvious signs of gnomish workmanship, were clearly the storage sheds he'd originally assumed, many of the miners entering them to emerge a moment later with barrows, tools, or other objects he couldn't make out at this distance. The ones further away were of cruder construction, looked older, and the people moving around in their vicinity were too tall and slender to be gnomes. Drago narrowed his eyes, already certain that these were elves, and carrying weapons to boot.

"That's where they process the ore," Clovis said, noting the direction of his gaze, "and the furnace where they melt down the gold and cast it into ingots, once they've extracted it." Sure enough, one of the largest buildings, on the shores of the bile green lake, was vomiting smoke from its chimney, and a dull red glow could be seen emanating from its open windows.

"How do they do that?" Drago asked. "Get it out of the rocks, I mean?"

The Gaffer shrugged. "Alchemy. In that shed over there." He pointed to the building adjoining the furnace, which also abutted the lake. "Trust me, you don't want to go anywhere near it."

"I wasn't planning to," Drago said truthfully. For one thing, the place was swarming with soldiers, and he was pretty sure their orders didn't include inviting curious strangers in for a mug of ale and a guided tour of the place. And for another, nothing down there looked likely to lead him to Gorash.

"Glad to hear it." The older gnome glared balefully in the direction of the lake. "Whatever they do down there, it's not good for the health."

"It certainly isn't," Clovis agreed. "That water'd kill you if you tried drinking it."

"I wasn't planning to," Drago said. He'd taken the bottle from his knapsack before leaving his room, and filled it with ale in the mess hall. You couldn't trust water to drink at the best of times: even in Fairhaven it could kill you or leave you so wracked with the flux you'd wish it had, and anything outside the city was bound to be even worse. The only safe thing to imbibe, unless a mage had been at it, was something that had previously been fermented. Everybody knew that.

"Glad to hear it." The Gaffer nodded. "Got your docky?"

Drago nodded confirmation. The packed lunches had been waiting on a table by the entrance to the mess hall, and every departing miner had been handed one as they filed past.

"You'll be glad of it come break time," Clovis assured him.

"I've no doubt I will," Drago agreed.

"Come on, then." The Gaffer beckoned the two younger gnomes to follow him, and set off down the sloping path. "Let's get you kitted out."

Drago followed him all the way down to the floor of the quarry, where dozens of gnomes were still bustling to and fro, and across to the nearest of the storage sheds. He paused, glancing up the way they'd come, marveling at how far they'd descended in so short a time. From here the cliff rose, almost sheer between the terraces cut into it, and he had to narrow his eyes again to pick out the entrances to the gnomish burrows a few yards below the top. Above that, the blocky stone buildings of the elvish garrison loomed, tiny figures no larger than his thumbnail going about their business, with nary a look down at the feverish activity they were there to protect.

No, not quite. One of the distant figures paused, turned its head, and, as if aware of his scrutiny, glanced down into the pit, right at where Drago was standing. Drago felt a sudden tightening of his stomach muscles. He couldn't be sure at this distance, but he was convinced he was looking at Graymane, and, irrational as it was, that the elf had recognized him too.

"You want a pick, or a shovel?" the Gaffer asked, and, brought back to himself, Drago turned to answer.

"Either, I suppose," he said, noting the glance of mutual amusement which passed between the Gaffer and Clovis in response. He looked back at the cliff top, but Graymane, if it really had been him, had disappeared from view. "What do you reckon?"

"Wheelbarrow," Clovis said, and the Gaffer nodded.

"Good idea. But you can have these too." He selected a pick and a shovel from a rack of tools just inside the shed, dropped them into a waiting barrow, and turned to Drago. "Bring them back at the end of your shift. Clovis will show you how to book them in."

"Will do," Clovis agreed, picking up a piece of chalk, and using it to scrawl his name on a slab of slate mounted on the wall just to the left of the tool rack. It had been divided up into a grid by neatly incised lines, with names and items of equipment chalked into the resulting spaces. Next to his name, he wrote Pick. "Basically, you sign on the board for everything you take out from here. I'll do yours too, save a bit of time." He added "Appleroot, Barrow, Spade, Pick" on the next line.

Drago nodded. "Thanks."

"No problem. You can take this for me." Clovis dropped the pick he'd signed for in the barrow, where it clattered against the tools the

Gaffer had selected for Drago. "When you finish your shift, you just put everything back where it came from, and rub out the chalk, ready for tomorrow."

"And don't forget," the Gaffer said, "the boss'll be checking who's got what later on, and if anything you signed for goes missing, it'll come out of your wages."

"Right," Drago said. At least three ways of pilfering tools and deflecting the blame onto somebody else had occurred to him already, and he was sure there would be others, but perhaps there were safeguards in the system he hadn't been told about yet. And gnomes tended to be honest, at least compared to the other races; something to do with living in a confined space underground, perhaps, where transgressing the social code would be swiftly noticed. Not that he hadn't met a few who could give a goblin or a human a run for their money in the venality stakes, but, like him, they'd lived in more cosmopolitan communities. "Is there anything else?"

"That's about it," the Gaffer said. "Just ask Clovis if you have any questions."

Clovis waited expectantly for a moment, and when none were forthcoming, strode out of the shed with a cheery wave. "This way."

Drago seized the handles of the barrow, and set out after him across the rough ground, the tools rattling and crashing together in raucous syncopation. It was harder to steer than he'd imagined, bouncing over the uneven surface, and tilting from one side to the other in response to every rut or large stone the single wheel encountered, or the shifting weight of the tools inside it.

Clovis glanced back. "You'll soon get the hang of it," he called encouragingly. Drago hoped so. Otherwise the next few days were going to be awkward, to say the least.

Clovis led the way into one of the tunnels, which, as Drago had expected, were both lower and narrower than the passageways of the burrow. The walls and ceiling were of rough, unfinished rock, but at least the floor was a little smoother than the surface of the quarry, and he found he was able to control the barrow a great deal more easily. Which was just as well, considering the number of other gnomes they passed. Several were pushing barrows like him, a steady stream of them going in the opposite direction, laden with chunks of stone, and a couple nodded greetings as they passed. The illumination was dim, the lanterns spaced three or four times further apart than in the burrow, but still more than adequate for gnomish eyes, and Drago was able to keep Clovis in sight easily as they penetrated deeper into the heart of the hill. Which was just as well, he reflected, as a number of side tunnels led off from the main shaft, which wasn't exactly straight itself, and he could easily have got lost without a guide.

"This one," Clovis said, disappearing down one of the turnoffs with barely a backward glance, and Drago followed, finding the going becoming a little rougher again. There was almost no light at all along here, but a little seeped in from the tunnel behind, and after a few moments he began to discern a faint glow up ahead, so he was able to remain orientated without much difficulty.

Then Clovis disappeared abruptly, his silhouette against the distant light vanishing, to be replaced by a diffuse illumination delineating the mouth of the tunnel. He must have reached whatever was at the end, and stepped aside into a wider space.

Having deduced that, Drago was more or less prepared for the cavern he entered after another dozen or so paces, but the size of it took him by surprise nevertheless. Some ten or twelve yards wide, and double that deep, it was well over six feet in height. At the far end, ladders led up to a ledge some three feet from the floor, where a trio of gnomes was digging into the rock face, throwing the lumps of stone they were extracting down to where a couple of others were loading them into barrows like the one Drago was pushing. Presumably at some point, when the ledge had been extended too far to drop the rocks down easily, the lower level would be dug into as well, extending the floor area, and making it easier to mine the upper level again.

"Right." Clovis waved in the direction of the burrowing gnomes, to make sure Drago was giving them his full attention, and raised his voice a little to carry over the constant clinking of steel against rock. "I'm not sure how you'd get on digging into the face, as you haven't got the experience of reading the rock yet, so you're on removal." He indicated the pile of spoil, which the other two gnomes on the ground were shoveling into their barrows, stopping every now and again to split a particularly large chunk of rock with a pickaxe. One of them looked familiar, and when she glanced up and waved, he recognized Della from the previous night. Deciding that she had enough for a decent load, she picked up the handles of her barrow and trotted away toward the tunnel mouth, steering with an effortless precision Drago could only envy.

"Seems simple enough," he said, moving over to the remaining spoil.

"It is." Clovis retrieved the tools from the barrow, lining them all up neatly against the nearby rock face. "Provided you remember to keep an eye out for falling rocks." As if to emphasize the point, a chunk of stone almost the same size as his head crashed to the ground a couple of feet away. Clovis didn't even flinch.

"I'll bear that in mind," Drago said feelingly. Gnome skulls were tough, something he'd had reason enough to be grateful for on more than one occasion in his line of work, but not tough enough to shrug off a blow like that.

"All you've got to do is load up, and run the ore outside," Clovis said.

"Right." Drago picked up the shovel, rammed it into the pile of stones, and lifted it. It felt unwieldy rather than heavy, and he pitched the shovelful into the barrow, spilling a couple of the smaller pieces onto the ground in the process. "What about the big ones?"

"That's what this is for," Clovis said, handing him the pick, and taking the shovel.

"Got it." Drago swung the blade of the pick at the head-sized rock which had almost brained his friend. It rebounded, with a judder which reverberated up his arms, a shower of sparks, and a loud clattering noise as the rock skittered away.

Clovis seemed to be holding in a grin. "Like this," he said. "Look for the flaws." He leaned the shovel against the barrow, swung his own pick, and the large rock shattered into three roughly equal chunks and a scattering of fragments. "There's always a flaw somewhere. That's what I meant about reading the rock."

"I see," Drago said, although he wasn't entirely sure that he did. Picking out another large piece he examined it carefully, this time noting a couple of hairline cracks in the surface. Feeling faintly self-conscious he swung the pick again, felt it connect cleanly with its target, and watched the rock split into two with a surprising sense of satisfaction.

"That's the way." Clovis nodded with evident approval. "I guess you can take the gnome out of the burrow . . ."

He watched Drago split another couple of rocks, then, apparently satisfied, clambered up the ladder to take his place alongside the gnomes working on the upper gallery. With a fresh appreciation of the skills involved, Drago watched them carving into the rock face for a moment or two, every stroke bringing down a new chunk of stone, before returning to his own job. Though it wasn't physically taxing for gnomish muscles, he found the process of loading the barrow required skill as well as strength, and was surprisingly tiring. By the time it was three quarters full he had to pause for breath, and to take a mouthful of ale to wash the dust from his throat.

"Not bad for a beginner." Della had come back while he was engrossed in his shoveling, the other barrow gnome departing in the interim, and she was watching him appraisingly. "Try not to overload the shovel, though. You'll spill less, then you won't have to collect it all up again."

"Right." Drago followed her advice, and found he got more in the barrow and less on the floor of the cavern. After a few more minutes he had a respectable load. "Where do I take this?"

Della grinned, her own barrow already more than half full. "Just follow the others. You'll know it when you see it."

"Be back soon, then," Drago said. He lifted the handles, and leaned into the barrow, which resisted for a moment before it started moving. If anything it seemed even harder to control than before, wobbling wildly until he managed to stabilize it. He made a mental note to try to even out the weight of the next load a little more carefully. Aiming at the mouth of the tunnel, he almost clipped the edge of it, but managed to get out of the cavern without any embarrassing collisions.

Now that it was rolling, the weight of his load made the barrow seem relatively easy to push, and he rattled and jolted along to the main shaft with surprisingly little effort. He tried to slow as he approached the wider tunnel, fearful of a collision, but the barrow resisted him; he had to lean back, tugging as hard as he could on the handles, to slow it down, and even then it trundled out into the shaft at a sluggish walking pace rather than stopping completely as he'd intended. Fortunately no one was coming, and he was able to wrestle the barrow round the corner and get it moving again without much more than a single anxious moment when it appeared as though the whole thing was about to topple sideways, spilling rocks everywhere.

Making a careful mental note of a distinctive seam of marbling in the tunnel wall next to the side passage he'd just emerged from, as getting lost on the way back to the work face would have been embarrassing in the extreme, Drago headed for the mine entrance at a brisk trot; partly because the barrowful of rock was building up a fair bit of momentum on the relatively level floor, and partly in response to the faint current of fresh air and the distant gleam of daylight.

As he moved out of the tunnel and hit the surface of the quarry, the barrow began to judder so much it felt as if his bones were rattling. The day was overcast, clouds almost the same color as the stone surrounding him, but after the gloom of the tunnels it seemed almost dazzling. The faint patch of lighter cloud, betraying the presence of the sun, was higher in the sky than he'd expected, leaving him surprised at how much time had passed while he was underground.

Drago glanced around, wondering where he was supposed to go, and loath to bring the hurtling barrow to a halt while he found out; getting it moving again on this uneven ground would be far from easy. Luckily, Della's assurance that he'd be sure to know the way seemed well-founded; a tangle of wheel ruts, their depth mute testament that the barrows which had made them were laden at least as heavily as his, ran straight from the mouth of the mine, and, once noticed, were easy to follow. As was the steady stream of other gnomes pushing barrows of their own, either in the same direction he was, or coming back the other way, a couple of yards to his right. A few of these smiled at him, either in friendly greeting or amusement at his evident inexperience and difficulty in controlling his barrow, but for the most part they seemed focused on nothing more than getting back to their work faces and picking up a fresh load.

Peering round the jolting barrow, Drago saw he was approaching the buildings guarded by the elven soldiers, most of whom carried crossbows in their hands. They formed a loose picket line, presumably intended to prevent any stray gnomes from wandering too close to the processing plant, but didn't seem particularly alert, watching the endlessly moving line of barrows with disdainful boredom.

"Watch it, shortarse," one of them said, his tone reasonably friendly by the standards he'd come to expect from Marchers, "you'll have that over the edge."

Distracted by his professional interest in the security arrangements around the buildings, Drago had reached his destination without realizing it. Leaning back against the momentum of the laden barrow, he brought it to a halt a few feet from the edge of a wooden platform which reminded him of the wharves the *Rippling Light* had tied up at along the Geltwash. There was no water below this one, though, apart from the scum-flecked surface of the foul-smelling lake a few dozen yards away, just a heap of rubble directly beneath where he was standing.

"Thanks." Drago tilted the barrow, letting the contents rattle down onto the pile below, where it instantly vanished as though it had never existed.

He straightened up, taking his time, using the opportunity to get a good look at the building Clovis had told him was used to extract the metal from the ore. Wide doors on the lower level were open, to admit the rocks the gnomes were delivering, this time conveyed by surly-looking elves who clearly felt the task was beneath them. The one in charge wore a thick leather apron, burned and stained, and with an interesting variety of scars on his face and hands, the universal signs of a practicing alchemist. He seemed irritated by something, glancing back into the depths of the building from time to time, talking to someone Drago couldn't see, and manifestly resenting having his attention diverted from the job in hand.

Then Graymane emerged into the light, nodding dismissively. "Thank you for your cooperation," he said, in tones which implied that cooperation had been scant to say the least. "I'll be sure to mention how helpful you've been to His Majesty." The alchemist bristled visibly, but was wise enough not to reply. Then Graymane glanced up, his attention attracted by the rattle of another barrowload of ore dropping onto the pile beside him, and noticed Drago loitering on the loading platform. He raised a hand, though whether in greeting or warning wasn't entirely clear. "Stay where you are," he said. "I want a word with you."

CHAPTER TWENTY-SIX
"You don't waste much time, do you?"

Drago hesitated, considering his options, while Graymane strolled unhurriedly to the end of the platform and began to climb a rickety-looking staircase leading to the upper level. The alchemist watched his retreating back for a moment with undisguised loathing, then snapped a few orders to his underlings and disappeared inside the building.

The way Drago saw it, he had two choices. Stay where he was, and see what the elf wanted, or leave now, keeping as far away from him as possible. Both had pros and cons: leaving would sidestep any potential confrontation in the short term, but if he read Graymane as well as he thought he did, would merely reinforce whatever interest the elf had in him. Better to have it out now, in daylight, with plenty of witnesses around. Although if it came to violence, that probably wouldn't mean much: the elven soldiers would back up whatever version of events Graymane chose to give. Unless Drago killed him, of course, which wouldn't be easy by any means, and was almost bound to end with a short dance at the end of a long rope; none of the watching gnomes would be likely to either intervene or give testimony on his behalf.

So he decided to stay where he was, waiting with as much of an air of disinterest as he could manage to project, and see what happened.

"They've put you to work, I see," Graymane greeted him, and Drago shrugged.

"That's what I came here for," he said.

"Oh, I sincerely doubt that." Graymane glanced in the direction of Drago's belt, and raised a quizzical eyebrow. "Not wearing your sword today?"

"I didn't think I'd need it," Drago said, keeping Graymane's in his peripheral vision. The leather covering its hilt was worn, like his own, but the elf's hand wasn't hovering near it, so he couldn't be intending to attack; at least not straight away. Drago resisted the temptation to scratch casually at his leg, just above his boot top, and surreptitiously ensure that his dagger was loose in its scabbard. Graymane was undoubtedly experienced enough to know what the gesture was meant to conceal, and if he didn't realize Drago was armed after all, tipping him off about it would be a really bad idea. Of course he probably took it for granted that the gnome had a hidden blade about him somewhere; Drago certainly would, if their positions were reversed. "What with the digging, and all."

"Getting anywhere with that?" Graymane asked, clearly not referring to the extraction of ore.

Drago permitted himself a faint smile. "About as well as you are, I suppose."

"Then we need to talk properly," Graymane said, his demeanor suddenly becoming businesslike. "Somewhere we can be candid with one another." He looked round, pointedly taking in the line of gnomes emptying their barrows, and the elven soldiers, who both seemed equally surprised at the sight of an elf and a gnome engaged in conversation. "Make sure we're not at cross purposes."

"That sounds reasonable," Drago conceded. Clearly Graymane wasn't about to buy his story about having travelled to the mine to look for work, and perhaps he should put his cards on the table. If the elf really was there to look for an agent of Gorash that would put them on the same side, more or less, and he might have information that Drago could use. On the other hand, Graymane didn't know he'd overheard his conversation with the elven officers the previous evening, so he could hardly come flat out and ask him. "When and where?"

"Midnight, top of the slope," Graymane said, with a wintery smile of his own. "Where you were eavesdropping last night. No one should see us up there."

"You spotted me," Drago pointed out.

Graymane shook his head. "Didn't see a thing. But I've got ears."

"Then how did you know it was me?" Drago said, a little too quickly, still angry with himself at falling into so simple a trap. Even more so, given the number of times he'd used variations of it to cozen felons into admitting their guilt without meaning to.

"I didn't," Graymane said, "until now. But it seemed the most likely guess." He turned away, and Drago felt a sudden pang of unexpected sympathy for the alchemist. "See you at midnight."

"What did he want?" Della asked, appearing suddenly at Drago's elbow, her words punctuated by a rattle of falling stone as she emptied her barrow onto the pile of rocks below.

"Nothing much," Drago said. "He just recognized me from yesterday."

"I'm not surprised," Della said. "You were definitely making an impression, fighting off those bandits like that. Surprised one of the lofties noticed you, though."

"I don't think that one misses much," Drago said as casually as he could, watching the elf diminish into the distance, his gray cloak rippling in the breeze.

"And Clovis will be missing us," Della said, hoisting the handle of her barrow. "Those rocks won't shift themselves, you know."

"Good point," Drago agreed, grateful for the change of subject, and shoving his own into motion. He wouldn't want to get sacked for idling just when he was on the point of making some progress.

Della grinned. "Race you back," she said.

Needless to say Della won the challenge easily; by the time Drago returned to the cavern, she was plying her shovel with an easy rhythm, and her barrow was already a quarter full. His empty one had been a little easier to control than before, even on the rubble-choked quarry floor, and Drago had been beginning to wonder if he was getting the hang of it at last; until he saw the progress his co-workers had made in his absence.

"You'll need to be a lot quicker than that," Clovis admonished, glancing down from the upper gallery, but his tone was light rather than serious. "Loads more to shift before we can take a break."

"I'd better get to it, then," Drago said, lifting his shovel. Della, he noticed, was scooping up a succession of smaller pieces, which probably accounted for the rapidity with which she was filling her barrow. He tried to follow suit, but after a couple of shovelfuls ran up against one of the larger rocks, and dropped the tool to seize hold of his pick. A swift blow was enough to shatter the stone, and he swapped the tool in his hands for the shovel again.

"Break them all up first," Della suggested, with a grin. "Or enough for a full load, at least," she added, as another cascade of raw material crashed down next to them.

"Good idea," Drago said, wondering why that hadn't occurred to him to begin with. Now she'd pointed it out it seemed obvious, and he lost no time in adopting the technique himself. Sure enough, he found himself filling his barrow far more quickly, and by the end of the shift he even found he was taking less time than he had that morning to make the run to the ore heap and back.

"Not bad," Clovis said, as he returned his tools to the shed that evening. "We'll make a miner of you yet." He smiled as he said it, though, and Drago realized it was merely a pleasantry rather than an accurate summation of his potential.

"Glad to hear it." The last time he'd felt as tired as this he'd just fought a drunken troll to a standstill, and he couldn't be sure whether his muscles had ached even more on that occasion than they did now. The work hadn't seemed particularly taxing while he'd been engaged in it, but it had been repetitive, gradually sapping his strength in tiny increments. Gritty dust was everywhere, coating his face and clothing, working its way into places he'd only dimly been aware he possessed until they started itching, and his eyes smarted. No doubt he'd get used to that too, if he stayed here long enough, but right now the prospect of facing a goblin bandit who'd ordered his murder seemed far more appealing.

"Right. Let's get you cleaned up and fed." Della wiped her name from the chalkboard, and returned her tools to the storage racks. She grinned at Clovis. "Coming?"

"I'll catch you later," the young supervisor said, already engrossed in making notes on a handheld slate. "Got to get these figures to the boss first."

"Course you do," Della said with a cheery wave, turning to follow the rest of their shift out of the door and back toward the ramps leading up to the burrows at the lip of the quarry. As they left the shed, she turned to Drago. "Not that she'll even notice. But he likes to do a proper job."

Drago expected her to lead him straight back to the mess hall, but she turned aside at the first tunnel entrance they came to on reaching the burrows. Most of the gnomes returning from the mines were heading that way, so he wasn't surprised to find the passageway wider and higher than he was used to. What was a surprise was the sound of running water echoing all around them, which seemed to be growing louder the deeper into the burrow they went.

"You can clean off in here," Della said, leading the way through an archway in one of the walls. A shelf had been neatly carved along one side of a long, narrow chamber, at which gnomes stood, hiding almost its entire length from view. As Drago and Della insinuated themselves into a gap, Drago realized that a channel had been gouged out in the gently sloping surface, along which a steady stream of water flowed; everyone was washing with great diligence, the thin stream gradually turning darker as it carried the accumulated grime of a score or more faces and pairs of hands away through a small, neatly carved arch.

Drago needed no further urging, plunging his face into the cold, reasonably clear water, feeling the grit dislodging from his skin under the gentle pressure of the current. He emerged spluttering, shaking the excess moisture from his face. "That feels better."

"You look better, too," Della said, pulling a handful of hair over her shoulder and wringing it out. Without its coating of rock dust, it was glossier than Drago had realized, a rich chestnut brown, almost the same color as her eyes. She began to braid it. "Feel like getting something to eat now?"

"What do you think?" Drago said. The hours of hard physical labor had left him famished, and the sooner he got to the mess hall the better, so far as he was concerned.

Della nodded. "We can wait a while if you're not hungry. I'll show you some more of the burrow instead." His dismay must have shown on his face, because she laughed loudly, and punched him lightly on the arm. "Gotcha."

"You certainly did," Drago said, as they emerged into the corridor again. It was less crowded now, fewer gnomes arriving to clean up, and most of the ones he could see were hurrying deeper into the burrow. He indicated another archway as they passed it. "What's in here?"

"Baths," Della told him. "But if you want to use them now, you can go in on your own. I don't know you that well yet."

"Food works for me," Drago told her, taken aback, and Della grinned again.

"Food it is, then," she agreed.

The rest of the evening passed more quickly than Drago realized; Della turned out to be pleasant company, and, rather more surprisingly, seemed to enjoy his in equal measure. A substantial meal was followed by several drinks, during which time Clovis joined them, his chin still stained with gravy from his hastily eaten supper. After that, Della introduced Drago to some of the dice players he'd seen on the previous evening, and he hardly lost anything; Della, on the other hand, ended the night several shillings up, which seemed to put her in an even better mood.

"You must have brought me luck," she said, as they turned away from the table. "What do you want to do now?"

Drago yawned, a sudden jaw-cracker which took him completely by surprise. "Go to bed, I suppose," he said.

Della's eyebrows rose, and she regarded him appraisingly. "You don't waste much time, do you?" she said. "Are all city boys that direct?"

Drago felt as though the floor had suddenly collapsed under him. "I didn't mean—" he began, before he realized she was laughing again.

"I know, but I couldn't resist. Your face!" She cracked up, Clovis joining in with his own hoots of merriment, and after a moment of indignation Drago saw the funny side too and began chuckling himself. He couldn't remember the last time he'd had anything to laugh about in earnest, and intended to make the most of it. "Not that you aren't interesting, and I've seen worse looking, but—nah. Can't see it, can you?"

For some reason, Drago found the question disconcerting. There were gnomish women in Fairhaven, of course, and the delvings where his relatives lived, and he'd had his fair share of romantic entanglements with a few of them—not to mention the odd human or goblin along the way—but his vocation wasn't exactly conducive to maintaining a long-term relationship. The thing was, under most other circumstances, Della would have been exactly the kind of woman who'd arouse his interest: astute, self-confident, and, if he was honest, not bad looking either under the patina of grime endemic to her occupation. But he was here with a purpose, to ensure his own survival, and couldn't afford to be distracted. So he simply shook his head. "No. Guess you're right."

"Of course I'm right," Della said, although she didn't seem all that happy about it.

CHAPTER TWENTY-SEVEN
"That'll be the day."

Despite the urge to sleep which had almost overwhelmed him, Drago forced himself to stay awake in his room until it was time for his rendezvous with Graymane. He wasn't exactly sure what the elf would do if he fell asleep and missed their meeting, but at the very least he'd lose the chance of gaining some useful information. At the worst, Graymane might consider him a suspect rather than a potential ally, and from what he'd seen and heard already, antagonizing the elf was unlikely to end well.

So, in spite of the siren call of his mattress, he remained sitting on the hard chair, carefully cleaning the blade of his sword. The familiar routine and the scent of the clove oil were soothing, and when he returned it to the scabbard with a satisfying *click!* he felt more alert again than he would have done after taking a brief nap.

After a moment's consideration, he added the weapon to his belt. Not that he expected to need it, but the familiar weight was comforting, and for the first time he realized how strange he'd felt without it. He didn't expect to meet many people this late at night, and after Clovis's enthusiastic description of his martial prowess he was quite sure that pretty much everyone around here knew he habitually carried a blade in any case. After a moment's consideration he draped a blanket around his shoulders, which more or less concealed it, and which he felt he could plausibly claim to have donned as protection from the chill night air.

In the event he need hardly have bothered; the few people he met
in the passageways leading to the outside were busy with concerns of
their own, and hardly gave him a glance as he passed by. Before long
he was standing on the slope leading up to the top of the quarry, and
glancing round to get his bearings. Everything seemed much the same
as it had the night before: the vast hole of the quarry falling away into
the darkness, the stars tinting everything with their faint blue radiance,
and the campfires of the elven garrison delineating the lip of the cliff
edge with their flickering orange glow.

Drago glanced up the slope. Sure enough, a darker patch of shadow
clung to the rock face, more or less where he'd been standing the night
before listening to Graymane castigate Oaktwig and his subordinates.
To any elves peering over the edge it would have been invisible, but to
Drago's gnomish night vision the silhouette of a cloaked elf stood out
clearly against the wall of stone.

"You're late," Graymane greeted him, and Drago shook his head,
forgetting for a moment that the elf probably couldn't see the gesture.

"You were early," he countered, and Graymane's mouth twitched
in a momentary smile he probably didn't realize was visible to the
gnome.

"I often am," he said evenly. "I don't like surprises." He paused for
a moment, to let his words sink in. "You were a surprise."

"So were you." Drago had decided to be as honest as he needed to
be, but that didn't mean he had to tell Graymane everything at once,
or even at all. "You're here to look for Gorash's people, right?"

Graymane nodded. "You heard as much last night. What are you
doing here?"

"I'm a bounty hunter from Fairhaven," Drago said. "An elf who
said he was working for your king hired me to find and kill Gorash."
Which was entirely true: no need to mention the qualms he still felt
about killing in cold blood, and the doubts he still harbored about his
ability to do so.

"Then we have a problem," Graymane said evenly. "What you
heard me telling Oaktwig was only partially true. My orders are to find
the traitor, have them lead me to Gorash, and kill him. I can hardly do
that if you've got to him first."

"I could say the same," Drago pointed out, in a reasonable tone,
which he hoped would be enough to mask the sudden surge of relief

he felt. If Graymane carried out the assassination his conscience would remain clear, and he'd still get the bandit chief's killers off his back. True, he wouldn't get the balance of his fee from Greenleaf, but that seemed a very minor consideration under the circumstances.

"You could," Graymane agreed. His hand was hovering close to his sword, but his posture was still relaxed, showing no inclination to draw it. If he did, of course, the advantage in the dark would be entirely with Drago, so the gnome kept his own hand away from his hilt as well. There was no telling how much Graymane could actually make out in the stars' weak glimmer, and he didn't want to make any moves that could be mistaken for threatening. "So what do you propose?"

"We work together," Drago said. "Pool information, find Gorash. Split the bounty between us."

"That might work," Graymane said, in a tone which clearly indicated that he didn't think it would, "except for one minor detail. I'm not after a bounty."

"Oh," Drago said, as a verbal placeholder, while he tried to think of something else to say that wouldn't seem trite or obvious. Then he decided he might as well be, under the circumstances. "What are you after him for, then?"

"I swore an oath," Graymane said, as matter-of-factly as if he was commenting on the weather, "to avenge the murder of my queen, on her brother's behalf. And I can't let anyone stand in the way of that."

"No, I suppose you can't," Drago said. He'd never had much use for oaths himself, preferring hard cash as a motivator, but in his experience the people who did took them very seriously. Particularly elves, for some reason. "Fine, then, when we catch up with him, you do the honors. I'll watch your back and keep the fleas off. Should be enough bounty on some of his followers to make it worth my while."

"There should indeed," Graymane agreed, after a moment's consideration. Then he stuck out his hand. "We're agreed, then. I kill Gorash, anyone standing between us is yours."

"Sounds good to me," Drago agreed, shaking the proffered hand. He hesitated a moment. "So what's our next move?" Despite cooperating with the Fairhaven City Watch from time to time, he'd never gone into an equal partnership with a fellow bounty hunter before, and wasn't quite sure how their collaboration was supposed to work. Although technically, as Graymane wasn't in it for the money, he supposed he wasn't really a bounty hunter either. "I've never worked with a partner before."

"Neither have I," Graymane admitted. "So I guess we'll just have to make it up as we go along."

Drago thought for a moment. "I suppose this informant you're looking for will be the key," he said. "Find them, and hope they'll lead us to Gorash." He hesitated. "I don't suppose you know who it is yet?"

"I'm narrowing it down," Graymane said, in a tone which clearly meant *not even close*. "But if they hold their nerve, it could be a long time before they reveal themselves. They're hardly going to contact the bandits about a supply convoy knowing I'm watching. Why take the risk?"

"Because they have some information that can't wait," Drago said, with a distinct sensation of *déjà vu*; it had been offering to act as bait which had got him into this mess in the first place. Ironic if it was the key to getting him out of it too. "Like the fact that a bounty hunter's arrived in camp, on his way to take out Gorash. His people in Fairhaven must have sent word they've lost track of me by now, and that's probably got them rattled. If his spy here picks up my trail, they just might break cover to warn him."

"It's possible," Graymane conceded. "But they might just decide to kill you instead, without waiting for orders."

Drago shrugged. "In which case I'll try not to kill them in self-defense." Which hadn't worked out so well in Fairhaven, but he didn't see any reason to mention that. "Then we can have a little chat with whoever it is."

Graymane was nodding thoughtfully, clearly liking the idea. "It's your neck," he said at last. "I'll pretend to let it slip in front of Oaktwig that I've found out there's a bounty hunter in the camp, but without any identifying details. If I ask him to keep it to himself, every elf in the garrison should know about it by nightfall." He turned away, heading back up the slope, then turned back, apparently struck by an afterthought. "Same time tomorrow."

"Right," Drago said, beginning to wonder if he was ever going to get enough sleep on this assignment.

The next day was a repeat of the previous one, even down to Clovis waking him far earlier than he would have liked. To his pleasant surprise, the work seemed a little easier today; the barrow went where he wanted to push it more frequently and seemed to fill faster, the rocks shattered under his pick with less effort and into more uniform lumps, and Della was always there with a joke or a pleasantry when he started to flag.

By the time the evening rolled around and he started back up the slope leading to the burrow, Drago had been concentrating on the job for so long, and with such fixity of purpose, that he'd almost forgotten about his conversation with Graymane the night before. Only when Della and Clovis joined him in the mess hall did his mind return to the real reason he was here, and the prompting for that was distinctly unwelcome.

"It's you, isn't it?" Della said, taking the next space on the bench, while Clovis squeezed in on his other side. Both dropped bowls of stew on the tabletop next to Drago's, which was already almost half finished. As before, the day-long physical exertion had left him ravenous.

"What is?" Drago asked, around a mouthful of turnip.

"This bounty hunter the lofties keep going on about. You must have heard them while you were doing the tip run."

Drago nodded, keeping his face expressionless, and swallowed enough to regain the power of speech. "Sounded to me like they thought it was another elf," he said neutrally.

Della emitted a derisive grunt around her mouthful of food. "Of course they did," she said, once the greater part of it was safely on its way toward her stomach. "It wouldn't occur to them that it might be one of us. But we've seen you fight."

"We have," Clovis agreed, "and you fight a lot better than you dig. If you were really looking for money you could easily have joined the city watch, or got a job as a bodyguard back in Fairhaven."

"Not for the kind of money I'm earning here," Drago said reasonably, wondering how Raegan and Waggoner would have reacted to the implied suggestion that their wages were overly lavish. With amusement, he strongly suspected, not unlaced with profanity.

"If you're going after Gorash, you'll earn every penny," Della said. "They say he's the finest swordsman for thirty leagues."

"You can't believe everything you hear in the ballads," Clovis demurred. Then he shrugged. "But he's definitely well hard. You don't get to lead a pack of bandits by being the best flower arranger."

Drago nodded. "I don't suppose you do," he said, although in his rather more extensive experience of criminal gangs, physical strength and fighting ability weren't necessarily the most important qualities for rising to the top. He'd often found the most effective leaders had been the ones with the wit and charisma to persuade other people to fight their battles for them.

Nevertheless, the conversation had unnerved him, and he retreated to his room as quickly as he could without making it obvious that he didn't want his friends' company. Even the dice game seemed a little less tempting than it had the previous evening, as he found himself wondering if the players were glancing speculatively in his direction.

"Think I'll get an early night," he said, to Della's evident disappointment. "See if I can get up before you two tomorrow."

"That'll be the day," Clovis said.

Sleep, of course, was the last thing on Drago's mind, and he loitered in his room obsessively checking his weapons until it was time to go and meet Graymane. That had been his intention, at least; in practice he found the waiting so onerous that he left as soon as the burrow grew quiet, hurrying through the almost deserted tunnels toward the open air. This time he hadn't bothered with the blanket, and the few gnomes he met glanced at his sword with open curiosity, followed almost at once by carefully composed indifference.

Stepping out into the chill of the night brought him back to himself, a faint tingle of renewed alertness that he knew well. He'd felt like this setting out in pursuit of a felon, or on an errand for the Tradesman's Association. He scanned his surroundings from force of habit, looking for anything out of the ordinary, and caught a flash of movement on the floor of the quarry.

For a moment he thought nothing of it, then the full implications of what he was seeing caught up with him. The figure was too large to be a gnome, but wasn't carrying a light, picking its way slowly and cautiously across the treacherous surface by the faint illumination offered by the stars overhead. Clearly whoever it was didn't want to be seen, and if he hadn't felt so restless, would probably have got away without being spotted at all.

"Graymane!" he called, in the loudest undertone he felt he could risk, sprinting up the slope toward the rendezvous point. As he'd hoped, the elf was already there, evidently not having exaggerated the night before about his habit of arriving early for meetings.

"What is it?" To his relief, Graymane didn't waste any time with unnecessary greetings or questions, his head turning in the direction of the sound of Drago's approach long before he could have made him out visually as anything other than a faint clump of deeper darkness.

"Someone's down in the quarry. Looks like an elf, but they're not carrying a light. Could be our spy."

"More than likely," Graymane agreed. He reached down and took hold of Drago's arm. "You'll have to guide me. If we show a light we'll tip our hand. Do you think you can catch up with whoever it is?"

"I think so," Drago agreed, with another glance down at the slowly moving figure in the distance. It seemed to be heading for the other side of the quarry, with a fixity of purpose undiminished by the arduous task of having to make its way across a litter of potentially ankle-turning detritus. Being able to see clearly in the dim light of the stars would allow him to make much faster progress. By the time whoever it was reached the distant rock face, he should be hard on their heels. He glanced at Graymane, as another thought occurred to him. "If you can keep up with me."

"I'll have to," Graymane replied, with what Drago hoped wouldn't turn out to be misplaced confidence.

"Come on then." He moved away as quickly as he dared, allowing Graymane to retain the light contact with his upper arm. "Try to stay away from the edge."

"Don't worry." The elf smiled, in what was probably intended to be a reassuring manner. "If I go over, so do you."

In the event, neither had to worry about taking a fatal shortcut to the quarry floor. Drago kept them well over to the rock-face side of the terraces and connecting ramps, and Graymane, despite being effectively blind, kept up with him easily on the relatively smooth surfaces. Only gradually did it begin to dawn on Drago that the elf trusted him, at least to some extent.

"Watch your step from here," Drago warned, as they reached the quarry floor, and began to make their way over the rougher, rubble-strewn surface. "It's going to get a lot harder."

He was right. Despite his best efforts to guide Graymane through the easiest going, his companion stumbled frequently, with a constant muffled clattering of displaced stones. To Drago's impressed surprise, though, the elf remained silent, despite what must have been a powerful urge to relieve his feelings verbally, although his lips moved on occasion with what looked like a selection of oaths which would have made a stevedore blush.

"Are we making too much noise?" Graymane asked at last, *sotto voce*, although nearly all the noise had been his, Drago being able to pick his way around the worst of the detritus in comparative silence.

Drago shook his head, then, unsure of whether the elf had been able to see the gesture in the darkness with his gaze fixed unrelentingly on his feet, added "I don't think so. They'll be making so much noise themselves they'll drown out anything we can do."

"Good." Graymane struggled on for a few more paces. "Are we catching up?"

"We are." The distant figure was almost at the rock face by now, although Drago couldn't imagine what they were hoping to find there. For a moment it crossed his mind that they were about to interrupt nothing more sinister than a romantic assignation, but that hardly seemed likely; there were plenty of more accessible venues for that sort of thing a lot closer to the main camp. "Do you want to challenge them?"

"No. Let's wait and see what's going on. They might be out here to meet someone."

"They're a he," Drago reported a few moments later, as the object of their interest paused by a particularly large boulder to relieve himself.

"Well, that narrows it down to about three quarters of the garrison," Graymane muttered, less happy with the news than Drago had expected. Reminded unexpectedly of Sergeant Waggoner, Drago strongly suspected that a prime suspect had just been eliminated.

"You were expecting a woman?" he asked.

Graymane shrugged, momentarily dislodging his hand from Drago's bicep. "Hoping, really. It's a much smaller group to whittle down. Besides, they're more fun to interrogate."

Drago found himself drawing away a little, and reminded himself that he didn't have to like the elf to work with him. Graymane must have felt him flinch, because he renewed the contact with something approaching diffidence. "Yes, I know, I'm a sick bastard. But I get the job done. Are you good with that, or do we go our own ways now?"

"Not good, exactly," Drago said, remembering his resolution to be as truthful with Graymane as seemed expedient, "but not bad enough to forget our agreement." After all, the elf thought he was willing to commit murder for money, so he could hardly come across as too squeamish. "So long as I can rely on you to focus on the job, and nothing else. Besides, we shook on it, remember?"

"And that matters to you?" Graymane asked, seeming faintly surprised.

"Why wouldn't it?" Drago asked. "Go back on your word in my business, and see how many clients you get."

"Fair point," Graymane said. "That hadn't occurred to me."

"Then perhaps it should have," Drago said, a little more curtly than he'd intended.

"Perhaps it should," Graymane conceded, and they went on in silence, both faintly relieved at the narrowing distance between them and the suspect which afforded them an excuse not to engage in any further conversation.

The shadowy figure had reached the far wall of the quarry by now, and began to move along it, hunching over to peer intently at the rock face in the enveloping darkness.

"He's looking for something," Drago murmured, pitching his voice so low it would barely carry to Graymane's ears, let alone the elf in the distance. "Can't tell what yet." Then, to his surprise, the unwitting fugitive reached up, grasped a protruding rock, placed a foot on a lower outcrop, and boosted himself up. "Bugger me! He's climbing!"

"Not to the top, surely?" Graymane whispered back, his tone incredulous. Scrambling all the way up the rock face would be incredibly dangerous even in daylight; in the dark it would be tantamount to suicide.

"Don't think so." The distant figure had scrambled onto a ledge, about eight feet from the ground, and begun walking again, rising steeply away from the quarry floor. "There's a path up there—or an easier route, at any rate."

"Then get after him," Graymane said, coming rapidly to the same conclusion that Drago had just reached. "You can see what you're doing, and I'll only hold you back. I'll follow on as quickly as I can."

"Right." Leaving the elf to make his way to the cliff face as best he could, Drago sprinted for the spot where the suspect had started to climb. Glancing up, he felt a momentary pang of alarm; the cloaked figure seemed to have vanished completely. Knowing that simply wasn't possible, he quelled his unease as best he could, and scanned the towering crag, beginning to breathe again as he noticed a flicker of movement near a cleft in the rock. The path, if such it was, must have disappeared into it, taking both the track and anyone traversing it out of sight of the ground almost at once.

The hand and footholds used by the skulking elf were, of course, out of his reach. He glanced round for alternatives, and failed to find any, settling instead for scrambling up onto the outcrop the suspect had used to stand on, and reaching up for the protruding rock above his head. He couldn't quite reach, and jumping was out of the question—if he missed, he'd probably break his leg, and if by some miracle he didn't, he'd just end up dangling by his hands and looking foolish.

"Need a boost?" Graymane asked, catching up with him, and Drago nodded, forgetting once again that the elf was unlikely to catch the gesture in the dark.

"What do you think?" he rejoined without heat, and stepped into the proffered stirrup of the elf's linked fingers.

Graymane was stronger than he looked. With one smooth motion of his arms, Drago's boot was level with his face, and the gnome was able to scramble onto the ledge above him. He reached down. "Need a hand?"

"You haven't got time," Graymane said, accurately enough. "If you lose him now we're right back where we started." He waited while Drago scrambled to his feet. "I'll catch you up."

"Right," Drago said, and began to trot along the path, already wondering how soon and how much he was going to regret this development.

CHAPTER TWENTY-EIGHT
"Neither did I."

The ledge turned out to be broad, sloping steeply upward, and Drago made good time along it, moving as lightly as he could, fearful of betraying his presence by any extraneous sound. Every now and then he paused, listening for the clatter of boot against stone, but heard nothing, either from the elf he pursued, or the one he fervently hoped would be feeling his way carefully along the ledge in the dark behind him by now. He'd lost sight of the quarry almost as soon as he'd turned into the cleft he'd noticed from the ground below, merely catching intermittent glimpses of the garrison fires far in the distance whenever the twists and turns he followed left a little clear space in the right direction. Every time he saw the faint orange glow it seemed to be less high above him, until finally the narrow track emerged onto level ground, where coarse grass clung grimly to the fringes of the narrow line of clear earth he now followed.

Glancing back, he saw that the distant fires were now on the same level as he was, apparently floating in mid-air. Any passing traveler unblessed with gnomish night vision could be readily forgiven for thinking nothing stood between his current vantage point and the apparently welcoming lights of the camp, and he found himself wondering how many unfortunates had plunged into the depths over the years, believing themselves mere minutes from a warm bed and a hearty supper.

Few, if any, his logical mind butted in. The Barrens weren't the sort of place people travelled on a whim, and anybody local would know the topography around here in intimate detail. The elf he pursued, who'd come into sight again as soon as they were back on the same level, certainly did. His hesitant progress across the quarry floor had changed into a rapid and confident stride as soon as he was on the path, despite being just as effectively blind as he had been before. Proof, if Drago needed it, that whoever he was following had been in regular contact for a long time with whoever he was on his way to meet.

Fearful of losing his quarry, he speeded up a little, keeping the mysterious elf in sight, a task which was beginning to become more difficult as the grassland gave way to denser undergrowth. A little farther ahead, the path disappeared into a belt of scrubby woodland, winding its way through the trees and the undergrowth between them, which he supposed wasn't altogether a bad thing; the going remained easy, he'd be able to find his way back to the mining camp without too much trouble, and Graymane, if he ever caught up, was unlikely to get lost either. Assuming he didn't blunder off the path in the dark and get tangled up in the undergrowth, of course, although Drago suspected that would be highly unlikely. Graymane struck him as the kind of person who'd had a lot of practice at sneaking around without getting caught.

As had Drago, of course, although his area of expertise was city streets, and, on occasion, other peoples' premises. Trying to move stealthily through woodlands was an entirely novel experience, and one he hoped he'd get the hang of in a hurry. Fallen leaves kept rustling under his feet, and the occasional twig snapped as he trod on it. Fortunately the elf he followed was still making enough noise of his own to mask that of his pursuer.

A faint odor of woodsmoke drifted into his nostrils, and he slowed down, warily. That could mean his quarry was nearing his destination. Either that, or there were charcoal burners active in the woods; the fuel for the furnaces used to cast the gold ingots must come from somewhere, after all.

No sooner had that thought occurred to him than he dismissed it, catching a glimpse of orange flame through the trees, an unmistakable campfire. Spotting it, the suspect picked up his pace even more, presumably in response to being able to see a little better, although it didn't make that much difference to Drago. Being careful to avoid the circle of firelight himself, the bounty hunter edged a little closer, drawn in by a murmur of voices.

"I didn't think you were coming tonight," a burly goblin said, glancing up from throwing another handful of sticks on the fire, the flickering flames striking highlights from his tusks. He was accompanied by three others, dressed like the goblins who'd attacked the convoy from the wharf, although Drago didn't recognize any of them. Not that he'd really noticed anyone apart from the three he'd fought, of course.

"Neither did I." Oaktwig strode into the illuminated circle, approached the fire, and crouched next to the goblin to warm his hands. "But this won't wait. The usurper's sent one of his attack dogs to sniff around. It seems it's finally dawned on him you're getting information from someone inside the camp." He seemed a lot less pompous and ineffectual than he had the previous night, Drago thought, although which persona was play acting, designed to hide his real motives, was difficult to tell. Perhaps they both were. One thing he'd learned early in his profession was that very few people were really all that they seemed.

"Then you shouldn't have taken the risk," one of the others said.

Oaktwig shrugged. "I'll be back before he even notices I'm gone, standing on my dignity and bleating about protocol after making him wait to talk to me. One thing I'll say for the troll shagger, he's fun to wind up."

The burly goblin stood, Oaktwig matching the movement, and shook his head dubiously. "Don't underestimate him. What's so important it couldn't wait?" He paused for a moment, mulling over his own words. "Apart from the fact that he's here, of course."

"He's dug something up already, or thinks he has. The usurper's agents in Fairhaven have been hiring bounty hunters to go after Gorash."

"We know." The goblin nodded. "We've got people there too. Who got to them first."

"Most of them," Oaktwig said. "One managed to give them the slip, got on a riverboat, and made it as far as the mine. If he's that resourceful and persistent, you should let Gorash know before he pays him a visit."

The goblins laughed, their leader the heartiest of all. "I don't think he's got that much to worry about. But I'll tell him what you said."

"Good." Oaktwig turned away, his eyes already on the path leading back to the quarry. "I'll keep my head down for a few days, and see what happens. Anything urgent I'll pass on as soon as I can."

"If you don't get caught," the burly goblin cautioned. "But we'll leave someone here just in case." The expressions on the faces surrounding him were ample evidence of just how much none of the other goblins wanted to be the one left behind in the woods on the off chance of receiving a message several days later.

"I won't be," Oaktwig assured the leader, blissfully unaware that Graymane was presumably still toiling up the path behind him, and that they were almost bound to meet head on.

Drago hesitated. If he followed the elf back he could assist Graymane in Oaktwig's apprehension, and presumably force the location of the bandits' camp out of him somehow. But that would take time. On the other hand, if he followed the bandits, who were now, with one sulky exception, preparing for departure, he'd find the camp for himself before the night was over. All he'd have to do then would be to sneak back to the mine undetected, and tell Graymane where to find it. After that they could raid it at their leisure, preferably with a goodly number of elven soldiers to keep the bandits occupied while Graymane fulfilled his oath, and Drago examined the bandit chief's dwelling for any readily portable valuables in lieu of the second installment of his payment from Greenleaf.

That, on balance, seemed the better option, offering the greatest possibility of success in the shortest possible time. If he was careful, there would be little or no risk, especially as he could see the goblins and they couldn't see him.

Then Oaktwig's foot brushed against a clump of fallen leaves, kicking them into the fire. They were tinder dry, and roared up, flickering brightly.

"Look! You were followed!" the burly goblin yelled, and Drago glanced reflexively at the pathway, expecting to see Graymane stumbling into an ambush. Only when he saw nothing there did he realize the goblin was pointing directly at him.

"Shag it!" Drago was moving even as the involuntary oath left his mouth, his hand going instinctively to the sword at his waist, although he hadn't the slightest intention of standing and fighting against so many. Turning on his heel, he plunged into the tangle of undergrowth surrounding the clearing, trusting to his smaller stature and ability to see in the dark to help him evade pursuit.

"Where did he go?" Oaktwig demanded, his own blade hissing from its scabbard. The goblins were turning their heads this way and that, hoping to catch a glimpse of him Drago supposed, although he didn't think they stood much of a chance so close to the fire; the light it threw out would merely intensify the surrounding darkness, making his cover even harder to penetrate.

"Over there," the burly goblin said, pointing almost exactly at Drago's position, and the gnome realized he'd badly underestimated the competence of his opposition. These bandits were as much at home in the woods as Drago was in the avenues and alleyways of the Wharfside district, and were perfectly able to track him by the noise he was making. Throwing himself flat he crawled under the low-hanging branches of a thicket of some shrub he didn't recognize, but the leaves of which were inordinately prickly, and emerged a moment later on the other side of a barrier he was fairly certain the larger beings would be unable to penetrate.

Rolling from beneath the bushes onto a patch of soft, rich leaf mould which muffled the sound of his movements, he stood cautiously, stilling his breathing as much as he could, and froze, looking back at the flickering fire. The silhouettes of Oaktwig and the goblins stood out clearly against the fluctuating light, blurring as they passed behind the intervening vegetation.

"I can't hear him," Oaktwig said, what Drago could see of his posture conveying the impression of listening intently.

One of the goblins shook her head. "Me neither."

Drago began to move away, placing each foot carefully on the cushioning loam, wary of treading on anything which looked as though it might snap and betray his position. Following the bandits when they left wasn't looking like such a good option anymore; they were bound to be wary from now on, alert to any suspicious sounds behind them, and would probably leave a rear guard in ambush in case he tried. That was what he'd do in their boots, anyway. Better to stick with his first idea, follow Oaktwig instead, and help Graymane apprehend him. If he hadn't fallen off the ledge trying to climb out of the quarry in the dark . . .

"We won't have to," the burly goblin said, taking something from his pocket, and Drago felt a sudden chill of apprehension. Gorash's agents in Fairhaven had used magic, as he remembered only too well; it shouldn't have come as that much of a surprise that his other followers had access to it too. "He must be around here somewhere." He threw the small object in his hand in roughly the right direction, presumably toward the last place he'd heard Drago moving.

After his encounter with the filth golem, Drago wasn't about to hang around and see what this spell was supposed to do; especially as the air was suddenly filled with the rustling of foliage. With one last glance back, he began to run, heedless of the noise he was making—which was probably being drowned out by now anyway. Suddenly the campfire was no longer visible, the thicket he'd crawled through denser and larger, the branches growing longer and thicker before his startled and horrified gaze.

Drago jinked sideways, making for a gap between the trees, but suddenly it was no longer there, fresh brambles shooting up from nowhere to fill the gap. As he turned aside they lashed out in his direction, snagging for a moment on the sleeve of his jacket before ripping free.

Writhing roots burst from the ground, entangling his feet, and he cut at them with his sword, heedless of the damage he was doing to the edge of his blade in the process. Right now, that seemed to be the least of his worries. He tore his boots free, but a low-lying tree branch whipped out, entangling his sword arm; before he could free it, another was round his throat. Reaching up with his free hand he tore frantically at the encircling wood, feeling the noose tighten in spite of his best efforts; then a bunch of flexible twigs seized his wrist, the scratchy bark feeling like the grasp of skeletal fingers against his skin. Darkness fell across his eyes, sparks flaring as his straining lungs gasped for non-existent air, the wooden noose biting into his carotid artery.

Then the darkness and the sparks were all there were, until even they faded into nothing.

CHAPTER TWENTY-NINE
"Just got someone to finish."

Drago's first surprise on coming round was that he didn't seem to be dead. The second was that he was lying on something soft, which gave slightly under him, and the third was that he managed not to throw up, despite the nausea and the pounding headache which all but overwhelmed him the moment the first surprise had kicked in.

"Take your time," a voice said, with what sounded like genuine solicitude, and Drago opened his eyes; he'd stirred without thinking as he began to regain consciousness, and cursed himself silently for forfeiting the chance to counterfeit oblivion while he got the measure of his surroundings. "Don't try to sit up too fast—told you so."

Overwhelmed by a sudden surge of nausea as he tried to push himself upright, Drago slumped back on what turned out to be a large, well-stuffed cushion. It was embroidered in an elaborate pattern which did nothing for the rippling lights which exploded across his vision in response to his attempt to move, and his pounding headache. Rolling over, he sat up a little more cautiously, and raised a hand to massage his neck, which, unsurprisingly, was uncomfortably stiff.

"Perhaps you should drink something." The speaker turned out to be a goblin, sitting in a folding camp chair, looking down at Drago with an expression of affable curiosity on his face. An expression Drago was far too wary to trust.

"Perhaps I should." His own voice surprised him, emerging in a husky croak, and he swallowed, finding his throat dry and sore, as if he was just getting over a severe cold. His sword was gone, of course, he'd known that instantly from the angle he'd been lying at when he woke. Had he dropped it when he lost consciousness? Probably, but the scabbard was missing too. He fought down the impulse to check his boot; somehow he doubted that the bandits would have missed the dagger hidden in it, but on the remote chance that they had, he wasn't about to reveal its presence.

"Then by all means, help yourself." The goblin indicated a folding table next to his chair, which seemed well stocked with food and drink.

Despite the aftereffects of being choked, which still lingered, Drago began to feel hungry again, which he supposed was a good sign. After a moment of struggling against the cushion, which seemed determined to suck him back down again like the mud exposed at low tide in the Geltwash estuary, he found his feet, with a little less difficulty than he pretended. He still didn't know who this goblin was, and why he was being so polite to someone he must have every reason to believe was there to assassinate his boss, but sooner or later he was probably going to have to fight his way out of here. If it turned out to be sooner, then it certainly wouldn't hurt to seem less able than he was.

Swaying a little on his feet, Drago took the opportunity to get a good look at his surroundings. As he'd surmised, he was in a tent, a large one; possibly even the murdered queen's royal pavilion, judging by the quality of the hangings, and the oak tree motif common to most of them. It was hard to judge the full size of it, as the sleeping area had been curtained off, leaving the living area they were now in all that he could see. Rugs covered the floor, but he could see grass beyond the open tent flap, and what looked like a surprisingly large camp; two or three tents were partially visible through the narrow gap, along with a couple of campfires. If the shadows they cast were anything to go by, the tent flap was flanked by guards, a guess confirmed a moment or two later by glimpses of mailed elbows.

Drago tried to extrapolate the full size of the camp from the tiny portion of it he could see, then gave it up as a bad job; there was still too much he didn't know, although if the line of trees he could see beyond the tents was anything to go by it was still somewhere in the woods, probably a clearing.

The food and drink, however, were definitely present, and he walked over to the table, careful to keep out of reach of any sudden moves by his enigmatic host. A second chair was already pulled up to it, into which he clambered, finding a second place setting already prepared opposite the goblin. Despite the real sense of menace he felt in this situation, the theatricality of that made him smile. This was someone who enjoyed playing mind games, which hinted at a sense of superiority, and an exaggerated opinion of their own cleverness. Someone, in other words, who could be outwitted a great deal more easily than they supposed.

"You shouldn't have gone to all this trouble," he said, reaching out to a flagon of wine which, from the sheen and the heft of it, was probably made of silver; the eyes and tongue of the dragon engraved on it were finely cut rubies. He poured a generous measure into a matching goblet, and swallowed appreciatively, his voice returning to something like normal. He'd never tasted anything like it; even the contents of Lady Selina's flask had been little better than dockside tavern dregs by comparison.

"It was no trouble," the goblin said, with evident amusement. He indicated the food. "Help yourself. I'm sure this evening's exertions have left you a little on the hungry side."

"They have." Drago contemplated a plateful of roast pigeons, transferred one to the platter in front of him, and began to dismember it. He tried to match his host's insouciant manner of speaking, hoping it didn't sound too forced. "I have to admit, I'm rather surprised to be here."

"Not half as surprised as we were," the goblin assured him. "But under the circumstances, Nug thought it would be better not to kill you once the trees had you under control. At least until after we've had a little chat, and decided what's best to be done."

Drago noted the implied threat, as he was supposed to do, and nodded politely, pretending to have missed it. "Nug?" he enquired. "I don't think we've met."

"Well, you certainly haven't been introduced," his host conceded. "Nug was in charge of the detachment you came across in the woods." Drago nodded again, picturing the burly goblin who'd conducted most of the business with Oaktwig. "Luckily he had a charm on him, or we might never have found you again." He poured himself a drink, and sipped at it, his eyes never leaving the gnome.

"I should have expected it," Drago said, around a mouthful of avian flesh. He swallowed, and continued a little more clearly. "Your people in Fairhaven were very fond of throwing spells around."

The goblin nodded. "Magic has its uses. If you don't get too reliant on it." He sipped his wine again. "From which, I take it, you're the one that got away."

"I am." Drago nodded too. "Drago Appleroot, at your service." He wasn't quite sure what "at your service" was supposed to mean, but it was one of the things people said to one another when formally introduced, and he thought it would be the right thing to say under the circumstances. Anything that helped this goblin fop believe he was buying his charade of good manners would work for him.

"And you know who I am, of course." The goblin chuckled quietly, as if sharing a private little joke he thought Drago was already in on. "If you'll pardon my bluntness, I really am most curious. Just how were you intending to kill me?"

"Kill you?" for the first time since he'd woken up, Drago felt his head spinning from something other than the aftereffects of being choked into unconsciousness. "You mean you're Gorash?"

The goblin stared at the gnome for a moment, while it dawned on him that Drago's astonishment was genuine, then burst out laughing so hard that one of the guards stuck his head round the tent flap to make sure everything was all right. Gorash waved him away.

"I've always thought I was. But perhaps we should ask my wife when she gets back, just to be on the safe side. After all the unexpected news we've been getting tonight, I wouldn't be in the least surprised to find I'm someone else entirely." He sat up straighter in his chair, directing a glance of keen intelligence at Drago. "What exactly were you expecting to find here?"

"If I'm honest?" Drago decided he might as well be. He'd misread the entire situation from the start, it seemed, even the second place at the table, and his head still felt too heavy, his thoughts too slow, to keep track of any attempts at misdirection. "Someone I could talk to."

"About what?" Clearly, whatever answer Gorash had been expecting, this wasn't it.

"Getting your people off my back. I turned Stargleam's offer down flat, but they didn't believe it, and kept coming after me anyway. I'm a bounty hunter, not an assassin. I've only ever killed in self-defense, and that's not a line I'm willing to cross unless I'm forced to."

"I see." Gorash looked thoughtful. "And what would force you to?"

"Saving my own neck," Drago said. "If you didn't call them off, then that would be self-defense in a way. Don't you think?"

"I think the legal profession or the priesthood has taken a bigger loss than either of them will ever know," Gorash said, an unmistakable glint of amusement kindling in his eyes. "But I take your point. I'll send word back to Fairhaven to leave you alone in future."

"Just like that?" Drago asked, completely wrong-footed. Somehow he'd expected things to be a lot more complicated.

"Just like that," Gorash assured him. He paused for a moment, in a manner Drago found far from reassuring. "Of course, you could do me a little favor in return."

"Could I?" Drago asked, not giving away any more than he could help.

Gorash nodded again. "You have the run of the mining camp, and you know your way here now. Or, at least from there to the meeting point Oaktwig uses to pass on information. It'll be dangerous for him to make contact, with this spy the usurper's sent sniffing around the place, but you could run messages for him instead without anyone even noticing. What do you say?"

"That sounds reasonable," Drago temporized. Graymane, he was sure, wasn't about to give up attempting to fulfill his oath, and wouldn't take kindly to his ally switching sides. If he ever found out, of course. Drago didn't have to tell him; but the elf seemed very good at what he did, and would probably work it out for himself given enough time. And if he did, would be in even less of a forgiving mood. On the other hand, he'd given his word to help Graymane achieve his objective; but if the elf assassinated Gorash now, before he'd dispatched his message to Fairhaven, he couldn't be entirely sure that the bandit's followers wouldn't be after him for revenge. After all, he'd really only been hoping that killing Gorash if he couldn't find any other way would be enough to dissuade his agents, but now he'd met the goblin in person, he could see how charismatic a leader he was: he definitely seemed the sort someone would want to avenge, rather than taking advantage of the resulting power vacuum like an ordinary bandit's lackeys would.

Then matters moved out of his hands entirely. The curtains dividing the tent twitched, and a stealthy figure slipped out between them. Graymane crept toward the table, signaling for silence as his eyes met Drago's.

"Splendid." Gorash nodded affably, and took another mouthful of wine. "If you've had enough to eat, we'd better get you back. It'll be sunrise soon, and we don't want anyone to miss you."

"I guess not," Drago said, his sluggish mind still trying to wrap itself around this latest unexpected development. The incongruous thought occurred to him that his shift in the mine today would be even more grueling after the excitement of the night, and an almost complete lack of sleep. As casually as he could, he dropped his hand to his boot, not entirely sure what having a knife in his hand would accomplish at this point, other than providing some reassurance, or even which of the two people facing him he'd be prepared to use it on. But, as he'd expected, his fingertips brushed against an empty sheath, taking the decision out of his hands.

"We'll let you have your weapons back when you leave, of course," Gorash said, picking up on the movement as astutely as Drago had suspected he would. Graymane nodded, apparently taking Drago's search for a blade as an attempt to divert his prey's attention, and took another stealthy step toward the oblivious goblin. A knife was in his hand, held ready to slit the bandit's throat; another pace and he'd be ready to strike.

Drago just couldn't let him. Whatever Gorash's crimes, he should be given a chance to answer for them; this wasn't justice as he understood it, just cold-blooded murder, no different from the one Graymane was supposedly here to avenge. He began to jump down from the chair, already knowing he would be too late to intervene by the time he got round the obstructing table.

But before his boots even hit the rug, Gorash was moving, twisting aside, and dashing the contents of his goblet into the elf's face. He must have been aware of Graymane's approach the whole time, watching it reflected in the silver surface of the drinking vessel.

Graymane flinched reflexively, blinking his eyes clear, but was too experienced to drop the dagger, turning to stab at Gorash's torso instead. But the bandit was too quick, pivoting out of the way of the thrust, seizing the elf's wrist, and pulling him off balance. Turning again, he got behind the blade and Graymane's extended arm, placed his free hand on the elf's elbow, and pushed out and down. Trapped by the momentum of his own attack, Graymane plunged to the floor; Gorash immediately went down too, his knees landing on the elf's ribcage with an audible *huff* of expelled breath. He might even have cracked a rib or two, Drago thought, but doubted that either combatant would even have noticed yet if he had, swept away as they both were on a riptide of adrenaline.

Astonishingly, Graymane had kept hold of the knife, and was attempting to twist round and use it, despite what must have been the agonizing lock Gorash was maintaining on his wrist. The goblin sighed, transferred a knee to Graymane's elbow, and shifted his now free arm to the elf's neck, applying a brutally efficient stranglehold instead.

"Wait," Drago said, as unwilling to stand by and see Gorash murder Graymane as he had been the other way around a few seconds before. "You don't have to kill him."

"No, but I want to." Gorash kept the pressure on unrelentingly. Graymane was clearly weakening, thrashing more feebly than he had been.

"He might have information you can use," Drago persisted, casting around for a weapon of some kind. If he jumped Gorash unarmed it could only end one way, probably quickly, as the guards outside responded to a shout for help. The heaviest thing he could see was the wine flagon, which was still mostly full, and he went up on tiptoes to snag it from the table as he skirted the piece of furniture.

"I'm sure he has," Gorash replied, in surprisingly reasonable tones. "And I'm sure he'd rather die than confide any of it to me. Isn't that right?" He released the pressure on Graymane's neck just enough to uncork a stream of expletives which almost scorched the rug. "Yes, I thought so." He reapplied the stranglehold, choking off the invective with a final gurgle.

With a pang of regret at having to waste so exceptional a vintage, Drago swung the flagon at Gorash's head; but before it could connect, he was thrown to the floor by a heavy blow against his back which left him sprawling.

"I'll take that," a clipped feminine voice said, snatching the flagon from his hand smoothly enough to keep most of its contents where they belonged, "before you make an unconscionable mess of my carpet."

Drago rolled onto his back, preparing to leap to his feet, and checked the motion suddenly as he became aware of the tip of a sword resting an inch above the hollow of his throat. The elven woman holding it placed the flagon delicately back on the table with her other hand, and glanced at Gorash with a hint of amusement.

"I can't leave you alone for a moment, can I?"

"Be right with you, darling." Gorash tightened his grip on Graymane's neck a little more, eliciting a rasping noise which didn't sound at all healthy. "Just got someone to finish."

The elven woman sighed, with what looked to Drago like genuinely fond exasperation. "We've talked about this, dear. We don't kill people in the tent. The stains are so hard to get out of the rugs."

"Right as always, my love." Gorash dropped what was left of Graymane, stood, looking faintly abashed, and kicked the fallen dagger across the room. Graymane stayed where he was, gasping for breath, and looking considerably the worse for wear. "But you know how annoying it is when somebody tries to assassinate you."

"Indeed." Violet eyes, framed by raven hair, stared down at Drago with evident distaste. "But you don't have to execute them yourself, you know. We have soldiers for that." She turned toward the tent flap, and raised her voice. "Boys, get in here. Couple of traitors to hang."

Immediately, the guards appeared from outside; the goblin who'd stuck his head in a few moments before, and, to Drago's surprise, another elf. Both were dressed in mail, with the oak tree motif emblazoned across their surcoats.

"Not that one." Gorash indicated Drago with a casual wave. "He only wanted to talk to me."

"He was doing a lot more than talking when I walked in," the elf woman demurred, but to Drago's relief she put up her sword anyway, returning it to the scabbard at her waist. "He was about to stove your head in with a flagon of the Kemmian Reserve."

"Then it's lucky you got back when you did," Gorash agreed. "It would have been a real shame to waste it." He poured himself a replacement for the drink he'd thrown at Graymane, and a second goblet for his wife; Drago, to his distinct lack of surprise, was pointedly excluded. When his attention returned to the gnome, he seemed considerably less affable than before. "And did you have any particular reason for doing that, or were you just lying to me about not being an assassin for hire?"

"I wasn't lying," Drago said, "but you were about to kill him. I had to do something."

"Why?" The elven woman's voice was hard with suspicion. "Were you working together?"

"Never seen this gnome before in my life," Graymane rasped, as the soldiers dragged him to his feet.

Drago shook his head. Graymane was probably about to be lynched, and there didn't seem anything he could do about that, but if he was going to survive the next few minutes himself he was going to have to be completely honest. That was the only thing he could be reasonably certain Gorash would respond to favorably, given their previous conversation. His wife, on the other hand, was a lot harder to read.

"I appreciate the gesture," he told Graymane, "but that isn't quite true." He turned back to Gorash and the elven woman. "When we found we were both looking for you we agreed to work together, although he insisted that he be the one to kill you. Something about an oath he'd sworn."

"Then the sooner he's in the ground the better," the woman said, addressing Gorash directly. "If he's taken an oath to kill you, he won't stop trying as long as he's drawing breath. You know what my people are like."

"Your people?" Graymane glared at her. "You're no Marcher. If you were, you'd strike him down in a heartbeat for murdering our queen."

"Really?" The woman looked back at him, amusement and surprise struggling for the possession of her face again. "And which queen would that be?"

"You know damn well," Graymane growled. "Ariella the Third, slain by treachery in the breach of truce. By this honorless caitiff!"

"I'm afraid you've been misinformed," the woman said dryly. "My husband is a man of his word, and has never breached the terms of a truce in his life. And the last time I looked, I was definitely not dead, despite the best efforts of my sapsucking brother."

CHAPTER THIRTY
"I always thought you'd be taller."

Drago gaped at her, feeling the ground falling out from beneath his feet for what seemed like the hundredth time since his impulsive offer to help Raegan find out who'd been targeting the bounty hunters of Fairhaven. None of the assumptions he'd started out with at the beginning of his journey seemed to be correct. Come to that, was this woman even telling the truth about being Ariella Stargleam, the missing queen?

That, at least, he could verify for himself. Ignoring Graymane's skeptical expostulations, Gorash's assurances that it was indeed so, and the would-be helpful interpolations of the two soldiers, he took out his purse. The fact that no one had taken it away from him while he was unconscious, and that it still held several of the gold coins he'd been given by Greenleaf, inclined him to believe the story; no self-respecting bandit he'd ever met would have hesitated to relieve an unconscious prisoner of everything of value they had about them. Fishing out the gold pieces the elven go-between had given him, he sorted through them rapidly.

Most bore the profile of the old king, Ariella and Lamiel's father, and the newest that of Lamiel Stargleam himself; but a couple had been struck before Ariella disappeared, and the resemblance between the portrait on the coins and the woman standing a few feet away from him was surely too striking to be merely a coincidence.

"It's true. Look." He held one of the gold pieces up where

Graymane could see it, flaring brightly as it caught the light from the candles illuminating the tent.

After glancing from the coin to the woman and back again a couple of times, Graymane nodded, and attempted to kneel, in spite of the soldiers holding him up; after a moment he simply bowed his head instead. "Your Majesty. Elerath Graymane, at your service."

"Graymane?" The name seemed to mean something to Ariella and the elven guard, who gave his prisoner a wary glance, although Gorash seemed to be as unfamiliar with his reputation as Drago was. "I always thought you'd be taller."

"A lot of people do, Your Majesty."

"Hm." Ariella nodded briskly. "Let's get one thing straight. If I decide not to hang you for attempting to murder my husband, you'll have to knock off that 'Majesty' stuff. We're not in a sodding ballroom. Are we clear?"

Graymane nodded, a trifle stiffly. "We are, yo—my lady."

Ariella sighed, and shook her head. "Nearly as bad. I've got a name, so just use it, all right? You can be as formal as you like once I'm back on the throne."

"As you wish." Graymane nodded again, even more awkwardly if possible, but didn't take her up on the offer. "And may I ask how you're planning to achieve that? You're a long way from the palace, and what I saw out there isn't much of an army."

"It'll just have to do," Ariella said. "We're gathering our strength slowly. That's why we're letting that usurping weasel think his plot worked, and I'm dead."

"The only problem with that," Drago said, "is that he isn't going to stop sending assassins after your husband. If you were really dead, that would make him the rightful king of the Marches, wouldn't it?"

"It would," Gorash agreed, glancing at him with renewed respect. "Which is why Lamiel's so desperate to see me put in the ground. So far as he knows, my claim to the throne's a lot stronger than his."

"A goblin on the throne of the Marches?" Graymane burst out laughing, so hard that he leaned into the guards holding him for additional support. "The traditionalists would have seizures at the very idea!"

"Quite," Ariella said, bitterly. "They objected strongly enough to me even opening negotiations with Gorash."

"Including your brother?" Drago asked. He was beginning to piece the whole sordid story together, but his record of accurate deduction so far wasn't all that encouraging—he wanted confirmation.

"Especially her brother," Gorash said. "He's about as traditional as an elf can get. So far as he's concerned, anyone without pointed ears is just talking livestock."

Drago thought of the Marchers he'd met on his way up the Geltwash, and nodded, recalling their arrogance and unshakable belief in their innate superiority. And those had been the ones willing to mingle with the other races; he could well believe the stay-at-homes were even worse.

"But he went along with it?" Graymane asked. The guards had let him go, at an almost imperceptible nod from the queen, and he seated himself, a little carefully, in one of the chairs. Still on the mend from a near-fatal choking himself, Drago couldn't help but sympathize.

"Of course he did. I'm the queen." Ariella smiled, without much discernible humor. "And so long as I allowed him enough money to indulge his little hobbies, he kept out of the way, and his opinions to himself. He never really wanted the throne; it's too much like hard work."

"Then why did he mount a *coup d'état*?" Drago asked, already sure of the answer.

For the first time, a faint frown of puzzlement appeared on the queen's face. "I'm not really sure. The last time we spoke, I told him the negotiations were going well, that was all."

"Very well," Gorash agreed. "To be honest I never expected them to come to anything, let alone bring me the love of my life." He smiled at his wife, in a manner which would have knocked a honey bee into a diabetic coma.

"Likewise." Ariella returned the look, with a simper the like of which Drago had last seen on the face of a besotted adolescent.

"And did you mention the, ah, personal dimension to these negotiations?" he asked.

"Of course not." Ariella shook her head emphatically. "That would have been playing right into the traditionalists' hands. They'd say I'd made too many concessions because I was thinking with my heart instead of my head."

Drago doubted that: in his experience people attributed what they saw as misjudgments of that kind to the influence of another organ entirely, although he didn't think it would be tactful to mention it.

"And your marriage?" he asked, feeling as though he was treading on conversational eggshells. "When did that take place?"

"As soon as I returned to the Barrens," Ariella said, looking even more puzzled than ever. "In the garrison temple."

"In front of the whole camp?" Graymane shook his head in disbelief. "Why didn't anyone mention it? The gossip would have spread like pox in a bawdy house." His brain suddenly caught up with his tongue, and he shot an awkward glance at the queen. "Begging your pardon, yo—Ariella. I wasn't thinking."

"No, it's a good point." She suppressed a smile, not altogether successfully. "But we married in secret. Only the priest and the witnesses knew. Then we set out for where Gorash was camped at the time, but a party of soldiers from the garrison ambushed us before we got there."

"Luckily some of my own people were on their way to meet us," Gorash added, "or it would have been all over. Her guard fought bravely, but we were outnumbered, and had already taken casualties before they turned up. Ariella was thrown from her horse in the confusion, and stunned." His voice became momentarily choked. "I thought I'd lost her."

"Luckily the traitors did too," Ariella chimed in. "They pulled back when our friends arrived, so they couldn't be sure, but Oaktwig confirmed the reports of my death as soon as he returned to the camp."

"Oaktwig was with you?" Drago digested this. "And he knew about the marriage in advance?"

"Of course he did," Ariella said, with a trace of impatience. "It's his garrison. Who did you think made the arrangements?"

Drago nodded. As soon as she'd said it, it seemed obvious.

"He seemed pretty traditional to me," Graymane said slowly, "and the traitors have left him in charge. How can you be sure he wasn't the one who set you up?"

"Because he knows where we are, and the camp hasn't been burned to the ground yet," Gorash said. "Not to mention the fact that every piece of information he's sent us has been accurate. He might not be completely comfortable with every decision she makes, but his loyalty's entirely to the crown." He grinned, with what seemed like genuine amusement. "And he's just uneasy enough about the queen being married to a goblin to pass for a traditional Marcher."

"He'll come round eventually," Ariella said, with a blithe optimism Drago found surprisingly endearing. "Everybody will."

"Let's hope so," Graymane said, in tones which betrayed just how unlikely he found the prospect.

"If the ambushers were waiting for you," Drago said, "they must have been sent before you set out. Did you leave right after the ceremony?"

Ariella shook her head. "There were still a few things to deal with. It was an hour or more before we were ready."

"Then anyone who knew could have sent them," Graymane concluded.

"No. Not anyone." A picture was starting to come together in Drago's head. "It had to have been an elf. One who knew about the marriage in advance."

"He's right." Graymane was nodding in agreement. "And someone who had the chance to talk to Lamiel. I've met him, remember, and the ballads are right; he's got no stomach for ruling, and turns every decision apart from what to order for dinner over to his ministers. Whoever it was must have accompanied you to Sylvandale, and convinced him to back their plan. Probably by promising him that with you gone, and Gorash out of the picture, all the gold would be his."

"That sounds like Lamiel," Ariella conceded. "He's always put his personal appetites ahead of the good of the kingdom."

"Then that narrows it down," Drago said. "Who went back to Sylvandale with you who knew about your plans, and had enough status to get an audience with the prince?"

Ariella and Gorash exchanged glances, and Drago wasn't in the least surprised by either of the names they uttered.

"The question is," Graymane said, after a short silence, "what you're intending to do about it." He waved a dismissive arm at the tent flap. "I've seen your army, and it's nowhere near ready to take back the Marches. You're only holding on to the Barrens because Oaktwig's feeding you enough information to outflank any attempt to wrinkle you out, and his soldiers' morale is so low they're not even trying anymore."

"I've already told you," Ariella said, a faintly icy tone creeping into her voice, "that's why we're playing the long game, building our strength up gradually."

"So gradually you'll have died of old age before they're ready to launch a counter coup," Graymane said. "And in the meantime, Lamiel's assassins will just keep coming."

"Yes, about that." Gorash regarded him thoughtfully. "Just how worried do I have to be about this oath of yours?"

"You don't." Graymane shook his head emphatically. "I swore to avenge the queen's death by killing you. As she isn't dead, there's no oath to fulfill."

"And I've got what I came for," Drago reminded him. As he spoke, he suddenly realized that it was all over. He could return home at once, and resume his life in Fairhaven, secure in the knowledge that only the usual lowlifes were trying to stab him in the back. The thought was oddly anticlimactic.

"How very reassuring." Gorash sounded anything but. He turned back to Graymane. "If our plans are so flawed, what would you suggest as an alternative?"

Graymane shrugged. "I haven't a clue. But I've been in wars before, and judging by what I've seen sneaking into your camp, you don't have the resources to win one. You've barely got enough to lose properly, instead of being massacred."

"Thank you. Most helpful." Ariella's tone effectively inverted the meaning of both phrases.

Drago hesitated. Common sense dictated, most emphatically, that he should walk out of the tent right now, and not stop until he reached the banks of the Geltwash somewhere within hailing distance of a boat heading downstream.

So it was with some surprise, not unmixed with resignation, that he heard his own voice say "I think I might have an idea."

CHAPTER THIRTY-ONE
"Not as such."

Dawn was breaking as Drago and Graymane made their way carefully down the path clinging to the cliff face, the quarry opening out beneath them in the soft gray light like a wound in the earth. No one seemed to be abroad yet; the only signs of life Drago could see were the bored and immobile sentries huddled around the doorways of the smelting and alchemical plants, and faint wisps of smoke rising from the campfires on the opposite cliff top.

Graymane shook his head ruefully. "If I could have seen where I was going last night, I would just have let you get on with it. I could have broken my neck scrambling up here."

"And saved Gorash a job," Drago joked, not entirely sure how serious the elf was.

"Not to mention the tentmaker who's having to sew up the rip you cut in the back of my home," Ariella put in, a little testily. She was following the others a pace or two behind, placing each foot carefully, even more uneasy about the precipitous drop than Graymane appeared to be; partly, Drago suspected, because the weight of the bulging satchel slung from one shoulder was affecting her balance. The hood of her cape was drawn up against the dawn chill, and whenever he glanced back, Drago found the face framed by it impossible to focus on, the image skittering from his eyes like a spun pebble bouncing from the water, leaving only a vague impression of unremarkable blandness. The queen and her husband had amassed quite a collection of spells, it seemed, finding them useful in their campaigns of guerilla warfare and espionage, and this one was supposed to obscure appearances in a slightly more subtle fashion than the shadow-weaving charms Quickfart had supplied to their agents in Fairhaven. Sometimes, it seemed, they couldn't wait until dark to embark on some piece of skullduggery.

"Sorry about that," Graymane said, with patent insincerity. "But it seemed like a good idea at the time, and the longer I was out in the open, the more likely it was that someone would spot me."

"I'm surprised the ones who caught me didn't notice you following them back," Drago said.

Graymane shook his head again, with evident amusement. "Believe me, you had their undivided attention. If they hadn't been making so much noise about it I'd just have taken out Oaktwig when he headed back, instead of hiding while he went by and going to see what was happening to you."

"I suppose I ought to feel flattered," Drago said, though in truth he felt anything but. Not for the first time, he was beginning to wonder if he'd made the right decision: he could have been on his way back to the river by now, instead of getting sucked even deeper into the quagmire of deception and duplicity in which he found himself. But he'd been lied to from the beginning of this affair, forced further out of his comfort zone than he'd ever believed possible, and his life endangered by the machinations of people to whom he and others like him were nothing more than convenient tools, to be used and discarded as it suited them. Before he went home, he intended to take control, show them in no uncertain terms that Drago Appleroot was nobody's catspaw. He turned back, addressing Ariella. "Are you sure about this? You're taking an enormous risk."

"No bigger than you are," she responded, in tones that made it clear that further discussion would not be welcome.

Drago shrugged. It had been his idea, after all, and no one had come up with a better one. Greenleaf was bound to have forwarded reports from Fairhaven, detailing his activities and the expenses incurred therein, but he didn't suppose Stargleam had read them with any attention. At least he hoped not; their lives depended on it.

They reached the floor of the quarry without incident, though

Drago had to scramble a bit more than the elves on the final drop from the end of the path, and began to pick their way through the scattering of detritus toward the ramps leading up to the garrison and the gnomish burrow nestling beneath it. As Drago had expected, a trio of people making their way across so wide an open space was hard to miss, and he began to notice figures on the cliff top glancing down at them with evident curiosity. A couple of armed and armored elves seemed to have taken up a station at the top of the ramp, observing their approach with more than casual interest. That was good: if someone in authority had placed sentries there to intercept them it would move things on nicely.

More gnomes were abroad now too, the first few to leave the burrow heading down the slope toward the mines. All of them gave Drago and his companions a curious glance as they passed in the opposite direction, but none spoke, intent on their own concerns. Until they were passing the burrows themselves, and a gnomish voice hailed them.

"Drago!" Clovis called out. Drago turned and saw his friend waving at him from the entrance to the main tunnel, the day's docky hanging from his other hand. "What's going on?"

"You're not usually up this early," Della agreed, appearing at Clovis's shoulder with a puzzled frown. "Is something wrong?"

"Where have you been?" Clovis added. "I went to get you up this morning, and your bed hadn't been slept in. We were getting worried."

"It's a long story," Drago said, with a quick glance at Ariella and Graymane, who clearly didn't have the patience for a full account. "The short version is, I'm a bounty hunter from Fairhaven, and last night I went out to take a crack at Gorash."

"You could have been killed!" Della said, looking gratifyingly horrified at the prospect.

"I nearly was. Luckily she'd got there first," Drago said, jerking a thumb at Ariella. "Caris Silverthorn. We're in the same line of work back home."

Clovis, Della, and a handful of openly eavesdropping gnomes glanced briefly at the queen, then back to Drago, who they clearly felt was of far greater interest. The glamor she'd invoked was evidently holding, although most of them probably wouldn't have recognized her if her own face was still visible anyway; the real test would come in a few minutes time, when they were talking to elves, some of whom had met Ariella before.

"You mean she killed Gorash?" Della asked, edging away from the elven woman a little despite her incredulous tone.

"As dead as the queen," Graymane said, with a straight face, and Drago nodded.

"Saw it myself," he agreed. The gathering miners looked at one another, then at Drago, still trying to take in the sudden transformation from rookie co-worker to hard-bitten gnome of action.

Clovis coughed, a little awkwardly. "Well," he said, "I'm sure you've got lots to do. And so do we. See you later. Probably."

"Yes. See you," Della said, turning away with a faintly forced air of casualness and a dismissive wave, which made it more than evident that she didn't really expect to do so.

"Count on it," Drago said, with equal sincerity, and a pang of regret which quite surprised him. He hadn't given his new friends so much as a passing thought when the idea of being able to go home had occurred to him a short while before, but now he'd seen them again he felt oddly reluctant to leave them. Della particularly. His profession didn't lend itself to lasting friendships so much as alliances of convenience with people whose company occasionally turned out to be enjoyable, as a kind of bonus, and the short time he'd spent here had given him a glimpse of a different way of interacting with people which had come as a pleasant change.

But then miners seldom had to worry about someone trying to kill them . . .

"You!" Ariella's voice brought him back to the present, and the realization that he was still a long way from being safe. She waved a peremptory hand, attracting the attention of the guards waiting at the top of the ramp. "Where's the commander of this pathetic excuse for an army?"

"You need to watch your mouth, girly." The tallest and most burly of the guards clearly didn't appreciate being addressed like that, particularly by a civilian, and even more particularly in front of an ever-growing throng of work-bound gnomes. "Or someone'll have to shut it for you."

"It's been tried," Ariella assured him, her hand drifting to the hilt of her sword. "But what do you know, I'm still talking." She began to walk up the slope toward the guard, and Drago felt his own hand drifting toward his weapon as he followed her. Graymane, too, was looking a little uneasy, and picked up his pace to walk beside her; recognizing him, the guard's demeanor became noticeably less challenging. He sketched an awkward salute.

"Begging your pardon, sir. I didn't realize she was with you."

"She isn't," Ariella snapped, "he's with me. Take us to your boss."

The guard looked at Graymane, who nodded a brusque confirmation.

"That's more or less the case. Tell Oaktwig we need to see him now. This won't wait."

"Of course." The guard glanced from elf to elf, clearly trying to work out which one he should be most wary of. Graymane he already knew wasn't to be trifled with, and although Ariella was an unknown quantity, the fact that she obviously had Graymane's tacit support was inclining him toward caution. Drago, to his complete lack of surprise, wasn't even registering as a potential threat. "This way." He turned, and began to lead the way into the heart of the encampment.

Ariella shifted the unwieldy bulk of the bulging satchel slung across her shoulder to a more comfortable position, and began to follow, Drago and Graymane falling in beside her. She nodded, in curt satisfaction. "That went well," she said.

"Can't this wait?" Oaktwig asked testily, as Ariella swept past the guard guiding them and into his office, a sparsely furnished room in a hut barely distinguishable to Drago's eyes from any of the ones surrounding it. He looked up at Graymane, who had entered hard on the queen's heels, and scowled, playing the part of the querulous and obstructive bureaucrat once more. "I have a great deal of work to get on with." Once again, Drago was not surprised to be entirely ignored.

"No, it can't," Graymane said, and Oaktwig laid his pen aside with a theatrically long-suffering sigh. "We've news of the bandit Gorash."

"There's always news of Gorash," Oaktwig said tolerantly, "and if you believe half of it you'll be chasing your own tail interminably. What's he supposed to have done now?"

"Died," Ariella said, dropping her satchel onto the commander's desk with an ominous thud.

Oaktwig glanced up at her curiously, and Drago tensed; but the glamor held, and the elf returned his gaze to Graymane almost at once. "And who's this, may I ask?"

"Caris Silverthorn," Graymane replied smoothly, with a cursory introductory wave. Apparently struck by an afterthought, he indicated Drago too. "And Drago Appleroot. They're bounty hunters from Fairhaven. The king's agents there hired them."

"Did he, indeed?" Oaktwig looked as affronted as he was supposed to. "Then why wasn't I informed?"

"Probably for the same reason I wasn't," Graymane replied, with a fair semblance of impatience. "His Majesty didn't think we needed to know."

Oaktwig nodded, pretending to accept that as readily as any mid-level functionary as unimaginative as he was trying to appear would. Now that he'd seen the mask slip, though, Drago could see the elf's mind racing behind the bland facade he was working to present; wondering if his connection to the rebels was known or suspected, whether the news of Gorash's death was genuine, and, most important of all, whether the queen was safe. "Quite so," he said blandly. "Bound to have had his reasons. Probably thought we'd just get in the way." He glanced at Drago. "So you're not a tunnel rat after all, then?"

"Not much of one," Drago agreed. "But it gave me a chance to keep my ears open. And my eyes." He smiled, in a manner he hoped would be vaguely disquieting. "Which can see in the dark, remember. Well enough to have spotted someone climbing the other side of the quarry last night."

"Really?" Oaktwig raised a disbelieving eyebrow. "Did you challenge them?"

"There wouldn't have been much point," Drago said. "By the time I got there, they'd disappeared. But I got close enough to where I'd seen them to find a pathway up the cliff, leading into the woods."

"Did you indeed?" Oaktwig injected just the right tone of faintly bored skepticism into his voice. "And that's where you met your confederate?" He nodded at Ariella. "Miss . . . Silverthorn, wasn't it?"

"It was," Ariella agreed untruthfully, "but we weren't working together. I left Fairhaven about a week before Drago was even hired, and hiked overland to the Barrens from Birch Glade. I'd been watching the bandits' camp for three nights, waiting for a chance to sneak in and scratch Gorash, but their sentries were too good to risk it. Then I got lucky." She nodded in Drago's direction.

"I got jumped by a band of goblins in the wood," Drago explained, keeping it simple, "and they dragged me off to their camp. Probably wanted to ask a few questions before they killed me."

"Which made the perfect diversion for me," Ariella said. "I just had to sneak in while the perimeter guards were distracted. I knew where Gorash was sleeping, so I cut a hole in the back of his tent and slit his throat before he even woke up."

"An interesting story," Oaktwig conceded, "but scarcely believable." He looked at Drago quizzically. "The bandits just let you go, did they?"

"Not as such," Drago told him, "but as soon as Gorash was found dead, they rather lost interest in me. Started turning the camp upside down looking for the assassin. Just left a couple of guards to keep me from making a run for it."

"Big mistake," Ariella said, nodding judiciously. "I thought I owed him something for giving me the chance to collect the bounty, so I took them out for him on my way back to the woods."

"You took one of them out," Drago said, nettled at the implied slur on his professional competence, despite the fact that the story was a complete fabrication. "I got the other two."

"If you say so." Ariella shrugged, not quite failing to hide her amusement. But the squabble seemed to have convinced Oaktwig that there was at least an element of truth to the story. He turned to Graymane.

"Forgive me if I seem a little slow on the uptake, but I don't quite see how you're involved in all this. Or what you're doing with these rapscallions."

"Because it seems my suspicions were right," Graymane said. "I told you someone in the camp was passing information to the bandits, and Drago confirmed that last night."

"So he says," Oaktwig pointed out, with just the right amount of carefully crafted skepticism. "But I wouldn't take a gnome's word for anything. Unless he happened to recognize this phantom traitor?" He glanced in Drago's direction again, with a scornful snort. "No, thought not."

"I was a long way away," Drago said, truthfully, "but it was certainly an elf."

"I'll make all the appropriate enquiries," Oaktwig said, in tones which made it abundantly clear that he expected the effort to be a waste of time. Which, of course, it would have been; Drago was certain the elf had relaxed a little as soon as he'd realized his secret was apparently safe. Oaktwig turned a condescending eye on Graymane. "Unless you would prefer to carry on truffling about for yourself?"

"That won't be necessary," Graymane said. "With Gorash dead, and no one else to lead them, the bandits will simply disperse. Your informant will have no one to report to. My duty now is to return to Sylvandale as quickly as possible to inform His Majesty that his sister has been avenged."

"Of course." Oaktwig's polite nod of understanding was a physical reminder not to let the door hit him on the way out. "You're quite sure the fellow's dead, then?"

"Pretty sure," Ariella said, opening the bag she'd dumped on Oaktwig's desk. "Unless he can manage without this."

Oaktwig blenched, and this time Drago was certain the elf wasn't play acting. The severed head had been Ariella's own idea, borrowed from one of the casualties of the raid on the supply convoy who had no further use for it, and was already looking somewhat the worse for wear. Getting kind of ripe, too, come to think of it.

Drago tensed, waiting for Oaktwig to realize that this wasn't Gorash's head at all, but fortunately the elf took no more than a cursory glance at the contents of the satchel before turning his face away.

"Very well," he said, with a dismissive wave toward the door. "Let me send a messenger to Sylvandale with the news, and you can follow on at your leisure with your—souvenir."

"Thanks." Ariella nodded again, curt and businesslike. "I'm not letting this out of my sight until I get the money I was promised for it." Drago had filled her in on the deal Greenleaf had been offering the bounty hunters in Fairhaven, with the bulk of the reward money due on the presentation of proof of Gorash's death, and she was playing the role to the hilt. The real Caris Silverthorn would have cracked a few more jokes in the course of the conversation, but been equally forthright. And probably have relished the irony of being impersonated by the wife of the warlord who'd ordered her death.

"Drago and I will be going with her," Graymane put in. "I take it you'll be able to provide us with an escort?"

"Of course." Oaktwig nodded stiffly.

If Drago was any judge of character, the elf would be quietly desperate to terminate the conversation as quickly as possible by now, eager to contact the rebels and confirm that Ariella, at least, was still safe. Which he had to prevent, if their plan was to work. "I think you should command the escort yourself," he said.

"Good idea," Graymane agreed. "And Moonshade and Meadowsweet as well. We are, after all, on the king's business. We ought to show him we're taking this seriously."

"Both my most senior officers?" This time Oaktwig's consternation clearly wasn't feigned. "That's ridiculous. Who'd take charge of the camp?"

"I'm sure there are one or two of the junior ones capable of rising to the challenge," Graymane said flatly. "Unless you'd rather explain to the king in person why you saw fit to ignore the direct instructions of his appointed representative."

"Of course not," Oaktwig said, through audibly gritted teeth.

"If none of the elves are up to it, you could always ask the mine manager," Drago suggested ingenuously. "Loma seems very organized."

"That won't be necessary," Oaktwig assured him, as though the suggestion had been a serious one. Very few of the elves here would have taken orders from a gnome under any circumstances. "I can think of a few names."

"Excellent," Graymane said. "Then the sooner we get started, the better."

CHAPTER THIRTY-TWO
"Don't get too much mud on my hands."

Despite Oaktwig's best attempts at delaying tactics, which Graymane brushed aside with a degree of brusqueness bordering on rudeness to the evident amusement of everyone who witnessed them, the cavalcade was ready to set out shortly before noon. Leaving the elves to their preparations, Drago returned to his quarters in the burrow to retrieve his possessions; he'd intended to be quick, but the lure of the bed after the exertions of the night before proved irresistible, and he slept for most of the morning, waking only in response to a peremptory rap on the door.

"Coming." Still not entirely awake, he expected to see Clovis as he pulled it open; but instead of his friend, Graymane was waiting, crouching uncomfortably in the corridor which seemed wide and high enough to the gnomes who habitually used it. "Oh, it's you." Strangely, he felt a vague sense of disappointment.

"It was the last time I looked. Got everything?" Graymane asked.

"I have now." Drago shouldered his rucksack, and left the room without a backward glance.

"Said your goodbyes?" Graymane shuffled along behind him, bent almost double, ignoring the incredulous or hostile stares from the gnomes they encountered along the way, who had to seek refuge in rooms or side passages to avoid being trampled by the elf. Almost as many stared at Drago, too, though in a more wary fashion; it seemed word about his real profession and reason for being there had got around fast. And been embellished along the way, he had no doubt.

"No." Again, he felt a momentary pang of regret; Della and Clovis deserved better. But that was how things were sometimes, and there wasn't a lot he could do about it now. If he hadn't fallen asleep, he'd have had time to walk down to the mine and back, but he couldn't think of anything he might have said to them that would ease the situation if he had.

"By the sap, that's better." Graymane straightened his back gratefully as they regained the open air. "Much longer down there and my spine would have locked up."

"I appreciate it," Drago said, settling the rucksack's shoulder straps a little more comfortably. "Not many elves would have gone in to wake me up."

"Neither would I, if she hadn't told me to," Graymane assured him. He didn't elaborate, confident that Drago would know who he meant, and Drago didn't blame him for that; there was no telling who might overhear their conversation.

"Hey! Appleroot!" The shout took him by surprise, and he turned, wondering who might want to speak to him. The voice was feminine, and for a moment he thought it might be Della intent on bidding him a proper farewell after all, although the timbre was subtly different; then he realized it came from Loma Claybed.

"Yes?" he asked, cautiously. The mine manager did not look happy.

"We had a talk when you arrived, remember?"

"I do." He nodded, trying to recall the details.

"It's just a technicality, seeing as you're leaving anyway, but I just wanted to tell you you're fired." She held out a handful of coins. "Here's what you're owed for the shifts you worked."

"Give it to Della and Clovis," Drago said. "Tell them to have a drink on me."

"I'm sure they'll be thrilled," Loma said sarcastically as she turned away, his existence already apparently forgotten.

Drago shrugged, and started up the slope. He supposed he should be feeling resentful at being so abruptly dismissed, but somehow he couldn't be bothered.

"Aren't you going to kill her, or something?" Graymane asked, and Drago stared up at him in astonishment. The elf smiled thinly. "Just kidding. If I thought you were liable to react like that to a few harsh words, I'd have taken you out myself a long time ago."

"Of course you would," Drago replied, not entirely sure how much Graymane was joking, but giving him the benefit of the doubt regardless. "Without her, you'd be getting a lot less out of the mine. Given your loyalty to the crown . . ."

"Exactly," Graymane agreed. "I can always get another thief-taker, but a good manager is hard to find."

They crested the top of the ramp, and Drago stopped short in astonishment. "You've been busy."

"Not just me," Graymane said. "There's only so much sand in the hourglass."

"Right." Drago nodded, taking his meaning at once. Spells like the one disguising Ariella's appearance—or any form of magic come to that—only had a finite duration, before reality reasserted itself. They could have permanent effects if judiciously applied, like the one which had extinguished the warehouse fire in Birch Glade, but even the strongest would fade in a couple of days: a fortuitous circumstance which enabled most mages to continue making a living. If they were to stand any chance of success in the desperate gamble he was already regretting having suggested, every minute counted. "Has the messenger left already?"

"Hours ago," Graymane assured him. "Oaktwig was efficient about that, anyway." He made the remark in Oaktwig's hearing, continuing to pretend that the garrison commander's pretense of posturing incompetence still had him fooled, and getting in a dig which would have nettled its target if the pose was real.

"On the fastest horse we could find," Oaktwig interpolated, from the saddle of his own mount. "The dispatch should have reached the quay by midmorning, and be well on its way up the river by now."

"Good," Drago said, a sense of unease growing in him by the moment as it began to sink in that everyone apart from Graymane and himself were on horseback. A foreboding that only increased as Graymane swung himself easily into the saddle of a roan gelding, and took the reins from the ostler holding them.

"Come on," Ariella said impatiently, reining in her own mount, which shied at the sight of the gnome—quite fairly in Drago's opinion, as he found the close proximity of so many of the huge animals distinctly disquieting himself. If one of them trampled him, he might never get up. "We haven't got all day."

"Quick change of plan," Drago said. He'd never ridden a horse in his life—in Fairhaven they tended to be used for pulling carts, and anyone foolish enough to flaunt their wealth and status by riding one in any of the districts he frequented would live to regret it. Though probably not for long. The local sausage vendors, on the other hand, would think all their birthdays had come at once. "You go on ahead. I'll walk to the quay and catch the next boat back to Fairhaven after all."

"Don't think so," Ariella said cheerfully. "Any messages on their way downriver can easily be altered, or lost in transit, if you take my meaning."

"I do," Drago said resignedly. The threat was clear enough; if he didn't help Ariella regain her throne, her husband wouldn't call off his assassins after all. Not that he could blame her, really; in her place he'd want everyone who knew who she really was within sight at all times. Which meant him and Graymane, basically. Graymane's loyalty she could count on, but so far as Ariella was concerned, Drago was simply a dagger for hire who'd switched sides as soon as it suited him. He had no intention of switching back, but she couldn't be sure of that, especially given the magnitude of her brother's wealth. "But I can't ride one of those." He indicated the horses milling around him. Ariella's wasn't the only one he seemed to be spooking, and Moonshade glared down at him from her own saddle, muttering something about shortarse troublemakers. "I couldn't even get my legs across one."

"You won't have to," Ariella said, turning her mount side on to him, and revealing a large wicker basket behind her. "Just hop up into this."

"Hop up how, exactly?" Drago asked, incredulous. Trying to clamber up the side of an animal almost three times his own height didn't strike him as something liable to end well.

Ariella shrugged. "Get someone to give you a boost." She pointed to the horse holder who'd been looking after Graymane's mount. "He'll do."

"I'm not chucking shortarses around," the elf protested. "They don't pay me enough for that."

"Who said anything about paying you?" Ariella asked, her hand dropping to the hilt of her sword. "When you've got your health you've got all the wealth you need. Am I right?"

"Yeah. Well put," the elf agreed hastily. He bent his knees, cupped his hands together, and glared at Drago. "Come on, then. Get on with it. And don't get too much mud on my hands."

"Much appreciated," Drago lied, thinking that bearing in mind what a stable boy normally got on his hands a bit of mud could only be an improvement. He got a foot into the makeshift stirrup, regaining his balance after a moment of frantic wobbling that sent a ripple of amusement around the onlookers, and suddenly found himself shooting skyward as the elf straightened his knees.

"Up you come," Ariella said, with a grin which seemed far from welcoming, and grabbed his arm, yanking him in like one of the fish he'd caught from the deck of the *Rippling Light*. Grabbing for a handhold, he grasped the rim of the basket, and scrambled in, finding there was just enough room to sit in it with his knees folded up under his chin, which was now more or less level with the lip. "Comfortable?"

"You are joking, right?" In some ways it was even worse than the barrel he'd sneaked out of Fairhaven in. For one thing, the rocking motion of the horse was far more pronounced than the hold of the riverboat had been, and was having interesting effects on his stomach. Not in a good way. And for another the rucksack was pushing him forwards, ramming his chin painfully against his kneecaps with every lurch. After a bit of wriggling he managed to slip the shoulder straps off and pull it round in front of him instead, where he held it against his chest, and leaned back against the enclosing wickerwork with a grateful sigh.

"Course I am," Ariella said, and spurred the animal into a brisk walk, which left Drago jolting even more uncomfortably than before. The good news was that at least the motion was more regular, which calmed his stomach and inner ear a little, used as they were to crossing the choppy waters of the Geltwash on a regular basis. "But if you throw up down my back I'll get to Sylvandale with two heads in my bag instead of one."

"I'm not going to throw up," Drago assured her, although if he was honest that was probably because he'd missed breakfast and didn't have much in his stomach to get rid of, rather than innate fortitude.

"Then we might as well move out," she said, catching Graymane's eye, and gesturing toward the gate.

Graymane nodded, rose in his stirrups, and lifted an arm, taking a deep breath as he did so.

"I believe I'm still the one giving the orders around here," Oaktwig interrupted, before Graymane could bellow the command he was preparing to give.

Graymane smiled sardonically. "For the moment," he agreed. He shot a disdainful look at Oaktwig, Meadowsweet and Moonshade, and the score of elven troopers accompanying them, whose uniforms were as presentable as could reasonably be expected given the suddenness of their call to action. "And they are your toy soldiers. Knock yourself out."

"Thank you." Oaktwig looked as if he'd rather knock Graymane out, but nodded with a fair semblance of courtesy. Then he rose in his saddle with surprising ease, waved a languid hand in the air, and called out something which sounded to Drago more like "Aderuer . . . . Hah!" than anything recognizable as words. The soldiers seemed to find it perfectly comprehensible, however, wheeling their mounts and setting off for the gates in a neat column, riding two abreast. Oaktwig took up his position at the front, riding alone, a little ahead of the main group, flanked by Moonshade and Meadowsweet, each of whom was leading one of the files of soldiers.

"Which leaves us at the back," Ariella said, with a trace of amusement, "where lowlifes like us belong."

"Couldn't have put it better myself," Meadowsweet said, as the head of the column moved out, leaving the civilian elves to tag onto the end.

Ariella glared at the elf's oblivious back. "The next time I get married," she said, *sotto voce*, "he's definitely not invited."

"I thought it was a once in a lifetime thing," Drago said, more to take his mind off the discomfort in his stomach as the horse picked up its pace, and the rocking movement increased accordingly, than because he felt like conversation. Meadowsweet had been one of the witnesses at the ceremony, when the queen married Gorash, Moonshade the other. What part Oaktwig had played, beyond smuggling the groom in and making sure the area round the garrison chapel was clear of potentially embarrassing onlookers, he wasn't sure, but that had probably been enough. Which meant one of the three elves was the traitor who had betrayed Ariella to her brother, and attempted to arrange her assassination. All had accompanied her on at least one trip between the Barrens and the palace in Sylvandale, and all had sufficient social connection to arrange a private audience with Stargleam. Which, in turn, meant that, despite the risk, they all had to be kept under observation. Perhaps whoever it was would tip their hand before the journey was over.

Ariella and Graymane exchanged a smile. "You're a romantic," Graymane said. "Who'd have thought it?"

"I'm a realist," Drago said, "and once was enough. You don't stick your hand in the bread oven twice." The topic made him uncomfortable, brought too many memories to the surface, and he really didn't want to talk about it.

"Sounds like a story there," Ariella said, conspicuously failing to take the hint. "Are you divorced, or widowed?"

Drago shrugged. "No, and haven't a clue. Haven't seen or heard from her in years."

"That's sad," Ariella said, sounding genuinely sympathetic, to his surprise. "Any children?"

Drago shrugged again. "Same answer. If she was expecting before she left, she never said."

They were picking up the pace again now, the horses cantering along a broad, well-defined track that might have seemed familiar if Drago hadn't been too shaken around by the motion of its hindquarters to take any notice of his surroundings.

"You're missing out," Graymane said, also with a surprising amount of sympathy. "There's nothing like a happy marriage to smooth life's little bumps."

"You're married?" Drago managed to get out in staccato bursts between the jolts, which at least masked his incredulity.

"Not at the moment, but I was happy when I was. Every time."

"How many is every?" Ariella asked, sounding intrigued.

"Five," Graymane said.

"Dear God in the earth," Drago said, with feeling, and took no further part in the conversation for the rest of the journey to the quay.

CHAPTER THIRTY-THREE
"The word you're looking for is 'gnome.'"

By the time they arrived at the riverside garrison, Drago was battered, disorientated, and felt sicker than he could ever remember without having drunk an excessive amount of alcohol the night before. As Ariella reined her horse in, and the jolting subsided to a merely unpleasant degree, he took a deep breath and hauled himself upright, leaning against the wickerwork frame enclosing him for support.

"Told you you'd be fine," Ariella said, although Drago couldn't remember any such assurances. Come to that, though, he was feeling so shaken at the moment that he could barely remember his own name.

Conscious that any reply he might make would undoubtedly fall under the heading of *lèse-majesté*, Drago chose to say nothing, using his elevated position instead to look for any potential threat as they passed through the gates. The camp by the waterside was exactly as he remembered it, even down to the scattered donkey droppings, but the soldiers manning it seemed different, conversing animatedly as they went about their duties. Everywhere he looked, the lassitude of a few days ago was gone, replaced, it seemed, by a sense of barely suppressed urgency. The messenger Oaktwig had dispatched had clearly not been reticent about his errand, and the news of Gorash's supposed death had swept through the camp like a surge tide.

"That must be her," one of the guards on the gate muttered to his companion as Ariella rode by, eyeing her with wary respect, and failing dismally in his attempt not to look as though he was staring at the satchel slung from the pommel of her saddle. "Who's the shortarse?"

"Her lunch?" the other guard suggested with heavy humor, determined not to seem intimidated, until Ariella glanced down at him with a smile which was far from reassuring.

"We work together," she said. "He kept Gorash's guards busy for me. Like to see how?"

Drago smiled lazily, in the fashion he'd discovered years ago made much bigger and stronger felons back down without a fight, and locked gazes with the guard. After a moment, the elf broke eye contact, and they passed fully inside the camp.

"Keeping a low profile I see," Graymane remarked, favoring them both with a wry smile.

"Don't think that's going to be an option," Ariella said, with a glance at the deputation coming to meet them. Judging by the amount of decoration on his tunic, and the size of the paunch it inadequately reined in, the elf leading it was clearly in charge here. A gaggle of aides accompanied him, casting appraising eyes at Moonshade and Meadowsweet, no doubt trying to work out their relative status. All were on foot, and the leader gazed up at Oaktwig with a faint air of resentment at having to crane his neck to converse.

"Welcome, in His Majesty's name," the overdressed elf said, raising a hand in formal greeting, the capitalization clearly audible.

"Quite so." Oaktwig raised a languid hand, and climbed down from the saddle, intent on continuing the conversation more comfortably now that his importance had been established. Graymane and Ariella followed his lead immediately, taking up a flanking position at each of his shoulders. The two officers from the mine remained where they were, until Oaktwig gestured irritably for them to join him; they clambered down a little more reluctantly, remaining as close to their mounts as they could without appearing to be deliberately insubordinate. "I take it a boat has been readied as I requested?"

"It has." The garrison commander smiled insincerely. "But I'm afraid it's a little smaller than you asked for."

"How small?" Graymane butted in, ignoring protocol as punctiliously as he always did.

The commander evidently remembered him from his arrival here on his way to the mine; judging by his faintly panicked air, Graymane had been just as tactful at the quayside as he had been on reaching his destination.

"Large enough for Miss Silverthorn, yourself, and whoever you choose to accompany you. But not, I'm afraid, to accommodate a full troop of soldiers."

"You mean it's not the cargo boat we specified," Graymane said. Drago thought about the *Rippling Light*, and the innumerable similar vessels he'd seen from its deck on his way up river. You could have squeezed everyone they'd brought with them on board a boat that size, but it would have been uncomfortably crowded to say the least. Anything smaller would be impossible.

"No. But on the plus side, it'll be a lot faster. You'll be in Sylvandale by dawn, if you leave now." The commander's tone betrayed just how much he hoped they would.

"Let's see it, then," Ariella said, and Graymane nodded his agreement.

"I suppose we'd better," he conceded.

Oaktwig turned to Moonshade and Meadowsweet. "Stay here while we find out what's going on. Get the troops fed and rested. We might still need them."

"By your command, sir," Meadowsweet said, with elaborate formality. He turned to the troopers behind them. "Dismount and fall out."

At which point, Drago realized he was still marooned on the back of Ariella's horse. He scrambled out of the basket, his rucksack in one hand, and clung to the rim of the wickerwork with the other as the animal shifted its weight irritably beneath him.

"A little help here?" he asked, trying not to sound too concerned, or notice the general amusement of the elves surrounding him.

"Just jump," Ariella said. She gestured impatiently to Moonshade, who was standing nearest to the horse. "She'll catch you."

"I'll do no such—" Moonshade began, before becoming belatedly aware that over four stone of gnome was already plummeting toward her. Not sanguine enough to expect her active assistance, Drago reached out, snagged her shoulders, and arrested his descent by sliding the rest of the way to the ground. Fortunately her mail shirt deflected any suspicion of opportunistic impropriety on his part, but she glared at him nevertheless, shoving him away impatiently. "If you ever touch me again I'll gut you like a fish. Clear?"

"As the forest stream," Drago said, quoting an expression he'd heard the elves use among themselves. The only one he'd ever come across, in the woods near Gorash's camp, had been muddy, with bits of dead leaf floating in it, but he supposed there were nicer ones in the forests of the Sylvan Marches. At any rate, it had been a lot more inviting than the side channels of Fairhaven, which weren't so much waterways as slow-moving trickles of semi-liquid ordure.

"Wouldn't fancy your chances much," Graymane said, with a snide smile. "I've seen him fight. I'd pay money to watch you try, though."

"I'm sure you would," Moonshade said witheringly, and turned to give orders to the soldiers, many of whom were trying to conceal their amusement at her discomfiture.

"This way." The garrison commander led the way down to the jetty Drago had disembarked at a few days before, and pointed out the boat moored there with a gesture of proprietorial pride. "There she is. The *Silverroad Messenger.*"

"It's a dispatch boat," Graymane said, taking in the sleek lines and neatly furled sail. It was less than half the size of the *Rippling Light*, but being from a maritime city Drago could appreciate the craftsmanship which had gone into the long, narrow hull. The rigging was simple, just a larger version of the sails on the dinghies which plied the waters of the lower Geltwash, ferrying passengers between the two halves of Fairhaven.

"You said time was of the essence," the overdressed and overweight elf said, trying to sound placating, "and there's nothing faster than this on the upper reaches. Apart from the others of her class, of course. She's identical to the one your dispatch went off on."

"Then the sooner we follow it, the better," Ariella said, with a meaningful glance at Drago and Graymane.

After a moment's thought, Graymane nodded briefly. "You're right," he said. "We'll just have to leave the escort behind. How many passengers can this tub take?"

"Three," the commander said, with a dismissive glance at Drago. "Though I don't suppose he'd slow you down much if you insist on taking him along too."

"We do," Ariella said. She glanced at Oaktwig, then back to Graymane. "And the two officers we brought with us from the mine."

"That'll slow us down a lot," Oaktwig said, "even if we can fit everyone aboard." He turned to Graymane, the picture of insincere helpfulness. "I appreciate the point you made earlier about the importance of our journey to His Majesty, but perhaps Meadowsweet and Moonshade would be better employed making their way back to the mine, and—"

"They would not," Graymane said, in tones of complete finality. "They're coming, and the matter is closed. You can, of course, raise the matter with the king in person, if you still wish to protest my handling of the commission he gave me once we reach Sylvandale."

"I'm sure that won't be necessary," Oaktwig said. He glanced at the boat again, with manifest distaste. "And I'm sure you'll still be able to find room for a crew, along with everyone else you seem to think is indispensable. Perhaps they can swim along behind, and push it."

"We won't need much of a crew," Drago said, his eyes still on the boat. "If whoever's on the tiller knows what they're doing, once the sails are set there shouldn't be a lot adjustment required along the way." He turned his face into the prevailing breeze. "The wind's steady enough, and in the right direction. We'll hardly need to tack at all, unless the river starts meandering upstream from here."

"It runs fairly straight as far as Sylvandale," Ariella said, glancing at Graymane, then speculatively at the gnome.

Graymane nodded. "Could you handle it?" he asked Drago.

"If I had to." He wasn't exactly an expert, but you didn't grow up in Fairhaven without acquiring the rudiments of controlling small watercraft. He must have spent hundreds of hours watching expert ferrymen ply their trade as he travelled around the city, and had taken the tiller of hire craft himself now and again when his business was better carried out without other eyes and ears in the vicinity. "It's a bit bigger than anything I'm used to, but the principle's the same."

"Good. Then you're our crew," Graymane said, an instant before it fully dawned on Drago what his response to the apparently idle query was letting him in for.

The garrison commander seemed to inflate, and his aides began to quack among themselves in indignant undertones. "I simply cannot allow one of His Majesty's courier boats to be left in the hands of a— of a—"

"The word you're looking for is 'gnome,'" Drago said mildly, his hand drifting to the hilt of his sword. "At least I hope it is. If it isn't, things could get very unpleasant." He was beginning to find the Marchers' constant and open disdain for anyone who wasn't an elf extremely tiresome, and combined with the lingering nausea and rising hunger clashing in his belly, it was making him more irritable than usual.

"I'm sure that was exactly the word my colleague was attempting to remember," Oaktwig said hastily. He hadn't seen Drago in action himself, but he knew he'd impressed Graymane, and that was enough for him to try and defuse the situation before blood was shed. Not that Drago would really commit murder for the sake of a petty insult, but Oaktwig didn't know that, still under the impression that he'd assisted the *faux* Caris Silverthorn to commit a cold-blooded assassination.

"And I'm the personally appointed emissary of the king," Graymane reminded everyone, pulling his now rather battered letter of commission from inside his jacket and waving it at the commander to emphasize the point. "I say he's taking the tiller, and that's the end of it." He smiled in a distinctly non-reassuring manner at the angry elf. "I'll be sure to let His Majesty know of your reluctance to relinquish the vessel when I speak to him, though. Are we all happy now?"

"Of course." The commander seemed anything but, if Drago was any judge, but wasn't fool enough to press the point. He turned to Oaktwig, whom he seemed to consider the most reasonable member of the party, and took several deep breaths. "I'll send for your officers, if you insist on taking them with you."

"That won't be necessary," Oaktwig said. "I'll fetch them myself. I'll need to give the troopers we're leaving behind their orders in any case."

"Don't take too long," Graymane admonished, and Ariella smiled at Oaktwig, with every appearance of friendliness.

"I'll come with you," she said. "See if we can grab some food for the journey."

"There's no need," Oaktwig said. "I'm sure Meadowsweet can take care of that."

"It's no bother." She was clearly not taking no for an answer, and

Oaktwig could see that as clearly as Drago could. He looked as though he was about to argue anyway, then turned and walked off without another word, Ariella trotting cheerfully at his heels. The other elves followed them, evidently having decided that anyone who'd contemplate trusting a gnome, let alone conversing with him as an equal, was beneath their notice however unassailable his authority was.

"Neatly done," Drago said, with a final glance at Ariella's retreating back. Graymane nodded, picking up his meaning at once. Left to his own devices, there was no telling what Oaktwig might say to Meadowsweet and Moonshade, or what orders he might leave for his soldiers. One of the three was definitely a traitor, who'd conspired to murder the queen and install her brother on the throne, and if one, then why not two: or even all three? Bringing the soldiers along, on the flimsy pretext of an honor guard, had been Graymane's insurance: if things had turned out really badly, the rank and file would have followed the orders of the king's emissary over their own commanders, even to the point of placing them under arrest if instructed to. But now that resource would be denied them. "Just between ourselves, I don't suppose we could leave the other two behind after all, could we?"

"No." Graymane's tone brooked no argument. "And Oaktwig has to stay with us, or he'll head straight back into the Barrens to look for her."

Drago nodded, and jumped down into the boat. The mast was already raised; all he had to do to get them moving was cast off the mooring lines and hoist the sails. "That he would," he agreed. And if anyone in the mining camp put two and two together, Ariella's life would be left hanging in the balance once again. Not to mention Gorash and his band, who were already in enough danger.

"And I want the other two where I can see them," Graymane went on. "Don't trust either of them further than I could throw a troll."

"Can't argue with that," Drago agreed, checking the ropes with more apparent confidence than he felt. It had been some time since he'd sailed by himself, and never in a boat this big. Everything had been designed for elves to handle, too, which meant the tiller loomed, huge and unwieldy, above his head; he'd have to stand on the stern thwart and lean into it in order to steer. Which meant trimming the sails exactly right before they set off, because he wouldn't be able to do it on the move, and he certainly wouldn't trust any of the elves to try. They'd probably be capsized in moments if they did.

Which was another thing, the extra passengers would leave the vessel uncomfortably low in the water. He'd just have to hope none of them moved around too much . . .

By the time he'd finished his inspection Ariella and Oaktwig had returned, accompanied by Moonshade and Meadowsweet, neither of whom seemed particularly enthusiastic about boarding the small craft. Meadowsweet, in particular, stopped short on the jetty, and stared at it with open distaste. "We can't all fit in that," he said.

"We can," Graymane said, "just not comfortably. And the sooner we get moving, the sooner we can get out at the other end."

"He's got a point," Moonshade told her fellow captain, and clambered awkwardly into the boat, setting it rocking.

Forewarned by decades of experience of boarding and disembarking from small boats, Drago held on to the tiller for support, allowing his sense of balance to adjust, and kept his feet easily. "Next," he said, carefully not noticing the gathering crowd of onlookers clearly hoping to see their betters taking an impromptu swim.

"Fine. Just don't blame me if we sink," Meadowsweet grumbled, and scrambled down too, settling next to Moonshade. The vessel listed alarmingly, the gunwales on that side sinking to within six inches of the water. A faint susurration, which might have been the wind rising, but which Drago strongly suspected was a murmur of anticipation from the onlookers, reached his ears.

"Alternate sides, keep the boat balanced," he instructed briskly. "Haven't you ever been on the river before?"

"Not in a bathtub," Meadowsweet grumbled. He began to move, and the boat rocked violently, shipping a couple of mugfuls of water.

"Just stay where you are," Drago snapped, a little more heatedly than he'd intended. "Next two on the other side."

Meadowsweet flushed, angry and embarrassed at being publicly upbraided by a non-elf, but had the good sense to hold his tongue.

"That would be me," Oaktwig said, boarding with surprising grace. The boat steadied as he settled opposite Moonshade, their knees almost touching. He glanced up at the jetty. "Miss Silverthorn?"

"Shouldn't she stay up there and cast off?" Moonshade asked. "She's from Fairhaven, so she ought to be used to this."

"Good point," Graymane agreed, swinging himself aboard before Ariella had a chance to argue. By this time the boat was sufficiently laden to remain reasonably steady, to the evident disappointment of the onlookers, who began to wander off. Ariella glared at his back, and began to fumble with the mooring lines. After a few moments of muffled cursing, they came loose.

"Heads below!" She lobbed her satchel down, everyone setting the small craft rocking again as they scrambled out of its way; it landed on the planking with a resonant thud, which made the three elves from the mine wince. "And again!" A sack of about the same size followed it; this time Graymane reached out a hand and caught it neatly. A second later Ariella followed, a little more sedately, and settled herself in the bow, leaning back into it as though it were a couch.

"Better haul the lines in before you get too comfortable," Drago said, putting the tiller about with some effort. The sails filled, and the overladen boat began to move slowly away from the shore. "Because I'm not going over the side to free them if they snag on something."

Ariella glared at him for a moment, then began hauling the sodden rope aboard, coiling it inelegantly on the boards between her feet. Meadowsweet shuffled a little further away, as river water spattered on his uniform, then back to where he'd started after Moonshade elbowed him in the ribs.

"I'll get the other one," Oaktwig said, reaching behind to begin hauling in the trailing stern line.

As the boat picked up speed, joining the steady stream of vessels heading upriver, Drago glanced at Ariella uneasily. Not because she'd been irritated by being pulled up on neglecting to stow the lines properly, but because he'd momentarily registered the expression on her face before the enchantment erased it from his notice again. The charm was beginning to weaken, and their whole plan relied on her not being recognized before they reached their destination.

He glanced at Graymane, who, engrossed in the contents of the sack, appeared not to have noticed anything untoward.

"Bread and cheese, mostly. And a couple of bottles of wine." Graymane nodded approval at Ariella. "Basic, but it'll get us there. Who's hungry?"

"Me," Drago said, realizing that it was true. He glanced at the open river ahead, then back to the quayside, already diminishing in the distance. The fresh air and open water were finally dispelling the last of the nausea induced by the journey on horseback, and his appetite was returning, even more so for having missed breakfast. That, at least, he could do something about. Everything else was now out of his hands.

CHAPTER THIRTY-FOUR
"The sooner we're done with this, the better I'll like it."

Despite being overladen, low in the water, and uncomfortably crowded, the courier boat still made good time on its journey upstream. Drago lacked the experience of river navigation to make an accurate assessment of their speed, but it seemed to compare well with what he remembered of the *Rippling Light*'s capabilities, and Clearspring had boasted of that particular vessel's exceptional handling on more than one occasion. Indeed, they overhauled several riverboats of a similar kind in the course of the afternoon, albeit slowly enough to arouse the curiosity of their crews; which meant either politely deflecting questions about their destination and business, or ignoring a flurry of jibes about their unusual appearance and fitness to be on the water, depending on whether the vessels were crewed by elves or not. This far upriver a few were even gnomish, ranging far downstream of the Delvings, although the majority were either elves on their way to the Marches, or humans, who, in the manner of their kind, seemed to be everywhere. By far the most scathing invective, and the occasional thrown object, however, came from the goblin boats, which Drago couldn't really claim to be surprised by; after the first one he learned to steer well clear of those, and hope no one aboard had a bow.

These interludes aside, the journey proceeded smoothly and easily, apart from Meadowsweet's incessant complaints about the lack of leg room, Moonshade's frequently expressed irritation with his "infantile whining," and Oaktwig's visibly waning patience with both of his subordinates. Ariella and Graymane kept quiet, on the whole, only speaking when one of them had something germane to say, which generally related to the steadily dwindling supply of foodstuffs, and Drago had even less inclination for idle conversation than he had the time and energy. After an entire afternoon of leaning into the tiller, or hauling it laboriously toward him, his back and shoulders ached as though they'd been trampled by a troll, and his neck felt as though it had been riveted straight to the top of his spine.

"We should put in for the night soon," Oaktwig said, as the light grayed around them, and a faint chill began to permeate the air. The sun hadn't quite set yet, but had already disappeared behind the ever-thickening forest lining the banks, the trees becoming taller and wider with every passing mile. "Otherwise it'll be too dark to find a landing place."

"Not for me," Drago said. He could still see perfectly clearly, and would be able to do so even after night fell in earnest. "How much longer to reach Sylvandale?" There were scattered lights along both banks, indicating either the presence of settlements or boats which had already moored for the night; mostly the latter, although without the benefit of his low-light vision, none of the others could be certain of that.

"That pompous oaf back at the quay said we'd be there by dawn," Oaktwig said. He shifted uncomfortably. "Though I'm not sure I can sit still for that long."

"He was factoring in an overnight stop," Graymane said, "or at least a comfort break or two along the way. This boat's faster than a regular cargo vessel."

"Not that much faster while it's as overloaded as this," Meadowsweet put in, "and I vote for a comfort break at least. We can't get much further anyway; it'll be completely dark soon."

"Which is where having a gnome at the tiller comes in handy," Graymane said. He glanced at Drago. "Can you keep going all night?"

"If I have to," Drago said. He wasn't exactly thrilled at the idea, but he could certainly see well enough to keep the boat moving for as long as the wind lasted. "Do we want to get there before daybreak?"

"Yes," Ariella said. "The fewer people around when we arrive, the better." Not to mention the advantage the darkness would give her if the spell concealing her identity had worn off by the time they arrived. Gorash had been confident that it would last for long enough, but he wasn't exactly an expert in thaumaturgy, and whoever had created the charm in the first place hadn't been around to ask.

"Then I'll put in briefly a little after nightfall," Drago said, ignoring the suppressed groan from Meadowsweet. If the elf thought sitting still for another hour or so was bad enough, he should try hauling on a tiller intended for a user twice his own size for half the day. "Wait until there's no chance of being spotted by anyone ashore." Which he couldn't entirely guarantee, of course, but if he chose a stretch of riverbank well away from any obvious habitation or moored vessels, the risk would be a small one.

"That would be best," Graymane agreed, with another glance at Drago which didn't quite manage to conceal his concern. "But can you last that long? You're looking all in."

"I'll be fine," Drago said. "Bit of food and a quick nap, and I'll be raring to go."

But Graymane didn't seem to believe him, which was fair enough, because Drago didn't really believe it either.

In the end it was his own fatigue which impelled him to steer the boat in toward the shore, rather than the increasingly frequent grumbling of the elves. Everyone was getting cold, tired, and short-tempered by this time, and more than ready to feel dirt under their feet again.

"Get the rond anchor out," he told Ariella, who merely shrugged in response.

"I would, if I had a clue what you're talking about."

"Big metal spike, tied to a rope. Should be in one of the lockers you're sitting on. Make the other end fast to the boat, and stick the spike in the bank when we reach it. Can you manage that?"

"I could if I could see anything," Ariella said testily, but began rummaging in the locker by her feet nevertheless. After a few moments of groping she found the anchor, and began making the rope fast, as instructed.

Drago nodded approval, even though she would barely be able to make out the movement of his head by now. "Good job," he said. "Stand by." The boat was heading straight into the bank, a little faster than he would have liked, but not enough to damage it when it hit. Bushes were growing out over the water, which would afford them a little extra concealment, and he trimmed the tiller a fraction to strike the bank at a more oblique angle. "Everyone duck." He wouldn't have to, of course, but most of the elves were still a few inches taller than him, even sitting down. They all complied, although a couple of muttered profanities indicated that someone hadn't been quick enough, and he glanced up to see Meadowsweet brushing a handful of leaves from his hair. Twigs and branches began rustling against the mast. "Any moment . . . Now!"

The boat jolted, Ariella jammed the spike hard into the muddy bank, and the boat came to rest, swinging round as the current pushed it broadside on to the shore. Drago jumped out, and stamped the aft line anchor firmly into the ground. He stretched gratefully, feeling his muscles crack.

"About time," Meadowsweet said, scrambling ashore as soon as Graymane and Oaktwig were out of the way, and vanishing into the bushes. The others dispersed a little more slowly, leaving Drago to take care of his own needs without interruption, although since none of them could see much further than their own noses, he didn't really know why they bothered. Keeping track of their whereabouts by the rustling, crackling, and occasional eruption of profanity, he returned to the boat for his rucksack and extricated the bedroll. Now he'd stopped concentrating on piloting the boat, exhaustion had him firmly in its grip.

"You should eat something first," Graymane said, kindling a small fire as he spoke; more for the light it afforded, Drago thought, than because it would provide much warmth. Glancing around, he noted with approval that the elf had placed the fire where a clump of trees would conceal it from anyone still out on the river, although he could see no running lights on the water; nor, to be honest, had he expected to. He'd seen very few boats sailing through the night while he'd been aboard the *Rippling Light*, and most of those had been too intent on delivering perishable cargoes to take any notice of what was going on along the shoreline in any case. But it never hurt to be cautious; they hadn't been showing any lights at all, conscious of the need to be inconspicuous, and there might be other boats abroad whose business made them equally wary of being visible.

"Thanks." Drago took the proffered food and ate mechanically, the flavor of the hard bread and past-its-best cheese barely registering; which, for a gnome, was a sign that something was seriously amiss. He must have been even more tired than he thought. "Wake me in an hour." That wouldn't be much, but a lot better than no rest at all.

"Will do," Graymane assured him, glancing up as Ariella appeared, refastening her breeks. "That'll should get us to the palace comfortably before dawn."

"Good." Ariella crouched down at the fire, warming her hands. "The sooner we're done with this, the better I'll like it." She glanced round, and lowered her voice. None of the rustling in the bushes seemed particularly close, but sound carried in the silence of the night. "Any idea who it is yet?"

Graymane shrugged. "Could be any of them. Oaktwig's not that likely, he could have betrayed you and Gorash at any time, or simply led his troops to the camp. But he might be playing the long game. Could be either of the others, but if I had to pick, I'd go for Moonshade. She's the brighter of the two, and a lot more cagey. Says a lot less than she thinks."

Ariella shook her head. "That's why I reckon it's Meadowsweet. Playing the fool's worked for Oaktwig. Maybe he's had the same idea."

Both elves looked at Drago, but before he could reply, he interrupted himself with a jaw-cracking yawn. Once it had passed, he shook his head. "Haven't a clue. Too knackered to think about it." He rolled himself up in his blanket and was asleep almost at once, dimly aware as he dozed off that the others were emerging from the bushes.

That prompted some dreams, which he forgot as soon as he woke, but which left him with a faint and nagging suspicion that he was missing something important.

"It's all right." Drago shrugged Graymane's hand from his shoulder. "I'm awake." The forest was silent, with the preternatural stillness of the pre-dawn, and he frowned, trying to cling to the rapidly evanescing thought which had come to him in the night.

"We should go," Ariella said, and he staggered to his feet, wrapping the blanket around himself against the chill.

"Right." It was no good. The thought had disappeared completely. All he could remember was something about his wedding, over a decade before, and that was an image which tended to figure in his dreams whenever he was involved in something he suspected wasn't likely to end well. Perhaps if he concentrated on something else it would return unprompted, but somehow he doubted that. He turned reluctantly toward the boat. "All aboard then. Try not to fall in." Which was less of a joke than he'd intended.

"It's all right for you," Meadowsweet grumbled, the short rest apparently having done very little to improve his temper. "You can see what you're doing." He scrambled in nevertheless, with enough bumping about to have attracted the attention of everyone within a mile of the clearing: fortunately, Drago suspected, that only meant the six of them. Moonshade followed, pointedly sitting opposite her fellow captain this time, then Oaktwig boarded as well.

"You next," Drago said to Graymane, who nodded, and complied, deferring to the gnome's greater expertise with water craft. He turned to Ariella. "Take the bowline. Sit in the same place as before."

He'd been expecting some argument, but she simply moved to comply, yanking the spike from the soggy turf and clambering back over the gunwale without a word. The boat bobbed, and the bow began to drift outward into the current. Throwing his kit into the boat, Drago pulled the second anchor out, and resumed his post by the tiller.

"The wind's dropped," Graymane said, as the sail flapped forlornly for a moment before reluctantly beginning to fill. "Can we still make it in time?"

"We should," Drago said, reluctant to commit himself. The elves might think him an expert, and compared to them he was, but his skills were rudimentary at best. "It'll be stronger further out, and the breeze should freshen by a bit before dawn." To his unspoken relief, the first part of his prediction turned out to be true. The second might have as well, for all he knew; but he never got the chance to put the matter to the test. After little more than another hour of scudding across the dark and silent water, a faint nimbus of light appeared up ahead, seeping through the trees where the river curved round to the left.

"That's it," Ariella said, her voice a strange amalgamation of determination and resignation. "The lights of Sylvandale."

CHAPTER THIRTY-FIVE
"And if she doesn't, I will."

Drago hadn't really thought about what Sylvandale would look like when he eventually got there; if anything, he supposed, he'd been expecting something like Fairhaven, though a bit more compact and probably a bit cleaner. The reality was completely different, so much so that it took him a while to assimilate what he was actually seeing.

The trees along both banks of the river had grown steadily in stature as their journey had progressed; now many of them were a couple of hundred feet or more in height, and several yards in girth. Drago had seen nothing like them before, and had been duly impressed. Now a grove of several dozen, taller and wider even than these, appeared on both sides of the river, leaning out across it until their branches met high over the water. Jetties and quays, many of them occupied by riverboats, nestled among roots a yard thick, or pushed out into the water on pilings.

At first, Drago thought these, and the scattering of timber buildings he could see between the forest giants, constituted the bulk of the town, and was mildly disappointed; then his eyes were drawn upward, by scores of flickering lights that at first he'd mistaken for fireflies, and the penny dropped. He'd been fooled by the vast scale of the trees into shrinking them in his mind's eye to the stature of normal ones: the lights were lanterns and sconces, flaring in the night, illuminating buildings and walkways clustered against the trunks and nestling among the branches. The whole town was higher than it was wide, a bewildering array of interlocking levels and courtyards within and around the trees. Here and there trunks had been hollowed out or tunneled through, so it was hard to tell where artifice ended and living wood began.

"Impressive, isn't it?" Ariella asked, with a hint of proprietorial pride.

Drago nodded, aware that he was gawping like a peasant fresh off the boat in Fairhaven, and not caring. It wasn't like any of the elves could see him anyway. He shrugged. "Seen one city, seen them all," he said, aware that he wasn't fooling anyone.

"Not like this," Oaktwig said, with what Drago had to admit was justified chauvinism.

"Bit different from Fairhaven," he admitted. If nothing else, his horizons had been well and truly expanded by his travels. But he was beginning to weary of novelty, and feel nostalgic for the fetid back alleys of his home. One last effort, though, and he'd be done, and able to return there. He began to look for a place to moor the boat. "Where do you want to land?"

"Over there." Ariella pointed toward the other side of the river. "That's the nearest dock to the palace."

"Of course it is. The one with all the soldiers on it." Sighing, Drago leaned into the tiller, bringing the boat hard about. "Mind your heads." To his relief, all the elves ducked in time, avoiding the swinging boom. He'd been exaggerating the number of guards waiting for them, but not by much; there were four armed and armored elves stationed on the jetty Ariella had indicated, already bending bows at the sight of the lightless watercraft bearing down on them. That was a Marcher habit he'd be glad to get away from.

"Leave this to me," Graymane said, getting unsteadily to his feet. The boat wallowed, the gunwales dipping uncomfortably close to the waterline, and Meadowsweet yelped. Ignoring him, Graymane cupped his hands and hailed the guards on the shore. "Stand down! We're on the king's business!"

"But not for much longer," Ariella muttered.

"Identify yourselves, or we shoot!" the officer in charge called back, with the air of someone who'd heard it all before and hadn't believed it the first time.

"Graymane, emissary of the king!" Graymane shouted back. "And Caris Silverthorn, the slayer of Gorash. His Majesty is expecting us!"

"Advance and be recognized!" the officer called back. His troops slackened their bowstrings, but kept the arrows nocked, and suspicious eyes on the boat as it drew in to the jetty. Moved more by a sense of mischief than any expectation of cooperation, Drago threw him a mooring line, which the surprised elf caught by reflex, handing it to the nearest soldier with a muttered imprecation.

"Take us to His Majesty at once," Graymane ordered, clambering onto the jetty with evident relief, and producing his letter of commission once again. The officer glanced at it, squinting as he tilted it to catch the light of the nearest torch, then at the rest of the elves as they scrambled onto the wooden planking. Meadowsweet was tugging at his tunic, trying to get the creases out, with limited effect.

"You and you, take them to the palace," the officer said, gesturing to the two closest guards. He took a step closer to the boat, barring Drago's way as he started to disembark. "Not you, shortarse. You stay where you are."

"He comes with us," Graymane said, "or you can explain his absence to His Majesty in person. And take it from me, he will not be pleased."

"If you say so," the officer said, with a further grimace of distaste at Drago. "Just keep an eye on him. Anything goes missing or gets grubby fingermarks on, it's down to you."

"That goes without saying," Graymane said. He waited for Drago to join the rest of the group, and gestured impatiently. "Shall we go?"

"The sooner the better," Ariella agreed, following the soldiers without waiting to see if anyone else joined them. Oaktwig, Moonshade and Meadowsweet looked distinctly uncomfortable, but followed, after glancing at one another for mutual reassurance.

"Don't get left behind," Graymane said, and Drago trailed in their wake, keeping a wary eye out for trouble. The vague sense of foreboding that had hung over him since his forgotten dream was intensifying, and the strangeness of the environment he found himself in wasn't exactly helping to overcome that. "If you got lost, we might never find you again."

"That I can believe," Drago said. There was a surprising number of people around, given the earliness of the hour, all of them elves, and all of them staring at him as they passed as though they'd just found him on the sole of their shoe. Most of the ones out of uniform were servants or artisans by their dress, although a few inebriated aristocrats tottered by giggling inanely, no doubt returning home from a night's carousing, the gender of several indeterminate under the extravagant fashions they wore.

The road, if that was quite the right word, rose in lazy spirals around and through the trees, splitting and merging with others, following branches wide enough to support it, or soaring over vertiginous drops on sturdy wooden bridges. All the buildings they passed seemed to be made of timber, like the causeway underfoot, larger and more lavishly decorated the higher they climbed. Used to the relatively level streets of Fairhaven, Drago soon found himself tiring and short of breath, which only became worse on the few occasions their way diverged from the main thoroughfares into shortcuts up flights of steps intended for elf-sized legs, but which were knee high to him.

"Won't Stargleam still be asleep?" he asked, pausing to catch his breath at the top of one such flight, as they regained the main street again. A high wall of smoothed timber, patrolled by sentries, ran along one side of it, a guarded gate about halfway along its length. It seemed they'd reached their destination at last.

Ariella shook her head. "He's probably not even gone to bed yet, if I know him." Abruptly conscious of the eyes suddenly on her, she shrugged theatrically. "If the rumors are true, of course."

"In my experience, rumors about people like that generally are," Graymane said, puncturing the awkward silence. He cleared his throat. "Perhaps we'd better get on. The quicker this business is concluded . . ."

"Quite so," Oaktwig said. "We should get back to the Barrens and start rounding up the rest of the brigands as soon as we can. I still don't see why you insisted on dragging us all the way here, instead of leaving us to get on with the job right away."

"No, I'm sure you don't." Graymane let the words hang in the air for a moment. "But you will, I can assure you."

"Here you are," one of the soldiers from the dock said, breaking into the conversation with scant regard for either the social niceties or their relative status. "Palace gate." His companion was already talking to the sentries, who glanced across at the group of visitors without much visible interest. "The guards will take you on from here."

"Is that it?" Moonshade glanced at the plain wall facing them with an air of faint disappointment. "I was expecting something a bit more spectacular."

"Then go round the front." The soldier glared at Drago. "Service entrance is good enough for traits and their pets."

Moonshade's hand went to the hilt of her sword, but before she could draw it, Meadowsweet reached out and forestalled her, gripping her wrist tightly. Moonshade glared at him.

"Move it or lose it. Your choice."

"This isn't the time or the place," Meadowsweet reminded her. After a moment Moonshade nodded curtly, and let go of the weapon. She turned to the soldier, who was looking a little less arrogant all of a sudden. "Be somewhere else when I leave. Because if I ever see you again I'll run you through where you stand, you jumped-up little prole."

"And if she doesn't, I will," Oaktwig said. "If you spoke like that to an officer of good family in my command I'd have you hanged for sedition." Turning his back on the now thoroughly cowed guard, he strode toward the gate. "Let us in at once. His Majesty is waiting."

"Exactly. What he said." Seemingly taken aback by Oaktwig's sudden decisiveness, Graymane followed, attempting to retrieve the initiative. He rounded on the sentries. "Get this gate open at once."

"I can't do that, sir." The elf in charge of the gate detail rallied, adopting the tone of obstructive politeness common to minor functionaries throughout the known world. "I'll need to send word to the palace that you're waiting, and require an escort."

"I need no such thing," Graymane said, waving his letter of commission for what Drago devoutly hoped would be the last time. "I'm here by the express command of the king, who is expecting us. Do you think I don't know the way to his private chambers?"

Which may or may not have been true, Drago reflected, but Ariella most certainly did. He glanced at her, catching a glimpse of anger and impatience on her face before the fading enchantment erased her expression again. The spell was fading fast: it was now or never. But before he could intervene, the sentry backed down in the face of Graymane's forceful manner.

"Very well, sir. If you insist." He stood aside, with visible reluctance, allowing them to enter.

CHAPTER THIRTY-SIX
"Not dead. That'll do."

It seemed Graymane hadn't been exaggerating about his familiarity with the layout of the palace, even Ariella having to hurry to keep up with him. He set a brisk pace through a labyrinth of richly carpeted floors and wood-paneled walls, cluttered at intervals with portraits and tapestries. Every now and again an occasional table or glass-fronted cabinet displayed expensive and over-ornamented knickknacks, which Drago passed too quickly to notice properly. The elves were walking so fast he had to jog to keep up, and even then he found himself lagging. So it was that he was a handful of yards behind the others when they turned and vanished through one of the doors leading off the corridor.

He was about to follow, when it suddenly occurred to him that they hadn't seen anyone since leaving the guards at the gate. In a building this size, even just before dawn, that couldn't be right. The servants would have their own doors and passageways, of course, so they could go about their business without disturbing their betters, but a few of them should have been abroad in the main part of the building, lighting fires and preparing for the day ahead. Come to that, there should have been guards in the palace, unobtrusive, to be sure, but not entirely absent. The sense of unease which had oppressed him since waking redoubled, and he slipped quietly into the room the others had entered, remaining close to the door. Fortunately it was well supplied with more of the cabinets he'd noticed in the corridor, which, for someone his height, meant he could easily be overlooked if he was quiet enough.

His sense of unease redoubled. The room was crowded with well-dressed elves, both men and women, most with visible weapons scabbarded at their waists. Two exceptions stood out: one whose paunch and general air of dissolution, not to mention a remarkable resemblance to his sister, identified him unmistakably as Stargleam, and a senior cleric, soberly and expensively dressed, who seemed surprisingly young to have reached such eminence in his calling.

Sudden understanding hit Drago like a footpad's bludgeon, an instant before Oaktwig caught sight of the ecclesiast's face, and his eyebrow twitched upward with surprise. "Rowanberry?"

"Your old chaplain indeed," Stargleam said. "Now my personal spiritual advisor."

"Oh." Oaktwig seemed as perplexed as his subordinates. "Then I suppose congratulations are in order."

"An advancement well merited," Stargleam said, as though the cleric had just won a prize for good penmanship which he'd found himself unexpectedly having to present. He held out his hand. "Show me the head."

"Of course." Ariella proffered the satchel, with its grisly contents. Stargleam winced, seemed about to take it, then changed his mind at the last minute, recoiling fastidiously after the most cursory of glances inside.

"Don't waste your time," Graymane said. "That's not Gorash. But I know where his camp is now. I'll return to the Barrens at first light and raze it to the ground. He won't escape twice."

Oaktwig, Moonshade and Meadowsweet all looked equally stunned. Ariella probably did too, but the enchantment was still holding, hiding whatever she felt.

"Your message was quite explicit," Stargleam said, frowning at Graymane. "You said he was dead. I don't appreciate being made a fool of."

"He couldn't do that," Ariella said, "nature beat him to it." Most of the elves surrounding them scowled or muttered, a few reaching for their weapons, but before anyone could act Graymane broke in again.

"A necessary stratagem, Your Highness. Your sister still lives. If that became generally known, the threat to your rule should be obvious."

"Ariella's alive?" Stargleam blinked, as though he'd just caught his head on a low beam he hadn't noticed was there. "Where? How?"

"Right here." Ariella reached into her pocket, pulled out a small leather bag, and threw it away. Instantly the illusion was dispelled. Oaktwig looked even more stunned than Stargleam, if that were possible, Moonshade and Meadowsweet bowed to her reflexively, gaping like freshly landed fish, and the background murmur of concerned muttering from the assembled elves intensified. Several grasped the hilts of their blades, seeming on the verge of drawing them, waiting only for someone else to take action first before committing themselves. She gestured imperiously to Oaktwig and the others. "Don't just stand there. Arrest these traitors!"

"I don't think so," Stargleam said, as Graymane's sword hissed from its scabbard. Emboldened, several of the others drew their weapons too. "You're the traitor, Ari, not me."

"Sorry, not quite following your reasoning," Ariella said dismissively. "But that's nothing new. If you can't drink it, eat it or sleep with it, it doesn't really cross your mental horizon, does it?"

"Lamiel knows his duty," Graymane said, "and that doesn't include polluting the royal blood line with goblin mongrels."

"He's right, you know. You brought this on yourself." Stargleam shook his head sorrowfully, and waved his hand at the elves surrounding him. "You think I wanted this job? I hate it. It's nothing but sign this, decide that, decree the other, and I never have a minute to myself. If it wasn't for the Council of Ministers telling me what to do, I'd be completely lost."

"And they suggested you have me murdered?" Ariella asked, with a pointed stare at the oldest and most richly dressed among the onlookers, who returned it unflinchingly.

"What? No! I cried for days when they told me you were dead." Stargleam frowned. "Anyway, you made them do it."

"I did what?" Ariella almost shouted.

"Marrying that—that—goblin. So long as you were just talking to him, they might have grumbled about it, but you were queen, you could do what you liked. But making him your heir, possibly even bearing his children—"

"Absolutely intolerable," the well-dressed elf confirmed. "Which is why we sent Graymane to discover who else knew about this marriage, and bring them back here to ensure their silence." Oaktwig, Moonshade and Meadowsweet exchanged grim looks.

"I can see Rowanberry has done very well for himself by telling you about the marriage, and keeping the secret from anyone else," Oaktwig said, stepping forward. Still concealed behind a credenza of staggering tastelessness, Drago silently nodded his agreement; it was the same conclusion his subconscious had been trying to prod him toward through the dream of his own wedding. If none of the three elves they suspected had been the one to betray the queen's confidence, the presiding priest had to have been the one who carried the news of the queen's marriage back to Sylvandale. "But I can assure you, my loyalty can't be bought so cheaply. My allegiance is to the crown, and to its rightful holder, while either of us still draws breath."

"Not for much longer then," Graymane said, lunging at Ariella with his sword as he spoke.

Drago leaped forward, with the horrified conviction that he was going to be too late, but Stargleam was closer and quicker.

"No," he shouted, shoving his sister off balance, and stumbling forward into the path of the blade. It pierced his chest with the hard, moist slapping sound Drago was all too familiar with.

"Lamiel!" Ariella shrieked, as her brother's blood sprayed across her face, and whirled, drawing her own sword. But before she could engage Graymane he was down, felled by the full weight of an angry, fast-moving gnome cannoning into his knees.

"Protect the queen!" Oaktwig yelled, drawing his own sword, while Moonshade and Meadowsweet followed suit.

Drago drove his forehead into the bridge of Graymane's nose, seeing momentary stars and hearing a surprisingly satisfying *crack!* Not that the Fairhaven kiss would slow someone like Graymane for long, of that he was certain, but the elf would stay down for a moment or two, and at the moment that was enough.

"Good luck with that," the elf who'd spoken before said, while more swords were drawn around him. "This entire wing has been cleared." He glanced dismissively at Stargleam, who was convulsing on the floor in a slowly widening pool of blood. Drago didn't give much for his chances; the stricken elf could only have minutes left to live. "You've got nowhere to go, and no one to help you."

"Run!" Stargleam gurgled, before his eyes rolled up in his head, and he said no more.

"What he said." Drago reached up, grabbing Ariella's arm, and yanked her into motion. "Unless you want what he just did to be futile."

"I swear my brother will be avenged," Ariella said, but fortunately she didn't seem inclined to hang around and see to it in person, much to Drago's relief. At his renewed urging, she hurried toward the door.

"Stop her! Kill them all!" the ringleader shouted, hanging back. The conspirators looked uncertainly at one another, while Oaktwig, Meadowsweet and Moonshade formed up in front of the door, barring their way. Clearly most of them considered swords as little more than badges of rank, and the idea of attempting to use them in earnest against trained soldiers held little appeal. But on the other hand, so did the prospect of being hanged for treason. Any second now they'd nerve themselves up for a concerted rush. Graymane, too, was beginning to rouse, lurching unsteadily to his feet.

Drago hesitated, wondering if he should stay and help in what was clearly going to be a pitched battle against overwhelming odds; he'd been in too many brawls not to know that with nothing to lose, sheer weight of numbers went a long way toward countering skill.

Oaktwig caught his eye. "Protect the queen! Get her to safety!" he called.

Drago nodded, and turned to leave.

"I can look after myself," Ariella snapped.

"Then prove it. Follow me," Drago riposted, and led the way down the corridor at a run. Behind him an ominous silence held for a second or two.

Then Meadowsweet's voice drifted after them. "Rinora. Bad timing I know, but might never get another chance to say this. I've loved you from the moment we met."

"Really?" Moonshade's voice sounded surprised, and not in a good way. "I've always thought you were a bit of a dick." Then the clash of steel against steel drowned out everything else.

"Where are we going?" Drago asked, as Ariella drew ahead of him, and the sounds of combat began to fade behind them.

"To get help," she snapped, as though that were obvious. "We can get to the guardroom through the kitchens, down the servant's stairs. There's a door through here." She stopped, next to a panel between two tapestries, and knocked on the wood; sure enough it echoed hollowly. "The knob's behind here . . ." she twisted and tugged at it. "Bugger."

"Locked," Drago said. The minister leading the coup had said the wing was sealed off, and it looked as though he hadn't been exaggerating. "Can you break it down?"

"Do I look like a troll to you?" Ariella snarled. "This is a royal palace, remember? Everything's built to last." She thumped the wood angrily with the hilt of her sword; the polished surface of the hidden door didn't even scratch. "And there's an enchantment on it. We're not getting out that way."

"You're not getting out at all," a new voice interjected. Drago turned. Graymane was charging up the corridor toward them, his sword still stained with Stargleam's blood; and possibly someone else's, Drago thought. The elf's clothing was ripped and bloodstained—getting out of the room to pursue them clearly hadn't been without cost.

"Neither are you," Drago assured him. "I'm pretty sure regicide is frowned on around here. Will you hang him?"

"Eventually," Ariella said, taking up a guard position.

Drago sighed. "You run, I fight, all right? That's what I get paid for."

Ariella scowled and took a step toward Graymane, raising her blade to parry a downward stroke, before pivoting and aiming a stroke at his kidneys as his forward momentum took him past her. "Don't remember hiring you for that."

"I'll bill you later." Drago stepped in as Graymane turned, blocking Ariella's stroke, and kicking out at her knee. While the elf was off balance Drago slashed at his leg, aiming for the femoral artery; he missed, but the blade cut deep into the muscle, and Graymane's leg folded. He crashed down onto one knee, and aimed a vicious swipe which would have decapitated the gnome if he hadn't leaped back at the last possible second.

"This piece of carrion killed my brother!"

"Then don't let him kill you too!" Drago jumped between them as Graymane rose to his feet, limping badly, but still determined to strike Ariella down. "You've a throne to protect!" That wasn't working, the lust for vengeance still written clearly on her face. Her skill with a sword had surprised him, but it was still straight out of a fencing master's manual; Graymane would know all the nasty little gutter tricks Drago did, which an honorable duelist would simply never think of. If he hadn't been wounded already, and facing two opponents instead of one, he might well have finished the woman by now. Evading another downward stroke, which gouged a nasty looking rip in the rug beneath his feet, Drago straightened up suddenly, headbutting Graymane in the groin. This time the impact jarred his entire body, and his head rang; the elf was wearing an armored codpiece. Always a wise precaution when brawling with a gnome. Drago tried a different tack to get Ariella to disengage. "And a husband who loves you! Don't make me have to tell him how you died!"

That did the trick. Ariella turned, and bolted for a nearby salon.

"I'll settle you later!" Graymane snarled, turning to pursue her.

"I'll settle you now," Drago said, stooping, and grabbing the rug he'd noticed a moment before. He yanked it hard, out from under the elf's feet. Graymane howled, and toppled like a felled tree, crashing into an occasional table laden with porcelain fruit. Drago darted in, and kicked him in the temple as he started to rise from the wreckage; with a groan, the elf lapsed into unconsciousness.

Drago hesitated for a moment, resting his sword against Graymane's carotid artery; one quick stroke and it would all be over. But he just couldn't do it; not in cold blood. The renegade was no threat to anyone now, at least for the moment. He turned away, and hurried after the queen.

"They didn't seal the window," Ariella said, as he entered the salon. She'd already yanked it open, admitting a blast of chill dawn air. Over the treetops below, the rising sun was beginning to tint the leaves the color of bronze.

"They didn't have to," Drago said, glancing down, and fighting a sudden surge of vertigo. "Not unless you can sprout wings." This part of the palace seemed to have been built along a side branch, with nothing beneath it except the forest floor, hundreds of feet below.

"I don't have to." Ariella already had one leg over the window sill. "There's a twig out here, leading to the courtyard on the south side." She swung the other leg over, and hesitated for a moment. "Not very wide, though." Then she took a deep breath, and jumped.

For a moment, Drago thought his heart had stopped. He leaned out, cautiously, and found Ariella about six feet below him, perfectly balanced on a side growth about eight inches wide. It seemed to be flexing in the wind, and his stomach lurched anew at the sight of it. Ariella seemed perfectly unconcerned, though, either about the shifting balance point, or the lethal drop beneath her.

"Come on," she said, in what she probably thought was an encouraging tone. "Almost there."

"You are, I'm not," Drago said. "I'm a gnome. I don't do heights." He hesitated. "Maybe I'd better go back and see how Oaktwig and the others are doing."

"Or maybe you'd just better die," Graymane said, staggering across the room with murder in his eye. He might have come round faster than Drago had expected, but he was still suffering from concussion judging by his uncoordinated gait. Before Drago could turn fully back into the room, the furious elf had grabbed him under the arms, shoving him upward and outward.

Drago felt an extraordinary sense of clarity as he spun out into thin air, time stretching around him, allowing every detail to imprint itself on his senses. The dappling of shadows from leaves higher up, the first golden rays of the rising sun piercing through them, the shimmering silver surface of the river bending lazily far below. His sword, glinting as it turned, catching the light as it tumbled toward the ground. The twig Ariella was standing on, drifting slowly past his face. He reached out toward it, already certain it was too far away, feeling the bark brush against the tips of his fingers . . .

"Gotcha," Ariella said, snagging his wrist, and yanking him back upward. He tumbled across the thin span of wood, clinging to it for dear life, arms and legs wrapped around it as though they'd never let go. After a moment he caught his breath, and opened his eyes, loosening his grip enough to sit cautiously upright. "Are you all right?"

"Not dead. That'll do," Drago said, his head still spinning. Graymane was glaring down at them, his face a mask of hatred. "Get moving. I'll hold him off."

"How, exactly? You're the one who doesn't do heights, remember?"

"I don't know! Maybe he'll trip over me." He tried getting to his knees, felt the twig sway under him, and gave it up, grabbing the narrow piece of wood with both hands again. This time it was easier.

Gripping as tightly as he could without completely immobilizing himself, and trying very hard not to look down, he shuffled along on his hands and knees. The courtyard Ariella had spoken of seemed a long way away.

"We're going together," Ariella said, slowing her pace to match his, although she seemed perfectly capable of running along the twig as easily as if it were solid ground. "My kingdom, my rules. If you don't like it, piss off back to Fairhaven."

"As soon as I can, believe me," Drago said, not quite managing to suppress an unexpected urge to laugh. He glanced back. Graymane was scrambling through the window after them, though a good deal less elegantly than Ariella had. "Doesn't he ever give up?"

"Not that anyone can remember," Ariella said. "That's why his services are in such demand around here."

"That's comforting," Drago said. Graymane was hanging by his hands now; as the gnome watched, he let go, landing on the twig as neatly as a falling cat. Then he swayed as he attempted to take his weight on his wounded leg, trying to regain his balance. Drago held his breath, willing the elf to fall; but Graymane recovered, and began to limp along the twig toward them, his breath rattling hoarsely in his chest.

"Out of the way, shortarse." Graymane made a cut with his sword at Ariella's head, overreaching to get past Drago, which she parried in the nick of time. He kicked out at the gnome, trying to knock him off the narrow perch; fortunately he needed to keep his good leg planted on the wood, and the wounded one lacked the strength to succeed.

"I'm getting really tired of people round here calling me that," Drago snarled, kicking out as hard as he could in response.

To his faint surprise, that was enough. Slightly off balance forward, in the attempt to reach Ariella, and with his weight on only one foot, Graymane wasn't stable enough to stay upright as the gnome's boot heel smashed into his kneecap. For a moment he swayed wildly, dropping his sword, arms flailing for equilibrium; then he vanished, dropping out of sight as his center of gravity shifted too far from the narrow strip of wood.

Despite himself Drago glanced down, his eye drawn to the rapidly shrinking figure plummeting into the depths, its face a death mask of anger and surprise, then closed his eyes reflexively as his head began to swim.

"Come on," Ariella said, reaching down a hand to squeeze his shoulder encouragingly. "We're almost there."

"I'll be right behind you," Drago said. Attracted by the commotion, faces were beginning to appear in the courtyard ahead of them. "I think you've got some guards to round up and some traitors to arrest."

Faint voices drifted toward them on the wind. "No, it can't be . . . Looks like her . . . Who's the shortarse? . . ."

"I think you're right." Ariella turned, and sprinted easily along the swaying twig, while Drago clung even more tightly to it, and was most ungnomishly grateful for the relative lack of food in his stomach. By the time he gained the welcome relief of solid woodwork underfoot, a few minutes later, the air was echoing to enthusiastic cries of "The Queen! The Queen! Long live the Queen!"

"I'll do my best to," she confided, as Drago joined her. "I owe Lamiel that much, at least."

"Maybe not," Drago said, as a small group of chastened and richly dressed elves appeared, surrounded by a much larger one of armed and surly looking soldiers. Two of the guards were carrying Stargleam on a stretcher, Rowanberry hovering anxiously at his side. After a moment Oaktwig detached himself from the group and came over. His clothes were disheveled, and he sported a few cuts and bruises, but looked remarkably healthy under the circumstances.

"Your brother still lives, ma'am. Rowanberry performed a healing ritual in the nick of time."

"Excellent news," Ariella said, in the tone of someone suddenly presented with an unexpected complication. "Then I suppose I'd better not have him executed like the others. I'm sure there's some useful missionary work he could be doing among the trolls." She caught sight of Moonshade and Meadowsweet, equally disheveled, and awkwardly not talking to one another. "I see your officers survived as well."

"The fight went out of most of the traitors as soon as Graymane left, and the first few felt the touch of our blades." Oaktwig glanced round the courtyard. "I can assure you, he won't get far."

"No, he won't. Drago killed him." Oaktwig's eyebrow rose in an expression of surprise, but he didn't interrupt. "He's somewhere down by the roots. If you send out a search party, they'll need a pail."

Oaktwig turned to Drago, proffering a hand, which, after a moment of surprise, Drago took. "You've done the Sylvan Marches a great service, Master Appleroot. If there's anything we can do for you in return, you have only to name it."

Drago nodded slowly, considering the offer. "As a matter of fact there is," he said. "You can find me a boat back to Fairhaven. The sooner the better."

CHAPTER THIRTY-SEVEN
"Thanks for the drink."

Of course it took a little longer than that to get home, almost another month having passed by the time Drago's boots hit the planks of a Fairhaven wharf once again. He hefted his rucksack, which, like most of the items in it, was of a far higher quality than the kit he'd set out with, and turned, savoring the familiar smells and noises of his hometown. For some reason everything seemed smaller and louder than he remembered.

"Drago! What a pleasant surprise!" He turned in response to the unexpected voice, finding himself face-to-face with Lady Selina, who looked no more surprised than he felt at the apparently fortuitous meeting. This time she was dressed as a well-to-do merchant, still prosperous, but not quite as much as she'd like to appear judging by the careful mending of her bodice. "I do hope you've a few minutes to catch up. It's been ages."

"It certainly feels like it," Drago agreed, allowing himself to be led to a nearby tavern—not one he was familiar with, but one which was familiar with Selina, judging by the way they were immediately ushered into a back room and left to their own devices. He sat, nursing the ale which had been left there for him, while Selina toyed with a glass of wine.

"And how are things in the Sylvan Marches?" Selina asked, after long enough had elapsed to make it clear he wasn't going to talk unprompted.

Drago shrugged. "Quiet, on the surface," he said. "But it's a tinderbox underneath. There are plenty of elves who feel the same way about Ariella and Gorash's marriage as the old Council of Ministers did. But at least the compromise has taken some of the heat out of it."

Selina nodded. "Oh yes, her abdication." She took a thoughtful sip of her wine. "Quite lucky her idiot brother didn't die after all when his own assassin ran him through."

Drago shook his head. "Graymane was never Stargleam's agent; he was acting entirely for the council. Stargleam was only ever a useful figurehead for them to rule through."

"And now he's performing the same service for his sister and her husband." Selina permitted herself a brief smile. "At least I suppose he's used to it."

"I suppose so," Drago agreed. "Anyway, with him back on the throne, the traditionalist Marchers won't have to worry about Ariella's half-goblin children inheriting the kingdom." He paused. "At least until it dawns on them that Lamiel's not going to be having any heirs of his own, so they'll be next in line anyway."

"Not our problem. And at least there won't be any civil wars disrupting trade along the Geltwash any time soon," Selina said. "Which from where I'm sitting is a definite result." She paused. "And the city council aren't exactly unappreciative of your contribution to that." A purse appeared on the table between them, which Drago reached out and hefted. It was as satisfyingly heavy as he'd expected. "I've no doubt the ex-queen expressed her appreciation as well."

"You'd have to ask her that," Drago said. "Client confidentiality."

"Of course. But confidentially, I've a pretty good idea of how much those clothes you're wearing would have cost. Not to mention that nice new sword of yours. And I'm presuming there was a cash bonus as well."

"You may well presume," Drago said, a little nettled at the reminder of his lost weapon. The new one was of exceptional quality, forged by a master craftsman, but he'd had the other one for years, and could wield it without conscious thought. The balance and heft of this one were subtly different, and however much he drilled with it, it didn't feel like an extension of his own body the way the old one had. No doubt he'd get the hang of it in the end, though, or die trying. "Did your spy hunt end well?"

Selina nodded. "Well for us, anyway. We've identified pretty much every Marcher asset in the city. Which includes Gorash's mob now, of course, which simplifies things. They won't be trying to kill one another on our turf anymore." She glanced at Drago with a hint of mischief. "Or any more of our bounty hunters either, you'll be pleased to hear."

"Good." Drago nodded. "You know the ministers were hiring assassins from here because they didn't want anyone from the Marches asking awkward questions about why it was suddenly so important to kill Gorash?" He'd worked that out for himself, but had still felt inordinately pleased when the convalescing Stargleam had confirmed it.

"That's what we'd thought," Selina said, "but it's good to have it corroborated. Any more news we should know about?"

"I don't think so," Drago said, after pretending to ponder for a moment. He'd stopped at the mine on his way back downriver, as he'd promised, but things had been awkward with Della and Clovis, particularly as they seemed to have formed an attachment in his absence, and he'd been glad to move on as soon as he decently could. He stood. "Thanks for the drink."

Selina smiled. "You're welcome. All in all, I think you've earned it."

✧ END ✧